Janet Fitch is a third-generation resident of Los Angeles. Her fiction has appeared in numerous publications including *A Room of One's Own*, *Black Warrior Review* and *Rain City Review*. An excerpt from *White Oleander* was selected as a notable story in Best American Short Stories 1994. She lives in Los Angeles.

white oleander

JANET FITCH

A *Virago* Book

Published by Virago Press 1999

First published in the United States by
Little, Brown & Company (US) 1999

Reprinted 1999 (seven times), 2000 (twice)

Copyright © 1999 by Janet Fitch

The moral right of the author has been asserted

A CIP catalogue record for this book is
available from the British Library

ISBN 1 86049 802 7

Printed and bound in Great Britain by
Clays Ltd, St Ives plc

Virago Press
A Division of
Little, Brown and Company (UK)
Brettenham House
Lancaster Place
London WC2E 7EN

To the man from Council Bluffs

white oleander

THE SANTA ANAS blew in hot from the desert, shriveling the last of the spring grass into whiskers of pale straw. Only the oleanders thrived, their delicate poisonous blooms, their dagger green leaves. We could not sleep in the hot dry nights, my mother and I. I woke up at midnight to find her bed empty. I climbed to the roof and easily spotted her blond hair like a white flame in the light of the three-quarter moon.

"Oleander time," she said. "Lovers who kill each other now will blame it on the wind." She held up her large hand and spread the fingers, let the desert dryness lick through. My mother was not herself in the time of the Santa Anas. I was twelve years old and I was afraid for her. I wished things were back the way they had been, that Barry was still here, that the wind would stop blowing.

"You should get some sleep," I offered.

"I never sleep," she said.

I sat next to her, and we stared out at the city that hummed and glittered like a computer chip deep in some unknowable machine, holding its secret like a poker hand. The edge of her white kimono flapped open in the wind and I could see her breast, low and full. Her beauty was like the edge of a very sharp knife.

I rested my head on her leg. She smelled like violets. "We are the wands," she said. "We strive for beauty and balance, the sensual over the sentimental."

"The wands," I repeated. I wanted her to know I was listening. Our tarot suit, the wands. She used to lay out the cards for me, explain the suits: wands and coins, cups and swords, but she had stopped reading them. She didn't want to know the future anymore.

"We received our coloring from Norsemen," she said. "Hairy savages who hacked their gods to pieces and hung the flesh from trees. We are the ones who sacked Rome. Fear only feeble old age and death in bed. Don't forget who you are."

"I promise," I said.

Down below us in the streets of Hollywood, sirens whined and sawed along my nerves. In the Santa Anas, eucalyptus trees burst into flames like giant candles, and oilfat chaparral hillsides went up in a rush, flushing starved coyotes and deer down onto Franklin Avenue.

She lifted her face to the singed moon, bathing in its glowering beams. "Raven's-eye moon."

"Baby-face moon," I countered, my head on her knee.

She softly stroked my hair. "It's a traitor's moon."

IN THE SPRING this wound had been unimaginable, this madness, but it had lain before us, undetectable as a land mine. We didn't even know the name Barry Kolker then.

Barry. When he appeared, he was so small. Smaller than a comma, insignificant as a cough. Someone she met at a poetry reading. It was at a wine garden in Venice. As always when she read, my mother wore white, and her hair was the color of new snow against her lightly tanned skin. She stood in the shade of a massive fig tree, its leaves like hands. I sat at the table behind stacks of books I was supposed to sell after the reading, slim books published by the Blue Shoe Press of Austin, Texas. I drew the hands of the tree and the way bees swarmed over the fallen figs, eating the sun-fermented fruit and getting drunk, trying to fly and falling back down. Her voice made me drunk — deep and sun-warmed, a hint of a foreign accent, Swedish singsong a generation removed. If you'd ever heard her, you knew the power of that hypnotic voice.

After the reading, people crowded around, gave me money to put in the cigar box, my mother signed a few books. "Ah, the writer's life," she said ironically, as they handed me the crumpled fives and ones. But she loved these readings, the way she loved evenings with her writer friends, trashing famous poets over a drink and a joint, and hated them, the way she hated the lousy job she had at *Cinema Scene* magazine, where she pasted up the copy of other writers, who, at fifty cents a word, bled shameless clichés, stock nouns and slack verbs, while my mother could agonize for hours over whether to write *an* or *the*.

As she signed her books, she wore her customary half-smile, more internal than outward, having a private joke while she thanked everybody for coming. I knew she was waiting for a certain man. I'd already seen him, a shy blond in a tank top with a bead-and-yarn necklace, who stood in the back, watching her, helpless, intoxicated. After twelve years as Ingrid's daughter, I could spot them in my sleep.

A chunky man, his dark hair pulled back in a curly ponytail, pushed in, offered his book to be signed. "Barry Kolker. Love your work." She signed his book, handed it back to him, not even looking into his face. "What are you doing after the reading?" he asked.

"I have a date," she said, reaching for the next book to sign.

"After that," he said, and I liked his self-confidence, though he wasn't her type, being chubby, dark, and dressed in a suit from the Salvation Army.

She wanted the shy blond, of course, way younger than her, who wanted to be a poet too. He was the one who came home with us.

I lay on my mattress on the screen porch and waited for him to leave, watching the blue of the evening turn velvet, indigo lingering like an unspoken hope, while my mother and the blond man murmured on the other side of the screens. Incense perfumed the air, a special kind she bought in Little Tokyo, without any sweetness, expensive; it smelled of wood and green tea. A handful of stars appeared in the sky, but in L.A. none of the constellations were the right ones, so I connected them up in new arrangements: the Spider, the Wave, the Guitar.

When he left, I came out into the big room. She was sitting cross-legged on her bed in her white kimono, writing in a notebook with an ink pen she dipped in a bottle. "Never let a man stay the night," she told me. "Dawn has a way of casting a pall on any night magic."

The night magic sounded lovely. Someday I would have lovers and write a poem after. I gazed at the white oleanders she had arranged on the coffee table that morning, three clusters of blossoms representing heaven, man, and earth, and thought about the music of her lovers' voices in the dark, their soft laughter, the smell of the incense. I touched the flowers. *Heaven. Man.* I felt on the verge of something, a mystery that surrounded me like gauze, something I was beginning to unwind.

ALL THAT SUMMER, I went with her to the magazine. She never thought far enough ahead to put me in a Y program, and I never mentioned the possibility of summer school. I enjoyed school itself, but it was torture for me to try to fit in as a girl among other girls. Girls my own age were a different species entirely, their concerns as foreign as the Dogons of Mali. Seventh grade had been particularly painful, and I waited for the moment I could be with my mother again. The art room of *Cinema Scene,* with its ink pens and a carousel of colored pencils, table-sized paper, overlays and benday dots, border tape, and discarded headlines and photographs that I could wax and collage, was my paradise. I liked the way the adults talked around me; they forgot I was there and said the most amazing things. Today, the writers and the art director, Marlene, gossiped about the affair between the publisher and the editor of the magazine. "A bizarre bit of Santa Ana madness," my mother commented from the pasteup table. "That beaky anorexic and the toupeed Chihuahua. It's beyond grotesque. Their children wouldn't know whether to peck or bark."

They laughed. My mother was the one who would say out loud what the others were thinking.

I sat at the empty drafting table next to my mother's, drawing the way the venetian blinds sliced the light like cheese. I waited to hear what my mother would say next, but she put her headphones back on, like a period at the end of a sentence. This was how she pasted up, listening to exotic music over headphones and pretending she was far away in some scented kingdom of fire and shadows, instead of sitting at a drafting table at a movie magazine pasting up actor interviews for eight dollars an hour. She concentrated on the motion of her steel X-acto knife, slicing through the galleys. She pulled up long strips that stuck to the knife. "It's their skins I'm peeling," she said. "The skins of the insipid scribblers, which I graft to the page, creating monsters of meaninglessness."

The writers laughed, uneasily.

Nobody took any note when Bob, the publisher, came in. I dropped my head and used the T square, as if I were doing something official. So far he hadn't said anything about my coming to work with my mother, but Marlene, the art director, told me to "fly low, avoid the radar." He never noticed me. Only my mother. That day he came and stood next to her stool, reading over her shoulder. He just wanted to stand close to her, touch her hair that was white as glacier milk, and see if he could look down her shirt. I could see the loathing on her face as he bent over her, and then, as if to steady himself, put his hand on her thigh.

She pretended to startle, and in one spare movement, cut his bare forearm with the razor-edged X-acto.

He looked down at his arm, astonished at the thread of blood that began to appear.

8

"Oh, Bob!" she said. "I'm so sorry, I didn't see you there. Are you all right?" But the look that she gave him with her cornflower eyes showed him she could have just as easily slit his throat.

"No problem, just a little accident." His arm bore a two-inch gash below his polo shirt sleeve. "Just an accident," he said a bit louder, as if reassuring everybody, and scuttled back to his office.

FOR LUNCH, we drove into the hills and parked in the dappled shade of a big sycamore, its powdery white bark like a woman's body against the uncanny blue sky. We ate yogurt from cartons and listened to Anne Sexton reading her own poetry on the tape deck in her scary ironic American drawl. She was reading about being in a mental home, ringing the bells. My mother stopped the tape. "Tell me the next line."

I liked it when my mother tried to teach me things, when she paid attention. So often when I was with her, she was unreachable. Whenever she turned her steep focus to me, I felt the warmth that flowers must feel when they bloom through the snow, under the first concentrated rays of the sun.

I didn't have to grope for the answer. It was like a song, and the light filtered through the sycamore tree as crazy Anne rang her bell, B-flat, and my mother nodded.

"Always learn poems by heart," she said. "They have to become the marrow in your bones. Like fluoride in the water, they'll make your soul impervious to the world's soft decay."

I imagined my soul taking in these words like silicated water in the Petrified Forest, turning my wood to patterned agate. I

9

liked it when my mother shaped me this way. I thought clay must feel happy in the good potter's hand.

In the afternoon, the editor descended on the art room, dragging scarves of Oriental perfume that lingered in the air long after she was gone. A thin woman with overbright eyes and the nervous gestures of a frightened bird, Kit smiled too widely in her red lipstick as she darted here and there, looking at the design, examining pages, stopping to read type over my mother's shoulder, and pointing out corrections. My mother flipped her hair back, a cat twitching before it clawed you.

"All that hair," Kit said. "Isn't it dangerous in your line of work? Around the waxer and all." Her own hairstyle was geometric, dyed an inky black and shaved at the neck.

My mother ignored her, but let the X-acto fall so it impaled the desktop like a javelin.

After Kit left, my mother said to the art director, "I'm sure she'd prefer me in a crew cut. Dyed to her own bituminous shade."

"Vampire 'n' Easy," Marlene said.

I didn't look up. I knew the only reason we were here was because of me. If it weren't for me, she wouldn't have to take jobs like this. She would be half a planet away, floating in a turquoise sea, dancing by moonlight to flamenco guitar. I felt my guilt like a brand.

That night she went out by herself. I drew for an hour, ate a peanut butter and mayonnaise sandwich, then drifted down to

Michael's, knocked on the hollow door. Three bolts fell back. "It's *Queen Christina*." He smiled, a gentle soft man about my mother's age, but puffy and pale from drinking and being inside all the time. He cleared a pile of dirty clothes and *Variety* from the couch so I could sit down.

The apartment was very different from ours, crammed with furniture and souvenirs and movie posters, *Variety* and newspapers and empty wine bottles, tomato plants straggling on the windowsills, groping for a little light. It was dark even in the daytime, because it faced north, but it had a spectacular view of the Hollywood sign, the reason he took it in the first place.

"*Snow again,*" he said along with Garbo, tilting his face up like hers. "*Eternal snow.*" He handed me a bowl of sunflower seeds. "I *am* Garbo."

I cracked seeds in my teeth and flicked off the rubber sandals I'd been wearing since April. I couldn't tell my mother I'd outgrown my shoes again. I didn't want to remind her that I was the reason she was trapped in electric bills and kid's shoes grown too small, the reason she was clawing at the windows like Michael's dying tomatoes. She was a beautiful woman dragging a crippled foot and I was that foot. I was bricks sewn into the hem of her clothes, I was a steel dress.

"What are you reading these days?" I asked Michael. He was an actor, but he didn't work that much, and he wouldn't do TV, so he made most of his money reading for Books on Tape. He had to do it under a pseudonym, Wolfram Malevich, because it was nonunion. We could hear him every morning, very early, through the wall. He knew German and Russian from the army, he'd been in army intelligence — an oxymoron, he always said — so they put him on German and Russian authors.

"Chekhov short stories." He leaned forward and handed me the book from the coffee table. It was full of notes and Post-its and underlines.

I leafed through the book. "My mother hates Chekhov. She says anybody who ever read him knows why there had to be a revolution."

"Your mother." Michael smiled. "Actually, you might really like him. There's a lovely melancholy in Chekhov." We both turned to the TV to catch the best line in *Queen Christina*, saying along with Garbo, *"The snow is like a white sea, one could go out and be lost in it . . . and forget the world."*

I thought of my mother as Queen Christina, cool and sad, eyes trained on some distant horizon. That was where she belonged, in furs and palaces of rare treasures, fireplaces large enough to roast a reindeer, ships of Swedish maple. My deepest fear was that someday she would find her way back there and never return. It was why I always waited up when she went out on nights like this, no matter how late she came home. I had to hear her key in the lock, smell her violet perfume again.

And I tried not to make it worse by asking for things, pulling her down with my thoughts. I had seen girls clamor for new clothes and complain about what their mothers made for dinner. I was always mortified. Didn't they know they were tying their mothers to the ground? Weren't chains ashamed of their prisoners?

But how I envied the way their mothers sat on their beds and asked what they were thinking. My mother was not in the least bit curious about me. I often wondered what she thought I was, a dog she could tie in front of the store, a parrot on her shoulder?

I never told her that I wished I had a father, that I wanted to go to camp in summertime, that sometimes she scared me. I was afraid she would fly away, and I would end up alone, living in some place where there were too many children, too many smells, where beauty and silence and the intoxication of her words rising in air would be as far away as Saturn.

Out the window, the glow of the Hollywood sign was slightly blurred with June fog, a soft wetness on the hills raising the smell of sage and chamise, moisture wiping the glass with dreams.

SHE CAME HOME at two when the bars closed, alone, her restlessness satisfied for the moment. I sat on her bed, watched her change clothes, adoring each gesture. Someday I would do this, the way she crossed her arms and pulled her dress over her head, kicked off her high heels. I put them on, admiring them on my feet. They were almost the right size. In another year or so, they would fit. She sat down next to me, handed me her brush, and I brushed her pale hair smooth, painting the air with her violets. "I saw the goat man again," she said.

"What goat man?"

"From the wine garden, remember? The grinning Pan, cloven hooves peeping out from under his pants?"

I could see the two of us in the round mirror on the wall, our long hair down, our blue eyes. Norsewomen. When I saw us like this, I could almost remember fishing in cold deep seas, the smell of cod, the charcoal of our fires, our felt boots and our strange alphabet, runes like sticks, a language like the ploughing of fields.

"He stared at me the entire time," she said. "Barry Kolker. Marlene says he's a writer of personal essays." Her fine lips turned into long commas of disapproval. "He was with that actress from *The Cactus Garden,* Jill Lewis."

Her white hair, like unbleached silk, flowed through the boar bristle brush.

"With that fat goat of a man. Can you imagine?" I knew she couldn't. Beauty was my mother's law, her religion. You could do anything you wanted, as long as you were beautiful, as long as you did things beautifully. If you weren't, you just didn't exist. She had drummed it into my head since I was small. Although I had noticed by now that reality didn't always conform to my mother's ideas.

"Maybe she likes him," I said.

"She must be insane," my mother said, taking the brush away from me and brushing my hair now, bearing down on the scalp hard. "She could have any man she wanted. What could she possibly be thinking?"

SHE SAW HIM again at her favorite artists' bar downtown with no sign by the tracks. She saw him at a party in Silverlake. Wherever she went, she complained, there he was, the goat man.

I thought it was only coincidence, but one night at a performance space in Santa Monica where we went to watch one of her friends beating on Sparkletts bottles and ranting about the drought, I saw him too, four rows back. He spent the whole time trying to catch her eye. He waved at me and I waved back, low, so she wouldn't see.

After it was over, I wanted to talk to him, but she dragged me out fast. "Don't encourage him," she hissed.

When he turned up at the annual publication party for *Cinema Scene*, I had to agree that he was following her. It was outside in the courtyard of an old hotel on the Strip. The heat of the day was beginning to dissipate. The women wore bare dresses, my mother like a moth in white silk. I threaded my way through the crowd to the hors d'oeuvres table, quickly loaded my purse with things I thought could stand a few hours unrefrigerated — crab claws and asparagus spears, liver in bacon — and there was Barry, piling a plate with shrimp. He saw me, and his eyes immediately swept the crowd for my mother. She was behind me, drinking white wine, gossiping with Miles, the photo editor, a gaunt, stubble-chinned Englishman whose fingers were stained with nicotine. She hadn't seen Barry yet. He started through the crowd toward her. I was close behind him.

"Ingrid," Barry said, penetrating her circle of two. "I've been looking for you." He smiled. Her eyes flicked cruelly over his mustard-colored tie hanging to one side, his brown shirt pulling at the buttons over his stomach, his uneven teeth, the shrimp in his chubby fist. I could hear the icy winds of Sweden, but he didn't seem to feel the chill.

"I've been thinking about you," he said, coming even closer.

"I'd rather you wouldn't," she said.

"You'll change your mind about me," he said. He put his

finger alongside his nose, winked at me, and walked on to another group of people, put his arm around a pretty girl, kissed her neck. My mother turned away. That kiss went against everything she believed. In her universe, it simply would never happen.

"You know Barry?" Miles asked.

"Who?" my mother said.

That night, she couldn't sleep. We went down to the apartment pool and swam slow quiet laps under the local stars, the Crab Claw, the Giant Shrimp.

MY MOTHER bent over her drafting table, cutting type without a ruler in long elegant strokes. "This is Zen," she said. "No flaw, no moment's hesitation. A window onto grace." She looked genuinely happy. It sometimes happened when she was pasting up just right, she forgot where she was, why she was there, where she'd been and would rather be, forgot about everything but the gift of cutting a perfectly straight freehand line, a pleasure as pure as when she'd just written a beautiful phrase.

But then I saw what she didn't see, the goat man enter the production room. I didn't want to be the one to ruin her moment of grace, so I kept making my Chinese tree out of benday dots and wrong-sized photo stills from *Salaam Bombay!* When I glanced up, he caught my eye and put his finger to his lips, crept up behind her and tapped her shoulder. Her knife went slicing through the type. She whirled around and I thought she was going to cut him, but he showed her something that stopped her, a small envelope he put on her table.

"For you and your daughter," he said.

She opened it, removed two tickets, blue-and-white. Her silence as she examined them astonished me. She stared at them, then him, jabbing the sharp end of her X-acto into the rubbery surface of the desk, a dart that stuck there for a moment before she pulled it out.

"Just the concert," she said. "No dinner, no dancing."

"Agreed," he said, but I could see he really didn't believe her. He didn't know her yet.

It was a gamelan concert at the art museum. Now I knew why she accepted. I only wondered how he knew exactly the right thing to propose, the one thing she would never turn down. Had he hidden in the oleanders outside our apartment? Interviewed her friends? Bribed somebody?

THE NIGHT crackled as my mother and I waited for him in the forecourt of the museum. Everything had turned to static electricity in the heat. I combed my hair to watch the sparks fly from the ends.

Forced to wait, my mother made small, jerky movements with her arms, her hands. "Late. How despicable. I should have known. He's probably off rutting in some field with the other goats. Remind me never to make plans with quadrupeds."

She still had on her work clothes, though she'd had time to change. It was a sign, to indicate to him that it wasn't a real date, that it meant nothing. All around us, women in bright summer silks and a shifting bouquet of expensive perfumes eyed her critically. Men admired her, smiled, stared. She stared back, blue eyes burning, until they grew awkward and turned away.

"Men," she said. "No matter how unappealing, each of them imagines he is somehow worthy."

I saw Barry across the plaza, his bulk jolting on his short legs. He grinned, flashing the gap between his teeth. "Sorry, but traffic was murder."

My mother turned away from the apology. Only peons made excuses for themselves, she taught me. Never apologize, never explain.

THE GAMELAN orchestra was twenty small slim men kneeling before elaborately carved sets of chimes and gongs and drums. The drum began, joined by one of the lower sets of chimes. Then more entered the growing mass of sound. Rhythms began to emerge, expand, complex as lianas. My mother said the gamelan created in the listener a brain wave beyond all alphas and betas and thetas, a brain wave that paralyzed the normal channels of thought and forced new ones to grow outside them, in the untouched regions of the mind, like parallel blood vessels that form to accommodate a damaged heart.

I closed my eyes to watch tiny dancers like jeweled birds cross the dark screen of my eyelids. They took me away, spoke to me in languages that had no words for strange mothers with ice-blue eyes and apartments with ugly sparkles on the front and dead leaves in the pool.

Afterward, the audience folded its plush velvet chairs and pressed to the exits, but my mother didn't move. She sat in her chair, her eyes closed. She liked to be the last one to leave. She despised crowds, and their opinions as they left a performance, or worse, discussed the wait for the bathroom or where do you want to eat? It spoiled her mood. She was still in that other world, she would stay there as long as she possibly could, the parallel channels twining and tunneling through her cortex like coral.

"It's over," Barry said.

She raised her hand for him to be quiet. He looked at me and I shrugged. I was used to it. We waited until the last sound had faded from the auditorium. Finally she opened her eyes.

"So, you want to grab a bite to eat?" he asked her.

"I never eat," she said.

I was hungry, but once my mother took a position, she never wavered from it. We went home, where I ate tuna out of a can while she wrote a poem using the rhythms of the gamelan, about shadow puppets and the gods of chance.

⮞

2

THE SUMMER I was twelve, I liked to wander in the complex where the movie magazine had its offices. It was called Crossroads of the World, a 1920s courtyard with a streamline-moderne ocean liner in the middle occupied by an ad agency. I sat on a stone bench and imagined Fred Astaire leaning on the liner's brass rail, wearing a yachting cap and blue blazer.

Along the outside ring of the brick-paved courtyard, fantasy bungalows built in styles from Brothers Grimm to Don Quixote were rented by photo studios, casting agents, typesetting shops. I sketched a laughing Carmen lounging under the hanging basket of red geraniums in the Sevillian doorway of the modeling agency, and a demure braided Gretel sweeping the Germanic steps of the photo studio with a twig broom.

While I drew, I watched the tall beautiful girls coming in and out of these doors, passing from the agency to the studio and back, where they bled a bit more of their hard-earned money from waitressing and temp jobs to further their careers. It was a scam, my mother said, and I wanted to tell them so, but their beauty seemed a charm. What ill could befall girls like that, long-legged in their hiphugger pants and diaphanous summer dresses, with their clear eyes and sculpted faces? The heat of the day never touched them, they were living in another climate.

At eleven or so one morning, my mother appeared in the tiled doorway of the *Cinema Scene* staircase and I closed my notebook, figuring she was taking an early lunch. But we didn't go to the car. Instead, I followed her around the corner, and there, leaning on an old gold Lincoln with suicide doors, stood Barry Kolker. He was wearing a bright plaid jacket.

My mother took one look at him and closed her eyes. "That jacket is so ugly I can't even look at you. Did you steal it from a dead man?"

Barry grinned, opening the doors for me and my mother. "Haven't you ever been to the races? You've got to wear something loud. It's traditional."

"You look like a couch in an old-age home," she said as we got in. "Thank God no one I know will see me with you."

We were going on a date with Barry. I was astonished. I was sure the gamelan concert would be the last we'd ever see him. And now he was holding open the back door of the Lincoln for me. I'd never been to the racetrack. It wasn't the kind of place my mother would think of taking me — outdoors, horses, nobody reading a book or thinking about Beauty and Fate.

"I normally wouldn't do this," my mother said, settling herself in the front seat, putting on her seat belt. "But the idea of the stolen hour is just too delicious."

"You'll love it." Barry climbed behind the wheel. "It's way too nice a day to be stuck in that sweatshop."

"Always," my mother said.

We picked up the freeway on Cahuenga, drove north out of Hollywood into the Valley, then east toward Pasadena. The heat lay on the city like a lid.

Santa Anita sat at the base of the San Gabriel Mountains, a sheer blue granite wall like a tidal wave. Bright banks of flowers and perfect green lawns breathed out a heavy perfume in the smoggy air. My mother walked a little ahead of Barry and pretended she didn't know him, until she finally realized that everybody was dressed like that, white shoes and green polyester.

The horses were fine-tuned machines on steel springs, shiny as metal, and the jockeys' satin shirts gleamed in the sun as they walked their mounts around the track, each horse coupled with an older, steadier partner. The horses shied at children at the rail, at flags, all nerves and heat.

"Pick a horse," Barry told my mother.

She picked number seven, a white horse, because of her name, Medea's Pride.

The jockeys had trouble getting them into the starting gates, but when the gates opened, the horses pounded the brown of the track in a unit.

"Come on, seven," we yelled. "Lucky seven."

She won. My mother laughed and hugged me, hugged Barry. I'd never seen her like this, excited, laughing, she seemed so young. Barry had bet twenty dollars for her, and handed her the money, one hundred dollars.

"How about dinner?" he asked her.

Yes, I prayed. Please say yes. After all, how could she refuse him now?

She took us to dinner at the nearby Surf 'n' Turf, where

Barry and I both ordered salads and steaks medium rare, baked potatoes with sour cream. My mother just had a glass of white wine. That was Ingrid Magnussen. She made up rules and suddenly they were engraved on the Rosetta Stone, they'd been brought to the surface from a cave under the Dead Sea, they were inscribed on scrolls from the T'ang Dynasty.

During the meal Barry told us of his travels in the Orient, where we had never been. The time he ordered magic mushrooms off the menu at a beachside shack in Bali and ended up wandering the turquoise shore hallucinating Paradise. His trip to the temples of Angkor Wat in the Cambodian jungle accompanied by Thai opium smugglers. His week spent in the floating brothels of Bangkok. He had forgotten me entirely, was too absorbed in hypnotizing my mother. His voice was cloves and nightingales, it took us to spice markets in the Celebes, we drifted with him on a houseboat beyond the Coral Sea. We were like cobras following a reed flute.

On the way home, she let him touch her waist as she got into the car.

BARRY ASKED US to dinner at his house, said he'd like to cook some Indonesian dishes he'd learned there. I waited until afternoon to tell her I wasn't feeling well, that she should go without me. I hungered for Barry, I thought he might be the one, someone who could feed us and hold us and make us real.

She spent an hour trying on clothes, white Indian pajamas, the blue gauze dress, the pineapples and hula girls. I'd never seen her so indecisive.

"The blue," I said. It had a low neck and the blue was

exactly the color of her eyes. No one could resist her in her blue dress.

She chose the Indian pajamas, which covered every inch of her golden skin. "I'll be home early," she said.

I lay on her bed after she was gone and imagined them together, their deep voices a duet in the dusk over the rijsttafel. I hadn't had any since we left Amsterdam, where we lived when I was seven; the smell of it used to permeate our neighborhood there. My mother always said we'd go to Bali. I imagined us in a house with an extravagantly peaked roof, overlooking green rice terraces and miraculously clear seas, where we'd wake to chimes and the baaing of goats.

After a while I made myself a cheese and sweet pickle sandwich and went next door to Michael's. He was halfway through a bottle of red wine from Trader Joe's — "poverty chic" he called it, because it had a cork — and he was crying, watching a Lana Turner movie. I didn't like Lana Turner and I couldn't stand looking at the dying tomatoes, so I read Chekhov until Michael passed out, then went downstairs and swam in the pool warm as tears. I floated on my back and looked up at the stars, the Goat, the Swan, and hoped my mother was falling in love.

All that weekend, she didn't say a thing about her date with Barry, but she wrote poems and crumpled them up, threw them at the wastebasket.

IN THE ART ROOM, Kit proofread over my mother's shoulder, while I sat at my table in the corner, making a collage about Chekhov, the lady with the little dog, cutting out figures from discarded photographs. Marlene answered the phone, covered the receiver with her hand.

"It's Barry Kolker."

Kit's head jerked up at the sound of the name, a marionette in the hands of a clumsy puppeteer. "I'll take it in my office."

"It's for Ingrid," Marlene said.

My mother didn't look up from her layout sheet. "Tell him I don't work here anymore."

Marlene told him, lying like oil.

"How do you know Barry Kolker?" the editor asked, her black eyes big as olives.

"Just someone I met," my mother said.

That evening, in the long summer twilight, people came out of their apartments, walked their dogs, drank blender drinks down by the pool, their feet in the water. The moon rose, squatting in the strained blue. My mother knelt at her table, writing, and a slight breeze brushed the wind chimes we'd hung in the old eucalyptus, while I lay on her bed. I wanted to freeze this moment forever, the chimes, the slight splash of water, the chink of dogs' leashes, laughter from the pool, the skritch of my mother's dip-pen, the smell of the tree, the stillness. I wished I could shut it in a locket to wear around my neck. I wished a thousand-year sleep would find us, at this absolute second, like the sleep over the castle of Sleeping Beauty.

There was a knock on the door, wrecking the peace. Nobody ever came to our door. My mother put down her pen and grabbed the folding knife she kept in the jar with the pencils, its dark carbon blade sharp enough to shave a cat. She unfolded it against her thigh and put her finger to her lips. She clutched her white kimono, her skin bare underneath.

It was Barry, calling her. "Ingrid!"

"How dare he," she said. "He cannot simply appear on my doorstep without an invitation."

She jerked the door open. Barry was wearing a wrinkled Hawaiian shirt and carrying a bottle of wine and a bag that smelled of something wonderful. "Hi," he said. "I was just in the neighborhood, thought I'd drop by."

She stood in the doorway, the open blade still against her thigh. "Oh, you did."

Then she did something I would never have imagined. She invited him in, closing the knife against her leg.

He looked around at our big room, elegantly bare. "Just move in?" She said nothing. We had lived there over a year.

THE SUN was hot through the screens when I woke up, illuminating the milky stagnant air wrapped like a towel around the morning. I could hear a man singing, the shower pipes clanking as he turned the water off. Barry had stayed the night. She was breaking her rules. They weren't stone after all, only small and fragile as paper cranes. I stared at her as she dressed for work, waiting for an explanation, but she just smiled.

After that night, the change was startling. Sunday, we went together to the Hollywood farmer's market, where she and Barry bought spinach and green beans, tomatoes and grapes no bigger than the head of a thumbtack, papery braids of garlic, while I trailed behind them, mute with amazement at the sight of my mother examining displays of produce like it was a trip to a bookstore. My mother, for whom a meal was a carton of yogurt or a can of sardines and soda crackers. She could eat

26

peanut butter for weeks on end without even noticing. I watched as she bypassed stands full of her favorite white flowers, lilies and chrysanthemums, and instead filled her arms with giant red poppies with black stains in the centers. On the walk home, she and Barry held hands and sang together in deep croony voices old songs from the sixties, "Wear Your Love Like Heaven" and "Waterloo Sunset."

So many things I would never have imagined. She wrote tiny haiku that she slipped into his pockets. I fished them out whenever I got a chance, to see what she had written. It made me blush to read them: *Poppies bleed petals of sheer excess. You and I, this sweet battleground.*

One morning at the magazine, she showed me a picture in the weekly throwaway *Caligula's Mother*, taken at a party after a play's opening night. They both looked bombed. The caption dubbed her Barry's new lady love. It was exactly the kind of thing she hated the most, a woman as a man's anything. Now it was as if she'd won a contest.

Passion. I never imagined it was something that could happen to her. These were days she couldn't recognize herself in a mirror, her eyes black with it, her hair forever tangled and smelling of musk, Barry's goat scent.

They went out and she told me about it afterward, laughing. "Women approach him, their peacock voices crying, 'Barry! Where have you been?' But it doesn't matter. He is with me now. I am the only one he wants."

Passion ruled her. Gone were the references to his physical goatishness, his need for dental work, his flabby physique, his

27

squalid taste in clothes, the wretchedness of his English, his shameless clichés, the criminal triteness of his oeuvre, a man who wrote "snuck." I never thought I'd see my mother plaster herself against a stout ponytailed man in the hallway outside our apartment, or let him inch his hand up her skirt under the table when we ate dinner one night at a dark Hunan restaurant in old Chinatown. I watched her close her eyes, I could feel the waves of her passion like perfume across the teacups.

In the mornings, he lay with her on the wide white mattress when I crossed the room on the way to the toilet. They would even talk to me, her head cradled on his arm, the room full of the scent of their lovemaking, as if it was the most natural thing in the world. It made me want to laugh out loud. In the courtyard at Crossroads of the World, I sat under a pepper tree and wrote "Mr. and Mrs. Barry Kolker" in my sketchbook. I practiced saying, "Can I call you Dad?"

I never told my mother I wanted a father. I had only questioned her once on the subject, I must have been in kindergarten. We were back in the States that year, living in Hollywood. A hot, smoggy day, and my mother was in a bad mood. She picked me up late from day care, we had to go to the market. We were driving in an old Datsun she had then, I still remember the hot waffled seat and how I could see the street through a hole in the floorboards.

School had just started, and our young teacher, Mrs. Williams, had asked us about our fathers. The fathers lived in Seattle or Panorama City or San Salvador, a couple were even dead. They had jobs like lawyers or drummers or installing car window glass.

"Where's my father?" I asked my mother.

She downshifted irritably, throwing me against the seat belt. "You have no father," she said.

"Everybody has a father," I said.

"Fathers are irrelevant. Believe me, you're lucky. I had one, I know. Just forget it." She turned on the radio, loud rock 'n' roll.

It was as if I was blind and she'd told me, sight doesn't matter, it's just as well you can't see. I began to watch fathers, in the stores, on the playgrounds, pushing their daughters on swings. I liked how they seemed to know what to do. They seemed like a dock, firmly attached to the world, you could be safe then, not always drifting like us. I prayed Barry Kolker would be that man.

Their murmured words of love were my lullabies, my hope chest. I was stacking in linens, summer camp, new shoes, Christmas. I was laying up sit-down dinners, a room of my own, a bicycle, parent-teacher nights. A year like the one before it, and the next like that, one after another, a bridge, and a thousand things more subtle and nameless that girls without fathers know.

Barry took us to the Fourth of July game at Dodger Stadium and bought us Dodger caps. We ate hot dogs and they drank beer from paper cups and he explained baseball to her like it was philosophy, the key to the American character. Barry threw money to the peanut vendor and caught the bag the man threw back. We littered the ground with peanut shells. I hardly recognized us in our peaked blue caps. We were like a family. I pretended we were just Mom, Dad, and the kid. We did the wave, and they kissed through the whole seventh inning, while I drew faces on the peanuts. The fireworks set off every car alarm in the parking lot.

Another weekend, he took us to Catalina. I was violently seasick on the ferry, and Barry held a cold handkerchief to my forehead and got me some mints to suck. I loved his brown eyes, the way he looked so worried, as if he'd never seen a kid throw up before. I tried not to hang around with them too much once we got there, hoping he would ask her while they strolled among the sailboats eating shrimp from a paper cone.

SOMETHING HAPPENED. All I remember is that the winds had started. The skeleton rattlings of wind in the palms. It was a night Barry said he would come at nine, but then it was eleven and he hadn't arrived. My mother played her Peruvian flute tape to soothe her nerves, Irish harp music, Bulgarian singers, but nothing worked. The calming, chiming tones ill suited her temper. Her gestures were anxious and unfinished.

"Let's go for a swim," I said.

"I can't," she said. "He might call."

Finally, she flipped out the tape and replaced it with one of Barry's, a jazz tape by Chet Baker, romantic, the kind of music she always hated before.

"Cocktail lounge music. For people to cry into their beer with," she said. "But I don't have any beer."

He went out of town on assignments for different magazines. He canceled their dates. My mother couldn't sleep, she jumped whenever the phone rang. I hated to see the look on her face when it wasn't Barry. A tone I'd never heard crept into her voice, serrated, like the edge of a saw.

I didn't understand how this could happen, how he could give us fireworks and Catalina, how he could hold that cold cloth to my forehead, and talk about taking us to Bali, and then forget our address.

ONE AFTERNOON, we stopped by his house unannounced.

"He's going to be mad," I said.

"We were just in the neighborhood. Just thought we'd stop by," she said.

I could no more keep her from doing this than I could keep the sun from coming up through the boiled smog on an August morning, but I didn't want to see it. I waited in the car. She knocked on the door and he answered wearing a seersucker bathrobe. I didn't have to hear her to know what she was saying. She wore her blue gauze dress, the hot wind ruffling her hem, the sun at her back, turning it transparent. He stood in his doorway, blocking it, and she held her head to one side, moving closer, touching her hair. I felt a rubber band stretching in my brain, tighter and tighter, until they disappeared into his house.

I played the radio, classical music. I couldn't stand to hear anything with words. I imagined my own ice-blue eyes looking at some man, telling him to go away, that I was busy. "You're not my type," I said coolly into the rearview mirror.

A half hour later she reappeared, stumbling out to the car, tripping over a sprinkler, as if she were blind. She got in and sat behind the steering wheel and rocked back and forth, her mouth open in a square, but there was no sound. My mother was crying. It was the final impossibility.

"He has a date," she finally said, whispering, her voice like there were hands around her throat. "He made love with me, and then said I had to leave. Because he has a date."

I knew we shouldn't have come. Now I wished she'd never broken any of her rules. I understood why she held to them so hard. Once you broke the first one, they all broke, one by one, like firecrackers exploding in your face in a parking lot on the Fourth of July.

I was afraid to let her drive like this, with her eyes wild, seeing nothing. She'd kill us before we got three blocks. But she didn't start the car. She sat there, staring through the windshield, rocking herself, holding herself around her waist.

A few minutes later, a car pulled up in the driveway, a new-model sports car, the top down, a blond girl driving. She was very young and wore a short skirt. She leaned over to get her bag out of the backseat.

"She's not as pretty as you," I said.

"But she's a simpler girl," my mother whispered bitterly.

KIT LEANED on the counter in the production room, her magenta lips a wolf's stained smile.

"Ingrid, guess who I saw last night at the Virgins," she said, her high voice breathless with malice. "Our old friend Barry Kolker." She stage-sighed. "With some cheap little blond half his age. Men have such short memories, don't they?" Her nostrils twitched as she stifled a laugh.

At lunchtime, my mother told me to take everything I wanted, art supplies, stationery. We were leaving and we weren't coming back.

3

⌐⌐

"I should shave my head," she said. "Paint my face with ashes."

Her eyes were strange, circled dark like bruises, and her hair was greasy and lank. She lay on her bed, or stared at herself in the mirror. "How can I shed tears for a man I should never have allowed to touch me in any way?"

She didn't go back to work. She wouldn't leave the darkened apartment except to go down to the pool, where she sat for hours watching the reflections in the shimmering blue, or swam silently underwater like a fish in an aquarium. It was time for me to go back to school. But I couldn't leave her alone, not when she was like this. She might not be there when I returned. So we stayed in, eating all the canned food in the apartment, then we were eating rice and oatmeal.

"What do I do?" I asked Michael as he fed me cheese and sardines at his battered coffee table. The TV news showed fires burning on the Angeles Crest.

Michael shook his head, at me, at the line of firemen

stradling the hillside. "Honey, this is what happens when you fall in love. You're looking at a natural disaster."

I vowed I would never fall in love. I hoped Barry died a slow lingering death for what he was doing to my mother.

A RED MOON rose over downtown, red from the fires burning to the north and out in Malibu. It was the season of fire, and we were trapped in the heart of the burning landscape. Ashes floated in the pool. We sat on the roof in the burnt wind.

"This ragged heart," she said, pulling at her kimono. "I should rip it out and bury it for compost."

I wished I could touch her, but she was inside her own isolation booth, like on Miss America. She couldn't hear me through the glass.

She doubled over, pressing her forearms against her chest, pressing the air out of herself. "I press it within my body," she said. "As the earth presses a lump of prehistoric dung in heat and crushing weight deep under the ground. I hate him. Hate. I hate him." She whispered this last, but ferociously. "A jewel is forming inside my body. No, it's not my heart. This is harder, cold and clean. I wrap myself around this new jewel, cradle it within me."

The next morning she got up. She took a shower, went to the market. And I thought things were going to be better now. She called Marlene and asked if she could come back to work. It was shipping week and they needed her desperately. She dropped me at school, to start the eighth grade at Le Conte Junior High. As if nothing had ever happened. And I thought it was over.

34

It was not over. She began to follow Barry, as he had followed her in the beginning. She went everywhere he might be, hunting him so that she could polish her hatred on the sight of him.

"My hatred gives me strength," she said.

She took Marlene to lunch at his favorite restaurant, where they found him eating at the bar, and she smiled at him. He pretended he didn't notice her, but he kept touching his face along the jaw. "Searching for acne that was no longer there," she told me that night. "The force of my gaze threatened to call it back into being."

She seemed so happy, and I didn't know which was worse, this or before, when she wanted to shave her head.

We shopped at his market, driving miles out of our way to meet him over the cantaloupes. We browsed at his favorite music store. We went to book signings for books written by his friends.

SHE CAME HOME one night after three. It was a school night but I'd stayed up watching a white hunter movie starring Stewart Granger on cable. Michael was passed out on the couch. The hot winds tested the windows like burglars looking for a way in. Finally I went home and fell asleep on my mother's bed, dreaming about carrying supplies on my head through the jungle, the white hunter nowhere to be seen.

She sat on the edge of the bed and took off her shoes. "I found him. A party at Gracie Kelleher's. We crossed paths by the diving board." She lay down next to me, whispering in my ear. "He and a chubby redhead in a transparent blouse were having a little tête-à-tête. He got up and grabbed me by the arm." She pushed up her sleeve and showed me the marks on her arm, angry, red.

"'Are you following me?' he hissed. I could have cut his throat right there. 'I don't have to follow you,' I replied. 'I can read your mind. I know every move you make. I know your future, Barry, and it doesn't look good.' 'I want you to leave,' he said. I smiled. 'I'm sure you do.' I could see his red flush even in the dark. 'It's not going to work,' he said. 'I'm warning you, Ingrid, it's not going to work.'" My mother laughed, her arms twined behind her head. "He doesn't understand. It's already working."

A SATURDAY AFTERNOON, hot and scented with fire, a parched sky. The time of year you couldn't even go to the beach because of the toxic red tide, the time when the city dropped to its knees like ancient Sodom, praying for redemption. We sat in the car down the block from Barry's house, under a carob tree. I hated the way she watched his house, her calm that was not even sane, like a patient hawk on top of a lightning-struck tree. But there was no point in trying to convince her to go home. She no longer spoke the language I did. I broke a carob pod under my nose and smelled the musky scent and pretended I was waiting for my father, a plumber inspecting some pipes in this small brick house with its dandelion-dotted lawn, its leaded picture window with a lamp in it.

Then Barry came out, wearing Bermuda shorts and a T-shirt that said Local Motion, funky little John Lennon sunglasses, his hair in its ponytail. He got in the old gold Lincoln and drove away. "Come on," my mother said. She put on a pair of white cotton gloves, the kind the photo editor used when he handled stills, and threw me a pair. I didn't want to go with her but didn't want to be left in the car either, so I went.

We walked up the path to his house as if we belonged there, and my mother reached into the Balinese spirit house he kept on the porch and pulled out a key. Inside, I was seized again by the sadness of what had happened, the finality. Once I had thought I might even live there, with the big wayang kulit puppets, batik pillows, and dragon kites hanging from the ceiling. His statues of Shiva and Parvati in their eternal embrace hadn't bothered me before, when I thought he and my mother would be like that, that it would last forever and engender a new universe. But now I hated them.

My mother turned on his computer at the great carved desk. The machine whirred. She typed something in and all the things on the screen disappeared. I understood why she did it. At that moment I knew why people tagged graffiti on the walls of neat little houses and scratched the paint on new cars and beat up well-tended children. It was only natural to want to destroy something you could never have. She took a horseshoe magnet from her purse and wiped it over all his floppy diskettes marked "backup."

"I almost feel sorry for him," she said as she turned the computer off. "But not quite."

She took her X-acto knife and selected a shirt from his closet, his favorite brown shirt. "How right he should wear clothing the color of excrement." She laid it on the bed and slashed it into fringe. Then she tucked a white oleander into a buttonhole.

SOMEONE WAS pounding on our door. She looked up from a new poem she was writing. She wrote all the time now. "Do you think he lost something valuable on that hard disk? Maybe a collection of essays due at the publisher this fall?" It frightened me, watching the door jump on its hinges. I thought of the marks on my mother's arms. Barry wasn't a brutal person, but everyone has a limit. If he got in, she was dead.

But my mother didn't seem upset. In fact, the harder he pounded, the happier she looked, pink-cheeked, bright-eyed. She had brought him back to her. She got out the folding knife from her pencil can and unfolded it against her thigh. We could hear him screaming, crying, his velvet voice rubbed threadbare. "I'm going to kill you, Ingrid, so help me God."

The pounding stopped. My mother listened, holding the knife open against the white silk of her robe. Suddenly he was on the other side of the apartment, pounding on the windows, we could see him, his face distorted with rage, huge and terrifying in the oleanders. I shrank back against the wall, but my mother just stood in the center of the room, gleaming, like a grassfire.

"I'm going to kill you!" he screamed.

"So helpless in his fury," my mother said to me. "Impotent, one might say."

He broke a windowpane. I could tell he hadn't intended to because he hesitated, and then, in a sudden burst of courage, he thrust his arm through the window and fumbled for the latch. She crossed the room faster than I could have believed possible, lifted her arm and stabbed him in the hand. The knife struck home. She had to jerk it out, and his arm raced back through the hole in the window. "You bloody bitch!" he was screaming.

I wanted to hide, to stop up my ears, but I couldn't stop watching. This was how love and passion ended. The lights were going on in the next building.

"My neighbors are calling the police," she said out the broken window. "You better go."

He stumbled away, and in a moment we heard him kick the front door. "You fucking cunt. You won't get away with this. You can't do this to me."

She threw open the front door then, and stood there in her white kimono, his blood on her knife. "You don't know what I can do," she said softly.

AFTER THAT NIGHT, she couldn't find him anymore, at the Virgins or Barney's, at parties or club dates. He changed his locks. We had to use a metal pasteup ruler to open a window. This time she put a sprig of oleander in his milk, another in his oyster sauce, in his cottage cheese. She stuck one in his toothpaste. She made an arrangement of white oleanders in a hand-blown vase on his coffee table, and scattered blooms on his bed.

I was torn. He deserved to be punished, but now she had crossed over some line. This wasn't revenge. She'd had her revenge, she had won, but it was like she didn't even know it. She was drifting outside the limit of all reason, where the next stop was light-years away through nothing but darkness. How lovingly she arranged the dark leaves, the white blooms.

A POLICE OFFICER showed up at our apartment. The officer, Inspector Ramirez, informed her that Barry was accusing her of breaking and entering and of trying to poison him. She was completely calm. "Barry is terribly angry with me," she said, posing in the doorway, her arms crossed. "I ended our relationship several weeks ago, and he just can't let go of it. He's obsessed with me. He even tried to break into this apartment. This is my daughter, Astrid, she can tell you what happened."

I shrugged. I didn't like this. It was going way too far.

My mother kept going without missing a comma. "The neighbors even called the police that night. You must have a record of it. And now he's accusing me of breaking into his house? That poor man, really, he's not all that attractive, it must be hard for him."

Her hatred glittered irresistibly. I could see it, the jewel, it was sapphire, it was the cold lakes of Norway. Oh Inspector Ramirez, her eyes said, you're a good-looking man, how could you understand someone as desperate as Barry Kolker?

After he left, how she laughed.

THE NEXT TIME we saw Barry was at the Rose Bowl Flea Market, where he liked to shop for ugly gag gifts for his friends. My mother wore a hat that dappled her face with light. He saw her and turned away quickly, fear plain as billboards, but then he thought again, turned back, smiled at us.

"A change of tactic," she whispered. "Here he comes."

He walked right over to us, a papier-mâché Oscar in his hands. "Congratulations on your performance with Ramirez," he said, and held it out to her. "Best actress of the year."

"I don't know what you mean," my mother said. She was holding my hand, squeezing it too tight, but her face was smiling and relaxed.

"Sure you do," he said. He tucked Oscar under his arm. "But that's not why I came over. I thought we could bury the hatchet. Look, I'll admit I went too far calling the cops. I know I was an asshole, but for Christ's sake, you tried to destroy the better part of a year's work. Of course my agent had a preliminary draft, thank God, but even so. Why don't we just call it a draw?"

My mother smiled, shifted to the other foot. She was waiting for him to do something, say something.

"It's not like I don't respect you as a person," he said. "And as a writer. We all know you're a great poet. I've even talked you up at some of the magazines. Can't we move on to the next phase now, and be friends?"

She bit her lip as if she was seriously considering what he was saying, while all the while she poked the center of my palm with her nail until I thought it would go right through my hand. Finally she said in her low rich voice, "Sure we can. Well, why not."

They shook hands on it. He looked a little suspicious but relieved as he went back to his bargain hunting. And I thought, he still didn't know her at all.

We showed up at his house that night. He had bars on all the windows now. She stroked his new security door with the pads

41

of her fingers like it was fur. "Taste his fear. It tastes just like champagne. Cold and crisp and absolutely without sweetness."

She rang the bell. He opened the inner door, gazed at us through the security mesh. Smiled uncertainly. The wind rippled through the silk of her dress, through her moon-pale hair. She held up the bottle of Riesling she'd brought. "Seeing we're friends and all."

"Ingrid, I can't let you in," he said.

She smiled, slid her finger down one of the bars, flirting. "Now is that any way to treat a friend?"

WE SWAM in the hot aquamarine of the pool late at night, in the clatter of palms and the twinkle of the new-scoured sky. My mother floated on her back, humming to herself. "God, I love this." She splashed gently with her fingers, letting her body drift in a slow circle. "Isn't it funny. I'm enjoying my hatred so much more than I ever enjoyed love. Love is temperamental. Tiring. It makes demands. Love uses you. Changes its mind." Her eyes were closed. Beads of water decorated her face, and her hair spread out from her head like jellyfish tendrils. "But hatred, now. That's something you can use. Sculpt. Wield. It's hard or soft, however you need it. Love humiliates you, but hatred cradles you. It's so soothing. I feel infinitely better now."

"I'm glad," I said. I was glad she felt happier, but I didn't like the kind of happiness it was, I didn't believe in it, I believed it would crack open sooner or later and terrible things would come flying out.

*

WE DROVE down to Tijuana. We didn't stop to buy piñatas or crepe paper flowers or earrings or purses. She kept looking at a scrap of paper in her hand as we wandered around the side streets past the burros painted like zebras and the tiny Indian women begging with their children. I gave them my change until it was all gone, and chewed the stale gum they gave me. She paid no attention. Then she found what she was looking for, a pharmacy, just like a pharmacy in L.A., brightly lit, the pharmacist in a white coat.

"*Por favor, tiene usted* DMSO?" she asked.

"You have arthritis?" he asked in easy English.

"Yes," she said. "As a matter of fact. A friend of mine told me you carry it."

"What size would you like?" He pulled out three bottles, one the size of a bottle of vanilla, one the same as nail polish remover, and the largest like a bottle of vinegar. She chose the big one.

"How much?"

"Eighty dollars, miss."

"Eighty." My mother hesitated. Eighty dollars was food money for two weeks, eighty dollars was two months' worth of gas for the car. What could be worth eighty dollars, that we drove down to Tijuana to buy?

"Let's go," I said. "Let's get in the car and just drive. Let's go to La Paz."

She looked at me. I'd caught her by surprise, so I kept talking, thinking maybe I could get us back onto some planet I recognized. "We could take the first ferry in the morning. Can't we just do that? Drive to Jalisco. San Miguel de Allende. We could close our accounts, have the money wired to the American Express, and just keep going."

How easy it could be. She knew where all the gas stations were from here to Panama, the cheap grand hotels with high ceilings and carved wooden headboards just off the main plazas. In three days we could put a thousand miles between us and this bottle of disaster. "You always liked it down there. You never wanted to come back to the States."

For an instant, I had her. I knew she was remembering the years we had spent down there, her lovers, the color of the sea. But it wasn't a strong enough spell, I wasn't a word spinner like her, not good enough, and the image faded, returning to the screen of her obsession: Barry and the blond, Barry and the redhead, Barry in a seersucker bathrobe.

"Too late," she said. She pulled out her wallet, counted four twenties onto the counter.

AT NIGHT she began cooking things in the kitchen, things too strange to mention. She steeped oleander in boiling water, and the roots of a vine with white trumpet flowers that glowed like faces. She soaked a plant collected in moonlight from the neighbors' fence, with little heart-shaped flowers. Then she cooked the water down; the whole kitchen smelled like green and rotting leaves. She threw out pounds of the wet spinach-green stuff into somebody else's dumpster. She wasn't talking to me anymore. She sat on the roof and talked to the moon.

"WHAT'S DMSO?" I asked Michael one night when she had gone out. He was drinking scotch, real Johnnie Walker, celebrating because he'd gotten a job at the Music Center in

Macbeth, though he couldn't call it that, it was bad luck. All the witches and stuff. You were supposed to call it the Scottish play. Michael was taking no chances, it had been a year since he'd done anything but Books on Tape.

"People use it for arthritis," he said.

I leafed through a *Variety* and tried to ask casually, "Is it dangerous?"

"Completely harmless," he said. He raised his glass and examined the amber liquor, then sipped slowly, his eyes closing in satisfaction.

I hadn't expected good news. "What's it for, then?"

"It helps drugs absorb through your skin. That's how the nicotine patch works, and those seasickness patches. You put it on and the DMSO lets it get through your skin into the bloodstream. Marvelous stuff. I remember when they used to worry that hippies would mix it with LSD and paint the doorknobs of public buildings." He laughed into his drink. "As if anybody would waste their acid on a bunch of straights."

I LOOKED FOR the bottle of DMSO. I couldn't find it anywhere. I looked under the kitchen sink and in the bathroom, in the drawers — there just weren't many places to hide things in our apartment, and anyway, hiding things wasn't my mother's style. I waited up for her. She came back late, with a handsome young man whose dark curls trailed halfway down his back. She held his hand.

"This is Jesus," she said. "He's a poet. My daughter, Astrid."

"Hi," I said. "Mom, can I talk to you for a second?"

"You should be in bed," she said. "I'll be right back." She smiled at Jesus, let go of his hand, and walked me out onto the screen porch. She looked beautiful again, no circles under her eyes, hair like falling water.

I lay down in my bed and she covered me with a sheet, stroked my face. "Mom, what happened to that stuff from Mexico?"

She just kept smiling, but her eyes told me everything.

"Don't do it," I said.

She kissed me and stroked my hair with her cool hand, always cool, despite the heat, despite the wind and the fires, and then she was gone.

THE NEXT DAY I called Barry's number.

"Tunnel of Love," a girl answered, stoned, giggling. I heard his voice, velvet, in the background. Then he came on the line. "Hello?"

I was going to warn him, but now all I could remember was my mother's face when she came out of his house that day. The way she rocked, the square of her mouth. Anyway, what could I tell him — don't touch anything, don't eat anything, watch out? He was already suspicious of her. If I told him, they might arrest her, and I would not hurt my mother, not for Barry Kolker and his screwing Shivas. He deserved it. He had it coming.

"Hello," he said, as she said something and laughed, stupidly. "Well, fuck you too," he said, and hung up.

I didn't call again.

*

WE SAT ON the roof and watched the moon, red and huge in the ash-laden air, hovering over the city laid out like a Ouija board. All around us was a Greek chorus of sirens, while my mother's mad low voice murmured, "They can't touch us. We're the Vikings. We go into battle without armor for the flush and the blood of it." She leaned down and kissed my head, smelling of metal and smoke.

The hot wind blew and blew and would not stop.

4

⌒

THEN CAME A TIME I can hardly describe, a season underground. A bird trapped in a sewer, wings beating against the ceiling in that dark wet place, while the city rumbled on overhead. Her name was Lost. Her name was Nobody's Daughter.

In my dreams, my mother walked through a city of bricks and rubble, a city after war, and she was blind, her eyes empty and white as stones. There were tall apartments all around her, with triangles over windows, all bricked up and burning. Blind windows, and her blind eyes, and yet still she came toward me, inevitable and insane. I saw that her face was melted and horribly pliable. There were hollows in the tops of her cheeks, under her eyes, as if someone had pressed into soft clay with their thumbs.

Those heavy days, how heavy the low gray sky, my wings were so heavy, so heavy my panicked flight under the ground. So many faces, so many lips, wanting me to tell, it made me tired, I fell asleep as they spoke. *Just tell us what happened.* What could I tell? When I opened my mouth, a stone fell out. Her poor white eyeballs. Just where I hoped to find mercy. I dreamed of white milk in the street, white milk and glass. Milk down the gutter, milk like tears. I kept her kimono against my face, her scent of violets and ash. I rubbed the silk between my fingers.

In that place under the ground lived many children, babies, teenagers, and the rooms echoed noise like a subway. Music like a train wreck, arguing, crying, the ceaseless TV. The heavy smell of cooking, thin sickly urine, pine cleaner. The woman who ran it made me get out of bed at regular intervals, sit at the table with the others before platters of beans and greens, meat. I dutifully came out, sat, ate, then returned to the cocoon of bed and sleep, plastic sheet crinkling under me. I woke up soaked to the armpits more nights than not.

The girl in the other bed had seizures. The niece told me, "There's more money in disability children like you all."

Roses drifted down the walls in brownish slants in the room. I counted roses. Diagonal rows of forty, ninety-two across. Over the dresser, Jesus, JFK, and Martin Luther King, Jr., all in profile, facing left, like racehorses at the starting gate, Jesus on the outside. The woman who ran the home, Mrs. Campbell, thin and raisinish, dusted with a yellow T-shirt. The horses all lined up, straining at the barrier. Hers was number seven, Medea's Pride. That was a day with a trapdoor, and we all fell through. I ran the belt of her kimono over my mouth, over and over, all day long, the taste of what had been lost.

THE DAY OF her arrest returned in my dreams, they were tunnels that kept coming around to the same place. The knock on the door. It had been very early, still dark. Another knock, and then voices, pounding. I ran into her room as the cops, cops in uniform, not in uniform, burst in. The manager stood in the doorway, his head in a shower cap. They pulled my mother out of bed, voices like snapping dogs. She yelled at them in German, calling them Nazis, calling them blackshirts. *"Schutzstaffel. Durch Ihre Verordnung, mein Führer."* Her naked body, tender breasts swaying, stomach welted red from the sheets. It was impossible, a faked photograph. Someone had cut out these policemen and stuck them on our apartment. They kept looking at her, a dirty magazine. Her body like moonlight.

"Astrid, they can't keep me," she said. "Don't worry, I'll be back in an hour."

She said. She said.

I sat on Michael's couch, slept and waited, the way dogs wait, all day, and then the next. A week went by, but she didn't come. She said she would, but she never did.

WHEN THEY CAME to get me, they gave me fifteen minutes to make up my mind what to take from our apartment. We never had many things. I took her four books, a box of her journals, the white kimono, her tarot cards, and her folding knife.

"I'm sorry," Michael said. "I'd keep you if I could. But you know how it is."

How it was. How it was that the earth could open up under you and swallow you whole, close above you as if you never were. Like Persephone snatched by the god. The ground opened up and out he came, sweeping her into the black chariot. Then down they plunged, under the ground, into the darkness, and the earth closed over her head, and she was gone, as if she had never been.

So I came to live underground, in the house of sleep, in the house of plastic sheets and crying babies and brown roses in drifts, forty down, ninety-two across. Three thousand six hundred and eighty brown roses.

ONCE THEY BROUGHT me to see her behind glass. She wore an orange jumpsuit, like a car mechanic, and there was something wrong with her. Her eyes were all clouded over. I told her I loved her, but she didn't recognize me. I saw her there in my dreams, again and again, her blind eyes.

It was a year of mouths, opening and closing, asking the same questions, saying the same things. *Just tell us what happened. Tell us what we want to know.* I wanted to help her, but I didn't know how. I couldn't find words, I had no words. In the courtroom she wore a white shirt. I saw that shirt when I was awake and I saw it when I slept. I saw her on the stand in that shirt, her eyes blank as a doll's. I saw her back in that white shirt walking away. Thirty-five to life, someone said. I came home and counted roses, and slept.

WHEN I WAS AWAKE, I tried to remember the things she taught me. We were the wands. We hung our gods from trees. Never let a man stay the night. Don't forget who you are. But I couldn't remember. I was the disability girl, stones in my mouth, lost on the battlefield, plastic sheets on the bed. I was the laundry monitor, I helped the niece take the laundry to the Laundromat. I watched the laundry go around. I liked the smell of it, it made me feel safe. I slept until sleep seemed like waking and waking like sleep. Sometimes I lay on my bed in the room with the roses and watched the girl in the other bed make scar tattoos on her ashy dark skin with a safety pin, a diaper pin with a yellow duck. She opened her skin in lines and loops. It healed over into pink pillowy tissue. She opened them again. It took me a while, but finally I understood. She wanted it to show.

I dreamed my mother was hunting me in the burnt-out city, blind, relentless. *The whole truth and nothing but the truth.* I wanted to lie, but the words deserted me. She was the one who always spoke for us. She was the goddess who threw out the golden apples. They would stoop to pick them up, and we'd make our escape. But when I reached into my pocket, there was only dust and dried leaves. I had nothing to protect her with, to cover her naked body. I had condemned her by my silence, condemned us both.

ONE DAY I woke to find the girl from the other bed going through my drawer in the dresser. Looking at a book, flicking through the pages. My mother's book. My slender, naked mother, alone among the blackshirts. She was pawing my mother's words. "Get out of my stuff," I said.

The girl looked up at me, startled. She didn't know I could talk. We had been in this room for months now and I'd never said a word.

"Put it back," I said.

She broke out in a grin. Grabbed a page, crumpled it and tore it out of the book, watching me. What would I do. My mother's words in her scaly-knuckled hand. What would I do, what would I do. She took another page, tore it out and stuffed it in her mouth, the pieces hanging from her blistered lips, grinning.

I fell on her, knocked her down. Sat on her, my knees in her back, the dark blade of my mother's knife jabbed at her spine. A song in the blood. *Don't forget who you are.*

I wanted to cut her. I could feel the tip of the knife in her, slipping into her neck, the indentation at the base of her skull like a well. She lay very still, waiting to see what came next. I looked at my hand, a hand that knew how to hold a knife, how to shove it into a crazy girl's spine. It wasn't mine. I wasn't this. I wasn't.

"Spit it out," I whispered in her ear.

She spit out the pieces, her lips buzzing like a horse's.

"Don't touch my stuff," I said.

She nodded.

I let her up.

She went back to her bed and started poking herself with the safety pin. I put the knife in my pocket and picked up the crumpled page, the torn pieces.

In the kitchen, the niece and her boyfriend were sitting at the table, drinking Colt 45, listening to the radio. Having an argument. "You're never going to see that money, fool," she said. They didn't see me. They didn't see any of us. I got the tape and went back to my room.

I taped the torn page together, taped them both back into the book. It was her first book, an indigo cover with a silver moonflower, an art nouveau flower, I traced my finger along the silver line like smoke, whiplash curves. It was her reading copy, soft pencil notes in the margins. *Pause. Upward Inflect.* I touched the pages her hands touched, I pressed them to my lips, the soft thick old paper, yellow now, fragile as skin. I stuck my nose between the bindings and smelled all the readings she had given, the smell of unfiltered cigarettes and the espresso machine, beaches and incense and whispered words in the night. I could hear her voice rising from the pages. The cover curled outward like sails.

The picture on the back. My mother in a short dress with long graceful sleeves, her hair cut in long bangs, eyes peeking out underneath. Like a cat peering out from under a bed. That beautiful girl, she was a universe, bearer of these words that rang like gongs, that tumbled like flutes made of human bones. In the picture, none of this had ever happened. I was safe then, a tiny pinhead egg buried in her right-side ovary, and we never were apart.

WHEN I STARTED talking, they sent me to school. My name was White Girl. I was an albino, a freak. I had no skin at all. I was transparent, you could see the circulation of the blood. I drew pictures in every class. I drew pictures on the computer cards, connecting the dots into new constellations.

5

⌐

CASEWORKERS CHANGED but were always the same. They took me to McDonald's, opened their files, asked their questions. McDonald's scared me. There were too many children, screaming and crying and sliding into pits filled with colored balls. I had nothing to say. This one was a man, white, with a clipped beard like the jack of spades. His hands square as a shovel, he wore a signet on his pinkie finger.

He found me a permanent placement. When I left the group home on Crenshaw Boulevard, nobody said good-bye. But the girl with the scar tattoos stood on the front porch and watched me drive away. Clusters of lavender jacarandas emerged from the ranks of trees as we stitched along the gray-and-white streets.

It took four freeways to get to my new home. We exited onto a street that sloped upward like a ramp. Tujunga, the signs said. I watched the low ranch houses get larger, then smaller, the yards chaotic. The sidewalks disappeared. Furniture grew on the porches like toadstools. A washing machine, scrap lumber, a white hen, a goat. Finally we were no longer in town.

We came over a rise and we could see the wash, half a mile across, kids on dirt bikes cutting trails in the open land, kicking up pale plumes of dust. In contrast, the air seemed listless, defeated.

We stopped in the dirt yard of a house, part trailer, but so many parts added on, you had to call it a house. A plastic garden pinwheel stood motionless in a patch of geraniums. Spider plants hung from pots on the wide trailer porch. Three little boys sat, watching. One held a jar with some kind of animal. The biggest one pushed his glasses up on his nose, called back over his shoulder, through the screen door. The woman who came through it was busty and leggy, with a big smile, her teeth white and shallow, all in the front. Her nose was flat at the bridge, like a boxer's.

Her name was Starr and it was dark inside her trailer. She gave us sugary Cokes we drank out of the can as the caseworker talked. When she spoke, Starr moved her whole body, throwing her head back to laugh. A small gold cross glittered between her breasts, and the caseworker couldn't keep his eyes off that deep secret place. She and the caseworker didn't even notice when I went outside.

There were no fringy jacarandas here, only oleanders and palms, pear cactus and a big weeping pepper. The dust that covered everything was the pinkish beige of sandstone, but the sky was broad as an untroubled forehead, the pure leaded blue of stained glass. It was the first time the ceiling wasn't pressing on my head.

The biggest boy, the one with the glasses, stood up. "We're catching lizards, you want to?"

They trapped the lizards with shoebox snares down in the

wash. The patience of such small boys as they waited, silent, still, for a green lizard to enter the trap. They pulled the string and the box fell down. The biggest boy slid a sheet of cardboard under the box and turned it over, and the middle one grabbed the tiny living thing and put it in the glass jar.

"What do you do with them?" I asked.

The boy with the glasses looked at me in surprise. "We study them, of course."

The lizard in the jar did push-ups, then grew very still. Isolated, you could see how perfect it was, every small scale, its row of etched toenails. Made special by virtue of its imprisonment. Above us the mountain loomed, a solemn presence. I found if I looked at it a certain way, I could feel its huge-shouldered mass moving toward me, green polka dots of sage clinging to its flanks. A puff of breeze came up. A bird screamed. The chaparral gave off a hot fresh smell.

I walked down the wash, wandering between boulders warmed in the sun. I leaned my cheek against one, imagining becoming so still, so quiet as this, indifferent to where the river dumped me after the last storm. The biggest boy was suddenly beside me. "Careful of the rattlesnakes. They like those rocks."

I moved away from the rock.

"The western diamondback is the largest of the American vipers," he said. "But they rarely strike above the ankle. Just watch where you're going, and don't climb on the rocks, or if you do, watch where you put your hands. Do like this." He took a small rock and knocked it on the nearest boulder, as if knocking on a door. "They'll avoid you if they can. Also look out for scorpions. Shake your shoes before you put them on, especially outside."

I looked at him closely, this skinny freckled boy, a bit younger than me, trying to decide if he wanted to scare me. But he seemed more interested in impressing me with how smart he was. I kept walking along, looking at the shapes the boulders made, the blue of their shadows. I had the sense that they were inhabited, like people in hiding. The boy followed me.

"Rabbit," he said, pointing down at the dust.

I could barely make out the blurred markings, two larger prints followed by a smaller one and then another. He smiled, his teeth slightly pushed back, vaguely rabbitlike himself. He was a boy who should have been in front of a TV or in a library, but he could read the pale dust the way another kid would read a comic book, the way my mother read cards. I wished he could read my fortune in the dust.

"You see a lot," I said.

He smiled. He was a boy who wanted to be seen. He told me his name was Davey, he was Starr's real son. There was a daughter too, Carolee. The other two, Owen and Peter, were foster like me. But even her natural children had been in foster care, when Starr was in rehab.

How many children had this happened to? How many children were like me, floating like plankton in the wide ocean? I thought how tenuous the links were between mother and children, between friends, family, things you think are eternal. Everything could be lost, more easily than anyone could imagine.

We walked on. Davey pulled at a bush with bright yellow flowers. "Deerweed. Pea family." The breeze came up the canyon, making the trees flicker green and gray. "Paloverde's got the green bark. The other's ironwood."

The quiet, the solidness of the mountain, the white butter-flies. Green scent of laurel sumac, which Davey informed me the local Indians had used to sweeten the air in their wickiups. Clumps of giant ryegrass, still green, but already crackling like fire. Two hawks circled the seamless blue sky, screaming.

THAT NIGHT, motifs of cowboys on broncos, lariats, and spurs decorated my sleeping bag bed, where I lay zipper open to the coolness watching Carolee, sixteen years old and tall as her mother, a sullen girl with pouty lips, zipping her top. "Thinks she's going to ground me," Carolee said to her reflection. "That's what she thinks."

On the other side of our thin wall, the mother and her hippie boyfriend were making love, the headboard knocking against the partition. It was not the night magic, my mother and her young men, murmuring to strains of imperial koto in the scented dusk.

"Lord almighty!" Starr wailed.

Carolee's mouth twisted into something not quite a smile, her boot on her bed, she was doing the laces. "Christians don't say, 'Fuck me baby.' Actually they're not supposed to do it at all, but she's got the sin virus in her blood." She posed in front of the mirror, lowered the zipper of her top an inch, so it showed the well between her breasts. She bared her teeth and wiped them with her finger.

A dirt bike whined, and she pushed the screen out, climbed onto the dresser, narrowly missing her basket of makeup. "See you in the morning. Don't close the window."

I got up and watched her on the dirt bike disappearing up

the road. It was wide and white in the moonlight, the darkness of mountains darker than the sky, a perfect vanishing point of the road and the telephone poles. I imagined you could follow that road through the vanishing point, come out somewhere else entirely.

"WITHOUT JESUS, I'd be dead today," Starr was saying as she cut in front of a semi, which punished us with its air horn. "That's the God's honest truth. They'd taken my kids, I was ready for roadkill."

I sat in the passenger seat of Starr's Ford Torino while Carolee slouched in the back, ankle bracelet glittering, a present from her boyfriend, Derrick. Starr drove too fast, bumping up the road, and chain-smoked Benson and Hedges 100s from a gold pack, listening to Christian radio. She was talking about how she used to be an alcoholic and a cokehead and topless waitress at a club called the Trop.

She wasn't beautiful like my mother, but you couldn't help looking at her. I'd never seen anyone with a figure like that. Only in the back pages of the *L.A. Weekly*, chewing on a phone cord. But her energy was overwhelming. She never stopped talking, laughing, lecturing, smoking. I wondered what she was like on cocaine.

"I can't wait for you to meet Reverend Thomas. Have you accepted Christ as your personal savior?"

I considered telling her that we hung our gods from trees, but thought better of it.

"Well, you will. Lord, once you hear that man, you'll be saved on the spot."

Carolee lit a Marlboro, lowered the back window. "That phony-ass con. How can you swallow such shit."

"He who believeth in me, though he was dead, yet he will live, and don't you forget it, missy," Starr said. She never called us by our names, not even her own children, only "mister" or "missy."

She was taking us to the Clothestime in the next town, Sunland, she wanted to get me a few things for my new life. I'd never been into a store like that. My mother and I got our clothes on the boardwalk in Venice. Inside the Clothestime, colors assaulted us from every side. Magenta! they screamed. Turquoise! Battery acid! under the flicker of fluorescent lighting. Starr filled my arms with clothes to try on, herded me into a dressing room with her, so we could continue our chat.

In the cubicle, she wriggled into a tiny striped minidress and smoothed it over her ribs, turning to the side to see what it looked like in profile. The stripes widened and tapered over her breasts and bottom like op art. I tried not to stare, but how could you not be astounded. I wondered what Reverend Thomas would think of her in a dress like that.

She frowned, pulled the dress over her head, and hung it back up. It still was stretched to fit her figure. Her body in the small dressing room was almost too much to bear. I could only look at her in the mirror, her breasts falling out of the top of her underwired brassiere, the cross hiding between them like a snake in a rock.

"Sin's a virus, that's what Reverend Thomas says. Infecting the whole country, like the clap," she told me. "They've got clap now you can't get rid of. Sin's just exactly the same. We've got every excuse in the book. Like what difference does it make

61

if I shovel coke up my nose or not? What's wrong with wanting to feel good all the time? Who does it hurt?"

She opened her eyes wide, I could see the glue on her false eyelashes. "It hurts us and it hurts Jesus. Because it's wrong." She said it soft and sweet, like a nursery school teacher. I tried to imagine what it was like working in a gentleman's club. Walking naked into a room full of men.

She tried on a pink stretchy dress, rolling it down over her hips. "It's a virus that eats you up from the inside out, you infect everything around you. Oh, wait till you hear Reverend Thomas."

She frowned at the dress in the mirror, the way it looked in the back, it was so tight it rose up between her legs. "This would look better on you."

She stripped it off and handed it to me. It smelled of her heavy perfume. Obsession. When I took off my clothes, she looked at my body closely, like she was trying to decide if she wanted to buy it or not. My underwear was torn. "You'd better start wearing a bra, missy. Thirteen years old, I should say. I had my first bra in the fourth grade. You don't want 'em hanging to your knees when you're thirty, do you?"

Thirteen? The shock of it made me drop a stack of clothes off the hook. I thought back through the past year. My mother's trial, all the sessions and questions, medication and caseworkers. Sometime in there I'd turned thirteen. I had crossed a frontier in my sleep, and nobody had woken me to stamp my passport. Thirteen. The idea so stunned me I didn't even argue when Starr insisted on buying me the pink dress to wear to church, and two bras so they wouldn't hang down to my knees when I was thirty, and a package of panties, some other things.

We went next door to Payless for shoes. Starr took a sample red high heel down from the display and put it on without a sock, stood on it, smoothed her shorts over her hips, cocked her head to one side, made a face, and put it back on the stand. "I mean, I really thought like that. Who cares if I stick my tits in some stranger's face? It's nobody's business but mine."

Carolee whispered, "Mother, please shut up. People are staring."

Starr handed me a pair of pink high heels that would match my dress. I tried them on. They made my feet look like Daisy Duck's, but Starr loved them and pressed them on me.

"She could really use some goddamn sneakers or something," Carolee said. "All she's got are those thongs."

I decided on a pair of hiking boots, hoping they weren't too expensive. Starr looked pained when I showed them to her. "They're not very . . . flattering."

But snakes rarely struck above the ankle.

On Sunday morning, Carolee was up early. I was surprised. On Saturday she'd slept until noon. But here she was, up at eight, dressed, her little backpack on her back.

"Where are you going?"

She brushed her sandy hair. "Are you kidding? I'm not going to spend my day listening to Reverend Creephead talk about the Blood of the Lamb." She put her brush down and rushed out of the room. "Sayonara." I heard the screen door slam.

I took the hint from Carolee and pretended I was sick. Starr looked at me hard, and said, "Next week, missy." She wore a short white skirt and a peach blouse and four-inch spike heels. I could smell a big waft of Obsession. "No excuses."

It was only when I heard Starr's Torino heave itself onto the road that I dared dress and come out, make myself some breakfast. It was nice being alone, the boys hiding somewhere down in the wash, the distant whine of dirt bikes. I was just eating when Starr's hippie boyfriend came out of the bedroom, barefoot in jeans, pulled a T-shirt over his head. His chest was lean and hairy, sandy threaded with gray, his shaggy hair out of its usual ponytail. He staggered down the hall. I could hear the sound of his piss, the water coming on. Splashing, flushing. He came into the main room and found a cigarette in a pack on the table, lit it. The hand that held the cigarette was missing one finger and the fingertip of the next.

He smiled when he saw me looking at it. "You ever see a carpenter get a table in a restaurant? Table for three, please." He held up his damaged hand.

At least he wasn't sensitive about it. I kind of liked him, though it embarrassed me that he was the one causing the "Christ almighties" through the wall. He was a plain man, lean-faced, sad-eyed, long graying hair. We were supposed to call him Uncle Ray. He opened the refrigerator, pulled out a beer. *Shhhhht,* it sighed when he popped the top.

"You're missing the Jesus show." He didn't drink his beer so much as pour it down his throat.

"So are you," I said.

"I'd rather be shot," he said. "Here's my theory. If there's a God, he's so fucked up he doesn't deserve to be prayed to." He belched loudly and smiled.

I'd never thought much about God. We had the Twilight of

64

the Gods, we had the world tree. We had Olympus and its scandals, Ariadne and Bacchus, the rape of Danaë. I knew about Shiva and Parvati and Kali, and Pele the volcano goddess, but my mother had banned the least mention of Christ. She wouldn't even come to the Christmas pageant at school. She made me beg a ride off some other kid.

The nearest I'd come to feeling anything like God was the plain blue cloudless sky and a certain silence, but how do you pray to that?

Uncle Ray leaned up against the doorjamb, smoking, looking out at the big pepper tree and his pickup truck in the yard. He sipped his beer, which he held in the same hand as the cigarette, dexterous for a person missing two fingers. He crinkled his eyes against the smoke as he exhaled out the screen. "He just wants to ball her. Pretty soon he's gonna tell her to get rid of me, that's when I get my thirty-eight, teach him a fucking thing or two. Then you'll see a little Blood of the Lamb."

I picked the marshmallows out of my cereal, arranged them on the rim of the bowl, purple moons, green clovers. "It's not a sin if you're married," I said. I didn't think he'd hear me but he did.

"I'm already married," he said, looking out the screen toward the pepper tree, its boughs blowing like a woman's long hair. He shot a grin back over his shoulder. "I got the virus big time."

I alternated the moons and clovers, eating the ones that fell in the bowl. "Where's your wife?"

"I don't know. Haven't seen her in two, three years."

He seemed so calm about it, that someone was walking around with his name and his history and he didn't even know where she was. It made me feel dizzy, like I wanted to grab hold of something heavy and hang on. This was the life I was going to be living, everybody separated from everybody else, hanging on for a moment, only to be washed away. I could grow up and drift away too. My mother might never know where I was, and in a few years, if someone asked her about me, she might shrug like this and say, "Haven't seen her in two, three years."

It hit me, like a punch in the stomach. I could go for years and never see her again. Just like this. People losing each other, their hands slipping loose in a crowd. I might never see her again. Those dull eyes behind the dry aquarium, the shape of her back. My God, how could I have avoided knowing this all these months? I wanted my mother, I wanted something to hold on to me, not let me slip away.

"Hey, what's all this?" Uncle Ray came over and sat next to me at the table. He stuck his cigarette in his beer can and took my hands in his. "Don't cry, kid. What's wrong? You can tell Uncle Ray."

All I could do was shake my head, raw sobs like razors.

"You miss your mom?"

I nodded. My throat felt like there were two hands wrapped around it, squeezing, forcing water out of my eyes. Snot ran from my nose. Ray scooted his chair so he could put his arm around me, handed me a napkin off the table. I buried my face in his chest, and let my tears and snot wet the front of his T-shirt. It felt good to be held. I breathed in his smell, cigarettes and stale body and beer and fresh-cut wood, something green.

He held me, he was solid, he wouldn't let me drift away.

Talking to me, telling me nobody was going to hurt me, I was a great kid, nothing was going to happen. After a while he wiped my cheeks with the back of his hand, lifting my chin so he could look at me, pushing my hair out of my eyes. "You really miss her, huh. Tell me, is she as pretty as you?"

I smiled a little, his eyes were so sad and kind. "I have a picture." I ran down to my room, brought back a copy of my mother's last book, *Dust*. I gently stroked my hand over her picture on the back cover, on the beach at Big Sur. Huge rocks in the water, driftwood. She wore a fisherman sweater, her hair swept back by the wind. She looked like a Lorelei, cause of shipwreck. Odysseus would have had to lash himself to the mast.

"You're going to be prettier," he said.

I wiped my nose on the short sleeve of my T-shirt, smiled. My mother was a woman people stopped in the market to wonder at. Not like Starr, but just at the sheer beauty. They seemed startled she had to shop and eat like anyone else. I couldn't imagine owning beauty like my mother's. I wouldn't dare. It would be too scary. "No way."

"Hey, way. You're just a different type. You're the sweetheart type. Your mother looks like she could take a bite out of ya — not that I'd mind, I can take it rough too, but you know what I mean. For you, they'll just fall down like flies." He peered into my lowered face with his kind eyes, speaking so gently. "You hear me? You're going to have to push the bodies out of the way if you want to go down the street."

Nobody had ever said anything like that to me before. Even if he was just lying to make me feel better, who bothered to do that now?

He flipped through some of the pages, reading. "Look, this one's about you."

I snatched it away, my face flaming. I knew the poem.

> Shhh
> Astrid's sleeping
> Pink well of her wordless mouth
> One long leg trails off the bed
> Like an unfinished sentence
> Fine freckles hold a constellation of second chances
> Her cowrie shell
> Where the unopened woman whispers . . .

She used to recite it at poetry readings. I would sit drawing at my table as if I didn't hear her, as if it weren't me she was talking about, my body, my childish girl parts. I hated that poem. What did she think, I didn't know what she was talking about? I didn't care who she read it to? No, she thought because I was her daughter that I belonged to her, that she could do anything she wanted with me. Make me into poetry, expose my chicken bones and my cowrie shell, my unopened woman.

"What happened to her?" he asked.

"She killed her boyfriend," I said, looking down at her photo, her profile a spear under my ribs, piercing my liver, my right lung. A tear ran off my eyelash and fell on her picture. I wiped it off. "She's in prison."

He shrugged. As if that was something people did. Not good, but not shocking.

*

I FINISHED OUT the eighth grade at Mount Gleason Junior High, my third school this year. I didn't know anyone, didn't want to. I ate lunch with Davey. We quizzed each other using flash cards he'd made for himself. What's a baby ferret called? A kitten. How many kittens in a litter? Six to nine. Constellation Andromeda. Major feature? The Great Andromeda Nebula. Favorite object for observation? The double star Gamma Andromedae. Distance to earth? Two million light-years. Anomaly? Unlike the other spiral nebulae, which are receding from us at high velocities, Andromeda is approaching us at a rate of three hundred kilometers per second.

My caseworker visited our trailer often, sat with Starr, trying to look handsome on the porch under the spider plants. One day he said my mother was settled at the women's prison in Chino now, and could have visitors starting Thursday. There was a group that brought children to see their parents in prison, and I was going to have a visit.

After the last visit, I was afraid. I didn't know if I could do that again. What if she was still like that, a zombie? I couldn't stand that. And I was afraid of the prison, the bars and hands snaking between them. Clanging their cups. How could my mother live there, my mother who arranged white flowers in a crackle-glass vase, who could argue for hours about whether Frost was an important poet?

But I knew how. Drugged, sitting in a corner, vaguely reciting her poems, plucking pills of fuzz off the blanket, that's how. Or beaten senseless by guards, or other prisoners. She didn't know when to lie low, avoid the radar.

And what if she didn't want to see me? What if she blamed me for not being able to help her? It had been eight months since that day at the jail, when she didn't even recognize me. At one point in the night, I even thought of not going. But at five I got up, showered, dressed.

"Remember, no jeans, nothing blue," Starr reminded me the night before. "You want to walk back out of there, don't you?" I didn't need reminding. I wore my new pink dress, my bra and my Daisy Duck shoes. I wanted to show her I was growing up, I could take care of myself.

THE VAN CAME at seven. Starr got up and signed the papers while the driver eyed her figure in her bathrobe. There was one other kid in the van. I took the seat in front of him, also by the window. We picked up three more on the way out.

The day was overcast, June gloom, the moisture in the air beading on the windshield. You couldn't see down the freeway as far as the next overpass. It came out of the mist and then it vanished, the world creating and erasing itself. It made me carsick. I cracked the window. We drove a long way, through suburbs and more suburbs. If only I knew what she would be like when I got there. I couldn't imagine my mother in prison. She didn't smoke or chew on toothpicks. She didn't say "bitch" or "fuck." She spoke four languages, quoted T. S. Eliot and Dylan Thomas, drank Lapsang souchong out of a porcelain cup. She had never even been inside a McDonald's. She had lived in Paris and Amsterdam. Freiburg and Martinique. How could she be in prison?

At Chino, we turned off the freeway and drove south. I tried to memorize this, so I could find it again in my dreams. We drove past nice suburbs, then not-so-nice ones, then brand-new subdivisions alternating with lumberyards and farm equipment rentals. Finally we came to real country, and drove along roads with no signals, just dairies and fields, the smell of manure.

There was a big complex of buildings on the right. "Is that it?" I asked the girl next to me.

"CYA," she said.

I shook my head.

"Youth Authority."

All the kids eyed it grimly as we passed. We could be there, behind that razor wire. We were silent as death when we went by the California Institution for Men, set way back from the road in the middle of a field. Finally, we turned onto a fresh blacktopped road, past a little market, case of Bud $5.99. I wanted to remember it all. The kids got their bags, their backpacks. Now I could see the prison — a steam stack, a water tower, the guard tower. It was aluminum-sided, like Starr's trailer. Frontera wasn't at all as I had imagined. I'd been picturing *Birdman of Alcatraz*, or *I Want to Live!* with my mother as Susan Hayward. Its low brick buildings were widely spaced and landscaped with trees and roses and acres of green lawn. It was more like a suburban high school than a prison. Except for the guard towers, the razor wire.

Crows squawked raucously in the trees. It sounded like they were tearing something apart, something they didn't even want, just for the fun of destroying it. We filed through the guard tower, signed in. They searched our backpacks and passed us through the metal detector. They took a package away from one girl. No gifts. You had to mail them, a package from family was allowed four times a year. The slam of the gate behind us made us jump. We were locked in.

71

They told me to wait at an orange picnic table under a tree. I was nervous and sick from the ride. I didn't even know if I'd recognize her. I shivered, wishing I'd brought a sweater. And what would she think of me, in my bra and high heels?

Women milled around behind the covered area of the visiting yard. Prisoners, their faces like masks. They jeered at us. One woman whistled at me and licked between her fingers, and the others laughed. They kept laughing, they wouldn't stop. They sounded like the crows.

The mothers started coming in from the prison through a different gate. They wore jeans and T-shirts, gray sweaters, sweatsuits. I saw my mother waiting for the woman guard to bring her through. She wore a plain denim dress, button front, but on her the blue was a color, like a song. Her white blond hair had been hacked off at the neck by someone who had no feeling for the work, but her blue eyes were as clear as a high note on a violin. She had never looked more beautiful. I stood up and then I couldn't move, I waited trembling as she came over and hugged me to her.

Just to feel her touch, to hold her, after all those months! I put my head on her chest and she kissed me, smelled my hair, she didn't smell of violets anymore, only the smell of detergent on denim. She lifted my face in her hands and kissed me all over, wiped my tears with her strong thumbs. She pulled me to sit down next to her.

I was thirsty for the way she felt, the way she looked, the sound of her voice, the way her front teeth were square but her second teeth turned slightly, her one dimple, left side, her half-smile, her wonderfully blue eyes flecked with white, like new galaxies, the firm intact planes of her face. She didn't even look like she should be in prison, she looked like she could have just walked off the Venice boardwalk with a book under her arm, ready to settle in at an oceanside café.

She pulled me down to sit next to her at the picnic table, whispered to me, "Don't cry. We're not like that. We're the Vikings, remember?"

I nodded, but my tears dripped on the orange vinyl table. Lois, someone had scratched into it. 18th Street. Cunt.

One of the women in the concrete courtyard behind the visitors covered area whistled and shouted out, something about my mother or me. My mother looked up and the woman caught her gaze full in the face like a punch. It stopped her cold. She turned away quickly, like it wasn't she who'd said it.

"You're so beautiful," I said, touching her hair, her collar, her cheek. Not pliable at all.

"Prison agrees with me," she said. "There's no hypocrisy here. Kill or be killed, and everybody knows it."

"I missed you so much," I whispered.

She put her arm around me, her head right next to mine. She pressed my forehead with her hand, her lips against my temple. "I won't be here forever. It'll take more than this to keep me behind bars. I promise you. I will get out, one way or another. One day you'll look out your window and I'll be there."

I looked into her determined face, cheekbones like razors, her eyes making me believe. "I was afraid you'd be mad at me."

She stretched me out at arm's length to look at me, her hands gripping my shoulders. "Why would you think that?"

Because I couldn't lie well enough. But I couldn't say it.

73

She hugged me again. Those arms around me made me want to stay there forever. I'd rob a bank and get convicted so we could always be together. I wanted to curl up in her lap, I wanted to disappear into her body, I wanted to be one of her eyelashes, or a blood vessel in her thigh, a mole on her neck.

"Is it terrible here? Do they hurt you?"

"Not as much as I hurt them," she said, and I knew she was smiling, though all I could see was the denim of her sleeve and her arm, still lightly tanned. I had to pull away a little to see her. Yes, she was smiling, her half-smile, the little comma-shaped curve at the corner of her mouth. I touched her mouth. She kissed my fingers.

"They assigned me to office work. I told them I'd rather clean toilets than type their bureaucratic vomit. Oh, they don't much care for me. I'm on grounds crew. I sweep, pull weeds, though of course only inside the wire. I'm considered a poor security risk. Imagine. I won't tutor their illiterates, teach writing classes, or otherwise feed the machine. *I will not serve*." She stuck her nose in my hair, she was smelling me. "Your hair smells of bread. Clover and nutmeg. I want to remember you just like this, in that sadly hopeful pink dress, and those brides-maid, promise-of-prom-night pumps. Your foster mother's, no doubt. Pink being the ultimate cliché."

I told her about Starr and Uncle Ray, the other kids, dirt bikes and paloverde and ironwood, the colors of the boulders in the wash, the mountain and the hawks. I told her about the sin virus. I loved the sound of her laughter.

"You must send me drawings," she said. "You always drew better than you wrote. I can't think of any other reason you haven't written."

74

I could write? "You never did."

"You haven't been getting my letters?" she said. And her smile was gone, her face deflated, masklike, like the women behind the fence. "Give me your address. I'll write you directly. And you write to me, don't go through your social worker. My mistake. Oh, we'll learn." And the vigor returned to her eyes. "We're smarter than they are, *ma petite.*"

I didn't know my address, but she told me hers, had me repeat it over and over so I would remember. My mind rebelled against my mother's address. Ingrid Magnussen, Inmate W99235, California Institution for Women, Corona-Frontera.

"Wherever you go, write to me. Write at least once a week. Or send drawings, God knows the visual stimulation in this place leaves something to be desired. I especially want to see the ex–topless dancer and Uncle Ernie, the clumsy carpenter."

It hurt my feelings. Uncle Ray had been there when I needed him. She didn't even know him. "It's Ray, and he's nice."

"Oh," she said. "You stay away from Uncle Ray, especially if he's oh so nice."

But she was in here, and I was out there. I had a friend. She wasn't going to take him away from me.

"I think of you all the time," she said. "Especially at night. I imagine where you are. When the prison's still and everyone's asleep, I imagine I can see you. I try to contact you. Have you ever heard me calling, felt my presence in your room?" She stroked a strand of my hair between her fingers, stretched it to see how long it was against my arm. It came to my elbow.

I had felt her, I had. I'd heard her call. *Astrid? Are you awake?* "Late at night. You never could sleep."

She kissed the top of my head, right in the part. "Neither could you. Now, tell me more about yourself. I want to know everything about you."

It was a strange idea. She never wanted to know about me before. But the long days of sameness had led her back to me, to remembering she had a daughter tied up somewhere. The sun was starting to come out and the ground fog glowed like a paper lantern.

6

─◆─

THE NEXT SUNDAY, I slept too late. If only I hadn't been dreaming about my mother. It was a sweet dream. We were in Arles, walking down the allée of dark cypress trees, past tombs and wildflowers. She had escaped from prison — she was pushing a lawn mower in front of the building and just walked away. Arles was deep shade and sunshine like honey, Roman ruins and our little pension. If I had not been hungry for that dream, for the sunflowers of Arles, I would have got up when the boys ran off into the wash.

But now I was sitting in the front seat of the Torino. Carolee groaned in the back, she had a hangover from doing drugs all night with her friends. Starr had caught her sleeping too. Amy Grant played on the radio, and Starr sang along, wearing her hair in a sort of messy French twist like Brigitte Bardot, and long dangling earrings. She looked like she was going to a cocktail lounge, and not to the Truth Assembly of Christ.

"I hate this," my foster sister said in my ear as we followed her mother into church. "I'd kill for some 'ludes."

The Assembly met in a concrete-block building with

linoleum-tiled floors and a high frosted glass window instead of stained. A modern fruitwood cross loomed in front, and a woman with a puffy hairdo played the organ. We sat on white folding chairs, Carolee on my left, face dark with sullenness and headache, Starr on the aisle, glowing with excitement. Her skirt was so short I could see where the dark part of her panty-hose started.

The organ playing crescendoed and a man walked to the lectern wearing a dark suit and tie with shiny black shoes, like a businessman. I thought he would wear a graduation-type robe. His short, side-parted brown hair glistened like cellophane under the colored lights. Now Starr sat very straight, hoping he would notice her.

As he spoke, I was surprised that he had a sort of speech defect. He swallowed his *l*'s, so it came out "alyive" instead of "alive." "Though we were dead in our error, He made us alive together in Christ. By the Cross, we have been saved. He lifts us up to the life . . . everlasting." He raised his hands, lifting us. He was good. He knew when to build and when to let off, and when he got quiet, that's when he came in for the kill, with big shiny eyes and little flat nose, and a lipless mouth so wide he looked like a Muppet, like his whole head opened and closed when he talked. "Yes, we can live again, even when we are dying of . . . the sin virus."

Carolee shifted, making her chair squeak on purpose. Starr flapped her hand, nudged me and pointed at the Reverend, as if there was anything else to look at.

Reverend Thomas started telling a story of a young man in the sixties, a good-hearted boy, who thought he could go his own way, as long as he didn't hurt anyone. "He met a guru who

78

taught him to look for the truth within himself." The preacher paused and smiled, as if the idea of truth within yourself was absurd, ridiculous, the red light warning of doom. "You are the judge of what is true." He smiled again, and I began to see that he always paused to smile when he said something he disapproved of. He reminded me of someone who put your fingers in the door and smiled and talked to you while he was smashing them.

"Oh, he was by no means alone in his philosophy at the time," Reverend Thomas continued, his button eyes shining. "'Do your own thing, man,' was the wisdom of the day. If there was something you wanted, it was good, because you wanted it. There was no God, no dying. There was only your own pleasure." He smiled at the word "pleasure," as if pleasure was hideous, an abomination, and he felt pity for anyone who would be so weak as to value it. "And if anyone spoke of responsibility or consequences, they were held up to ridicule. 'Lighten up, man. Don't be square.'

"Yes, the young man had unwittingly contracted the deadly virus. It had infiltrated his heart, weakening the structure of his conscience, liquefying his judgment." Reverend Thomas seemed positively overjoyed. "After a while, there just didn't seem much difference between right and wrong."

So how could the kid have ended up as anything but one of the Manson killers?

I had sunk back in my chair as far as Carolee by now, and Starr's perfume and the hissing words of the Reverend were making me sick to my stomach.

Luckily, in prison, the young man had a revelation. He realized he was a part of a raging epidemic of the sin virus, and through another inmate discovered the Lord and the life-giving serum of His Blood. Now he was preaching to the other inmates and doing good works among the hopeless. Although he was twenty-five years into a life sentence, his life was not a waste. He had a reason for being, to help others, and bring the Good News to people who had never looked an inch beyond their own momentary desires. He was redeemed, a new man, reborn in the Lord.

It wasn't hard for me to imagine the Manson kid in prison, his hardness, his warped thinking, a killer. Then something had happened. A light had come on, which let him see the awful reality of his crime. I imagined his agony, when he saw what a monster he had become and knew that he had ruined his life for nothing. He could have killed himself, how very close he must have come. But then came the ray of hope, that there might be another way to live, some meaning after all. And he prayed, and the spirit came into his heart.

And now, instead of living out his years as a walking corpse in San Quentin, hating and more hate, he had become someone with a purpose, someone with the light within him. I understood that. I believed it.

"There is an answer to this deadly epidemic laying waste our vital substance," Reverend Thomas was saying, lifting his arms, like an embrace. "A powerful vaccine for the devastating infection within the human heart. But we have to recognize the danger we are in. We have to accept the grave diagnosis, that by acting upon our own desires instead of following God's plan, we have become infected by this terrible plague. We have to receive the knowledge of our responsibility to the heavenly power, and our own vulnerability."

Suddenly, a scene that I had kept at bay all these months came flooding in. The day I'd phoned Barry to warn him, and then hung up. I could feel the weight of the receiver as I put it on the cradle. My responsibility. My infection.

"We need Christ's antibodies, to overcome this contagion within our souls. And those who choose to serve themselves instead of the Heavenly Father will experience the deadly consequences."

It wasn't surreal anymore. What Reverend Thomas was saying was true. I had contracted the virus. I had been infected all the while. There was blood on my hands. I thought of my beautiful mother, sitting in her tiny cell, her life at full stop. She was just like the Manson kid. She didn't believe in anything but herself, no higher law, no morality. She thought she could justify anything, even murder, just because it was what she wanted. She didn't even use the excuse of who was she hurting. She had no conscience. *I will not serve.* That's what Stephen Dedalus said in *Portrait of the Artist,* but it meant Satan. That's what the Fall was. Satan would not serve.

An old lady stepped forward from the choir and began to sing, "The blood that Jesus shed for me, way back at Calvary . . ." and she could really sing. And I was crying, my tears coming down. We were dying inside, my mother and I. If only we had God, Jesus, something larger than ourselves to believe in, we could be healed. We could still have a new life.

IN JULY, I was baptized into the Truth Assembly of Christ. It didn't even matter that it was Reverend Thomas, how fake he was, how he looked down Starr's dress, the way his eyes

81

fondled her when she walked up the stairs in front of him. I closed my eyes as he laid me back in the square pool behind the Assembly building, my nose filling with chlorine. I wanted the spirit to enter me, to wash me clean. I wanted to follow God's plan for me. I knew where following my own would get me.

Afterward, we went out to Church's Fried Chicken to celebrate. Nobody had ever given me a party before. Starr gave me a white leatherette Bible with passages highlighted in red. From Carolee and the boys I got a box of stationery with a dove in the corner, trailing a banner in its beak that said, "Praise the Lord," but I knew Starr must have picked it out. Uncle Ray gave me a tiny gold cross on a chain. Even though he thought I was nuts to be baptized.

"You can't really believe in this crap," he whispered in my ear as he helped me put the necklace on.

I held up my hair so he could fasten it. "I've got to believe in something," I said, low.

His hand rested on my neck, warm, heavy. His good plain face, sad hazel eyes. And I realized he wanted to kiss me. I felt it inside me. And when he saw that I felt it, he reddened and looked away.

Dear Astrid,

ARE YOU OUT OF YOUR MIND?? You may not 1) be baptized, 2) call yourself a Christian, and 3) write to me on that ridiculous stationery. You will not sign your letters "born again in Christ"! God is dead, haven't you heard, he died a hundred years ago, gave out from sheer lack of interest, decided to play golf instead. I raised you to have some self-respect, and now you're telling me you've given it all away to a *3-D postcard Jesus? I would laugh if it weren't so desperately sad.*

Don't you dare ask me to accept Jesus as my savior, wash my soul in the Blood of the Lamb. Don't even think of trying to redeem me. I regret NOTHING. No woman with any self-respect would have done less.

The question of good and the nature of evil will always be one of philosophy's most intriguing problems, up there with the problem of existence itself. I'm not quarreling with your choice of issues, only with your intellectually diminished approach. If evil means to be self-motivated, to be the center of one's own universe, to live on one's own terms, then every artist, every thinker, every original mind, is evil. Because we dare to look through our own eyes rather than mouth clichés lent us from the so-called Fathers. To dare to see is to steal fire from the Gods. This is mankind's destiny, the engine which fuels us as a race.

Three cheers for Eve.

> *Mother.*

I prayed for her redemption. She took a life because someone humiliated her, hurt her image of herself as the Valkyrie, the stainless warrior. Exposed her weakness, which was only love. So she avenged herself. So easy to justify, I wrote to her. It's because you felt like a victim you did it. If you were really strong, you could have tolerated the humiliation. Only Jesus can make us strong enough to fight the temptations of sin.

She wrote back, a quotation from Milton, Satan's part in *Paradise Lost*:

What though the field be lost?
All is not lost; the unconquerable will,
And study of revenge, immortal hate,
And courage never to submit or yield.

UNCLE RAY was teaching me to play chess from a book, *Bobby Fischer Teaches Chess*. He had taught himself in Vietnam. "I had a lot of time to kill there," he said, running his fingers over the peaked hat of the white pawn. He'd carved the set there, Vietnamese kings and Buddhas for bishops, horses with sculpted cheeks and combed manes. I couldn't imagine the months it must have taken him, patiently carving with a Swiss Army knife while all the bombs blasted around him.

I liked the order of chess, the coolness of reason, the joy of its patient steps. We played most nights when Starr was at AA or CA meetings or at Bible study, while the boys watched TV. Uncle Ray kept a little pipe of dope next to him on the arm of the chair to smoke while he waited for me to make my move.

That night the boys were watching a nature show. The littlest one, Owen, sucked his thumb, holding his stuffed giraffe, while Peter twined a bit of his hair around his finger, over and over again. Davey narrated the show for them, pointing to the screen. "That's Smokey, he's the alpha male." The light from the screen reflected in his glasses.

Uncle Ray waited for my move, looking at me in a way that made my heart open like a moonflower — his eyes on my face, my throat, my hair over my shoulders, changing color in the TV lights. On TV I saw the white of snow, the wolves hunting in pairs, their strange yellow eyes. I felt like an undeveloped photograph that he was printing, my image rising to the surface under his gaze.

"Oh, don't," Owen said, clutching his giraffe with the broken neck as the wolves leapt on their deer, pulling it down by the throat.

"It's the law of nature," Davey said.

"There, look at that." Ray pointed with the black bishop he was moving. "It's like, if God saved that deer, he'd starve the wolf. Why would he favor one person over another?" He had never quite resigned himself to my becoming a Christian. "The good don't get any better a break than anybody else. You could be a fucking saint, and still, you got the plague or stepped on a Bouncing Betty."

"At least you have something larger to fall back on," I said, touching the cross around my neck, zipping it back and forth along the chain. "You have a compass and a map."

"And if there's no God?"

"You act as if there is, and it's the same thing."

He sucked at his pipe, filling the room with its skunky smell, while I examined the board. "What does your mother have to say about that?" he asked.

"She says, 'Better to reign in Hell than serve in Heaven.'"

"My kind of woman."

I didn't say that she called him Uncle Ernie. Through the screen door, the summer crickets sang. I flicked my hair behind my shoulders, moved my bishop to queen's knight 3, threatening his knight. I sensed how he looked at my bare arm, the shoulder, my lips. To know I was beautiful in his eyes made me beautiful. I had never been beautiful before. I didn't think it went against Christ. Everybody needed to feel love.

We heard the crunch of Starr's Torino turning into the yard, car tires in the gravel, earlier than she normally came home. I was disappointed. Ray paid attention to me when she was gone, but when she came home I went back to being just one of the kids. What was she doing home so early anyway? She usually stayed out until eleven, drinking coffee with the addicts, or discussing Matthew 20 verse 13 with the old ladies at the church.

"Shit." Uncle Ray quickly pocketed his stash and small pipe just as the screen door swung open and the bug zapper zapped a big one at the same time.

Starr stopped for a second at the door, seeing us, and the boys sitting on the couch, mesmerized by the TV. Then it was like she was confused to find herself home so soon. She dropped her keys and picked them up. Uncle Ray watched her, her breasts practically coming out of the scooped neck of her dress.

Then her smile came on, and she kicked off her shoes and sat on the arm of his chair, kissed him. I could see her sticking her tongue in his ear.

"Was it canceled?" he asked.

It was my move, but he wasn't paying attention.

She draped herself over his shoulder, her breast squashed into his neck. "Sometimes I just get so tired of hearing them complain. Taking everybody else's darn inventory." She picked up my remaining white knight. "I love this," she said. "Why don't you ever teach me, Ray baby?"

"I did once," he said in a murmuring, tender voice, turning his head and kissing her breast, right in front of me. "Don't you remember? You got so mad you turned the board over." He plucked the knight from her hand and put it back down on the board. King 5.

"That was in my drinking days," she said.

"'Can white mate in one move?'" he repeated out of the Bobby Fischer book.

"One move?" she said, tickling his nose with a strand of her hair. "That doesn't sound too exciting."

White knight to king's bishop 6. I rode the delicately carved knight into place. "Mate."

But they were kissing and then she told the boys to go to bed when they were done and led Uncle Ray back to her bedroom.

ALL NIGHT LONG as I lay in my sleeping bag with its bucking broncos and lariats, I heard their headboard smacking the wall, their laughter. And I wondered whether real daughters were jealous of their mothers and fathers, if it made them sick to see their fathers kiss their mothers, squeeze their breasts. I squeezed my own small breast, hot from the sleeping bag, and imagined how it might feel to another hand, imagined having a body like Starr's. She was almost a different species with her narrow waist, her breasts round as grapefruit, her bottom round like that too. I imagined taking off my clothes and having a man like Uncle Ray look at me the way he looked at her.

God, it was so hot. I opened the zipper of the sleeping bag, lay on top of the hot flannel.

And she didn't even hide it, she wasn't that Christian. Always the shortest of shorts, the tightest of tops. You could see where her jeans crept up inside her labia. I wanted someone to want me that way, touch me the way Uncle Ray did her, like Barry and my mother.

I wished Carolee were there. She would make funny comments about the headboard or joke about Uncle Ray having a heart attack — he was almost fifty, for Christ's sake, lucky if he didn't die with his boots on. He met Starr at the club when she was still waitressing, and what kind of sleazy guys went to places like that anyway. But Carolee was never home at night anymore. She climbed out the window as soon as Starr said good night and went to meet her friends in the wash. She never invited me to come with her. It hurt my feelings, but I didn't like her friends much — girls with mean laughter and boys with shaved heads, awkward and boasting.

I stroked my hands under my nightgown and felt the different skins against my fingertips — the hair on my legs, the smoothness between my thighs, and the slippery, fragrant skin of my private parts. I felt the folds, the peak, and thought of rough hands with missing fingers tracing all the secret places. On the other side of the pressboard wall, the headboard banged.

MY MOTHER sent me a reading list that summer with four hundred books on it, Colette and Chinua Achebe and Mishima, Dostoyevsky and Anaïs Nin, D. H. Lawrence and Henry Miller. I imagined her lying in bed reciting their names like a rosary, running her tongue over them, round as beads. Sometimes Starr took us to the library. She waited in the car and gave us ten minutes to get our books or she'd leave without us. "I've got the only book I need, missy," she said.

Davey and I grabbed our books like Supermarket Sweep while Peter and Owen wistfully hovered near the library grandpa who read stories to kids. It had been better when Ray was home — he would drop us off, go have a few beers, and pick us up an hour or two later. Then the little boys would listen to the grandpa's stories as long as he held out.

But now Ray had a job doing finish carpentry in a new sub-development. I was used to him being home all day and missed him. He hadn't had steady work since he'd quit his job as the shop teacher at the high school over in Sunland. He'd gotten into a fight with the principal when he wouldn't stand up for the Pledge of Allegiance at assembly. "I fought in fucking Vietnam, got a fucking Purple Heart," he said. "What did that asshole do? Went to goddamn Valley State. What a goddamn sterling hero."

The owner of the development lived in Maryland and didn't care about the Pledge of Allegiance. Ray knew someone who knew the subcontractor. So I was stuck at the height of summer in the trailer watching Starr knit a gigantic afghan that looked like a rainbow threw up on it. I read, drew. Ray bought me some kid's watercolors from the drugstore and I started painting. I stopped trying to persuade my mother to accept Jesus. It was hopeless, she would have to come to it herself. It was God's will, like Dmitry in *The Brothers Karamazov*, one of the books from her reading list.

Instead of letters, I sent her drawings and watercolors: Starr in shorts and high heels, watering the geraniums with a hose. Ray drinking a beer watching the sun set from the porch. The boys wandering the wash in the warm tender nights with flashlights, surprising a horned owl. Ray's chess set. The way he studied the board, fist under chin. The paloverde trees in the cool of early morning, a rattlesnake lying across a rock at full length.

I painted pictures for everybody that summer, lizards for Peter and children riding white giraffes and unicorns for Owen, raptors for Davey, both perched and in flight, from pictures in magazines: golden eagles, red-shouldered hawks, peregrine falcons, elf owls. I painted a head-and-shoulders portrait of Carolee for her to give to her boyfriend, and some for Starr, angels mostly, Jesus walking on water. Also her in different poses, wearing a bathing suit, in the style of World War II poster girls.

Uncle Ray just wanted a picture of his truck. It was an old Ford, high and aqua green, with a feather roach clip hanging from the rearview mirror, and a bumper sticker that said, This Property Protected by Smith & Wesson. I painted it against the mountains in the clear morning, aqua and salmon and pale blue.

THE SUMMER climaxed in Santa Anas like nothing I'd ever seen before. Fire came up over the ridges and burned down the flanks of the mountains a mile away. This was no mere smudge on the horizon with miles of concrete separating you. We could see a thousand acres burning off the Big Tujunga. We kept our things packed in Ray's truck and in the trunk of the Torino. The winds blew like hurricanes and the burn area was being reported in square miles and there were riots down in the city. Uncle Ray took to cleaning his guns on the patio after work, as the ash from the fires sifted a fine powder over everything. He handed me the small gun, a Beretta. It was like a toy in my hand. "Want to shoot?"

"Sure," I said. He never let the boys touch his guns. Starr hated to even look at them, though now the riots were going on, she'd stopped asking him to get rid of them. He took a can of green Rust-Oleum and spray-painted a human figure on a board, and for fun made it carrying a TV. He set it up against an oleander at the far end of the yard. "He's taking your TV, Astrid. Plug him."

It was fun, the little Beretta .22. I landed four out of nine shots. He put tape over the bullet holes so I'd know which were old, which were new. I got to try all the guns eventually — the rifle, the short-nosed .38 Police Special, Smith & Wesson, even the twelve-gauge pump-action shotgun. I liked the Beretta best, but Ray insisted the Smith & Wesson was the thing to shoot, it had "stopping power." He'd put it in my hands, showing me how to sight it, how to squeeze the trigger with my mind. The .38 was the hardest of the four to shoot and be accurate with. You had to use both hands, and keep your arms very straight, or it came back and hit you in the face.

Each gun had a purpose, like a hammer or a screwdriver. The rifle was for hunting, the Beretta for potentially touchy situations — a bar, a meeting with the ex, a date, what Ray called close-in work. The shotgun was for home protection. "Get behind me, kids!" he'd say in a grandmothery voice, and we'd all run behind him as he demonstrated, spraying the oleanders with buckshot.

And the .38? "Only one reason for a thirty-eight. And that's to kill your man."

I felt like an Israeli girl soldier, in shorts and the hot wind, sighting down the barrel of the rifle, holding the .38 with both hands. It was a strange feeling, him looking at me as I aimed. I found I couldn't quite lose myself in the target. His eyes split my attention between the C in Coke and my awareness of him watching me.

And I thought, this was what it was like to be beautiful. What my mother felt. The tug of eyes, pulling you back from your flight to the target. I was in two places at once, not only in my thought, my aim, but my bare feet on the dusty yard, my legs growing stronger, my breasts in the new bra, my long tanned arms, my hair flowing white in the hot wind. He was taking my silence but giving me something in return, a fullness of being recognized. I felt beautiful, but also interrupted. I wasn't used to being so complicated.

7

In November, when the air held blue in the afternoons and the sunlight washed the boulders in gold, I turned fourteen. Starr threw me a party, with hats and streamers, and invited Carolee's boyfriend and even my caseworker, the Jack of Spades. There was a cake from Ralph's Market with a hula girl in a grass skirt and my name written in blue, and they all sang "Happy Birthday." The cake had a trick candle that wouldn't go out, so I didn't get my wish. Which was just that it would always be like this, that my life could be a party just for me.

Carolee bought me a mirror for my purse and Owen and Peter gave me a lizard in a jar with a bow. From Davey I got a big sheet of cardboard on which he'd taped animal scat and Xeroxes of animal tracks to match, with carefully printed labels. Starr's gift was a green stretchy sweater, and the social worker brought me a set of rhinestone barrettes.

The last gift was from Ray. I carefully opened the paper, and saw the wood, carved and inlaid in the pattern of an art nouveau moonflower, the cover motif of my mother's first book. I held my breath and took it out of the paper, a wooden jewelry box. It smelled of new wood. I ran my fingers over the moonflower, thought of Ray cutting the pieces, the sinuous edges, fitting them so perfectly you couldn't feel the transitions in the woods. He must have done it late at night, when I was asleep. I was afraid to show how much I loved it. So I just said, "Thanks." But I hoped he could tell.

WHEN THE RAINS CAME, the yard turned to deep mud, and the river rose, filling its enormous channel. What had been a big dry wash littered with rocks and chaparral was transformed into a huge dirty torrent the color of a coffee milkshake. Parts of the burnt mountain sighed and gave way. I never thought it could rain so much. We kept putting pots and cartons and jugs under the leaks in Starr's roof, emptying them in the yard.

It was the break in a seven-year drought, and the rain that had been held back was being delivered, all at once. It lasted without a break through Christmas, leaving us crammed inside the trailer, the boys playing road race and Nintendo and watching a National Geographic double video of tornados, over and over again.

I spent my days out on the porch swing, staring out at the rain, listening to its voices on the metal roof and the runoff thundering down the Tujunga, boulders tumbling, trees washed away whole, knocking into one another like bowling pins. Every color turned to a pale brownish gray.

When there was no color, and I was lonely, I thought of Jesus. Jesus knew my thoughts, knew everything, even if I couldn't see Him, or really feel Him, He would keep me from falling, from being washed away. Sometimes I read the tarot cards, but they were always the same, the swords, the moon, the hanged man, the burn-ing tower with its toppled crown and people falling. Sometimes when Ray was home, he'd come out with his chess set, and we played and he got high, or we'd go out to the shed where he had his workbench set up and he'd show me how to make little things, a birdhouse, a picture frame. Sometimes we'd just talk on the porch, listening to the street-fighting sound effect of the boys' Double Dragons and Zaxxon video games muffled by rain. Ray propped himself against one of the posts, while I lay on the porch glider, swinging it with one foot.

One day, he came out and smoked his pipe a while, leaning one shoulder on the porch upright, not looking at me. He seemed moody, his face troubled.

"You ever think about your dad?" he asked.

"I never met him," I said, stirring with my dangling foot slightly to keep the glider moving. "I was two when he left, or she left him, whatever."

"She tell you about him?"

My father, that silhouette, a form comprised of all I did not know, a shape filled with rain. "Whenever I asked, she'd say, 'You had no father. I'm your father. You sprang full-blown from my forehead, like Athena.'"

He laughed, but sadly. "Some character."

"I found my birth certificate once. 'Father: Anders, Klaus no middle name. Birthplace: Copenhagen, Denmark. Residing in Venice Beach, California.' He'd be fifty-four now." Ray was younger than that.

Thunder rolled, but the clouds were too thick to see light-ning. The glider squeaked as I rocked myself, thinking of my father, Klaus Anders, no middle name. I'd found a Polaroid picture of him stuck in a book of my mother's, *Windward Avenue*. They were sitting together in a beachside café with a bunch of other people who looked like they'd all just come in off the beach — tanned, long-haired people wearing beads, the table covered with beer bottles. Klaus had his arm across the back of her chair, careless and proprietary. They looked like they were sitting in a special patch of sunlight, an aura of beauty around them. They could have been brother and sister. A leonine blond with sensual lips, he smiled all the way and his eyes turned up at the corners. Neither my mother nor I smiled like that.

The picture and the birth certificate were all I had of him, that and the question mark in my genetic code, all that I didn't know about myself. "Mostly I think about what he would think of me."

We looked out at the sepia pepper tree, the mud in the yard thick as memory. Ray turned so he could lean his back flat against the post, lifted his hands over his head. His shirt crawled up, I could see his hairy stomach. "He probably thinks you're still two. That's how I think of Seth. When the boys are down by the river, I imagine he's down there with them. I have to remind myself he's too big for frogs now."

Klaus thought of me as two. My hair like white feathers, my diaper full of sand. He never imagined that I was grown. I could walk right past him, he might even look at me the way Ray did, and never know it was his own daughter. I shivered, pulled the sleeves of my sweater over my hands.

"Have you ever thought to call him, find him?" I asked.

Ray shook his head. "I'm sure he hates my guts. I know his mother fed him all kinds of crap about me."

"I bet he misses you, though," I said. "I miss Klaus and I never even met him. He was an artist too. A painter. I imagine he'd be proud of me."

"He would be," Ray said. "Maybe someday you'll meet him."

"I think about that sometimes. That when I'm an artist, he'll read about me in the paper, and see how I turned out. When I see a middle-aged blond man sometimes, I want to call out, Klaus! And see if he turns his head." I made the glider creak as I pushed myself slowly.

My mother once told me she chose him because he looked like her, so it was as if she were having her own child. But there was a different story in the red Tibetan notebook with the orange binding dated Venice Beach, 1972.

July 12. Ran into K. at Small World this afternoon. Saw him before he saw me. Thrill at the sight of him, the slight slouch of broad shoulders, paint in his hair. That thread-bare shirt, so ancient it is more an idea than a shirt. I wanted him to discover me the same way, so I turned away, browsed an Illuminati chapbook. Knowing how I looked against the light through the window, my hair on fire, my dress barely there. Waiting to stop his heart.

I looked at Ray, gazing out into the rain — and I knew how she felt. I loved his smoke, his smell, his sad hazel eyes. I couldn't have him as a father, but at least we could talk like this out on the porch. He relit his pipe, toked, coughed.

"You might be disappointed," he said. "He might be a jerk. Most guys are jerks."

I rocked myself, knowing it wasn't true. "You're not."

"Ask my ex."

"What you doing out there?" Starr opened the screen door, slammed it behind her. She was wearing a sweater she knitted herself, fuzzy and yellow as a chick. "Is this a party anybody can come to?"

"I'm going to blast that fucking TV set," Ray said evenly.

She pulled at the brown tassels of spider plants over her head, plucking the dried leaves and throwing them off the porch, her breasts pushing out of the V neck. "Look at you, smoking in front of the kids. You always were a bad influence." But she smiled when she said it, soft and flirting. "Do me a favor, Ray baby? I'm out of cigs, could you run down to the store and get me a carton?" She flashed him her flat wide smile.

"I need some beer anyway," he said. "You want to come, Astrid?"

As if her smile couldn't stretch anymore, it sprang back to the center, then she stretched it again. "You can go yourself, can't you, big boy? Astrid needs to help me for a minute." Pluck, pluck, tearing the baby spiders off with the dead leaves.

Ray got his jacket and ducked out under the waterfall of water coming off the corrugated steel porch roof, the jacket pulled up to cover his head.

"You and me need to talk, missy," Starr said to me as Ray closed the cab door to the truck and started the motor.

Reluctantly, I followed her back into the house, into her bedroom. Starr never talked to the kids. Her room was dark and held the smell of unwashed grown-ups, dense and loamy, a woman and a man. The bed was unmade. A kid's room never smelled like that, no matter how many were sleeping there. I wanted to open a window.

She sat down on the unmade bed and reached for the pack of Benson and Hedges 100s, saw it was empty, threw it away. "You're having a good time here, aren't you," she said, peering into the drawer of the bedside table, rummaging inside. "Making yourself at home? Getting comfortable?"

I traced the flower pattern on her sheets, it was a poppy. My fingers followed the aureole, and then the feelers in the middle. Poppy, the shape of my mother's undoing.

"A little too darn comfortable, I'd say." She shut the drawer, the little ring of the pull clicking. She tugged the blanket up, so I couldn't trace the flower anymore. "I may not be some genius, but I'm getting your game. Believe me, it takes one to know one."

"One what?" I couldn't help but be curious about what I was that Starr recognized in herself.

"Going after my man." She straightened out a cigarette butt from the plaid beanbag ashtray on the nightstand and lit it.

I had to laugh. "I wasn't." That was what she saw? Bang bang bang, Lord almighty? "I didn't."

"Always hanging around, handling his 'tools' — 'What's this for, Uncle Ray?' Playing with his guns? I've seen the two of you. Everybody asleep except the two of you, cuddling up, just as sweet as you please." She exhaled the stale butt-smoke into the close, humid air.

"He's old," I said. "We're not doing anything."

"He's not that old," Starr said. "He's a man, missy. He sees what he sees and he does what he can. I've got to talk fast before he gets back, but I got to tell you, I decided I'm calling

Children's Services, so whatever you were thinking, it's all over now, Baby Blue. You're history."

I stared at her, her furry lashes. She couldn't be that mean, could she? I hadn't done anything. Sure, I loved him, but I couldn't help that. I loved her too, and Davey, all of them. It was unfair. She couldn't be serious.

I started to protest, but she held up her hand, the butt smoldering between her fingers. "Don't try to argue me out of it. I got a nice thing going here now. Ray's the best man I ever had, treats me nice. Maybe you haven't been trying, but I smell S-E-X, missy, and I'm not taking any chances. I lived too long and come too far to blow it now."

I sat like a fish in that airless room, flopping, as the rain battered the metal roof and walls. She was kicking me out, for nothing. I felt the ocean tugging me from my tiny little place on the rock. I could hear the river, carrying its tons of debris. I tried to think of an explanation, a reason that might satisfy her.

"I never had a father," I said.

"Don't." She crushed the twice-smoked butt out in the ashtray, watched her fingers. "I've got myself and my own kids to worry about. You and me, we hardly know each other. I don't owe you a thing." She looked down at the front of her fuzzy sweater and brushed at some ash that had fallen on her full breast.

I was slipping, falling. I had trusted Starr and I'd never given her a reason to doubt me. It wasn't fair. She was a Christian, but she wasn't acting on faith, on goodness. "What about charity?" I said, like a falling man reaching for a branch. "Jesus would give me a chance."

She stood up. "I'm not Jesus," she said. "Not even close."

I sat on the bed, praying to the voice in the rain. Please, Jesus, don't let her do this to me. Jesus, if you can see this, open up her heart. Please Jesus, don't let it be like this.

"I'm sorry, you were a good kid," she said. "But that's life."

The only answer was rain. Silence and tears. Nothing. I thought of my mother. What she would do if she were me. She would not hesitate. She would spare nothing to have what she wanted. And thinking of her, I felt something flow into my emptiness like a flexible rod of rebar climbing up my spine. I knew it was evil, what I was feeling, self-will, but if it was, then it was. I suddenly saw us on a giant chessboard, and saw my move.

"He might be mad," I said. "You thought of that? If he knew you sent me away, because you were jealous."

Starr had been halfway to the door, but she stopped and turned around. She looked at me as if she'd never seen me before. I was surprised at how fast the words poured out of me then. I was the one who never had words. "Men don't like jealous women. You're trying to make him a prisoner. He's going to hate you. He might even break up with you."

And I liked the way she flinched, knowing I had caused the lines in her forehead. There was power in me now, where there had been none.

She pulled down her sweater so her breasts were even more prominent, glanced at herself in the mirror. Then she laughed. "What do you know about men. You baby."

But I felt the doubt that had made her turn to the mirror, and kept going. "I know that men don't like women who try to own them. They dump them."

Starr hovered by her dresser, uncertain now whether she should stop listening to me and get rid of me quick, or let me go on mining the possibilities of her doubts. She busied herself looking for another butt in the ashtray, found one that wasn't so long, straightened it out between her fingers, and lit it with her powder-blue Bic lighter.

"Especially when there's nothing going on. I like you, I like him, I like the kids, I would never do anything to screw it up. Don't you know that?" The more I said it, the less true it was. The angel on her bureau looked down, ashamed, afraid to see me. The rain drummed on the roof.

"Swear you're not interested in him?" she said finally, squinting against the vile smoke. She grabbed the Bible off the bedside table, a white leather Bible with red ribbons and a gilded edge. "Swear on the Bible?"

I put my hand on it. It could have been the phone book for all I cared now. "I swear to God," I said.

SHE NEVER CALLED Children's Services, but she watched my every move, every gesture. I wasn't used to being watched, it made me feel important. I sensed a layer of myself had been peeled off that day in her bedroom, and what was under it glowed.

One night she was late getting dinner, and as we were finishing, Uncle Ray glanced at the clock. "You're going to be tardy if you don't get a move on."

Starr leaned back in her seat and reached for the coffeepot behind her on the counter, poured herself a cup. "I guess they can get on without me for one night, don't you think, baby?"

The following week, she skipped two more meetings, and the third week, she actually missed church. Instead, they made love all morning, and when they finally did get up, she took us all out to the IHOP, where we ate chocolate pancakes and waffles with whipped cream in a big corner booth. Everyone was laughing and having a good time, but all I could see was Ray's arm around her shoulder on the back of the leatherette booth. I felt strange, and moved the waffle around on my plate. I wasn't hungry anymore.

THE RAINS PASSED, and now in the nights the new-washed sky showed all its stars. The boys and I stood out in the darkest part of the clay-muddy yard, listening to the runoff on the Tujunga out in the dark beyond the trees. Heavy pancakes of mud congealed around my boots as I craned my head back in the vapor-breath cold and tried to pick out the dippers and the crosses. Davey's books didn't show so many stars. I couldn't separate them.

I thought I saw a streak of light. I wasn't sure if I even saw it. I gazed upward, trying not to blink, waited.

"There!" Davey pointed.

In a different quadrant of the sky, another star broke loose. It was eerie, the one thing you didn't plan on, stellar movement. I tried to keep my eyes open without blinking. When you blinked, you missed them. I held them open for the light to develop on them like a photograph.

The little boys shivered despite the jackets over their pajamas and muddy boots, chattering and giggling in the cold and the excitement of being up so late as they gazed at the stars that started pinging like pinballs, mouths opened in case one should fall in. It was completely dark except for the line of Christmas lights that twinkled along the edge of the trailer porch.

The screen door opened and slammed. I didn't have to look to know it was him. The flare of a match, the warm stinky pot smell. "Ought to take down those Christmas lights," he said. He came out on the yard where we were, the ember glow, and then the sharpness of his body, the smell of new wood.

"It's the Quadrantid shower," Davey said. "We'll be getting forty an hour pretty soon. It's the shortest-lived meteorite display, but the densest except for the Perseids."

I could hear the mud sucking at his boots as he shifted his weight. I was glad it was dark, that he couldn't see the flush of pleasure on my face as he drew closer, looking up at the sky, as if he cared about the Quadrantids, as if that's why he'd come out.

"There!" Owen said. "Did you see it, Uncle Ray? Did you?"

"Yeah, I saw it buddy. I saw it."

He was standing right next to me. If I shifted just an inch to my left, I could brush him with my sleeve. I felt the radiant heat of him across the narrow gap between us in the darkness. We had never stood so close.

"You and Starr having a beef?" he asked me softly.

I exhaled vapor, imagined I was smoking, like Dietrich in *The Blue Angel*. "What did she say?"

"Nothing. She's just been acting funny lately."

Shooting stars hurled themselves into the empty places, burned up. Just for the pleasure of it. Just like this. I could have swallowed the night whole.

Ray toked too hard, coughed, spat. "Must be hard on her, getting older, pretty girls coming up in the same house."

I gazed up as if I hadn't heard, but what I was thinking was, tell me more about the pretty girls. I was embarrassed for wanting it, it was base, what did pretty matter? I had thought that so many times with my mother. A person didn't need to be beautiful, they just needed to be loved. But I couldn't help wanting it. If that was the way I could be loved, to be beautiful, I'd take it.

"She still looks good," I said, thinking that it wouldn't be so hard on her if he didn't follow me out into the star-filled night, if he didn't watch me the way he did, touching his mouth with his fingertips.

But I didn't want him to stop. I was sorry for Starr, but not enough. I had the sin virus. I was the center of my own universe, it was the stars that were moving, rearranging themselves around me, and I liked the way he looked at me. Who had ever looked at me, who had ever noticed me? If this was evil, let God change my mind.

Dear Astrid,

Do not tell me how much you admire this man, how he cares for you! I don't know which is worse, your Jesus phase or the advent of a middle-aged suitor. You must find a boy your own age, someone mild and beautiful to be your lover. Someone who will tremble for your touch, offer you a marguerite by its long stem with his eyes lowered, someone whose fingers are a poem. Never lie down for the father. I forbid it, do you understand?

Mother.

You couldn't stop it, Mother. I didn't have to listen to you anymore.

IT WAS SPRING, painting the hillsides with orange drifts of California poppies, dotting the cracks in gas stations and parking lots with poppies and blue lupine and Indian paintbrush. Even in the burn zones, the passes were matted with yellow mustard as we jounced along in Ray's old pickup truck.

I told him I wanted to see the new development up in Lancaster, the custom cabinetry he'd been working on. Maybe he could pick me up after school sometime. "You know how funny Starr's been," I said. Every day I came out of school hoping I would see his truck with the feathered roach clip hanging from the rearview mirror. Finally he had come.

The development itself was bare as a scar, with torn and dusty streets of big new houses. Some were already roofed and sided, others finished to the insulation, some skeletal and open to the sky. Ray led me through the house where he was working, clean, the exterior finished, smelling of raw sawdust. He showed me the solid maple cabinetry in the eat-in kitchen, the bay window, the built-in bookcases, the backyard gazebo. I felt the sun glinting off my hair, knew how my mother felt that day long ago at the Small World bookstore, when she had seen my father and stood in the window, beautiful in the light.

I let him show me around like a real estate agent — the living room's two-story picture window, the streamlined toilets in the two and a half baths, the turned banister, the carved newel post. "I lived in a house like this when I was married," he said, running his hand along the flank of the heavy banister, pushing against the solidity of the post. I tried to imagine Ray in a two-and-a-half-bath life, dinner on the table at six, the regular job, the wife, the kid. But I couldn't. Anyway, even when he was doing it, he was going to the Trop instead of coming home, falling in love with strippers.

I followed him upstairs, where he showed me the finish work, cedar-lined linen closets and window seats. In the master bedroom we could hear the hammering from the other houses and the sound of the bulldozer cutting a pad for a new one. Ray looked out the smudgy casement at the surrounding construction. I imagined what the room would look like once the people moved in. Lilac carpets and blue roses on the bedspread, white-and-gold double dresser, headboard. I liked it better the way it was, pink wood, the sweet raw smell. I watched the browns and greens of his Pendleton shirt, his hands spread on either side of the window frame, as he looked down into the unplanted yard. "What are you thinking?" I asked him.

"That they won't be happy," he said quietly.

"Who?"

"People who buy these houses. I'm building houses for people who won't be happy in them." His good face looked so sad.

I came closer to him. "Why can't they?"

He pressed his forehead to the window, so new there was still a sticker on it. "Because it's always wrong. They don't want to hurt anyone."

I could smell his sweat, sharp and strong, a man's smell, and it was hot in the room with the new windows, heady with the fragrance of raw wood. I put my hands around his waist, pressed my face into the scratchy wool between his shoulder blades, something I'd wanted to do since he held me that first Sunday when I'd ditched church and stayed behind in the trailer. I closed my eyes and breathed in his scent, dope and sweat and new wood. He didn't move, just gave a shuddering sigh.

"You're a kid," he said.

"I'm a fish swimming by, Ray," I whispered into his neck. "Catch me if you want me."

For a moment he stood still as a suspect, his hands open on the window frame. Then he caught my hands, turned them over and kissed the palms, pressed them to his face. And I was the one who was trembling, it was me and my marguerite.

He turned and held me. It was precisely how I had wanted to be held, all my life — by strong arms and a broad, wool-shirted chest smelling of tobacco and pot. I threw my head back and it was my first kiss, I opened my mouth for him to taste me, my lips, my tongue. I couldn't stop shaking unless he held me very tight.

He pushed me away then, gently. "Look, maybe we should go back. It isn't right."

I didn't care what was right anymore. I had a condom from Carolee's drawer in my pocket, and the man I'd always wanted for once in a place we could be alone.

I took off my plaid shirt, tossed it onto the floor. I took off my T-shirt. I took off my bra and let him see me, small and very pale, not Starr, but me, all I had. I untied my hiking boots, kicked them off. I unbuttoned my jeans and let them fall.

Ray looked sad right then, like someone was dying, his back pressed against the smudged window. "I never wanted this to happen," he said.

"You're a liar, Ray," I said.

Then he was kneeling in front of me, his arms around my hips, kissing my belly, my thighs, his hands on my bare bottom, fingers in the silky wetness between my legs, tasting me there. My smell on his mouth as I knelt down with him, ran my hands over his body, opened his clothes, felt for him, hard, larger than I'd thought it would be. And I thought, there was no God, there was only what you wanted.

8

ALL DAY AT SCHOOL, and in the Ray-less afternoons down the wash, or at dinner with Starr and the kids, or when we watched TV at night, Ray was my only thought, my singular obsession. How soft his skin was, softer than you'd think a man's skin could be, and the thickness of his arms, the sinews tracing along his forearms like tree roots, and the sad way he looked at me when my clothes were gone.

I sketched the way he looked nude, gazing out the window after we'd made love, or lying on the pile of carpet padding he'd dragged into the corner of the new bedroom. On our afternoons we'd lie on those pads, our legs entwined, smooth over hairy, his fingers lightly covering my breast and playing with my nipple, making it stand up like a pencil eraser. I hid the drawings in the box with my mother's journals, a place Starr would never think to look. I knew I should throw them out, but I couldn't bear to.

"Why are you with Starr?" I asked him one afternoon, tracing the white scar under his ribs where a Vietcong bullet had left its mark.

He ran his fingertips over my ribs so the goose bumps came up. "She's the only woman who ever let me just be myself," he said.

"I would," I said, doing the same on his balls with the back of my fingernails, making him jump. "Is she good in bed, is that it?"

"That's personal," he said. He covered my hand with his and held it to his groin. I felt him growing hard again. "I don't talk about one woman to another. That's plain bad manners."

He ran his finger between my legs, into the wet like silk, then put his finger in his mouth. I never imagined it would be like this, to be desired. Everything was possible. He pulled me on top of him and I rode him like a horse in the surf, my forehead against his chest, riding through a spray of sparks. If my mother were free, would this be one of her lovers, filling me up with his stars? And would my mother watch me the way Starr did, realizing I was no longer transparent as an encyclopedia overlay?

No. If she were free, I wouldn't be here. She would never have allowed me to have this. She kept everything good for herself.

"I love you, Ray," I said.

"Shhh," he said, holding my hips. His eyelids fluttered. "Don't say anything."

So I just rode, the ocean spray tingling all over me, the tide rising, filled with starfish and phosphorescence, into the dawn.

STARR'S EDGINESS spilled over, mostly at the kids. She was accusing her daughter of all the things she wanted to accuse me of. Carolee barely ever came home, she went dirt biking with Derrick in the afternoon, the drone of the bikes like a nagging doubt. When I wasn't with Ray, I stayed at school or went to the library, or hunted frogs with the boys as the Big Tujunga's winter flow slowly dried up into rivulets and muddy pools. The frogs looked like the mud and you had to be very still to see them. Mostly I just sat on a rock in the sun and painted.

But one day I came home from the wash to find Starr curled up on the porch swing, her hair in hot rollers, wearing a blue blouse tied up tight under her breasts and tiny cutoffs that bunched up at her crotch. She was playing with the kittens the cat had had under the house that spring, fishing for them with ribbons Davey had tied to a stick. She was laughing and talking to them, it wasn't like her. She usually called them rats with fur.

"Well, the artiste. Come talk to me, missy, I'm so bored I'm talking to cats."

She never wanted to talk to me, and there was something about her mouth that seemed slower than the words she was saying. She gave me the stick and took a cigarette out of the Benson and Hedges pack. She stuck the wrong end in her mouth, and I watched to see if she would light it. She caught it just in time. "Don't know which end is up," she joked, and took a sip from her coffee cup. I dragged the ribbons along the carpet, luring a little gray-and-white furball out from beneath the swing. It hopped, pounced, ran off.

"So talk to me," she said, taking an exaggerated drag from her cigarette and blowing it out in a long stream. She bared her lovely throat as she arched back her neck, her head huge with hot curlers like a dandelion puff. "We used to talk all the time. Everybody's so darn busy, that's what's wrong with life. You seen Carolee?"

Up the road, we could both see the plumes of dust from the dirt bikes rising into the thin blue sky. I wanted to be dust, smoke, the wind, sun glimmering over the chaparral, anywhere but sitting here with the woman whose man I was stealing.

"Carolee's trouble," Starr said, holding out her foot to look at the silvery pedicure. "You stay away from her. I'm going to have to talk to that girl, stop the downward spiral. Needs a big dose of the Word." She pulled out a curler, looked cross-eyed at the ringlet over her forehead, started pulling out the other ones, dropping them into her lap. "You're the good girl. I'm making my amends to you. A-mend. Where's Carolee, you seen her?" she asked again.

"I think she's with Derrick," I said, wiggling the ribbon end near the glider where the kitten was hiding.

She leaned her head forward to get the curlers at the back. "Of all the white trash. His mama's so dumb she puts the TV dinner in the oven with the box still on." She laughed and dropped the curler, and the kitten that had just come out dashed back underneath the glider.

That's when I realized Starr was drunk. She'd been sober eighteen months, kept the AA chips on her key ring, red, yellow, blue, purple. It was such a big deal to her, too. I never quite understood it. Ray drank. My mother drank. Michael drank from the moment he finished reading his Books on Tape at noon until he passed out at midnight. It didn't seem to hurt him any. If anything, Starr looked happier now. I wondered why she'd tried so hard to be some kind of saint, when it wasn't really her nature. What was the big deal?

"He's crazy about me, you know," she said. "That Ray. There's a man that needs a *real* woman." She rolled her hips in their tight cutoffs as if she were sitting on him right now. "His wife wouldn't do shit for him." She took another hit on her cigarette, lowering her mascaraed eyelashes, remembering. "That man was starving for a piece. I saw her once, you know. The wife." She drank from her coffee cup, and now I could smell it. "Sailor's delight. Sensible shoes, you know what I'm saying. Wouldn't give head or anything. He'd come to the Trop and just sit and watch us girls with those sad eyes, like a starving man in a supermarket." She squared her shoulders, rolled them forward, so I'd get an idea of what Ray had been watching, the cross caught in her cleavage, Jesus drowning in flesh. She laughed, dropped cigarette ash on the white-patched kitten. "I just had to fall in love with him."

It made me queasy thinking of Ray in some strip club, goggling at the girls with their enormous breasts. He just didn't know where else to go. I picked up the stick again, rustled the ribbons, trying to get the kitten interested so she wouldn't see my red face.

"I must have been crazy to think you and him . . . ," she said into her coffee cup, drained it and put it on the mosaic-topped table with a thud. "I mean, look at you, you're just a baby. You didn't even wear a bra until I got you that one."

She was convincing herself there was nothing between Ray and me, that nothing could possibly be going on, because she was a woman and I was nothing. But I could still feel how he knelt in front of me on the unfinished floor, how he held me around the thighs, kissed my bare belly. I could smell the odor of the raw wood, feel the clutch of his fingers, and we burst into flame like oilfat chaparral in oleander time.

A FULL MOON poured white through the curtains. The refrigerator cycled around in the kitchen, ice cubes dropping in the icemaker. "I can't believe she'd go out after all this time," Carolee said. "Never trust an alcoholic, Astrid. Rules one, two, and three."

Carolee sat up in bed, peeled off her nightgown, put on her miniskirt, nylons, and a shiny shirt. She opened the window, pushed the screen out, and clambered onto the dresser, high-heeled shoes in her hand. I heard her drop down on the porch outside.

"And where you think you're goin', missy?" Starr's voice came from out of the darkness.

"Since when did you care," I could hear Carolee reply.

I went to the window. I couldn't see Starr, only Carolee's hip jutting out in her white skirt, hands on her hips, her elbows defiant.

"Goin' out to spread 'em for every Tom, Dick, and Harry." Starr must have had a few on the porch, in the lawn chair over by the living room.

Carolee put on her high heels, one at a time, and walked out into the yard, which was full-moon lit, bright as a stage. "So what if I am." I wished I could draw the way her broad-shouldered body threw a shadow on the moon-pale dust. How brave she looked just then.

Starr wouldn't let it go at that. "You know what they say.

'Call Carolee, she does it for free.' Whores are supposed to get paid, don't you know anything?"

"You should know better than me." Carolee turned and started walking to the road.

Starr lurched across my field of vision, staggering down the stairs in a shortie nightgown, and smacked Carolee in the face. The sound of the blow reverberated in the still night, irrevocable.

Carolee's arm drew back and struck. Starr's head jerked to one side. It was ugly, but fascinating, like a movie, like I didn't even know them. Starr grabbed her by the hair and dragged her around as Carolee screamed and tried to hit her, but she couldn't straighten up far enough to reach her. So she took off a high heel and hit her with that, and Starr let her go.

I saw Ray come down the steps wearing just a pair of jeans. I knew he had nothing on underneath, that body I loved so much, as Carolee grabbed Starr by the front of her nightgown and shoved her down hard in the dirt. She stood above Starr so she had to look up at Carolee's legs in their nylons, her high-heeled shoes. How bad could this get, could a daughter kick a mother in the face? I could see that she wanted to.

I was relieved when Ray got between them and helped Starr to her feet. "Let's go back to bed, baby."

"You lousy drunk," Carolee yelled after them. "I hate you."

"Get lost then," Starr said, staggering unsteadily on Ray's arm. "Bug off. Who needs you."

"You don't mean that," Ray said. "Let's just sleep it off, okay?"

"I'll leave," Carolee said. "You bet I will."

"You leave, you are never coming back, missy."

"Who'd the fuck want to?" Carolee said.

She slammed into our room, opening drawers, pulling stuff onto the bed, cramming what would fit into a flowered suitcase. "Bye, Astrid. It's been real."

Davey and the little boys were waiting in the hall, scared, blinking from sleep. "Don't go," Davey said.

"I can't stay. Not in this nuthouse." Carolee gave him a quick one-armed hug and went out, banging her suitcase against her knee. She walked right past Ray and Starr, never turning her head, strode out of the yard on her high heels and walked down the road, smaller and smaller.

I watched her for a long time, memorizing her shoulders, her long-legged gait. This was how girls left. They packed up their suitcases and walked away in high heels. They pretended they weren't crying, that it wasn't the worst day of their lives. That they didn't want their mothers to come running after them, begging their forgiveness, that they wouldn't have gone down on their knees and thanked God if they could stay.

WHEN CAROLEE LEFT, Starr lost something essential, something she needed, like a gyroscope that kept the plane from flipping over or a depth gauge that told you whether you were going deeper or coming up. She might suddenly want to go out dancing, or stay home and drink and complain, or get all sweet and sloppy and want to be a family and play games and cook brownies that burned, and you never knew which it would be. Peter didn't eat her casserole one night and she took his plate and turned it over on his head. And I knew it was my defiance, my sin. I took it all, never said a word.

If only I hadn't started with Ray. I made her go off her program. I was the snake in the garden.

But knowing it wasn't enough to make me stop. I had the virus. Ray and I made love in the new houses, we made love in his woodshop behind the garage, sometimes even in the wash among the boulders. We tried not to be in the same room at the same time when Starr was home, we set the air on fire between us.

THEN ONE DAY Starr was yelling at the boys for their mess in the living room, some plastic lizards and Legos and an exhibit Davey was working on. It was a painstakingly accurate model of Vasquez Rocks and the fossils he'd found there on a field trip with his class, turritella shells and trilobites from the Cambrian era. Starr threw toys and puzzles and then marched over to Davey, lifted her foot and crushed his project in two fast stomps. "I told you to clean this crap up!"

The other boys ran out the screen door, but Davey knelt by his ruined exhibit, touching the crushed shells. He looked up, and I didn't have to see his eyes behind his glasses to know he was crying. "I hate you!" Davey yelled. "You ruin everything! You can't even comprehend —"

Starr grabbed him, started hitting him, holding him by one arm so he couldn't get away, screaming, "Who do you think I am? Don't you call me stupid! I'm your mother! I'm a person! I can't do all this by myself! Have some respect!"

It started as a spanking, but it turned into just a beating. The little boys had run away, but I couldn't. This was because of me.

"Starr," I said, trying to pull her off. "Don't."

"You shut up!" she screeched, and threw me off. Her hair was in her face, her eyes white all the way around the pupil. "You have nothing to say, you hear me?"

Finally she stumbled away, crying into her hands. Davey just sat by the devastation of his project, and I could see the tears rolling down his face. I crouched next to him, seeing if there was anything that could be salvaged.

Starr opened the Jim Beam she'd started keeping in the cabinet with the breakfast cereal, poured herself a glass, threw in a few ice cubes. She was drinking right in front of us now. "You just can't talk to people like that," she said, wiping her eyes, her mouth. "Little shit."

Davey's arm hung at a funny angle. "Does your arm hurt?" I asked softly.

He nodded, but he wouldn't look at me. Did he know, could he guess?

Starr sat on a molded kitchen chair, slumped with exhaustion after the beating. Sullen, drinking her booze. She took a cigarette from the gold package and lit it.

"I think it's dislocated," Davey said.

"Whine, whine, whine. Why don't you go somewhere and whine."

I filled a bag with ice, put it against Davey's shoulder. It looked bad. His mouth was all puckery. He never whined.

"He needs to go to the hospital," I said, afraid, trying not to sound accusing.

"Well I can't drive him. You drive him." She fumbled in her purse for the keys and threw them at me. She had forgotten I was only fourteen.

"Call Uncle Ray."

"No."

"Mom?" Davey was sobbing now. "Help me."

She looked at him, and now she saw the angle of his arm, the way he held it out by the elbow in front of him. "Oh Lord." She ran over to Davey, knocking her shin into the coffee table, crouched by her son where he sat on the couch, holding his arm. "Oh, mister, I'm sorry. Mommy's sorry, baby." The more she thought about it, the more upset she got, running at the nose, trying to comb his hair back with her awkward hands, making jerky, meaningless gestures. He turned his head away.

She crossed her arms across her chest, but low, more toward the belly, and huddled next to the couch on the floor, rocking herself, hitting her forehead with her fist. "What do I do, Lord, what do I do?"

"I'm calling Uncle Ray," I said.

Davey knew the number, recited it while I called him at the new houses. Half an hour later, he was home, his mouth set in a thin line.

"I didn't mean it," Starr said, her hands in front of her like an opera singer. "It was an accident. You've got to believe me."

Nobody said anything. We left Starr crying in monotonous sobs, took Davey to the emergency hospital, where they popped his shoulder back in, taped it down. We concocted a story about how we were playing on the river. *He jumped off a rock and fell.* It sounded stupid even to me, but Davey made us promise not to say it was Starr. He still loved her, after everything.

*

EASTER. A pure crystalline morning where you could see every bush and boulder on the mountain. The air was so clean it hurt. Starr was in the kitchen fixing a ham, pushing little points of cloves into the squares she'd scored into the top. She'd been sober for two weeks, taking a meeting a day. We were all making an effort. Davey's sling was a constant reminder of how bad it could get.

Starr put the ham in the oven, and we all went to church, even Uncle Ray, though he stayed behind in the car for a minute to get stoned before he came in, I could smell it as he passed by me to take the seat between Owen and Starr. Her eyes begged Reverend Thomas for a dose of the Blood. I tried to pray, to feel once again that there was something bigger than just me, someone who cared what I did, but it was gone, I could no longer detect the presence of God in that cinder-block church or in what was left of my soul. Starr yearned toward the sagging Jesus on the pearwood cross, while Uncle Ray cleaned his fingernails with his Swiss Army knife and I waited for the singing to start.

Afterward we stopped at a gas station and Uncle Ray bought her an Easter lily, the promise of a new life.

At home, the trailer smelled of ham. Starr served up lunch, creamed corn, canned pineapple rings, brown-and-serve rolls. Ray and I couldn't look at each other, or it would all start again. We looked at the little kids, we played with our food, congratulated Starr on her cooking. Ray said Reverend Thomas wasn't half bad. We had to put our eyes anywhere but on the other one's face. I studied the little bowl of pink peppermint ice cream with jelly beans sprinkled over, and the Easter lily in the middle of the table in its foil-wrapped pot.

We hadn't been together since we took Davey to the emergency room. We hadn't talked about it, how it had all gone too far.

All afternoon, we watched Easter shows on TV. Pink-skinned evangelists and choirs in matching sateen gowns. Congregations the size of rock 'n' roll concerts. Hands waved in the air like sunflowers. He is risen, Christ the Lord. I wished I believed in Him again.

"We should be there," Starr said. "Next year, we'll do the Crystal Cathedral, Ray, let's."

"Sure," Ray said. He had changed out of his church clothes, back into his regular T-shirt and jeans. We played Chinese checkers with the boys and avoided each other's glances, but it was work, being in the same room without touching, especially with Starr sitting next to him, one hand up high on his soft-washed jeans. I couldn't stand it. After Davey won, I went outside and walked around down in the wash. All I could think of was her hand on his jeans.

I was bad, I had done bad things, I had hurt people, and the worst of it was, I didn't want to stop.

Blue shadows climbed the tawny round slopes of the mountain, like hands modeling the shape of a lover's thighs. A lizard perched on a rock, thinking he was invisible. I threw a pebble at him, watched him dart away into the chaparral. I tore up a leaf of laurel sumac and held it to my nose, hoping it would clear my head.

I smelled him first, the smell of dope wafting on the twilight air. He was in the yard, sunlight striking his face and warming it like a stone. The sight of him caught in my throat. Now I knew I'd been waiting for him. I climbed onto a rise so he could see me, to the east, on the blind side of the trailer, then descended into a bowl of sand between the boulders.

A minute later, I heard him walking up the riverbed, dry already though it was only April. I knew Davey would read all this tomorrow in our tracks. But the moment I touched Ray, I knew we could never be apart, no matter how much we wanted to, no matter who we hurt. His lips on my neck, his hands under my shirt, pulling my pants open, peeling them down. My thighs craved the naked touch of his hips, we fit together like magnets as we sank into the sand. I didn't care about scorpions or the western diamondback. I didn't care about rocks or who might see us.

"Baby, what are you doing to me," he whispered into my hair.

THE LAST TIME I had heard two adults fight was the night my mother stabbed Barry in the hand. Smashing, crashing. I covered my head with the pillow, but I could still hear every word through the thin walls, Starr's drunken screeching, Ray's murmuring rebuttals.

"You used to get it up fine, before you started fucking that little bitch. Admit it, you bastard, you've been fucking her!"

I crouched deeper into my sleeping bag, sweating, pretending it wasn't me, it was some other girl, I was just a kid, I had nothing to do with this.

"Fuck my sponsor! God, I should have got rid of her when I had the chance!"

I imagined Ray sitting on the edge of the bed, his back

slouched, hands dangling between his thighs, not interrupting her, just letting her blow it off, warding off her drunken slaps, wishing she would pass out. I could hear his voice, still calm, soothing, reasonable. "Starr, you're shitfaced."

"You perv. You like fucking kids? What's next, dogs? You really like that skinny twat better than me? That no-tit baby?"

The shame, knowing that the boys were listening, now they knew everything.

"She got a tighter pussy than me? She suck you off like me? Does she take it up the ass? No, really, I want to know what kid fuckers do."

How long did I think I was going to get away with it? I wished I'd never come here, I wished I'd never been born. Yet I had to admit there was a part of me that was proud, even excited, that Ray couldn't get it up for Starr. He couldn't fuck her, no matter how big her tits were, no matter if she let him put it up her ass. It was me he wanted.

"Fuck my sponsor, *you* call my fucking sponsor. I'm going in there and I'm going to cash her check."

I heard more crashing, yelling, and then suddenly the door to my room flew open. Starr in her Victoria's Secret rose negligee all twisted around, both huge tits exposed, was waving the .38. I would see that sight for years in my dreams. She fired without aiming, one arm extended. I rolled onto the floor and the room was full of the smell of gunfire and flying chipboard. I tried to wedge myself under the bed.

"You crazy." Ray and Starr struggled. I moved out where I could see them. He twisted her arm behind her back and took the gun away. He was naked, and bent her backwards by her arm, so that his cock pressed into her buttocks, her tits pointing at the ceiling, shivering like small scared animals as he pushed her with his hips toward the door.

"Fuck you, Ray, fuck you!"

"Anytime," he said as he shoved her out.

Maybe they would do it now and forget all about me. There was a hole in the closet wall. I started to get dressed. I wasn't going to stick around anymore, not with that crazy drunk and a houseful of guns. I was going to call my caseworker tonight. I'd let Ray know where I was, but I couldn't stay here.

Then I heard fighting in their room, and Starr was back, firing at me as I was struggling into my clothes. Pain bloomed in my shoulder, raced fire across my ribs. I staggered for the dresser, to climb up and out the window, but then she fired again, and my hip exploded. I fell onto the floor. I could see her coral painted toenails. "I told you to leave him alone." The ceiling, no air, the metallic smell of static and gunpowder and my own blood.

LIGHT IN MY EYES. Hands moving me. Someone was screaming. God — uniforms, questions. Bearded man, woman, shirt buttoned wrong. Flashlight in my eyes. "Where's Ray?" I asked, turning my head from the light.

"Astrid?" Davey, the light in his glasses. Holding me together. "She's coming to."

Another face. Blond, doll-like. False eyelashes. Black shirt. Schutzstaffel. "Astrid, who did this? Who shot you?" Just tell us, tell us who.

Davey shoved his glasses up his nose. Stared into my eyes. He shook his head, imperceptibly, but I saw.

In the doorway, the two little boys huddled. Jackets over their pajamas. Owen with his broken-necked giraffe, head sagging over his arm. Peter with the jar of lizards. The foster kids. They knew what came next.

"Astrid, what happened. Who did this to you?" I closed my eyes. Where could I begin to answer such a question anyway.

Beard Man swabbed my arm, stuck the needle in, IV.

"She going to be okay?" Davey asked.

"Great job, son. Without you she'd have already bled to death."

Hands under me. Firestorms of pain as they lifted me onto the stretcher. Screaming. Fire. Fire. Beard Man held up the IV bag.

"That's it," he said. "Just relax."

I stared into Davey's eyes, knowing that who felt worse was a toss-up. He held my hand, and I held his, as hard as I could though the painkillers were knocking me out. "My stuff."

"We'll get it later." Caseworker. Couldn't even button her shirt right.

Davey started grabbing things, my mother's books, my sketchbook, some paintings, the animal scat poster. But Ray . . . "Davey, my box."

Davey's face darkened. He'd read the tracks. My brain fading into blue-greens and yellows, a coruscating flicker of Tiffany glass. "Please," I whispered.

"Let go now, sweetheart. You need to come with us."

He grabbed the wooden jewelry box, his face twisted like when his shoulder was dislocated. He stayed with me as they wheeled me out to the ambulance, shrugging off the blackshirt doll woman as she tried to lead him away. Overhead, the cradle moon shone like a silver hoop. Beard Man talking to me as he loaded me in the back of the ambulance. "Relax, you've got to relax now. We've got your stuff." Then the rear doors closed, Davey went away, the night swallowed him, swallowed them all.

9

＊

HER FINGERS MOVED among barnacles and mussels, blue-black, sharp-edged. Neon red starfish were limp Dalis on the rocks, surrounded by bouquets of stinging anemones and purple bursts of spiny sea urchins. Her fingers touched an urchin's stiff bristles and I watched inert plant spines move, animate, and reach for my mother, feeling for her shape and intent. She wanted me to touch it too, but I was afraid. It amazed me to see the white flesh and purple spines communicating across a gap no less enormous than deep space, a miracle in six inches of water. She touched me that way, my cheeks, my arms, and I too reached out to her.

El cielo es azul. We were on Isla Mujeres, the Island of Women. I was a little girl in a faded dress, sunburned, barefoot, hair white as dandelion floss. The streets were crushed shell where we stood in line at the tortilla shop every morning with the Mexican women. *¿Quál es su nombre? Su hija es más guapa,* they said, Your daughter is too pretty, and touched my hair. My mother's skin peeling like paint. Her eyes bluer than the sky, *azul claro.*

In a big hotel colored pink and orange, a man with a dark mustache smelled like crushed flowers. There were taxis and music, and my mother went out in embroidered dresses pulled low off the shoulders. But then he was gone, and we moved on to the Island of Women.

My mother was waiting for something there, I didn't know what. We bought our tortillas every day, walked back to the little whitewashed bungalow with our string bag, past small houses with grated windows and the doors opened like frames. Inside were pictures on the walls, grandmothers with fans, sometimes there were books. We ate shrimp with garlic in outdoor restaurants on the beach. *Camarones con ajo.* Some fishermen caught a hammerhead shark and dragged it up onto the beach. It was twice the size of the little boats the fishermen used, and everyone came to the beach to look at it, to pose alongside its monstrous head, as wide as I was tall. Battalions of teeth showed in its humorless grin. I was afraid when my mother left me on the beach to swim out on the soft blue. What happened if the shark came, and the water turned red and the bones came through?

WHENEVER I WOKE, there was Demerol. Doctors in masks, nurses with soft hands. Flowers. Their smiles like nectar. There were IVs and other children, dressings and Tom and Jerry on the TV, balloons and strangers. *Just tell us, just tell.* Schutzstaffel. Plainclothes. How could I begin to describe Starr, with her nightgown all twisted around, unloading a .38 into my room. I preferred to think about Mexico. In Mexico the faces were weathered and soft as soap. These buzzing noises in my room were only the mosquitoes in our bungalow on the Island of Women.

ON A FULL MOON NIGHT, something moved her, and we left with only our passports and money in a belt under her dress. I threw up on the ferry. We slept on a new beach, far to the south. The next day, she danced with a young man, Eduardo, on the rooftop, it was his hotel, all the windows were open and I could see the reef, the sea like a lens. The top floor wasn't done yet, there were hammocks under a palm roof, and we could stay as long as we liked. We were happy in Playa del Carmen, driving with Eduardo around town in his black Volare, feeling very rich, *¡qué rico!*, though the town only had two paved roads and a Michoacán ice-cream stand. Painted pictures of snow-capped volcanoes. The tourist boat stopped at Playa del Carmen twice a week, bobbing five stories high like an offshore wedding cake. My mother read tarot cards in the café perfumed with the fat smoke of grilled pollo and carnitas. I watched the man shave the stacks of meat onto tortillas with a machete. We ate well there.

At night Eduardo played guitar and sang gypsy songs with the guests at his hotel, as I rocked in my hammock like a bat folded into leathery wings. At night the air was full of bats. The fruit, my mother said, mangos and *plátanos* and papayas. Fairy circles of ringworm came out all over my body. A doctor in a block concrete clinic gave me medicine. Can't we ever go home? I asked my mother. We have no home, she told me. I am your home.

How beautiful she was barefoot in a bathing suit and a

tablecloth wrapped around her hips. My mother loved me. Even now, I could feel myself rocking in that hammock while Eduardo and my mother danced. You were my home.

But the weather turned and Eduardo closed the hotel for the season, went back to Mexico City, where his parents lived. He said we could stay on if we liked. It was sad and scary. We closed the shutters and the wind began to blow, the gentle sea rose and ate the beach, running into the grape hyacinth. There were no tourists now. We ate from cans, *frijoles refritos*, evaporated milk. Cats poured into the hotel, skinny, feral, or just abandoned for the season. My mother let them all in and the sky was a yellow-tinged bruise.

The rain when it came arrived sideways, bleeding in through the shutters and under the doors. The cats hid in the shadows. Occasionally we felt the brush of their bodies or tails as we sat at the table, my mother writing by the light of a kerosene lantern. The cats were hungry but my mother ignored their mewing as we ate.

In the end, my mother locked up the hotel and some students took us to Progreso on the Gulf. The boat from Texas stank of fish. The captain gave me a pill, and I woke up on somebody's couch in Galveston.

"WE GOT HER," said the plainclothesman in his white socks. "We caught her trying to see the kid. Says she was visiting her sister. You know damn well she shot you. Why make up a story about burglars? She's not even your mother."

If I were Starr, maybe I would have shot me too. Maybe I would have painted the doorknobs with oleander like my mother, if Ray had said he didn't love me anymore. It was hard for me to focus. Starr in her nightgown, my mother in her blue dress. Barry holding a cloth to my forehead. Why did it seem all the same, why did it melt together like crayons left in the car on a summer day? The only one who stood distinct was Davey. This cop was giving me a headache and I needed more Demerol.

LETTERS CAME from my mother. A girl my age, a hospital volunteer, with fluffy brown hair and pale green eye shadow, tried to read them to me, but it was way too surreal, my mother's words in her high ignorant voice, I made her stop.

> Dear Astrid,
>   They say they don't know if you will last until morning. I pace the cell's three steps, back and forth, all night. A chaplain just came by, I told him I'd rip out his liver if he bothered me again. I love you so much, Astrid. I can't bear it. There is no one else in the world but you and me, don't you know that? Please don't leave me alone here. By all the powers of light and darkness, please, please don't leave.

I read that paragraph over and over again, savoring each word, the way Starr would read her Bible. I drifted off to sleep hearing it in my head. You were my home, Mother. I had no home but you.

> *Freude! Beethoven's ninth, Ode to Joy, the Solti version, Chicago Symphony. To think that I almost lost you! I live for*

you, the thought that you're alive gives me the strength to go on. I wish I could hold you now, I want to touch you, hold you, feel your heartbeat. I'm writing a poem for you, I'm calling it "For Astrid, Who Will Live After All."

News travels fast in prison, and women I've never spoken to inquire after your condition. I feel akin to each one of them. I could kneel down and kiss the stale earth in gratitude. I will try for a compassionate visit, but I have no illusions about the extent of compassion here.

What can I say about life? Do I praise it for letting you live or damn it for allowing the rest? Have you heard of the Stockholm syndrome? Hostages begin taking the side of their captors, in their gratitude not to have been killed outright. Let us not thank some hypothetical God. Instead, rest and gain strength for the new campaign. Though I know, it's candystripers and <u>Highlights</u>, maybe a morphine drip if you're a good girl.

Be strong.

Mother.

And she never once said I told you so.

A MAGICIAN CAME to entertain us, and I was mesmerized by his beautiful hands, his fluid, round gestures. I couldn't stop watching his hands. They were better than any of his tricks. He pulled a bouquet of paper flowers out of the air and gave them to me with a courtly bow, and I thought love was like that, pulled out of the air, something bright and unlikely. Like Ray, molding me in his fingers like soft wax.

Ray. I tried not to think of him, what had made him run when I lay bleeding on my bedroom floor, shot by his lover. I knew why he wasn't there when the ambulance came. It was how I felt when I thought of Davey, that I had ruined his life for him. Ray couldn't face it. He hadn't wanted us to happen in the first place, I was the one who created it, out of nothing but my own desire. It was like Ray knew it was going to happen from the very first time we touched. Every time he looked at me his eyes pleaded with me to leave him alone. I wished I could see him, just once, and tell him I didn't blame him.

Sometimes I woke up and I was sure he would come, disguised, that we would be together again. There would be a glimpse of a strange intern, an unfamiliar orderly, a visitor searching for the right bed in the children's ward, and I was sure it would be him. I didn't blame any of them. I should have known what could happen. After my mother and Barry, how could I not have known.

The only innocent one was Davey. At first I wondered why Starr had left him behind. Probably thought she could make an easier getaway. Maybe she was so freaked out she completely forgot him. But now I knew it was Davey. That he had refused to go and leave me to bleed to death on the bedroom floor. He had refused to go. He had given up his mother to keep me alive for the ambulance. Knowing Davey, that was it. And I was deluged by fresh waves of shame and regret. He never knew when he met me that first day, when the little boys sat on the porch, that I would be the one to ruin his life the way Starr crushed his model in the living room. I stepped on it running to meet Ray.

*

MY MOTHER SENT me her poem "For Astrid, Who Will Live After All." There were a couple of lines I couldn't get out of my head:

> *After all the fears, the warnings*
> *After all*
> *A woman's mistakes are different from a girl's*
> *They are written by fire on stone*
> *They are a trait and not an error . . .*

It was worse than I told you so. I didn't want to believe it. I was still a girl, only fourteen. I could still be saved, couldn't I? Redeemed. I could live a different life, I would go and sin no more. I scowled when the physical therapist flirted with me, a lean young man, kind, handsome. It took half the day to walk up and down the corridor. They moved me from Demerol to oral Percodan.

IF I HAD had anywhere to go to, I could have been released after two weeks, but as it was, I recuperated on the county dollar until I could walk with a cane and the bandages came off. Then I was given a new placement, sent off with a thirty-day prescription for Percodan and my mother's letters and books, the wooden box, and a lost boy's poster of animal turds.

⟶

10

THE AIR IN VAN NUYS was thicker than in Sunland-Tujunga. It was a kingdom of strip malls and boulevards a quarter-mile across, neighborhoods of ground-hugging tracts dwarfed by full-growth peppers and sweet gums fifty feet high. It looked hopeful, until I saw a house down the street, and prayed, please Jesus, don't let it be the turquoise one with the yard paved in blacktop behind the chain-link fence.

The social worker parked in front of it. I stared. It was the color of a tropical lagoon on a postcard thirty years out of date, a Gauguin syphilitic nightmare. It was the gap in the chain of deciduous trees that cradled every other house on the block, defiantly ugly in its nakedness.

The bubble-glass door was also turquoise, and the foster mother was a wide, hard-faced blond woman who held a dumbfounded toddler on her hip. A little boy stuck his tongue out at me from behind his mother. She glanced at my metal hospital cane, narrowed her small eyes. "You didn't say she was lame."

The caseworker shrugged her narrow shoulders. I was glad I was high on Percodan, or I might have cried.

Marvel Turlock led us through her living room dominated by a television set the size of Arizona, where a talk show hostess admonished a huge bearded man with a tattoo, and down a long hall to my new room, a made-over laundry porch with navy-and-green-striped curtains and a ripcord spread on the narrow rollaway bed. The little boy tugged at her oversized shirt and whined, like music played on a saw.

Back in the TV room, the caseworker spread her papers on the coffee table, ready to bare the details of my life to this hard-faced woman, who told me to take Justin out to play in the backyard in a voice that was used to telling girls what to do.

The paved backyard was thick with heat and littered with enough toys for a preschool. I saw a cat bury something in the sandbox, run away. I didn't do anything about it. Justin roared around on his Big Wheel trike, smashing into the playhouse every round or two. I hoped he would decide to make a few mud pies. Mmm.

After a while, the toddler came out, a little blond girl with large, transparent blue eyes. She didn't know how much I feared the color turquoise, that I wanted to vomit thinking of her mother reading my file. If only I could have stayed in the hospital, with a steady Demerol drip. The baby headed for the sandbox. I wanted not to care, but found myself getting up, scooping out the catshit with a pail, throwing it over the fence.

ED AND MARVEL Turlock were my first real family. We ate chicken with our hands, sucking barbecue sauce off our fingers as if forks had not yet been invented. Ed was tall and red-faced, quiet, with sandy hair going bald. He worked in the paint department of Home Depot. It didn't surprise me to learn they got the turquoise paint at cost. We watched TV all through the meal and everybody talked and nobody listened, and I thought about Ray, and Starr, and the last time I saw Davey. Boulders and green paloverde, red-shouldered hawks. The beauty of stones, the river in flood, the stillness. My longing seesawed with hot prickling shame. Fourteen, and I'd already destroyed something I could never repair. I deserved this.

I finished out the ninth grade at Madison Junior High, limping from class to class on my cane. My fractured hip was mending, but it was the slowest thing to heal. My shoulder was already functional, and even the chest wound that cracked my rib had stopped burning every time I straightened or bent. But the hip was slow. I was always late to class. My days passed in a haze of Percodan. Bells and desks, shuffling to the next class. The teachers' mouths opened and butterflies burst out, too fast to capture. I liked the shifting colors of groups on the court-yard, but could not distinguish one student from the next. They were too young and undamaged, sure of themselves. To them, pain was a country they had heard of, maybe watched a show about on TV, but one whose stamp had not yet been made in their passports. Where could I find a place where my world connected to theirs?

IT WASN'T LONG before my role in the turquoise house was revealed to me: baby-sitter, pot scrubber, laundry maid, beautician. This last I dreaded the most. Marvel would sit in the bathroom like a toad under a rock, calling for me just the way Justin called for her, relentlessly. I tried to escape by thinking of gamelan orchestras, creatures in tide pools, even the shape of the curtains, navy and green, noticing how the stripes created the curtain by the way they flowed or broke. I thought there was a meaning there, but she kept calling.

"Astrid! Damn it, where is that girl?"

There was no point in pretending, she'd keep calling until I came, exaggerating my limp like a servant in a horror movie.

Her face was red when I got there, hands on her wide hips. "Where the hell have you been?"

I never answered, just turned on the water, tested the temperature.

"Not too hot," she reminded me. "I've got a sensitive scalp."

I made sure it felt a little cold to me, because the Percodan I was doing around the clock made it hard to sense temperature. She knelt on the rug and stuck her head under the faucet and I washed her hair, stiff with dirt and hair spray. Her roots needed touching up. She went for a blond shade that on the package looked like soft butter gold, but on her more closely resembled the yellow shredded cellophane lining kids' Easter baskets.

I worked in a conditioner that smelled of rancid fat, rinsed, and sat her on the stool she'd dragged in from the kitchen. I covered the sink with newspaper and started to comb. It was like combing tangled pasta. One good yank and it would all come out. I combed starting at the bottom and worked my way up, thinking how I used to brush my mother's hair at night. It was shiny as glass.

Marvel talked continuously, about her friends, her Mary

Kay customers, something a woman saw on Oprah — not that Marvel watched Oprah, only Sally Jessy because Oprah was a fat nignog and not good enough to scrub Marvel's floor, though she made ten million a season, blah blah blah. I pretended she was speaking Hungarian and that I couldn't understand a word as I put on the gloves and mixed the contents of the two bottles. The smell of ammonia was overwhelming in the small windowless bathroom, but Marvel wouldn't let me open the door. She didn't want Ed to know she dyed her hair.

I separated the shreds of hair, applied bleach to the roots, set the timer. If I left the mixture too long, it would eat huge bloody sores into her scalp and all her hair would fall out. I thought that might be interesting, but I knew there were places worse than the Turlocks'. At least Marvel didn't drink, and Ed was unattractive and barely noticed me. There wasn't much damage I could do here.

"This is good practice for you," Marvel said as we waited the last five minutes before working in the color to the ends. "You could go to beauty school. That's a good living for a woman."

She had big plans for me, Marvel Turlock. Looking out after my welfare. I'd rather drink bleach. I rinsed off the dye, leaning over her like a rock. She showed me a page in a hairdo magazine, a setting diagram intricate as an electrical schematic. A style called The Cosmopolitan. Upswept on the sides, with curls in the back and curled bangs, like Barbara Stanwyck in *Meet John Doe*. I thought of Michael, how he would shudder. He adored Stanwyck. I wondered how the Scottish play went. I wondered if he ever thought of me. You could not even imagine how it was, Michael.

The pink sticky setting gel added to the stench in the hot bathroom as I wrapped the strings of hair around the curlers. I was getting faint. As soon as I was done rolling, I wrapped the scarf over her pink curlers and finally was allowed to open the bathroom door. I felt like I hadn't breathed in an hour. Marvel went out to the family room. "Ed?" I heard her calling.

The TV was on, but Ed had slipped out to the Good Knight bar, where he drank beer and watched the game on pay-per-view.

"Damn him," she said without bitterness. She turned the station to a show about middle-aged sisters and settled onto the couch with a carton of ice cream.

Dear Astrid,

Don't tell me how you hate your new foster home. If they're not beating you, consider yourself lucky. Loneliness is the human condition. Cultivate it. The way it tunnels into you allows your soul room to grow. Never expect to outgrow loneliness. Never hope to find people who will understand you, someone to fill that space. An intelligent, sensitive person is the exception, the very great exception. If you expect to find people who will understand you, you will grow murderous with disappointment. The best you'll ever do is to understand yourself, know what it is that you want, and not let the cattle stand in your way.

Moo.

IT HADN'T OCCURRED to me the worst was yet to come, until my prescription ran out. I had foolishly doubled my dose, and now I lay shipwrecked on a desolate shore littered with broken glass. I caught a cold from the air-conditioning, which worked too well in my small porch room. All I could think of was how alone I was. My loneliness tasted like pennies. I thought about dying. A boy in the hospital had told me the best way was an air bubble in the bloodstream. He had bone cancer and had stolen a syringe he kept in an Archie comic book. He said if it ever got too bad, he'd shoot up some air, and it'd be over in seconds. If it weren't for my mother's letters, I would have thought of something. I reread them until they were soft and divided along the creases.

When I couldn't sleep, I'd go out in the backyard, where the crickets sang duets and the blacktop was warm as an animal under my bare feet. The crushed white gravel flowerbeds glowed in the moonlight, their sterile length punctuated by white plastic dahlias stuck into the gravel at regular intervals. I once sent my mother a painting of the house set in its sea of blacktop and white gravel edges, and she sent me a poem about the infant Achilles, whose mother dipped him in black water to make him immortal. It didn't make me feel any better.

I sat on the redwood picnic table and listened to music coming through the closed shutters of the house next door. They were always closed, but a jazz saxophone worked its way out from between the wood slats, music personal as a touch. I ran my fingertips over the dark carbon blade of my mother's old knife, imagining opening my wrists. If you did it in the bathtub, they said, you didn't even feel it. I wouldn't have hesitated, except for my mother. But the scales were in precarious balance, everything on one side but my mother's letters, light as good night, a hand touching my hair.

I played with the knife, spread out my hand on top of the slide, and jabbed the point past my fingers. Johnny johnny johnny whoops! Johnny johnny whoops! Johnny johnny johnny johnny. I liked it just as well when it stabbed me.

Dear Astrid,

I know what you are learning to endure. There is nothing to be done. Just make sure nothing is wasted. Take notes. Remember it all, every insult, every tear. Tattoo it on the inside of your mind. In life, knowledge of poisons is essential. I've told you, nobody becomes an artist unless they have to.

Mother.

WITHOUT PERCODAN, I began to see why mothers abandoned their children, left them in supermarkets and at playgrounds. I had never imagined the whining, the constancy of those tiny demands, the endless watch. I told Marvel I had papers and reports to write, and buried myself in after-school library shelves, working my way through the book lists that came in my mother's letters, sharing table space with old men reading newspapers on sticks and Catholic school girls hiding teen magazines inside their history books.

I read everything — Colette, Françoise Sagan, Anaïs Nin's *Spy in the House of Love, Portrait of the Artist as a Young Man.* I read *The Moon and Sixpence,* about Gauguin, and the Chekhov short stories Michael had recommended. They didn't have Miller but there was Kerouac. I read *Lolita,* but the man was nothing like Ray. I wandered through the stacks, running my hands along the spines of the books on the shelves, they reminded me of cultured or opinionated guests at a wonderful party, whispering to each other.

One day a title jumped out at me from a shelf of adventure books. I took the volume to a table, opened its soft, ivory pages, ignoring the dark glances of the girls in their white shirts and plaid jumpers, and fell into it as into a pool during a dry season.

The name of the book was *The Art of Survival*.

Every religion needs its bible, and I had found mine, not a moment too soon. I read it in eighteen hours, and then started over again. I learned how to stay alive for long weeks on the open sea when my white ocean liner went down. When shipwrecked, you catch fish, press their juices to drink. You sponge up morning dew off your life raft's rubberized deck. Adrift on a sailboat, you catch rainwater on the canvas. But if the sails were dirty, the book pointed out, the decks crusted with salt, what water you caught would be worthless. You had to keep the decks clean, the sails rinsed, you had to be ready.

I looked at my life and saw quite clearly that I was not surviving it in the turquoise house. I was letting my sails crust up with salt. I had to stop playing johnny johnny and concentrate on preparing for rain, preparing for rescue. I decided I would take daily walks, stop overdoing the limp, retire my cane. I would pull myself together.

I SAT ON THE BUS on the way home from school, head aching from the shrill laughter of the other kids, and recounted the grim means to survive disaster at sea. You make fishhooks from any kind of bent metal, form line from the thread in your clothes, bait the hook with bits of fish or dead fellow passengers, even a strip of your own flesh if you have to. I forced myself to imagine it, taking the sharp edge of a C ration and piercing my thigh. It hurt so much I could hardly stay conscious, but I knew I had to finish the job, there was no point passing out, it would just heal and I'd have to do it all over again. So I kept on until I had the yellow worm in my hand, bloodbacked and warm. Hooked it onto the sharpened shred from the can, threw it into the sea on my handmade thread.

Panic was the worst thing. When you panicked, you couldn't see possibilities. Then came despair. A man from Japan was adrift four days in a boat when he panicked and hung himself. He was found twenty minutes later. A sailor from Soochow floated 116 days on a life raft before he was found. You never knew when rescue might come.

And if my life had come to this — shame and long bus rides and the stink of diesel-soaked air, trying not to get beat up at Madison Junior High, Justin's sweater and Caitlin's red rash — people had gone through far worse and survived. Despair was the killer. I had to prepare, hold hope between my palms like the flame of the last match in a long Arctic night.

When I couldn't sleep, I'd sit on the picnic table in the backyard, listening to the music from our next-door neighbor's house and imagine my mother, awake in her cell just like me. Would I want her around if I'd crashed my plane in Papua New Guinea or Pará, Brazil? We'd slog through a hundred-mile labyrinth of mangrove forest, covered with leeches like in *The African Queen*, maybe even pierced with a long native spear. My mother wouldn't panic, rip out the spear, and die of blood loss. I knew she could do the right thing, let the maggots feed in the wound, clearing out the hole, and then in five days or a week, pull out the spear. She would even write a poem about it.

But I could also see her making a terrible mistake, a failure in judgment. I imagined us adrift in a life raft ten days outside shipping lanes, pressing fish juice, sponging each drop of water from the clean morning deck, when suddenly she determined seawater wasn't undrinkable after all. I saw her going swimming among sharks.

"ASTRID, come help me," Marvel called. She came out from the kitchen to where I sat on the back steps watching the kids, and twisted her neck around to see the picture, five blackened Frenchmen who tried to cross the Qaza basin in Egypt by day. "Still reading that book? You ought to think about the army, you like that kind of stuff. They take care of their people fine. Now they let women in, you'd probably get along. You work hard, you keep your mouth shut. Come on, help me with the groceries."

I went with her to unload the cans of soup and bottles of soda, cheese slices and family-pack pork chops, more food than I'd ever seen in my life. The army, I thought. How little she knew me. I appreciated her interest, I'd come to believe she really did want me somewhere comfortable, with a decent paycheck. But I would rather live out on the desert alone, like an old prospector. All I needed was a small water source. What was the point in such loneliness among people. At least if you were by yourself, you had a good reason to be lonely.

Or even better, I thought, stashing packaged cocoa mix and

Tang in the cupboards, a cabin in the woods, snow in the winter, jagged mountains all around, you'd have to hike in. I'd cut my own wood, have a few dogs, maybe a horse, put in bushels of food and stay there for years. I'd have a cow, plant a garden, it was a short growing season, but I'd raise enough to get by.

My mother hated the country, couldn't wait to get out. When I had her, the city was fine, it was free Thursday afternoons at the museum downtown, concerts on Sundays, poetry readings, her friends acting or painting or casting their private parts in plaster of Paris. But now, what was the point. I hadn't been to a museum since her arrest. Just that morning I saw a piece in the paper about a Georgia O'Keeffe show at the L.A. County Art Museum, asked Marvel if she'd take me.

"Well, pardon me, Princess Grace," Marvel said. "What's next, the opera? Change Caitlin's diaper, will you, I got to take a leak."

I called the bus company, they said it would take me three hours there, three hours back. It dawned on me how far I was from where I'd begun.

When you broke down in the desert, you had to work fast. In the Mojave, it could be 140 degrees in the shade. In an hour, you might sweat two and a half pints. People went crazy from thirst. You danced and sang and finally embraced a saguaro, thinking it was quite something else. A lover, a mother, a Christ. Then you ran away bleeding to die. To survive in the desert, you had to drink a quart of water a day. There was no sense in rationing — all those movies were lies. To drink less was just to commit slow suicide.

I thought about that, what it meant, as I took the giant box of disposable diapers and toilet paper back to the bathroom. It was one thing to hope, but you had to take care of yourself in the present, or you wouldn't survive. You put out your hubcaps to catch morning dew, drank radiator water, and buried yourself to the neck in the sand. Then you set off at nightfall, retracing your steps. Overhead, the sky would be full of stars. You needed a flashlight, a compass, you had to have watched how you came.

Davey had known all of these things. I suddenly knew he would also survive.

In the prolonged twilight of the lengthening day, I started dinner, thinking about the desert, imagining myself buried to the neck, when I heard the mechanical purr of the neighbor's Corvette turning into her driveway. I looked up in time to see her, a striking black woman in a white linen suit. I'd only seen her a couple of times, picking up her magazines, leaving her house in the evening in silk and pearls. She never spoke to us or anyone in the neighborhood.

Marvel heard the car too, and stopped making a bottle for Caitlin to stare out over my shoulder and glare. "That damn whore. Thinks she's the Duchess of Windsor. Makes me want to puke." We watched the neighbor pull her two small bags of groceries from Whole Foods out of the champagne-colored sports car.

"Mommy, *juice*," the baby whined, tugging on Marvel's T-shirt.

Marvel yanked her shirt from the baby's hands. "Don't you ever let me catch you talking to her," she said to me. "Christ, I remember when this was a good neighborhood. Now it's the blacks and the whores, chinks and beaners with chickens in the yard. I mean, what next?"

It bothered me that Marvel told me all this stuff, like I sympathized with her, like we were some Aryan secret society out here in the Valley. "I'll make up some juice," I said. I didn't even want to stand next to her.

While I mixed the juice, I watched the neighbor, stopping to pick up the magazines from her porch, slip them inside her grocery bag. She wore white slingbacks with black tips, like deer's hooves.

Then she disappeared inside the shuttered house. I was sad to see her go but glad she was out of sight of Marvel's talk like hot tar, that fumed and stank as it left her lips. I wondered if the woman in the linen suit thought we were all like Marvel, that I was like that too. It made me cringe to think that probably she did.

Marvel grabbed the juice and filled the bottle, handed it to Caitlin, who toddled off, clutching her special velvet pillow that said Guam. "Traipsing around in that car," Marvel grumbled. "Flaunting it in decent people's faces. Like we didn't know how she got it. Flat on her back is how."

The car gleamed like the flanks of a man, soft and muscular, supple. I wanted to lie down on the hood, I thought I could probably come just lying on it. I gazed past the carport to the door where she went in, wished I didn't have anything to do and could just stand there all evening to see if she'd come out again.

When the dishes were done and the kids put to bed, I slipped out the side door and stood next to her jacaranda, which dripped purple flowers over the fence onto Marvel's blacktop and perfumed the warm night. Music seeped out, a singer, at first I thought she was drunk but then knew it wasn't that at all, she had her own way with the words, played with them in her mouth like cherry chocolates.

I don't know how long I stood in the dark, swaying to this music, the woman with a voice like a horn. It seemed impossible that a woman so elegant could live right next door to us with our fifty-inch TV. I wanted to crawl under her windows, peep through a crack in her fat-slatted shutters, and see what she was doing in there. But I didn't have the nerve. I picked up a handful of her jacaranda blooms from the ground and pressed them to my face.

THE NEXT DAY, I got off the bus in the four o'clock heat, walked the last mile home. I didn't need the cane anymore, but the long blocks of walking still made my hip ache, bringing back my limp. I felt dirty and awkward as I trudged up our block, chafed in my Council of Jewish Women thrift store clothes, a white blouse that never softened in the wash, an unsuccessful homemade skirt.

In the shade in front of the house next door, our elegant neighbor was cutting some lily of the Nile, the same color as the jacaranda bloom. She was barefoot in a simple dress, and her feet and the palms of her hands showed pale pink against her burnt caramel skin. They looked ornamental, as if she came from a place where women dipped hands and feet in pink powder. She didn't smile. She was wholly absorbed in her shears, clipping a stem of rosemary, a stem of mint, in the dappled light and shade. A fallen jacaranda bloom clung to her dark hair, which was up in a careless French twist. I loved that one stray blossom.

I felt clumsy, ashamed of my limp and my ugly clothes. I hoped she wouldn't see me, that I could get to the house before she looked up. But when I'd reached our chain link and black-top, and she still hadn't glanced in my direction, I was disappointed. I wished she would see me, so I could tell her, I'm not like them. Talk to me. Look up, I thought.

But she didn't, only stopped and picked a sprig of alyssum to smell the honey. I cut a shred from my heart and dangled it on a homemade hook before her.

"I like your yard," I called out.

She looked up, startled, as if she knew I was there but didn't think I'd speak to her. Her eyes were large and almond-shaped, the color of root beer. She wore a thin scar on her left cheek, and a gold watch on her narrow wrist. She pushed a strand of marcel-waved hair from her face and threw me a quick smile, which faded just as quickly. She turned back to her lilies. "You better not be seen talking to me. She's going to burn a cross on my lawn."

"You don't have a lawn," I said.

She smiled, but she didn't look at me again.

"My name's Astrid," I said.

"You go inside now," she said. "Astrid."

⌐

11

HER NAME WAS Olivia Johnstone. That was the name on the magazines and catalogs on her doormat. She took *Condé Nast Traveler* and French *Vogue*, thick as a phone book. I babysat the kids in the front yard now, not to miss the least glimpse of her leaving the house in her Jackie O sunglasses, returning from shopping, clipping her herbs. Hoping our eyes would meet again. Packages came for her almost daily, the handsome UPS man lingering in her doorway. I wondered if he was in love with her, his legs like tree trunks in his UPS brown shorts.

At night, from the kitchen window, I began to take note of her visitors. Always men. A black man whose white French cuffs lay bright against his dark skin, gold cuff links glimmering. He drove a black BMW, came around seven-thirty, and was always gone by midnight. A young man with Rasta hair and Birkenstocks came in a Porsche. Sometimes he was still there when I got up in the morning. A large balding white man who wore striped shirts and double-breasted suits with big lapels. He drove a monstrous Mercedes, and came every day for a week.

What I noticed especially was the way they hurried from

their shining cars, their excitement. I wondered what she must do that put such urgency in their steps. I wondered which she liked best. I thought about what she must know about men, how she must shine for them like a lighthouse.

I refused to think for a second that Marvel might be right about anything, let alone Olivia Johnstone. I lived for the sight of her, taking out her trash or alighting from her car in the dim light of dawn while I was making my breakfast. It was just enough dew on my decks to keep me another day.

I picked sprigs of her rosemary and tucked them in my pockets. I went through her garbage when I knew she was out, thirsty to know more, to touch the things she touched. I found a wide-toothed tortoiseshell comb from Kent of London, good as new except for a single broken tooth, and a soap box, Crabtree and Evelyn's Elderflower. She drank Myers's rum, used extra virgin olive oil in a tall bottle. One of her boyfriends smoked cigars. I found an impossibly soft stocking, the garter kind, cloud taupe, laddered, and an empty flagon of Ma Griffe perfume, its label decorated with a scribble of black lines on white. It smelled of whispery black organdy dresses, of spotted green orchids and the Bois de Boulogne after rain, where my mother and I once walked for hours. I thrilled to share Paris with Olivia Johnstone. I saved the bottle in my drawer to scent my clothes.

THEN ONE DAY Olivia's newspapers and magazines lay on her doorstep, untouched. The Corvette sat sullen under a tan canvas cover dotted with fallen jacaranda flowers like mementos of loss. Just the sight of the landlocked Corvette made me wish I had some Percodan left. I settled for some leftover codeine cough syrup Marvel had in her medicine chest. The sticky cloying taste lingered as I sat on my ripcord bedspread and combed my hair with Olivia's comb. I was in awe of her perfection. A woman who would throw out a handmade tortoiseshell comb just because it was missing a tooth. I wondered if she really made love to men for money, what that was like. *Prostitute. Whore.* What did they really mean anyway? Only words. My mother would hate that, but it was true. Words trailing their streamers of judgment. A wife got money from her husband and nobody said anything. And if Olivia's boyfriends gave her money? So what?

I combed my hair and made a French twist, imagining myself as Olivia. I stalked the small room, walking the way she walked, hips first, like a runway model. What difference did it make if she was a whore. It sounded like ventriloquism to even say it. I hated labels anyway. People didn't fit in slots — prostitute, housewife, saint — like sorting the mail. We were so mutable, fluid with fear and desire, ideals and angles, changeable as water. I ran her stocking up my leg, smelled the Ma Griffe.

I imagined she'd gone to Paris, that she was sitting at a café, having a cloudy Pernod and water, scarf tied to her purse like the women in her French *Vogue.* I imagined she was with the BMW man, the quiet one with gold cuff links who liked jazz. I'd imagined them often, dancing in the old-fashioned way in her living room, hardly moving their feet, his cheek resting on the top of her close-waved hair. That's how I saw her in Paris. Staying up late in a jazz club only black Parisians knew, in a cellar on the Rive Gauche, dancing. I could see the champagne and the way their eyes closed, and they weren't thinking of anything but more of the same.

I sat in the sun's blistering glare off the blacktop after school, doing my homework and listening to Justin and Caitlin splash in the inflatable pool, shrieking, squabbling over the toys. I was waiting, thinking ahead, setting out my hubcaps. At 4:25 the UPS man stopped in front of Olivia's and began to write up a delivery slip.

I stepped up to the chain-link fence. "Excuse me," I said. "Olivia said you could leave the package with me." I smiled, trying to project a neighborly trustworthiness. I was the girl next door, after all. "She told me she was expecting it."

He brought the clipboard and I signed. The shipment was a small box marked Williams-Sonoma. I wondered what it could be, but my curiosity about what was in the box paled when compared to my determination to make friends with Olivia Johnstone, to someday enter the shuttered house.

THE DAY SHE returned, I made up a story about a project I had to finish with a classmate in the neighborhood. I wasn't a good liar. My mother always said I had no imagination. But I kept it short, and Marvel gave me an hour. "I need you home at five, I've got a party." She sold Mary Kay, and though she didn't make much money at it, it made her feel important.

I took the box out of my laundry bag, where I'd kept it hidden, and walked up Olivia's steps, onto her porch. I rang the doorbell.

Almost immediately, her shape appeared behind the bubble-glass diamonds of her door, just like ours except the inserts were yellow instead of turquoise. I could feel her looking at me through the spyhole. I tried to look calm. Just a neighbor doing a favor. The door opened. Olivia Johnstone was wearing a long print halter dress, her hair in a low chignon, her bare cinnamon shoulders smooth as bedposts.

I held the box out to her. "The UPS man left this." One tooth on the comb, one tooth. She was perfect.

Olivia smiled and took the box. Her nails were short, white-tipped. She thanked me in an amused voice. I could tell she knew it was just a ploy, that I wanted to climb into her life. I tried to look past her but could only see a mirror and a small red-lacquered table.

Then she said the words I'd been dreaming of, hoping for. "Would you like to come in? I was just pouring some tea."

Was there anything as elegant as Olivia's house? In the living room, the walls were covered with a gold paper burnished to the quality of cork. She had a taupe velvet couch with a curved back and a leopard throw pillow, a tan leather armchair, and a carved daybed with a striped cotton cover. A wood table with smaller tables tucked underneath it held a dull green ceramic planter bearing a white spray of orchids like moths. Jazz music quickened the pace of the room, the kind the BMW man liked, complicated trumpet runs full of masculine yearning.

"What's this music?" I asked her.

"Miles Davis," she said. "'Seven Steps to Heaven.'"

Seven steps, I thought, was that all it took?

Where we had sliding glass doors, Olivia had casements, open to the backyard. Instead of the air-conditioning, ceiling fans turned lazily. Upon closer examination, a big gilded birdcage held a fake parrot wearing a tiny sombrero, a cigar clamped in its beak. "That's Charlie," Olivia said. "Be careful, he bites." She smiled. She had a slight overbite. I could understand how a man would want to kiss her.

We sat on the velvet couch and drank iced tea sweetened with honey and mint. Now that I was here, I was at a loss to begin. I'd had so many questions, but I couldn't think of one. The decor bowled me over. Everywhere I looked, there was something more to see. Botanical prints, a cross section of pomegranates, a passionflower vine and its fruit. Stacks of thick books on art and design and a collection of glass paperweights filled the coffee table. It was enormously beautiful, a sensibility I'd never encountered anywhere, a relaxed luxury. I could feel my mother's contemptuous gaze falling on the cluttered surfaces, but I was tired of three white flowers in a glass vase. There was more to life than that.

"How long have you been over there?" Olivia asked, stroking down the condensation on her glass with a manicured forefinger. Her profile was slightly dish-shaped, her forehead high and round.

"Not long. A couple months." I nodded to the UPS package untouched on the coffee table. "What'd they send you?"

Olivia walked to a small secretary desk, opened it and found a letter opener. She slit the side of the box and lifted out two terra-cotta hearts. "They're breadwarmers. You heat them and put them in the basket to keep the rolls warm."

I was disappointed. I thought it would be something secret and sexual. Breadwarmers didn't go with my fantasy of Olivia Johnstone.

She sat closer to me this time, arm across the back of the

couch. I liked it though it made me nervous. She seemed to know exactly the effect she had on me. I couldn't stop staring at her skin, which gleamed as if polished, exactly the color of the wallpaper, and I could smell Ma Griffe.

"Where did you go?" I asked.

"Back east. New York, Washington," she said. "A friend had business there."

"The BMW?"

She smiled, her overbite winking at me. She had an impish quality up close, not so perfect, but better. "No, not the BMW. He's very married. You don't see this man here."

I'd been afraid she would talk about breadwarmers, but here she was, telling me about the men, as if it was the weather. Encouraged, I pressed for more. "Don't you worry they're going to run into each other?"

She pursed her lips, raised her eyebrows. "I do try to avoid it."

Maybe it was true. Maybe she was. But if she was, it was nothing like the girls on Van Nuys Boulevard in their hot pants and satin baseball jackets. Olivia was linen and champagne and terra-cotta, botanical prints and "Seven Steps to Heaven."

"Do you like one of them best?" I asked.

She stirred her iced tea with a long-handled spoon, letting Miles Davis seep into our pores. "No. Not really. How about you, do you have a boyfriend, someone special?"

I was going to tell her that I did, an older man, make it sound glamorous, but I ended up telling her my sorry life history, Starr and Ray, my mother, Marvel Turlock. She was easy to talk to, sympathetic. She asked questions, listened, and kept the music coming, tea and lemon cookies. I felt I had woken up on my raft to find a yacht dropping a ladder. *You never knew when rescue might come.*

"It won't always be so hard, Astrid," she told me, brushing a lock of my hair behind my ear. "Beautiful girls have certain advantages."

I wanted to believe her. I wanted to know those things she knew, so I wouldn't be afraid anymore, so I'd believe there was an end to it all. "Like what?"

She looked at me close, examining the planes of my face, the bangs I cut myself now. My stubborn chin, my fat, chapped lips. I tried to look ready. She picked up my hand and held it in hers. Her hands were more delicate than I'd thought, no larger than mine, warm and surprisingly dry, but a bit rough. She twined her fingers in mine, as if we had always held hands.

"It's a man's world, Astrid," she said. "You ever hear that?"

I nodded. A man's world. But what did it mean? That men whistled and stared and yelled things at you, and you had to take it, or you could get raped or beat up. A man's world meant places men could go but not women. It meant they had more money, and didn't have kids, not the way women did, to look after every second. And it meant that women loved them more than they loved the women, that they could want something with all their hearts, and then not.

But I didn't know much more about a man's world. That place where men wore suits and watches and cuff links and went into office buildings, ate in restaurants, drove down the street talking on cell phones. I'd seen them, but their lives were as incomprehensible as the lives of Tibetan Sherpas or Amazonian chiefs.

Olivia took my hand and turned it over, brushed the tips of

her dry fingers down my moist palm, sending waves of electricity up my arms. "Who has the money?" she asked, softly. "Who has the power? You have a good mind, you're artistic, you're very sensitive, see?" She showed me lines in my hand, her fingertips like a grainy fabric stroking my skin. "Don't fight the world. Your carpenter friend, he didn't fight the wood, did he? He made love to it, and what he made was beautiful."

I thought about that. My mother fought the wood, hacking at it, trying to slam it into place with a hammer. She considered it the essence of cowardice not to. "What else do you see?" I asked.

Olivia curled my fingers up, wrapping my fate, handing it back to me.

I picked at a burn blister on my middle finger and thought about fighting the grain or not. Women like my mother, alone as tigers, fighting every step. Women with men, like Marvel and Starr, trying to please. Neither one seemed to have the advantage. But Olivia didn't mean men like Ed Turlock or even Ray. She meant men with money. That man's world. The cuff links and offices.

"You'll figure out what men want and how to give it to them. And how not to." She smiled her naughty crooked grin. "And when to do which."

The little brass clock whirred and struck five, a music box tune, tiny chimes. So many pretty things, but it was getting late, I didn't want to go, I wanted to find out more, I wanted Olivia to handle my future like wax, softening it in the heat of her parched hands, shaping it into something I didn't have to dread. "You mean sex."

"Not necessarily." She glanced at the round mirror over

the fireplace, at the drop-top desk with its secret drawers and pigeonholes. "It's magic, Astrid. You have to know how to reach up and pull beauty out of thin air." She pretended to reach up and grab a firefly, then opened her palms slowly and watched it fly out. "People want a little magic. Sex is its theater. There are sliding panels and trapdoors."

The night magic. *Never let a man stay the night.* But my mother's theater was her own pleasure. This was something quite different. I was excited that I knew this.

"The secret is — a magician doesn't buy magic. Admire the skill of a fellow magician, but never fall under his spell." She rose and collected our glasses. And I thought of how Barry seduced my mother, his smoked mirrors and hidden trained doves. She never chose him, not really, but she gave him everything. She would always be his, even if he was dead. He had shaped her destiny.

"So what about love?" I asked.

She had started toward the kitchen but stopped, turned back, glasses in her hands. "What about it?" When Olivia frowned, two vertical lines sliced between her eyebrows and cut into her rounded forehead.

I flushed red, but I wanted to know. If only I could ask without falling all over myself like a clown in size fourteen shoes. "Don't you believe in it?"

"I don't believe in it the way people believe in God or the tooth fairy. It's more like the *National Enquirer*. A big headline and a very dull story."

I followed her into the kitchen, exactly like ours yet light-years away, a parallel universe. Her pots and pans dangled overhead from a restaurant rack — copper pots, iron. Ours were Corning Ware with the little blue flowers. I ran my hands over Olivia's terra-cotta counters, inset with painted ceramics, where ours were mottled green and white, like a bad cold.

"So what do you believe in?" I asked her.

Her dark gaze ran with pleasure along the warm cinnamon tile, the beaten copper hood over the range. "I believe in living as I like. I see a Stickley lamp, a cashmere sweater, and I know I can have it. I own two houses besides this. When the ashtrays are full in my car, I'll sell it."

I laughed, imagining her bringing it back to the dealer, explaining why she was selling. She probably would. I could hardly fathom someone living so close to her own desire.

"I just spent three weeks in Tuscany. I saw the Palio in Siena," she said, strumming the words like the strings of a guitar. "It's a fifteenth-century horse race through the cobbled streets. Would I exchange that for a husband and kids and happily-ever-after? Not to mention the likely outcome, divorce and overtime at the bank and shaky child support. Let me show you something."

She picked up the small quilted bag on her counter, found her wallet, opened it for me to see the wad of cash as thick as my finger. She spread the bills, at least a dozen hundreds among the others. "Love's an illusion. It's a dream you wake up from with an enormous hangover and net credit debt. I'd rather have cash." She put her money away, zipped her purse.

Then she put her arm around my shoulder and led me to the door. The amber light fell through the bubble glass against our cheeks. She hugged me lightly. I smelled Ma Griffe, it was warmer on her. "Come again, anytime. I don't know many women. I'd like to know you."

I left walking backwards so I wouldn't miss a moment of her. I hated the idea of going back to Marvel's, so I walked around the block, feeling Olivia's arms around me, my nose full of perfume and the smell of her skin, my head swirling with what I had seen and heard in the house so much like ours, and yet not at all. And I realized as I walked through the neighborhood how each house could contain a completely different reality. In a single block, there could be fifty separate worlds. Nobody ever really knew what was going on just next door.

12

I LAY ON MY BED, wondering what I would be like when I was a woman. I'd never thought much about it before, my possible futures. I'd been too busy sucking fish juice, burying myself in the sand against the killing rays of desert sun. But now I was intrigued by this future Astrid that Olivia had seen in me. I saw myself sort of like Catherine Deneuve, pale and stoic, the way she was in *Belle de Jour*. Or maybe Dietrich, *Shanghai Express*, all shimmer and smoke. Would I be fascinating, the star of my own magic theater? What would I do with a wad of hundred-dollar bills?

I imagined that money in my hand. My mind went blank. So far, my fantasies had centered completely on survival. Luxury had been beyond imagining, let alone beauty. I let my eyes rest on the striped curtains, until the stripes themselves formed a sculptural shape. Ray had seen it in me. With Olivia's help, I could own it, create it, use it. I could work in beauty as an artist worked in paint or language.

I would have three lovers, I decided. An older man, distinguished, with silver hair and a gray suit, who would take me traveling with him, for company on long first-class flights to Europe, and stuffy cocktail receptions for visiting dignitaries. I called him the Swedish ambassador. Yes, Mother, I would lie down for the father, gladly.

Then there was Xavier, my Mexican lover, Mother's Eduardo reconstituted, but more tender and passionate, less silly and spoiled. Xavier spread camellias on the bed, he swore he would marry me if he could, but he had been engaged since birth to a girl with a harelip. It was fine with me, I didn't want to live with his overbearing parents in Mexico City and bear his ten Catholic children. I had a room of my own in the hotel, and a maid who brought me Mexican chocolate for breakfast in bed.

The third man was Ray. I met him in secret in big-city hotels, he sat in the bar with his sad face, and I would come in in a white linen suit with black-tipped shoes, my hair back in a chignon, a scarf tied to my purse. "I wasn't sure you'd come," I said in a deep, slightly humorous voice, like Dietrich. "But I came anyway."

I heard Marvel calling to me, but she was in another country, too far away. She didn't mean me. She meant some other girl, some drab hopeless thing destined for the army or else beauty school. I lay with my legs wrapped around Ray in a room with tall windows, a bouquet of full-bloom red roses in a vase on the dresser.

"Astrid!"

Her voice was like a drill, penetrating, relentless. If I had a choice, I'd rather be a man's slave than a woman's. I pulled myself out of bed, stumbled into the living room where Marvel and her friends sat on the flowered couch, their heads pressed together over sodas tinted space-alien colors, hands in the snack mixture I'd made from a recipe on the cereal box.

"Here she is." Debby raised her horsey face under her curly perm, eye shadow layered like strata in sedimentary rock. "Ask her."

"I'm telling you, the car," Marvel said. "You come back and you're still living in the same dump, still driving around the same old shitbox. What good does it do?"

Linda took a hit on her cigarette, fanning the smoke away with a pearl-nailed hand. A blond with blue eyes perpetually wide with surprise, she wore shiny eye shadow like the inside of shells. They all went to Birmingham High together, were bridesmaids at each other's weddings, and now sold Mary Kay.

It was the new Mary Kay brochure, illustrating the prizes they could win if they sold enough mascara wands and lip liners and face-firming masques, that they'd been arguing about. "They used to have Cadillacs." Linda sniffed.

Marvel finished her soda, smacked it down on the coffee table. "Just once in my life, I'd like a goddamn new car. Is that too much to ask? Everybody's got a new car, the kids at the high school. The slut next door's got a goddamn Corvette." She handed me her glass. "Astrid, get me some more Tiki Punch."

Debby handed me hers too. I took them back to the kitchen, and poured Tiki Punch from the big Shasta bottle, getting momentarily lost in its irradiated Venusian pinkness.

"Astrid," Linda called, her feet tucked under herself on the flower-print couch. "If you had a choice between two weeks in Paris France, all expenses paid, or a car —"

"Shitty Buick," Debby interjected.

"What's wrong with a Buick?" Marvel said.

"— which would you take?" Linda picked something out of the corner of her eye with a long press-on nail.

I brought their drinks, suppressing the desire to limp theatrically, the deformed servant, and fit all the glasses into hands without spilling. They couldn't be serious. Paris? My Paris? Elegant fruit shops and filterless Gitanes, dark woolen coats, the Bois de Boulogne? "Take the car," I said. "Definitely."

"Smart girl," Marvel said, toasting me with her Shasta. "You always had a good head on your shoulders."

"You know, we should do Astrid," Debby said.

Three sets of eyes, all those circles, looking at me. It was unnerving. Invisibility was my normal state in the turquoise house.

They seated me on a stool in the kitchen. Suddenly, I was a valued guest. Was the gooseneck lamp in my face too bright? Did I want something to drink? Linda turned me from side to side. They were examining my pores, touching my skin with tissue to see if I was oily, normal, or dry. I liked being the center of so much attention. It made me feel close to them. My freckles were a matter of concern, the shape of my forehead. The merits of foundations were discussed, samples streaked along my jaw.

"Too ruddy," Linda said.

The others nodded sagely. I needed correction. Correction was important. Pots and tubes of white and brown. Anything could be corrected. My Danish nose, my square jaw, my fat lips, so far from ideal. And I thought of a mannequin I saw once in a store window, bald and nude, as two men dressed her, laughing and talking under her nippleless breasts. One man, I remembered, had a pincushion stuck to his shaved head.

"You've got the perfect face for makeup," Debby said, applying base with a sponge, turning me back and forth like a sculptor turning the clay.

Of course I did, I was blank, anyone could fill me in. I waited to see who I would be, what they would create on my delicious vacancy. The woman in first class, reading French *Vogue* and sipping champagne? Catherine Deneuve walking her dog in the Bois, admired by strangers?

Linda outlined my eyes on the inside, rolling back my lids, dabbing tenderly at my tears with the corner of a Q-tip when it made me cry. She gave me four coats of mascara, until I was seeing through a tangle of spiders. I was going to be so beautiful, I could feel it. Marvel redefined my big lips smaller, penciling them inside the lines and filling in Piquant Peach.

"God, she could be Miss America," Debby said.

Linda said. "No shit. Go look in the mirror."

"Hair," Debby said. "Let me get my curling wand."

"We don't have to get carried away, now," Marvel said. She'd suddenly remembered who I was, not Miss America at all, only the kid who did her wash and set.

But Debby overrode her objections with the phrase "total effect." Heat and the smell of burning hair tangled in the spikes of the curling wand, section by section.

Then I was done. They led me into Marvel's bedroom by both arms, my eyes closed. My skin crawled with anticipation. Who would I be? "And here, representing the great State of California — Astrid!"

They pulled me in front of the mirror.

My hair curled and frizzed around my shoulders and rose three inches above my scalp. White stripes raced down my forehead and nose like Hindu caste marks. Brown patches appeared under my cheekbones, white on the ridges, dividing my otherwise dead beige face into a paint-by-number kit. Blusher broke out on my cheeks like a rash, my lips reduced to a geisha's tiny bow. My eyebrows glared in dark wings, protecting the glistening bands of eye shadow, purple, blue, and pink, like a child's rainbow. I never cried, but now tears sprang unbidden to my eyes, threatening a mud slide if they were to break out of their pool.

"She looks just like Brigitte what's-her-name, the model." Linda held me by the shoulders, her face next to mine in the mirror. I tried to smile, they'd been so nice.

Debby's brown eyes went soft with pride. "We should send Mary Kay her picture. Maybe they'll give us a prize."

At the thought of reward, Marvel quickly rummaged in her closet, found her Polaroid, and arranged me in front of the mirror. It was the only picture she ever took of me. You could see the unmade bed, the bureautop clutter. They congratulated themselves and went back out to their sodas and Chex mix, leaving me in front of the mirror, a toddler's fussed-over Barbie abandoned in the sandbox. I blinked back my tears and forced myself to look in the mirror.

Looking back at me was a thirty-year-old hostess at Denny's. Anything else I can get you, hon? I could feel this vision burning itself into my soul, burning away Deneuve and Dietrich like acid thrown in my face. The woman in the mirror would not have to orchestrate three different lovers. She would not dance on rooftops in Mexico, fly first class to London over the pole. She was in for varicose veins and a single apartment with cat litter and Lana Turner movies. She would drink by herself with tomatoes dying on the windowsills. She would buy magic every day of the week. Love me, that face said. I'm so lonely, so desperate. I'll give you whatever you want.

SCHOOL LET OUT at the end of June under a marine layer heavy as wet towels. The pencil-gray days were broken only by the blue flowers in Olivia's yard. I babysat, ran errands, reread *A Spy in the House of Love*. I longed to see Olivia, but Marvel kept me working. If I so much as walked outside, she gave me four other things to do. Sometimes I'd see Olivia picking herbs in her garden, and our eyes would meet, but she gave no indication she knew me. She would have been a good secret agent, I thought, and tried to do the same, but after a while, I wondered if it was a good act or if she had forgotten me entirely.

Dear Astrid,

The all-prison issue of Witness *is out, you must buy it, they printed my whole poem. It ran seven pages, illustrated with photographs by Ellen Mary McConnell. The response has been tremendous. I had them include a brief note in which I humbly mentioned that gifts of stamps, books, and money would be deeply appreciated.*

Already I've made new fast friends. For instance, the delightful Dan Wiley, #M143522, a strong-arm robber serving twelve years at San Quentin. Dan the Man, as he calls himself, writes almost daily, a series of rough-trade fantasies in which I am the starring player. The best to date is one in which he sodomizes me on the hood of his '72 Mustang while watching the sun go down over Malibu. Doesn't that sound romantic? Did it have a hood ornament that year?

A woman just had the Collected Anne Sexton sent. Hallelujah. Finally something else to read. The only books in the prison library without heaving bodices on the covers are a large-print edition of War and Peace *and a tattered Jack London. Arf. Arf.*

Of course, this admirer also had to send a sheaf of the most dreadful po-e-tree for my approval. She lives on a farm in Wisconsin, some sort of aged hippie commune, where she spins her own sheep. How could anyone who loves Sexton produce work so unrelievedly bad? I am Womannn, hear me Roarrr. So just roar, please, it would be far less embarrassing for all concerned.

However, she believes me to be a prisoner of the patriarchy, a martyr in my own small way. So long as her solidarity includes gifts — power to the people. Free Huey! Free Ingrid Magnussen.

Not one word about me. How are you, Astrid? Are you happy? I miss you. It seemed like years since she'd considered the possibility of losing me. I'd returned to the shadows. My job once again was to share in her triumphs, to snicker at her unfortunate admirers with her, a sort of pocket mirror and studio audience. I realized I was exactly where she wanted me, safely unhappy with Marvel Turlock, a prisoner in turquoise, brewing into an artist, someone she might want to know some- day. When all I wanted was for her to see me now, the way she saw me that day at the prison. To want to know me, what I thought, how I felt.

I wrote to her about Olivia, about another way to be in the world. I inserted drawings of Olivia, lying on the couch pulling magic out of the air. You're not the only beauty in the world, Mother. There is burnished teak as well as alabaster, rippling mahogany as well as silk. And a world of satisfaction where you found only fury and desire. The world parts for Olivia, it lies down at her feet, where you hack through it like a thorn forest.

MARVEL MADE ME sit the kids at the park in the long dull summer afternoons, sometimes not picking us up until dinner-time. I was supposed to buy their snacks and help them on the slides, adjudicate their sandbox wars, push them on the swings. Mostly I sat on the rim of the sandbox with the mothers, who ignored me, each in her own way — the Latina teen mothers importantly, proud of their strollers and made up as formally as Kabuki actors, and the older Anglo moms, plain as pancakes, smoking cigarettes and talking about car trouble, man trouble, son trouble. I sketched the women talking, their heads together and apart. They looked like mourners crouched around the foot of the Cross.

One of those afternoons, I smelled marijuana on the sluggish air and looked around the playground for the source. Over by the parking lot a group of boys sat on a yellow car, doors cocked, their music piercing the dullness of the day. What I wouldn't give to get high. To be mellow and sympathetic, not jagged and spiteful and ready to smack

Justin in the head with his shovel if he whined to me one more time about some kid throwing sand or pushing him off the bars. He was relentless, just like his mother. I tried to remind myself he was only four, but after a while it didn't seem like any excuse.

I pulled out the letter that had arrived that morning from my mother, unfolded the scrap of notebook paper. At least she was paying attention now.

Dear Astrid,

Wasn't Uncle Ernie bad enough? No, you had to locate the most detestable kind of creature to attach yourself to. Don't you dare allow her to seduce you. All Ernie wanted was your body. If you possess the slightest hint of common sense, RUN from this woman as you would a flesh-eating virus.

Yes, the patriarchy has created this reprehensible world, a world of prisons and Wall Streets and welfare mothers, but it's not something in which one should collude! My God, the woman is a prostitute, what would you expect her to say? "Stand up for your rights"? You'd think, as a black woman, she would be ashamed to lick the master's boots, say it's Whitey's world, make the best of it. If she was a Nazi collaborator, they'd shave her head and march her through the streets. A woman like her is a parasite, she fattens on injustice like a tick on a hog. Of course, to the tick, it's a hog's world.

You'd think any daughter of mine would be far too intelligent to be taken in by such ancient offal. Get Germaine Greer's The Female Eunuch, *read some Ai. Even your tragically limited local library must have a copy of* Leaves of Grass.

Mother.

Mother prescribing her books like medicines. A good dose of Whitman would set me straight, like castor oil. But at least she was thinking of me. I existed once more.

The smell of that pot on the sullen air was driving me crazy. I watched the boys around the yellow car enviously. I would normally go out of my way to avoid boys like that, gangly, pimply groups bonded by crude comments and a posture of entitlement. Reminding me of their ownership of this world. But Olivia would not be afraid of them. She would make magic there. She knew what they wanted, she could give it to them or not. Did I have the nerve?

I turned to the mother of the child playing with Justin. "Could you watch him a second? I'll be right back."

"I'll be here," she sighed, stubbing out her cigarette in the sand.

I carried Caitlin across the grass to where the boys clustered around the car. A man's world. I saw myself as they would see me, as Ray saw me, a tall pale girl with long floating hair, a shy smile on my big lips, my legs bare in summer cutoffs. I hitched Caitlin up higher on my hip as I came near, they were all watching me. I glanced back to see if Justin's keeper was looking. She was busy putting sunblock on her kid.

"Mind if I have a hit?" I asked. "I've been babysitting all day, I'm desperate."

A boy with skin that looked like it had been grated handed me the joint. "We saw you get here," he said. "I'm Brian, that's

PJ, and Big Al. And Mr. Natural." The boys ducked, nodded. They waited for me to introduce myself, but I didn't. I could give it to them or not. I liked that.

The pot wasn't first class, not like Ray's, which you could smell right through the Baggie. This smelled like burning straw and tasted dry and brown, but it was sweet as sunshine to me. I sucked in the smoke, turning my head away from Caitlin so she wouldn't get stoned. She squirmed in my arms but I couldn't set her down, she'd be under the first car that drove by.

"Wanna buy some?" The boy named PJ had dyed his hair blond. His T-shirt said Stone Temple Pilots in orange psychedelic writing.

I had three dollars in my pocket, for ice cream for the kids. "How much?"

The others turned to the chunky boy, Mr. Natural, seated in the passenger seat of the car. "Five a gram," he said.

I switched Caitlin to the other hip, the bad one, took the joint from the Stoned Temple Pilot. It felt so good to be high. I felt the lid of the pencil-gray sky lift and I could breathe, I didn't dread the rest of the afternoon now. "I have three."

"How come I never saw you before? You go to Birmingham?" the chunky boy said, getting out of the car. He had rosy cheeks and wavy brown hair, he looked about twelve.

I shook my head, aware of how he was looking at me, and for once I wasn't embarrassed. He was interested. It was my currency, my barter goods. I exhaled away from Caitlin, in a way that showed my neck, drawing his eyes where I wanted.

"Got a boyfriend?" he asked.

175

"Juice," Caitlin said, tugging on my shirt, pulling the strap off my shoulder. "Assi, juice."

I changed hips, jiggled her quiet, feeling their eyes stroking the smooth ball of my shoulder. "No," I told the boy, watching him touch his lips with his fingers.

He leaned against the open car door, foot on the sill, thinking. "Suck my dick, I'll give you a quarter O-Z."

The Stoned Pilot laughed. "Shut the fuck up, dickhead," he told him, turned back to me. "Half," he said softly. "Half a bag, that's a lot for head."

The other boys watched to see what would happen.

I hitched Caitlin high on my hip, looked back at the playground, how far away it was, the swings opposing, like a machine in a factory, the product hurled down the slides. Did I want to? The fat boy bit his lower lip, chapped, unkissed. He was blushing under his light tan, trying so hard to look tough. Suck his dick for half a bag? If anyone had suggested this before, I would have been disgusted. But now my lips could remember holding Ray's column of vein, jerk, and pulse, soft skin of the head, the salty come. I looked at the fat boy and wondered how it would feel.

Caitlin burrowed herself in my neck, trying to make farts, wet and buzzing, against my skin, laughing to herself. I didn't know these boys, I would never see them again. The pot made me brave, curious at how far I would go, as if I was somebody else, someone Olivia would be proud of. "Somebody's got to hold Caitlin. You can't put her down, she'll run off in a second."

"Al's got four little brothers."

I gave her to the quiet boy with short cropped hair and

straggly beard, followed the fat boy back into the bushes behind the bathrooms. He unbuckled his pants, pushed them down over his hips. I knelt on a bed of pine needles, like a supplicant, like a sinner. Not like a lover. He leaned against the rough stucco wall of the bathroom as I prayed with him in my mouth, his hands in my hair. *Just like Miss America.*

With Ray it was never like this. Then it was one pleasure after another, mouths, hands, the richness of skin, every surprise. This was the opposite of sex. I felt nothing for this boy, for his body moving. It felt like working. It cut the heart out of making love, turned it into something no more exciting than brushing your teeth. When the boy was done, I spat out the bitter come, wiped my mouth on my shirt. I thought he would walk away, but he gave me his hand, pulled me up. "My name's Conrad," he said. He was a foreign taste in my mouth, a scent in my hair. He gave me the half-bag of pot. "If you ever want anything, I'm always around."

"I'll keep it in mind," I said as we walked back to the car and I collected Caitlin. My first trick, I thought, trying out the sound of it.

THROUGH the kitchen window, I watched Olivia emerge from her house, cinnamon and beige silk, hair sleeked back. I was peeling apple slices for Justin and Caitlin's snack. I watched her climb into the champagne Corvette, back it out, and I understood.

For her, it was a job. She was earning her car, her copper pots, just as much as someone pasting up magazines or delivering mail. These men weren't lovers, the Rastaman, the BMW.

177

They were customers. The kneeling was just more subtle, the service more discreet, the illusion more substantial, and the payoff no half-bag of dope.

I ANNOUNCED to Marvel that I was starting an exercise program, so I could be ready for the army. I tied on my gym shoes on a cloudy morning, put my hair back, did a couple of jumping jacks, touched my toes, stretched my hamstrings against the fence, the full display for her approval. The army would be a good place, job security, benefits.

Then I ran around the block once and knocked on Olivia's door.

She was dressed in white jeans and a sweater, loafers. On her it looked sexy, I tried to see why. The shoes weren't quite school shoes, they were slimmer, with a tassel. The sweater lightly skimmed her body, the neckline showing one shoulder. I had drawn that shoulder, which gleamed as if polished as it slid out from the soft ginger wool. Her hair was caught in a long silver pin, which probably cost more than the pot I'd just earned.

"I need to talk to you," I said.

She invited me in, glanced over my shoulder as she shut the door. On the stereo, a man was singing in French, sexy, half talking. "I'm glad you came," she said. "I've wanted to see you, but I've been so busy. Excuse me, I was just cleaning up." She loaded glasses and plates on a lacquered tray, emptied a crystal ashtray with cigar butts. I wondered which man was the cigar smoker. The Mercedes had been there again. The fan turned slowly, stirring cigar-sour air. She carried the tray to the kitchen, poured some coffee. "Milk?"

The coffee was so strong it didn't change color when she poured the milk in. "You look different," she said. We sat down at her dining room table, gilded chairs with harp backs. She pulled out small mats with Dutch tulips for our cups.

I took out the bag of pot from my pocket, put it on the table. "I sucked a fat kid's dick at the park. He gave me this."

She held the bag in her hand, in the palm, the fingers lightly cupped around it, and I thought it was the way she would hold a man's penis. She turned her hand over, knuckles to the table, and shook her head. The two vertical lines scored her brow. "Astrid. That's not what I meant."

"I wanted to see how it felt."

"How did it feel?" she asked softly.

"Not great," I said.

She handed it back to me. "Roll one, we'll smoke together."

I rolled a joint on the elegant mat, a parrot-striped bloom. I wasn't good, but she didn't offer to help. While we smoked, I looked around and thought how much come all this must equate to, the framed botanical prints and harp-backed chairs and fat wooden shutters. It must be an ocean. If I were Olivia, I would have nightmares about it at night, a white sea of sperm, and the albino monsters that lived in its depths.

"Do you like having sex?" I asked her. "I mean, do you enjoy it?"

"You enjoy anything you're good at," she said. "Like an ice skater. Or a poet." She got up, stretched, yawned. I could see her slim belly as she lifted her arms. "I've got to run an errand, would you like to come?"

I wasn't sure. Maybe my mother was right, maybe I should run. She could steal my soul. She was already doing it. But who else did I have, what other beauty was there? We agreed to meet down the block, so Marvel wouldn't see me in her Corvette.

She had the top down, a white polka-dot scarf tied over her hair and around her neck, front and back, Grace Kelly–style. Was there ever a woman so glamorous as Olivia Johnstone? I slid into the passenger seat, so low it was like lying down, buckled my seat belt, keeping my head ducked in case anybody saw me as we sped away.

I fell in love that cloudy afternoon. With the speed and the road and the spin of scenery like a fast film pan. I usually got carsick, but the pot lifted me out of it, and the road and the pines peeled away the gloom I'd been carrying around since the park, leaving nothing but the tenor song of the engine and the wind in my face, Olivia's dished profile, her big sunglasses, Coltrane's "Naima" unfolding like a story on the CD player. *The slut next door's got a goddamn Corvette.* And I loved Olivia for sharing it with me, this champagne pearl she'd brought up from the depths of the white sea.

We drove down Ventura, up Coldwater Canyon, the twists in the road like the rise and fall of Coltrane's alto sax. We were dancing it, embodying it as we climbed past overblown Valley ranch homes, white cinder block pierced ornamentally, black cypresses planted in unimaginative rows and geometrically trimmed, up over the top into Beverly Hills.

Now it was tree ferns and banks of impatiens and houses with two-story front doors, grass the radiant green of pool tables, the gardeners with blowguns the only humans in sight. We were entirely free. No children, no job, no foster mothers, just speed and our beauty and the soulful breath of Coltrane's sax. Who could touch us.

She valet-parked at a hotel on Rodeo Drive, and we walked past the expensive shops, stopping to look in the windows. We went into a store so fancy it had a doorman. Olivia took a liking to a black crocodile bag, bought it with cash. She wanted to buy me something. She pulled me into a store that had nothing but sweaters, scarves, and knit hats. She held a sweater up against my cheek. The softness was startling. I realized I had not thought enough about the possibilities of physical reality.

"Cashmere." She smiled, her overbite twinkling. "Like it?"

I sighed. I had seen the price tag.

"Good girl. But not peach." She handed the sweater back to the shopgirl, an eighteen-year-old who smiled placidly. The store smelled of money, soft as a dream.

"Aqua is pretty," the girl said, holding a cable knit sweater the color of spring.

"Too obvious," I said.

Olivia knew what I meant. She found one in French blue, without cables, gave it to me to try on. It turned my eyes blueberry, brought out the rose in my cheeks. Yet in my drawer, it could pass for something from the Jewish Women thrift store. It cost five hundred dollars. Olivia didn't blink as she counted out fifties and hundreds. "What's real is always worth it," she explained to me. "Look how it's made." She showed me the shoulders, the way they were knit together with a separate yoke instead of a seam. "You'll wear it your whole life."

What was real. That's what I learned as we moved from shop to shop. The Georg Jensen silver bangle. The Roblin pottery vase. Stores like churches in worship of the real. The quiet voices as the women handled Steuben glass, Hermès scarves.

To own the real was to be real. I rubbed my cheek against my sweater, soft as a blue Persian cat.

She treated me to lunch in a restaurant under yellow-and-white-striped umbrellas, ordered us a meal composed solely of appetizers: oysters, gravlax, carpaccio. Hearts of palm salad. She explained how each dish was prepared as she sipped a glass of cold white wine and tasted first one, then another, putting her fork down between bites. I'd never seen anything so elegant as Olivia eating. As if she had all the time in the world.

"Life should always be like this." She sighed. "Don't you agree? Like lingering over a good meal. Unfortunately, most people have no talent for it." She pointed out my empty water goblet to the white-jacketed busboy. "As soon as they start one thing, they want it to be over with, so they can start on the next." He got a pitcher and refilled the glass.

"I used to go with a man who took me to the finest restaurants in the city," Olivia continued. "And after we'd eaten, he'd stand up and say, 'Now where shall we go?' And we'd move on to another restaurant, where he'd eat a second complete meal, soup to dessert. Sometimes three in a row."

She cut a small piece of the gravlax and put it on a piece of black bread, daintily spooned a bit of dill sauce onto it, and ate it like it was the last piece of food in the world. I tried to imitate her, eating so slowly, tasting the raw pink fish and the coarse, sour bread, salt and sugar around the rind, flavors and scents like colors on a palette, like the tones in music.

"A lovely man too. Intelligent, rich as Croesus," she said, blotting her lips and taking a sip of wine. "But he lived like a tapeworm." She gazed into her straw-yellow wine, as if the solution to the man's greed was there. Then she shook her head when it wasn't. "Enormous man, probably weighed three hundred pounds. A very unhappy person. I felt sorry for him. Poor Mr. Fred."

I didn't want to imagine her making love to this three-hundred-pound man, lying under him as he hurriedly thrust into her, so he could go again. "How did you know him?"

She fanned away a bee that was exploring her wine. "I was a loan officer in one of his banks."

I laughed out loud, picturing Olivia as a bank employee. Nine to five, behind a desk, in gabardine and flat shoes. Eating lunch at the Soup Exchange. "You're kidding."

"Sure, what did you think, I was some honeychile walking Van Nuys Boulevard in a bunnyfur jacket? I have an MBA. Oh, I knew all about money, except how to get my hands on some. I was out there making payments on a Honda Accord and keeping my little apartment off Chandler, just like everybody else."

"And the big man saved you from yourself."

She sighed. "Poor Mr. Fred. He had a heart attack last year. His brother got everything." She shrugged her shoulders. "But what do you expect of a man who'll eat three dinners in a row?"

I SAT AT MARVEL'S, watching them eat. They stared at the television the whole time, raising their forks to their lips like windup toys, oblivious to whether it was tuna casserole or cat food gratiné. I'd begun to cook, told Marvel I might want to become a chef, it was a good living for a woman. I was gaining weight. My ribs smoothed into the buttery flesh of my torso. I admired my breasts in the mirror, wished Ray could have seen them, cupped them in his mauled hands. I liked the way my body moved as I walked down the street. Marvel thought it was just my age, filling out, she called it. But that wasn't it. I had been moving too fast. I had been too hungry to become a woman.

13

FULL-ON SUMMER fell like a hammer. By nine in the morning you could already start dreading how hot it was going to be. Olivia took me for rides in the Corvette, up the 101 and then out one of the canyons, Topanga, Kanan Dume, to the beach, then we'd cruise back down the coast highway, the wind against our skins bared to the sun, ignoring the shouts of men from other cars. I'd never felt so beautiful and unafraid.

Sometimes she'd make up a pitcher of rum punch and play Brazilian music on the stereo — Milton Nascimento, Gilberto Gil, Jobim. Astrud Gilberto sang interestingly flat, like she was half asleep in a hammock, singing to a child. We sat in the living room on the striped cotton daybed, the fans turning slowly overhead, eating mangos with ham and looking at Olivia's pictures of Brazil. She pronounced the names of the cities in their hushing Portuguese: Rio de Janeiro, Itaparica, Recife, Ouro Prêto, Salvador. Pictures of colonial cities painted popsicle colors, black women in white dresses sending candles out to sea. Pictures of Olivia at Carnival, wearing a dress of silver tinsel slit up to the armpits, her hair feathery and wild.

She held a white man's hand, he was tanned and had flat blue eyes.

"You'd love Carnival," she said. "You dance for three days straight."

"I hate crowds," I said, drunk on the rum punch she'd made, sweet and heavy as a brick. "I'm always afraid I'm going to be crushed."

"It happens," Olivia said, nodding to the samba music. "You better not fall down at Carnival."

After a while she got up to dance. I lay down and watched her in her head scarf and wrapped skirt, moving in time to the complex rhythms of the samba. I imagined her dressed only in tinsel and sweat, dancing with the throbbing crowd under the southern sun, the smells of rum and mangos and Ma Griffe. The music moved along her body in waves, her feet shuffling in small, hesitation steps, arms swaying like palms atop her raised elbows. Hundreds of thousands of people of every hue pulsing under the sun.

"Dance with me," she said.

"Can't dance," I said. "I'm a white girl."

"Don't say can't." She grinned, her hips shifting in subtle circles like a stream over rocks. She grabbed my hand and pulled me off the daybed.

I stood awkwardly before her, tried to copy her movements, but even slightly inebriated, I was aware of how ridiculous I was, how out of time with the music, how out of step. Her body moved in ten directions at once, all harmonized, supple as ribbon. She laughed, then covered her smile with her hand. "Feel the music, Astrid. Don't look at me. Close your eyes and be inside it."

I closed my eyes, and felt her hands on my hips, moving me. Each hip turned independently of the other. She let go, and I tried to keep the rhythm, letting my hips swing in big arcs to the complex beat. I lifted my arms and let the waves of motion travel along the length of me. I closed my eyes and imagined us in Brazil, on a beach with a palm-covered bar, dancing dangerously with men we would never see again.

"Oh Astrid, you've got to come to Carnival," Olivia said. "We'll tell your keeper your class is taking a trip to see the Liberty Bell, and steal you away. For three days in a row you don't sleep, you don't eat, you just dance. I promise, you'll never move like a white girl after Carnival."

When the songs turned quiet, she put her arm around my waist, danced with me close. Her perfume still smelled fresh, despite the heat and the sweat, like pine trees. I was as tall as Olivia now, and her holding me made me awkward, I was stepping on her feet.

"I'm the man," she said. "All you have to do is follow."

I could feel her leading me, her hand open on the small of my back, always dry, even in the heat.

"You're growing up so fast," she said softly in my ear as we danced like waves on Copacabana. "I'm so glad I found you now. In a year or two, it would have been different."

I imagined she was a man, dancing with me, whispering. "Different how?"

"Everything would have been decided," she said. "Now you're so open. You could go any number of ways." She danced me in slow circles, teaching my feet how to move, my hips to trace the sign of infinity.

*

THE WINDS of September fanned harvests of fire on the dry hills of Altadena, Malibu, San Fernando, feeding on chaparral and tract homes. The smell of the smoke always brought me back to my mother, to a rooftop under an untrustworthy moon. How beautiful she had been, how perfectly unhinged. It was my second season of fire without her. Oleander time. I read that the Jews celebrated their New Year now, and decided I too would calculate time from this season.

Coyotes drifted down into the city at night, driven by thirst. I saw them walking down the center line on Van Nuys Boulevard. The smoke and ash filled the basin like a gray bath. Ashes filtered into my dreams, I was the ash girl, born to these Santa Anas, born to char and aftermath.

At the height of the fires, 105 in the shade, I went back to school. The world burned, and I started the tenth grade at Birmingham High. Boys blew me kisses in the halls, waved money at me. They heard I would do things. But I could hardly see them, they were just shapes in the smoke. Conrad, the chunky boy from the park, was in my typing class. He slipped me joints in the hall. He didn't ask me to suck him off now. He could see the flames in my hair, he knew my lips would scorch him. I liked the feeling. I felt like my mother in oleander time. *Lovers who kill each other now will blame it on the wind.*

I sent my mother pictures of Olivia, making gumbo, stirring the huge pot, dancing the samba with her pink palms and feet, driving with her Grace Kelly scarf tied around her head, how bright her skin looked against the white.

Dear Astrid,
  I look at the fires that burn on the horizon and I only

pray they come closer, immolate me. You have proved every
bit as retarded as your school once claimed you were. You'll
attach yourself to anyone who shows you the least bit of
attention, won't you? I wash my hands of you. Do not re-
mind me that it has been two years since I last lived in the
world. Do you think I would forget how long it has been?
How many days hours minutes I have sat looking at the
walls of this cell, listening to women with a vocabulary of
twenty-five words or less? And you send pictures of your
Mulholland rides, your great good friend. Spare me your
enthusiasms. Are you trying to drive me mad?

Dial M.

IN OCTOBER the leaves began to redden and fall, the black
plums and cutleaf maples, the sweet gums. I came home from
school, planning what I would tell Olivia about a teacher who
had asked if I would stay after school, he wanted to talk to me
about my "home life situation," imagining how she would
laugh when I imitated his hangdog look. I wanted to know
which kind of man he was, when I saw something that sucked
the winds out of my sails, they flapped and then hung empty in
midocean. Olivia's car hidden under its canvas cover.

I'd just seen her, and she'd said nothing about leaving. How
could she go and not tell me? Maybe it was an emergency, I
thought, but she could have left a note for me somewhere, I'd
have found it. I waited two days, three, but still the leaves piled
up in her yard, floated in and lay on her car cover like Japanese
paper screens.

I sat in my room at Marvel's, sullen and stoned, sketching

the curtains. The stripes were the only thing that interested me now, that made sense. I didn't write to my mother, I couldn't stand for her to gloat over my loss. She wrote to me, and told me she was corresponding with a classics professor whose name had three initials. He was sending her original translations of some of the more obscene passages of Ovid and Aristophanes. She said she liked the contrast with Dan "The Man" Wylie's mash notes. She also had a lively exchange going with an editor of a small press in North Carolina, and Hana Gruen, a famous feminist in Cologne who had heard of her plight. She wrote me about her new cellmate, she had finally gotten rid of the last one, sent her off to the Special Care Unit babbling about witchcraft. Of course, none of it had anything to do with me, except teeth.

Dear Astrid,

I have a loose tooth garnered in a contretemps on Barneburg B. I cannot possibly lose a tooth here — the idea of a prison dentist is just too grotesque. I see a thin man palsied with early Parkinson's, florid with alcoholism, rife with malpractice. Or a stout woman, a real pig slaughterer, administering procedures without anesthesia, relishing the victim's screams.

Astrid, take care of your teeth. No one will take you to a decent dentist now. If anything goes wrong, they'll let them rot in your head and you'll have to pull the lot when you're 24. I floss every day, even in here, brush with salt, massage my gums. Try to get some vitamin C, if they won't buy it, eat oranges.

Mammy Yokum.

At least she couldn't vanish, I thought as I folded the letter back into the envelope. But she couldn't see me, either. I needed Olivia to come back and feed me.

THERE WAS a water ring around the moon, raven's eye in the mist. It was the first of November. I didn't tell anyone it was my birthday. To celebrate a birthday without Olivia was worse than having it forgotten. I felt like a painting of Icarus, falling into the sea, all you could see was his legs, and the peasant and the cow kept plowing.

I lay out in the backyard in the cold on the picnic table, brushed my cheek against my blue cashmere shoulder. There was already a seed hole in the front. I flaked the last of the joint into a beer can in the cold yard, then threw the can over the back fence, making the dog bark. I wished the BMW man were there, it was his time of night, and Olivia would be playing Oliver Nelson, "Stolen Moments." They would have a fire in the fireplace, they would dance slow, the way Olivia danced with me, he would whisper in her ear, the way she whispered in mine. Now I could dance, but she had left me without music.

I pulled my sweater close and stared up at the veiled moon. I heard laughter from the house, Marvel and Ed in their bedroom watching Leno. I'd just reddened her hair for the fall, Autumn Flame. I shivered under the wet sheets of fog on the picnic table, still smelling dye on my hands, thinking of the infant Achilles. But this was no intentional trial, and the only stars in the sky were lines of planes coming into Burbank from the west.

I thought how it was sunset right now in Hawaii, and hot

curried noon in Bombay. That's where I should be. I would dye my hair black and wear sunglasses, I would forget all about Olivia, Marvel, my mother, all of it. Why couldn't she tell me she was leaving? Did she think it didn't matter to me, didn't she know how entirely I depended on her? I felt hope slipping out from between my fingers like fish juice.

Was I the party jinx, a piece of space junk jettisoned from a capsule? No one to see me, no one to notice. I wished I was back with Ray, that he could hold me down with his eyes, bring me to earth again. It made me nauseous, to float, weightless and spinning in the moon rocks' white glare, the silent funeral of the cypresses. No more jacaranda bloom. It was a landscape Van Gogh could have painted.

I was tired of the moon staring at me so indifferently, tired of the lunar landscape with the white rocks. What I needed was more cover. I slipped through the cyclone fence, careful to close the gate without making noise. The unpicked oranges spread their resinous scent in the moist air, reminding me of her. And then I thought of my mother and her teeth, her vitamin C. My ridiculous life. I crunched through the leaves heaped on the unswept sidewalks, humming a sweet-sad Jobim tune. Back to sucking dew off the sails. I should have known how it would end. I should know enough by now not to expect anything from life, instead of giving in to Stockholm syndrome.

A white dog emerged from the mist and I called him, glad for a little company. Another stray. But he started barking at me, so intently that his front legs lifted off the sidewalk. "Don't bark, it's okay." I moved toward him, to pet him, but another dog appeared, a brown one, then a third, a blue-eyed husky.

The brown one showed his teeth. The big husky barked. I didn't know if I should keep walking or back slowly away.

"Go home," I said. They were blocking my path. I yelled, hoping to scare them off, or that someone would hear, but the houses turned their blank garage faces to the street. "Go home!" I started to back away, but now the little one ran forward, lunged, snapped at my leg.

"Please, someone, come get your dogs!" I begged, but the sound of my voice caromed off the houses, shut down tight behind iron bars and block fences, security doors. And as the brown dog came at me, growling, I remembered what I'd managed to forget for just a few months — that it would always be like this. The brown dog sank its teeth through my jeans.

I screamed for help. It seemed to excite them, the husky knocked me to the ground, biting the arms I'd held up to protect my face. I screamed, knowing there was no one. It was a dream I'd had before, but now there was no awakening, and I prayed to Jesus the hopeless way people pray who know there is no God.

Then — shouts in Spanish. Shoes pounded the ground. Metal clanged on bone. Teeth letting off, sharp painful barks. Snarling, whimpering, toenails scrambling on asphalt, ringing blows of a shovel. A man's face peered into mine, pockmarked, dark with alarm. I didn't know what he was saying, but he helped me up, put his arm around my waist, led me to his house. They had a row of china ducks on the windowsill. They were watching boxing in Spanish. His wife's frantic hands, clean towel running red. Her husband dialed the phone.

*

ED DROVE ME to the emergency room, a washcloth across my face and a towel on my lap to soak up the blood from my arms. He gave me a nip of the glove compartment Jim Beam. I knew it was bad if Ed was sharing his booze. He wouldn't come with me past the reception area of Emergency. There were limits. I wasn't his child, after all. He took a seat on the waiting room bench and looked up at the TV bolted into the wall, Leno shaking hands with the next guest. He hadn't missed much at all.

I was shaking as the woman filled out a chart. Then the redheaded nurse led me back. I told her it was my birthday, that I was fifteen, that Ed wasn't my father. She squeezed my hand and had me lie down on a crisp narrow bed, then gave me a shot, something good to relax me, or maybe because it was my birthday. I didn't tell her just how nice it felt. If you had to get mauled, at least there were drugs. She stripped off my clothes, and the shreds of cashmere made me cry.

"Don't throw it away," I begged. "Give it to me."

I held the bits of my luxurious life against the good side of my face as she cleaned out the wounds, injecting a beautiful numbness. She said if it hurt, just tell her. The redheaded angel. I loved nurses and hospitals. If only I could just lie inside a wrapping of gauze and have this gentle woman care for me. Katherine Drew, her tag said.

"You're lucky, we've got Dr. Singh on tonight," Katherine Drew said. "His father was a tailor. He does custom work. He's the best." Her mouth smiled, but her eyes pitied me.

The doctor came in, speaking with a lilt that sounded like joking, a movie I once saw starring Peter Sellers. But Dr. Singh's brown eyes carried the weight of all the emergencies he had ever seen, the blood, the torn flesh, the fever and gunshots, it was a wonder he could open them at all. He began to sew, starting with my face. I wondered if he was from Bombay, if he knew it was noon there right now. The needle was curved, the thread black. Nurse Drew held my hand. I almost passed out and she brought me apple juice sweet as cough syrup. She told me if they didn't find the dogs I'd have to come back.

Whenever I came close to feeling anything, I asked for another shot. No point in trying to be brave. No Vikings here. On the ceiling of the emergency room was a poster of fish. I wanted to go down under the sea, drift in the coral and kelp, hair like seaweed, ride on a manta ray in silent flight. Come with me, Mother. She loved to swim, her hair like a fan, musical staff for a mermaid's song. They sang on the rocks, combing their hair. Mother. . . . My tears flowed from nowhere, like a spring from a rock. All I wanted was her cool hand on my forehead. What else was there ever? Where you were, there was my home.

Thirty-two stitches later, Ed made his appearance, gray-faced, baseball cap in hand. "Can she go now? I gotta work in the morning."

The redheaded Nurse Drew held my hand while she gave Ed Turlock instructions about cleaning my sutures with hydrogen peroxide and ordered him to bring me back in two days to check healing, then back in a week to have the stitches removed. He nodded but he wasn't listening, explaining as he signed the papers that I was only his foster kid, it was a county health plan.

We didn't talk on the ride back. I watched the passing signs. Pic N Save, Psychic Adviser, AA. Hair Odyssey. Fish World. If I were his daughter he would have come with me. But I didn't want to be his daughter. I was thankful I didn't possess a single drop of his blood. I cradled the bloody cashmere in my hands.

When we got home, Marvel was waiting in the kitchen in her dirty blue robe, hair Autumn Flame. "What the hell were you thinking?" She waved her plump hands in the air. If it hadn't been for the bandages, she would have smacked me. "Walking around all hours of the night. What did you expect?"

I walked past her and took the first of the Vicodins, scooping water from the faucet. I went down to my room without saying a word, closed the door, and lay on my bed. In a perverse way, I was glad for the stitches, glad it would show, that there would be scars. What was the point in just being hurt on the inside? I thought of the girl with the scar tattoos at the Crenshaw group home. She was right, it should bloody well show.

14

SEAMS TRACED my jaw and cheek, arms and legs. Everyone at Birmingham High still stared at me, but differently, not because I was a baby hooker, but because I was a freak. I liked it better this way. Beauty was deceptive. I would rather wear my pain, my ugliness. Marvel wanted me to cover the weals with pancake, but I wouldn't do it. I was torn and stitched, I was a strip mine, and they would just have to look. I hoped I made them sick. I hoped they saw me in their dreams.

Olivia was still gone, her Corvette covered and silent, sprinklers coming on at eight in the morning for seven minutes exactly, lamps lighting at six P.M. by remote control. Magazines piled up on her doorstep. I left them there. I hoped it would rain on them, her sixteen-dollar *Vogue*.

How easy I was. Like a limpet I attached to anything, anyone who showed me the least attention. I promised myself that when she returned, I would stay away, I would learn to be alone, it was better than the disappointment when you found it out anyway. Loneliness was the human condition, I had to get used to it.

I thought about her as I sat under the bleachers with Conrad and his friends, getting stoned. Boys were easy, she was right about that. I knew what they wanted, could give it to them or not. What did she need me for, nothing. She could buy herself a Georg Jensen bangle, a Roblin vase.

AT CHRISTMASTIME, it was hot again, and smog lay thick over the Valley, like a vast headache over a defeated terrain, obscuring the mountains. Olivia was back, but I hadn't seen her, only her discernible patterns, deliveries and men. At Marvel's we went all out for the holidays. We dragged the green metal tree in from the garage, wound ropes of colored tinsel like bottle scrubbers around every door and window, put the plastic Frosty the Snowman on the blacktop, wired up the rooftop Santa-and-reindeer display.

Relatives came by and I wasn't introduced, I passed around the Chex mix, the nutty cheese ball. They took pictures in groups nobody asked me to be in. I drank eggnog from the grown-ups' punch bowl, fiery with bourbon, and went outside when I couldn't take it anymore.

I sat out in the playhouse in the dark, smoking a Tiparillo I'd found in a pack someone had left out. I could hear the Christmas tapes Marvel played round the clock, *Joey Bishop Christmas, Neil Diamond at Bethlehem*. At least Starr believed in Christ. We had gone to church, visited the fluffed straw in the manger, the baby Jesus, newborn King.

Of all the red-letter events of the American sentimental calendar, my mother hated Christmas the most. I remembered the year I came home with a paper angel I made in school, with golden sparkles on tissue paper wings, and she threw it straight into the trash. Didn't even wait until I went to bed. On Christmas Eve, she always read Yeats's "The Second Coming": *What rough beast . . . slouches towards Bethlehem . . .* We'd drink mulled wine and cast runestones. She wouldn't come to hear me sing "O Come All Ye Faithful," "God Rest Ye Merry," with my class at Cheremoya Elementary. She wouldn't drive me.

But now that I'd shadowed Marvel in and out of malls, heard the wall-to-wall canned Christmas carols, experienced Marvel's blinking Christmas light earrings, I was starting to come around to my mother's point of view.

I sat in the dark in the playhouse and imagined I was with her now, and we were in Lapland, in a cottage of painted wood, where the winter was nine months long and we wore felt boots and drank reindeer milk and celebrated the solstice. We tied forks and metal pans to the trees to frighten evil spirits, drank fermented honey and took mushrooms we collected in the fall and had visions. The reindeer followed us when we tried to pee, craving the salt of our bodies.

In the house, Ed's brother George was dressed as Santa, pink drunk. I could hear his laughter over the other voices. Ed sat on the couch next to him, even drunker, but he was a quiet drunk. Justin got a road race set that cost Ed a week's pay, Caitlin had a plastic ride-in Barbie car. All my gifts came from the 99-cent store. A flashlight on a keychain. A sweatshirt with a teddy bear on it. I was wearing the sweatshirt. Marvel insisted. I smoked my Tiparillo and turned the flashlight on and off, just a heartbeat ahead of Rudolph's nose on Marvel's rooftop Santa display. We were having a secret conversation, Rudy and I.

I thought how easily you could kill yourself when you were drunk. Take a bath, fall asleep, drown. No turtle would come floating by to rescue you, no spotter plane would find you. I took my mother's knife and played johnny johnny johnny on the playhouse floor. I was drunk, stabbed myself every few throws. I held my hand up and there was satisfaction at seeing my blood, the way there was when I saw the red gouges on my face that people stared at and turned away. They were thinking I was beautiful, but they were wrong, now they could see how ugly and mutilated I was.

I pressed the knife to my wrist, drew it softly across, imagining how it would feel, but I knew that wasn't the way. You opened the vein from top to bottom. You had to consider the underlying structure.

What was the underlying structure of this, that's what I needed to know: Joey Bishop singing "Jingle Bell Rock," poets sleeping in cots bolted to walls, and beautiful women lying under men who ate three dinners in a row. Where children hugged broken-necked giraffes and cried, or else drove around in plastic Barbie cars, and men with missing fingers longed for fourteen-year-old lovers, while women with porn-star figures cried out for the Holy Spirit.

If I could have one wish, Jesus, it was to let my mother come get me. I was tired of sucking the sails. Tired of being alone, of walking and eating and thinking for myself. I wasn't going to make it after all.

Slivers of light escaped through the shutters of Olivia's house. No men tonight. They were home with their good wives or girlfriends. Who wanted a whore on Christmas?

Oh Christ. I'd been spending so much time with Marvel, it

was starting to rub off. Next thing I knew I'd be making racist jokes. Olivia was Olivia. She had some nice pieces of furniture and some clocks, a rug and a stuffed parrot named Charlie, while I had some books and a box, and a torn cashmere sweater, a poster of animal turds. Not that much different. Neither of us had much, when you got down to it.

So I went next door. Nobody would notice tonight. Her yard smelled of chives. I knocked, heard her footsteps. She opened the door. The expression of shock on her face reminded me she hadn't seen me since November.

She pulled me inside and locked the door. She was wearing a silver-gray satin nightgown and peignoir. She'd been listening to the music I'd heard that first night, the woman with tears in her voice. Olivia sat on the couch and tugged at my hand but I resisted her. She could hardly look at me. Scarface, the kids said. Frank N. Stein.

"Good God, what happened?"

I wanted to think of something clever, something cool and sarcastic. I wanted to hurt her. She'd let me down, she'd abandoned me. She didn't think twice. "Where were you?" I asked.

"England. What happened to your face?"

"Did you have a good time in England?" I picked up the CD box on the table, a black woman with a face full of light, white flower behind her ear. She sang something sad, about moonlight through the pines. Billie Holiday, it said. I could feel Olivia staring at my face, the scars on my arms where my sleeves crept up. I wasn't beautiful anymore. Now I looked like what I was, a raw wound. She wouldn't want me around.

"Astrid, look at me."

I put the box down. There was a new paperweight, grainy

French blue with white raised figures. It was heavy and cool in my hand. I wondered what she'd do if I dropped it on the stone tabletop, let it go smash. I was drunk but not drunk enough. I put it down. "Actually, it's a dog's world. Did you know that? They do anything they want. It was my birthday too. I'm fifteen."

"What do you want, Astrid?" she asked me quietly, beautiful as always, still elegant, that smooth unbroken face.

I didn't know what I wanted. I wanted her to hold me, feel sorry for me. I wanted to hit her. I wanted her not to know how much I needed her, I wanted her to promise never to go away again.

"I'm so sorry."

"You aren't really," I said. "Don't pretend."

"Astrid! What did I do, go out of town?" Her pink palms were cupped, what was she expecting, for me to fill them? With what? Water? Blood? She smoothed her satin skirt. "It's not a crime. I'm sorry I wasn't here, okay? But it's not like I did something wrong."

I sat down on the couch, put my feet on the coffee table among the antiques. I felt like a spoiled child, and I liked it. She shifted toward me on the couch, I could smell her perfume, green and familiar. "Astrid, look at me. I am sorry. Why can't you believe me?"

"I don't buy magic. I'm not one of your tricks. Look, you got something to drink? I want to get really drunk," I said.

"I was going to have a coffee and cognac, and I'll let you have a small one."

She left me there listening to Billie Holiday sing while she made clicks and clatters in the kitchen. I didn't offer to help. In a minute, she was back with glasses, a bottle of brandy, and coffee on a tray. So perfect in every way, even the way she put the tray on the table, keeping her back straight, bending her knees.

"Look," she said, sitting down next to me. "Next time I'll send you a postcard, how's that. Wish you were here, love . . . Brandy." She poured cognac into the snifters.

I drank mine down in a swallow, not even trying to savor it. It was probably five hundred years old, brought over on the *Niña,* the *Pinta,* and the *Santa Maria.* She looked down into her glass, swirled it, smelled it, sipped.

"I'm not the world's most considerate person," Olivia said. "I'm not the type who sends birthday cards. But I'll try, Astrid. It's the best I can do." She reached her hand to touch my face but couldn't bring herself to do it. The hand fell on my shoulder instead. I ignored it there.

"Oh for Christ's sake," Olivia said, removing it, sitting back against the pillows. "Don't sulk. You're acting just like a man."

I looked away and caught our reflection in the mirror over the fireplace, the beauty of the room, of Olivia in her silver nightgown like mercury in moonlight. Then there was this wretched blond girl who looked like she had wandered in from another movie, her face scored with welts, her 99-cent sweatshirt, her unbrushed hair.

"I brought you something from England," Olivia said. "You want to see it?"

I wouldn't look at her. What, did she think presents would make it all better? But I couldn't help watching that beautiful slow walk as she went into the back of the house, silver satin trailing her like a pet dog. I poured myself some more brandy, swirled and watched the liquid separate into trails and meet in the amber pool at the bottom. The smell was fire and fruit, and it burned as it went down. I felt just the way Billie Holiday sounded, like I'd cried all I could and it wasn't enough.

She came back out with a small white box and dropped it into my lap.

"I don't want things," I said. "I just want to feel like someone gives a shit."

"So you don't want it?" she teased, moving to take it away.

I opened the box marked Penhaligon, and nested in tissue was an antique perfume bottle, silver and glass with a lace-covered bulb, filled with a perfume tinged a slight pink. I set it on the table. "Thanks."

"No, don't be like that. Here, smell it." She picked it up and squirted me with it, a fine mist propelled by the lace-covered bulb.

I was surprised at the scent, not at all like Ma Griffe, it smelled like small flowers that grew in leafy English woods, like a girl who would wear pinafores and pantaloons and make chains of wild daisies, a fairy-tale girl from the Victorian age.

When Olivia grinned, the charm of her overbite got to me in a way her perfection never could. "Now, isn't that you?"

I took it away from her and sprayed it over my head so the mist fell like light rain. Wash my sins away. Make me a girl who'd never seen the firestorms of September, who'd never been shot, who'd never gone down on a boy behind a bathroom in a park. A nursery-rhyme girl in a blue dress holding a pet lamb in a cottage garden. It was me, after all. I didn't know quite whether to laugh or to cry, so I poured some more brandy in my glass.

"That's enough," she said, taking the bottle away.

The threads of my scars throbbed with alcohol. I knew it wasn't up to Olivia to love me. She did the best she could, bought me a bit of childhood in a bottle, by appointment to the Queen. "Thanks, Olivia, really," I said.

"That's better," she said.

I WOKE UP the next morning painfully curled on Olivia's couch. Someone had taken my shoes off, the bottle of pink perfume still clutched in my hands. Either it was hot, or I had a fever, and a headache that beat the sides of my skull like an African drum. I slid my feet into my shoes, not tying the laces, and went looking for Olivia.

She lay on top of her bedspread in her crewel paisley canopy bed, completely passed out, still in her robe, bent legs at right angles like she was running in her dream. The clock past her pillow read eleven. I ran down the hall and hit the door.

I was halfway across Olivia's garden when Marvel came out of the turquoise house, Caitlin's Barbie car in her arms. She glanced up. Her mouth opened wide. The only color left on her face was the Autumn Flame of her hair.

If I hadn't been so hungover, something might have sprung to mind. But we stared at each other and I knew I was caught, knee-deep in rosemary and alyssum, frozen as a deer. Then it was all screaming and confusion. She ran out the gate as I took a few feeble steps back toward Olivia's. She seized me by my hair and yanked me back. Her head jerked as she smelled my breath.

"Drinking with the whore? Did you sleep with her too?"

She smacked me in the face, not caring about my scars, her voice reverberating in my tenderized skull like a shot in a cave. She smacked me as she dragged me back over to the turquoise house, head, arms, anywhere she could get me. "What were you doing over there? Is that where you spent the night? Is it? Is it?" She hit me square on the ear and the Penhaligon perfume leaped from my hands and smashed on the blacktop.

I broke away from her, knelt down, the bottle broken inside its silver cage, perfume already soaking the pavement. I put my hands in the puddle. My childhood, my English garden, that tiny piece of something real.

Marvel gripped my arm, hauled me to my feet, screaming, "You ungrateful thing!"

I grabbed her around her arms and yelled in her face. "I hate you so much, I could kill you!"

"How dare you raise your hand to me!" She was much stronger than I had thought. She broke my hold in a second, smacked my face so hard I saw patterns. She caught me under the armpit and marched me back home, kicking me every few feet. "Get in the house, get in there!"

She opened the door and shoved me inside. I sailed into the wreckage of Christmas Eve, dirty glasses and bowls and gift wrapping. The kids looked up from their new toys, Ed from his football game. I staggered into the knickknack shelf and Marvel's Little Women plate fell off and smashed.

She screamed and hit me on the side of my head, I saw patterns again. "You did that on purpose!" She shoved me on the floor, I was afraid she was going to grind my face in the broken glass. She kicked me in the ribs. "Pick it up!" The kids were screaming.

"Assi —" Caitlin ran toward me, arms spread. Marvel snatched her away. She bundled them out to the yard while I picked up the pieces, crying. I hadn't done it on purpose, but I might have if I'd thought of it. She'd broken my perfume, something real, by appointment to the Queen, made from pounds of English spring flowers, not a copy of a copy of a kid's book illustration. When she came back she threw the broom at me. "Now sweep up the rest." She turned to Ed. "God, you can't believe where I just found her. Coming out of that nigger's house, she spent the night there. This is what we get, for all the work and trouble?"

Ed turned the sound up on the game.

I threw out the big pieces, Jo and Amy and Beth, the other one, and Marmee. Broken. Well, that's the way it is, Marmee. One little accident, and it's all gone forever. Jo won't like foster care, she'll get moved around, shot. Amy'll get adopted, she's cute, but you'll never see her again. Beth'll croak and the other one'll turn tricks in a park for dope. Say good-bye to the fireside, welcome to my life.

I swept the shards into a pile, careful not to leave any slivers, Caitlin always went barefoot.

"And when you're done with that, start cleaning this place up. I'm going to go give that nignog whore a piece of my mind." I watched out the kitchen window as Marvel marched from our yard into Olivia's, heard the chain-link gate slam but not click, bang open again. She was hammering on Olivia's door, screaming, "Wake up, whore, you rat's ass, piece of living crap. You stay away from that girl, hear me, nigger?"

Everybody in the neighborhood was home on Christmas morning, listening to this as they celebrated the birth of the newborn King. Nice, Marvel. You go, girl. Show everybody what you're really made of. My only consolation was that Olivia couldn't hear it, passed out as she was at the back of the house.

Marvel tore out handfuls of Olivia's flowers as she stormed back to our house, flinging the uprooted plants at the shuttered windows.

Nauseated and headachy, I nevertheless spent the rest of the day wadding up foil gift wrap and stick-on bows, vacuuming popcorn and Styrofoam peanuts, hauling trash and washing sink after sink of dishes. Marvel wouldn't let me lie down. She kept saying, "You made your bed, now sleep in it."

Later in the day, the cops arrived. Schutzstaffel. The kids wanted to see them, but Marvel stepped out and closed the door. We watched from the living room as Marvel's mouth flew and she gestured to Olivia's with a meaty arm.

"What do they want?" Justin asked. It was three in the afternoon and he was in his pajamas, glassy-eyed from TV and sugar and new toys.

"Someone lost a dog," I said.

Marvel opened the door and called me.

I went out, burnishing the sapphire of my hatred. *"Jawohl,"* I said under my breath.

Marvel's eyes sprayed me with Mace, my skin blistered under her gaze. The older of the two white men drew me aside. "She says you spent the night with the woman next door. It's technically a runaway."

I shifted from leg to leg, the throb of my headache accompanying each heartbeat. If I breathed carefully, I could smell English flowers. The football announcer shouted excitedly from the house, and the cop's eyes flickered briefly in its direction. Then he remembered what he was supposed to be doing and they returned to me.

"This woman gave you alcohol?"

"No. Marvel and Ed had a big Christmas Eve party last night. The eggnog was spiked." The sparkle of my sapphire, Officer Moody. See how it shimmers. Nothing up my sleeve.

"They make you work on Christmas?"

"Triple overtime," he said. "I've got child support you wouldn't believe. So what did you do next door?"

"Listened to records, talked."

"And you spent the night?"

"Well, it was too noisy to sleep over here."

He pulled his fleshy earlobe. "You go over there a lot?"

I shrugged. "She's nice, but she's busy. She travels a lot."

"She ever introduce you to her friends?"

I shook my head, let my mouth go slack, a little moronic, as if I had no idea what he was getting at. You mean, did she ever set me up on a date with one of her johns? Did she ever sell me to the BMW man on a cake platter like *Pretty Baby*? I wanted to laugh in his face.

"She ever talk to you about what she does for a living?" He said it quietly, stroking his brushy mustache.

"She's a caterer, I think." It came out of nowhere.

"What a bunch of crap!" Marvel called out from where she was talking to the other cop, her eyes narrowed in disgust.

I turned my back to the turquoise house so Marvel couldn't read my lips. "Marvel hates her because she's pretty and doesn't have any kids to worry about. She's always calling her names — *nigger, whore*. It's embarrassing, but what am I supposed to do, I'm just a foster kid. She does it to all the neighbors, ask anybody. *Beaner* this, *Jew bitch* that, everybody hates her." He probably said *nigger* and *beaner* too, this Officer Moody, pulling his red earlobes, but not where anybody would write it up.

They sent me inside, but I watched through the kitchen window as the Schutzstaffel went through Olivia's garden, knocked at her door. Five minutes later, they were back. I could hear Marvel screaming. "Aren't you going to arrest her?"

The patrol car slowly pulled away from the curb without Olivia Johnstone.

THINGS WENT back to normal for the rest of the Christmas break, except Marvel watched me like a shoplifter. No more "runs" to the market or library, no more "workouts." But she mostly stopped yelling at me, and was back to just telling me what to do and otherwise treating me like a slave. She left me alone to babysit on New Year's Eve, though she called four times to make sure I was there. I left messages on Olivia's machine, but she never picked up.

15

ON THE FIRST DAY back at school after winter break, I was given a yellow summons slip during third period. It led to a sour, overweight caseworker waiting in the office with the girls' vice principal. The vice principal told me to clear my locker out and leave my books at the front desk. She never once looked at my face. The new caseworker said she had my things in the car.

I twirled my combination and emptied the books from my locker. I was stunned, and somehow not. How like Marvel to do this while I was at school, without a word of warning. I was there and then I wasn't. I would never see any of them again, would never have the chance to tell Olivia good-bye.

The caseworker, Ms. Cardoza, scolded me all the way back into town, down the Ventura Freeway. "Mrs. Turlock told me everything. That you was doing drugs, running around. With little kids in the house. I'm taking you somewhere you'll learn to act right." She was an ugly young woman with a broad, rough-skinned face and a set look about the jowls. I didn't bother to argue with her. I would never speak to anyone ever again.

I thought of the lies Marvel would tell the kids, why I didn't come home. That I died, or ran off. But no, that wasn't Marvel, the Hallmark card woman, dyeing her hair behind closed doors. She would think up something completely the opposite, something you could paint on a Franklin Mint plate. That I went to live with my grandma on a farm, where we had ponies and ate ice cream all day.

Though it hurt me to admit it, I realized Olivia would probably be relieved. She'd miss me a little, but it wasn't her style to miss anyone much. Too many gold badges knocking on her door. She would rather worship sweaters. I wrapped my arms around my waist and slumped against the door. If I had had more energy I would have opened the car door and fallen out under the sixteen-wheeler driving next to us.

THE NEW HOME was in Hollywood, a big wooden Craftsman with a deep eaved porch, too nice for foster care. I wondered what the story was. Ms. Cardoza was excited, she kept opening and closing her handbag. A Latina girl with a long braid let us in, eyed me guardedly. Inside it was dark, the windows covered with heavy curtains. The woodwork gleamed halfway up the walls, smelling of lemon oil.

In a moment, the foster mother appeared, chic and straight-backed, with a dramatic streak in her dark hair. She shook hands with us, and Ms. Cardoza's eyes shone as she took in Amelia's fitted suit and high heels. *"¿Qué pasa con su cara?"* the foster mother asked. What happened to my face. The social worker shrugged.

Amelia invited us to sit in the living room. It was beautiful, carved wood and claw-footed chairs, white damask and needlepoint. She served tea from a silver set, and butter cookies on flowered bone china. I put to work all I had learned at Olivia's, showing her how I could hold my cup and saucer and keep the spoon from falling. They spoke Spanish while I looked into the deodar cedar framing the bay window. It was quiet, no TV. I could hear the little clock on the mantel.

"It's beautiful, no? Not a dormitory," Amelia Ramos said with a smile. She sat on the edge of her chair, her legs crossed at the ankle. "This is my home, and I hope you will enjoy becoming part of our life."

Every once in a while a girl would pass by, cast an inscrutable glance through the doorway, as Amelia signed the papers and explained the rules in her lightly accented English. Each girl cooked and cleaned up one night a week. I would make my bed, shower every other day. The girls took turns doing the laundry and other chores. She was an interior decorator, she explained. She needed the girls to look after themselves. I nodded each time she paused, wondering why she took in girls at all. Maybe the house was too big for her, made her lonely.

OVER THE POLISHED dining table, the other girls spoke in Spanish to each other, laughing in lowered voices, and only stared at me. I was the White Girl. I had been here before, there was nothing you could do about it. Amelia introduced them. Kiki, Lina, Silvana. The girl with the long braid was Micaela, and the wiry, tough-looking girl with a crescent-moon scar on her forehead serving the meal was Nidia Diaz. We ate chiles rellenos, with a salad and cornbread.

"It's good," I said, hoping Nidia would stop glaring at me.

"I provide the recipes," Amelia said. "Some of these girls come to me, they cannot even open a can." She eyed Nidia and smiled.

Afterward, we took our plates into the kitchen, where Nidia was starting on the dishes. She took my plate and narrowed her eyes at me, but said nothing.

"Come in here, Astrid," Amelia called. She brought me into the sitting room, more feminine than the living room, with lace-edged tabletops and an old-fashioned couch. She had me sit in the armchair next to hers. She opened a large leather-bound album on the marble-topped coffee table. "This is my home. In Argentina. I had a splendid house there." There were photos of a pink house with a flagstone courtyard, a dinner party with candlelit tables set up around a rectangular pool. "I could seat two hundred for dinner," she said.

In the dark interior of the house were a heavy staircase, dark paintings of saints. In one photograph, Amelia in pearls sat in a thronelike chair before a painting of herself, she wore a ribbon diagonally across her ball gown, and flanking her chair were a man, also with ribbons, and a beautiful little boy. "This is my son, Cesar, and my husband."

I wondered what had happened in Argentina, if it was so great there, what was she doing here in Hollywood? What had happened to her husband, and her little boy? I was about to ask when she turned the page and pointed a lacquered nail at a picture of two girls in tan uniforms kneeling on a lawn. "My maids," she said, smiling nostalgically. "They were sitting around on their fat *culos,* so I made them pull weeds out of the lawn."

214

She gazed admiringly at the picture of the girls pulling weeds. It gave me the creeps. It was one thing to have somebody pull weeds, but why would anybody take a picture of it? I decided I was better off not knowing.

AT AMELIA'S, my room was large, two beds covered in white flower-sprinkled quilts, and a view into the deodar cedar. My roommate, Silvana, was an older girl, eyebrows plucked to a thin line, lips outlined in lip liner but not filled in. She lay on the bed farther from the door, filing her nails and watching me as I put my things away in the dresser, my boxes in the walk-in closet.

"Last place I slept was a laundry porch," I said. "This is nice."

"It's not what you think," Silvana said. "And don't think sucking up to that bitch is going to do you any good. You better side with us."

"She seems okay," I said.

Silvana laughed. "Stick around, *muchacha*."

In the morning I waited my turn to use the huge, white-tiled bathroom, then dressed and went downstairs. The girls were already leaving for school. "Did I miss breakfast?" I asked.

Silvana didn't answer, just shouldered her backpack, her eyebrows two indifferent arches. A horn honked, and she ran outside, got into a low-slung purple pickup truck and drove away.

"You like breakfast?" Nidia said, putting on her baseball jacket in the front hall. "It's in the fridge. We saved it for you."

Lina and Kiki Torrez laughed.

I walked back to the kitchen. The refrigerator was padlocked.

When I went out into the hall again, they were still standing there. "Was it good?" Nidia asked. Her eyes glittered under her moon-scar like a hawk's, amber-centered.

"Where's the key?" I asked.

Kiki Torrez, a petite girl with long glossy hair, laughed out loud. "With our lady of the keys. Your friend, the noblewoman."

"She's at work now," Lina, a tiny Central American with a broad Mayan face, said. "She'll be home by six."

"Adios, Blondie," Nidia said, holding the door open for them all to go out.

IT DIDN'T TAKE ME long to figure out why the girls called Amelia Cruella De Vil. In the beautiful wooden house, we went hungry all the time. On the weekends, when Amelia was home, we got fed, but during the week, we only had dinner. She kept a lock on the refrigerator, and had the phone and the TV in her room. You had to ask permission to use the phone. Her son, Cesar, lived in a room over the garage. He had AIDS and smoked pot all day. He felt sorry for us, knew how hungry we were, but on the other hand, he didn't pay rent, so he felt there was nothing he could do.

I sat in my tenth-grade health class at Hollywood High with a searing headache. I couldn't tell you whether we were studying VD or TB. Words buzzed like flies that would not land, words drifted across the pages of my book like columns of ants. All I could think of was the macaroni and cheese I would make that night for dinner, how I would devour as much of the cheese as I could without getting caught.

While I made the white sauce for the macaroni and cheese, I hid a stick of margarine behind a stack of plates. The girls told me right off that whoever had kitchen duty stole food for everybody, and if I didn't, they could make life hell for me. After the dishes, I carried it up to my room inside my shirt. Once we could hear Amelia in her room talking on the phone to a friend, they all came into our room and we ate the whole stick. I divided it into cubes with my knife. We ate it slowly, licking it, like candy. I could feel the calories enter my bloodstream, undiluted, making me high.

"Eighteen and out," Nidia said as she licked her fingers. "If I don't kill that bitch first."

But Amelia liked me. She had me sit next to her and finish the food on her plate when she was done eating. If I was really lucky, she invited me into the sitting room after dinner to talk about decorating, look at her fabric swatches and wallpaper patterns. I nodded to her endless anecdotes about aristocratic Argentina while scarfing down tea and butter cookies. The girls resented my collaborating with the enemy, and I didn't blame them. They didn't speak to me at school or on the street in the long hungry lockout afternoons before she got home. Nobody had a key — we might steal something, break into her room, use the phone.

WHAT CAN I tell you about that time in my life? Hunger dominated every moment, hunger and its silent twin, the constant

217

urge to sleep. School passed in a dream. I couldn't think. Logic fled, and memory drained away like motor oil. My stomach ached, my period stopped. I rose above the sidewalks, I was smoke. The rains came and I was sick and after school I had nowhere to go.

I drifted the streets of Hollywood. Everywhere were home-less kids, huddled in doorways, asking for dope, change, a cigarette, a kiss. I looked into their faces and saw my own. On Las Palmas, a girl with half her hair shaved started following me, calling me Wendy. "Don't you walk away from me, Wendy," she yelled after me. I opened my knife in my pocket, and when she grabbed the back of my jacket, I turned and stuck it under her chin.

"I'm not Wendy," I said.

Her face was streaked with tears. "Wendy," she whis-pered.

Another day I found myself walking west instead of east, then north, zigzagging through wet side streets, drinking the resinous smells of eucalyptus and pittosporum and leftover oranges on the trees. Water squished in my shoes, my face burned with fever. I knew vaguely I should get out of the rain, dry my feet, prevent pneumonia, but I felt a strange pull to go north and west. I picked an orange from somebody's tree, it was sour as vinegar, but I needed the vitamin C.

It was not until I emerged onto Hollywood Boulevard that I realized where I was going. I stood in front of our old apart-ment house, dingy white streaked with rain, water dripping from the bananas and the palms and the glossy oleanders. This was where our plane had crashed. I saw our windows, the ones that Barry had broken. Michael's windows. There was a light on in his apartment.

My heart came to life for a moment, beating with hope as I studied the names by the buzzers, imagining him opening the door, his surprise, he would smell of Johnnie Walker, and the warmth of his apartment, the ceiling crumbling, the piles of *Variety*, a great movie on the TV, how welcome I'd be. *Masaoka, Benoit/Rosnik, P. Henderson*. But no McMillan, no Magnussen.

I knew by my disappointment what I had really expected. That we would still be here. That I could go in and find my mother writing a poem, and I could wrap myself in her quilt and this would just be a dream I could tell her about. I was not really a girl one step from homeless, eating scraps off Amelia's plates. In that apartment, my mother had never met Barry Kolker, and prison was something she'd read about in the papers. I would brush her hair, smelling of violets, and swim again in the hot nights. We would rename the stars.

But we were gone. Michael was gone. The door was locked, and the pool was green with algae, its surface pimpled with rain.

I LEANED AGAINST the wall of the lunch court at Hollywood High, fevered and trying not to watch the other kids eat. A girl looked into her lunch bag, made a face, and threw away the offending meal. I was shocked. Of course, she would have a snack waiting when she got home. I wanted to smack her. Then I remembered *The Art of Survival*. When your plane crashed, you drank radiator water, you clubbed your sled dogs. This was no time to be fastidious.

I walked up to the garbage can and looked inside. I could see her brown paper bag on top of the trash. It stank, they never washed out the cans, but I could do this. I pretended I had dropped something in the garbage, and grabbed the lunch sack. It held a tuna sandwich with pickle relish on buttered white bread. The crusts were cut off. There were carrot sticks and even a can of apple juice fortified with vitamin C.

Compared with clubbing your sled dogs, this was easy. I learned to watch when the bell rang, when everybody threw their lunches away and rushed back to class. I was always tardy fifth period. But my hands didn't shake anymore.

Then one day I got busted. A girl pointed me out to her friend. "Look at that nasty girl. Eating garbage." And they all turned to look at me. I could see myself in their eyes, my scarred face, gobbling up a thrown-away yogurt with my finger. I would have stopped going to school, but I wouldn't have known where else to eat.

I found a library where I could safely pass the afternoons, looking at pictures in art books and sketching. I couldn't read anymore, the words wouldn't stay still. They drifted down the page, like roses on wallpaper. I drew samba figures on lined notebook paper, copied Michelangelo's muscular saints and Leonardo's wise Madonnas. I drew a picture of myself eating out of the garbage, furtive, with both hands, like a squirrel, and sent it to my mother. I got a letter back from her cellmate.

Dere Asrid,

*You dont know me, I am your mamas roomayt. Your
letters make her too sad. Send more chereful things, how
youre getten strate As, homecome queen. Shes here for life.
Why make it hardr.*

youre frend
Lydia Guzman

Why make it harder, Lydia? Because it was her fault I was
there. I would spare her nothing.

My mother's reply was more practical. She ordered me to
call Children's Services every day and yell my head off until
they changed my placement. Her writing was big and dark and
emphatic. I could feel her rage, I warmed myself by it. I needed
her strength, her fire. "Don't you let them forget about you,"
she said.

But this was not about being forgotten. This was about
being in a file cabinet with my name on it and they closed the
door. I was a corpse with a tag on my toe.

AS I HAD NO MONEY, I panhandled in the liquor store parking
lot and the supermarket, asking men for change so I could call
social services. Men always took pity on me. A couple of times,
I could have turned a trick. They were nice men who smelled
good, men from offices who looked like they'd have been good
for a fifty. But I didn't want to start. I knew how it would play.
I'd just buy a bunch of food and then be hungry again and
also a whore. When you started thinking it was easy, you were
forgetting what it cost.

AMELIA FOUND OUT I'd been asking for a new placement. I cringed on the uncomfortable wooden-edged sofa in the sitting room as she paced back and forth, ranting, her hands cutting the air. "How dare you tell such outrageous lies about my house! I treat you like my own daughter, and this is how you repay me? With these lies?" The whites of her eyes showed all around the black irises, and spittle accumulated in the corners of her thin lips. "You don't like my house? I send you to Mac. See how well you eat there. You're lucky I allow you to sit at the table with the other girls, with that hideous face. In Argentina you would not be allowed to walk through the front door." My face. I felt my scars throb along my jaw.

"What do you know about a noble home? Just a common piece of street garbage. Mother in prison. You know, you stink like garbage. When you come into a room, the girls hold their breath. You soil my home. Your presence insults me. I don't want to look at you." She turned away, pointed to the polished stairway. "Go to your room and stay there."

I stood but hesitated. "What about dinner?"

She turned on her patent leather heel, and laughed. "Maybe tomorrow."

I lay on my bed in the beautiful bedroom smelling of cedar, my stomach clawing inside me like a cat in a sack. During the day, all I wanted to do was sleep, but at night, images of my days returned like a slide show. Did I really smell? Was I garbage, hideous?

I heard Silvana come in, settle on her bed. "You thought you were something special, eh? Some hot shit. Now you see, you're no better than us. You better shut up, or you'll end up at Mac." She tossed a dinner roll onto my blanket.

I ate it in two bites. It was so good, I almost cried. "What's Mac?" I asked.

I heard her exasperated sigh. "Mac's where they put you when you got no place to go. You won't last a day. They'll eat you for breakfast, white girl."

"Least they get breakfast," I said.

Silvana chuckled in the dark.

A car went by outside, its headlights painting the ceiling in moving shadows. "Were you ever there?" I asked.

"Nidia," she said. "Even she said it was tough, and she's a *loca*. Better shut up and take it like everybody else. Remember, eighteen and out."

But I was only fifteen.

NOW KIKI TORREZ was the pet, the one who sat on Amelia's right and ate scraps off her plate like a dog. I was both envious and disgusted. It was Kiki who turned the pages of the Argentine scrapbooks and ate butter cookies, while I washed Amelia's dirty underwear by hand in the sink, scrubbed her bathtub, ironed her clothes and her lace-edged linens, and if I got any idea to ruin anything out of spite, then no dinner.

She played us off one another. I stole a can of yams one night, and she made Kiki tell her who did it. I lost more weight, my ribs stuck out like the staves of a boat. I was beginning to understand how one human being could kill another.

"You should take in girls," I heard her tell her friend Constanza one day while I was polishing the silver. "It's easy money. You can remodel. I'm remodeling the bathroom next."

I polished the intricate coils of the fork handle with a

toothbrush. I'd done it yesterday, but she didn't like that there was still tarnish in the crevices, so I had to redo them. I would have liked to plant it in her gut. I could have eaten her flesh raw.

Finally in the darkness of March, after weeks of near-daily phone calls, Ms. Cardoza dumped me and I got a new caseworker, an angel of the Lord called Joan Peeler. She was young, wore black, and had long hair dyed rock 'n' roll red. She had four silver rings on each hand. She looked more like a poet than a government drone. When it was time to go for our visit, I asked if she knew any coffeehouses.

She took me to one on Vermont. We ducked in past a few outside tables occupied by shivering smokers trying to stay dry, and into the warm, humid interior. Immediately, I was overcome by memories, the black walls and fragrance of hippie soup, the table by the cash register cluttered with handbills and flyers and free newspapers. Even the laughably ugly paintings in thick pigments seemed familiar — green women with long breasts and vampire teeth, men with baroque erections. And I could remember my mother's voice, her irritation when the roar of the cappuccino machine interrupted her reading, her books stacked on the table where I drew and took the money when someone bought one.

I wanted her back. I was overwhelmed with a need to hear her low, expressive voice. I wanted her to say something funny and cruel about the art, or tell a story about one of the other poets. I wanted to feel her hand on my hair, stroking me while she spoke.

Joan Peeler ordered peach tea. I took strong coffee with cream and sugar and the biggest pastry, a blueberry scone shaped like a heart. We sat at a table where we could see the street, the funereal umbrellas, hear the soft hiss of cars through puddles. She opened my case file on the sticky tabletop. I tried to eat slowly, to enjoy the buttery biscuit and the whole blueberries, but I was too hungry. I finished half of it before she even looked up.

"Ms. Cardoza recommended you not be moved," my new caseworker said. "She says the home is perfectly adequate. She says you have an attitude problem."

I could picture her writing it, Ms. Cardoza, her skin muddy with makeup applied like cake frosting. She never once took me out for a visit, always spent the whole time talking to Amelia in Spanish over plates of butter cookies and *yerbabuena* tea in matching flowered cups and saucers. She was so impressed by Amelia and the big house, the sparkling silver. All that remodeling. She never wondered where the money came from. Six girls bought a lot of remodeling, even antiques, especially if you didn't feed them.

I glanced up at a drippy, heavy painting of a woman lying on a bed, her legs spread, snakes crawling out of her vagina. Joan Peeler craned her neck around to see what I was looking at.

"Did she say why I asked to be moved?" I licked powdered sugar off my fingers.

"She said you complained about the food. And that Mrs. Ramos restricts use of the telephone. She found you bright but spoiled."

I laughed out loud, pulled up my sweater to show her my ribs. The men across the aisle looked too, a writer with a portable computer, a student making notes on a legal pad. Seeing if I'd pull it up any higher. Not that it mattered, I didn't

225

have much on top anymore. "We're starving," I said, covering myself again.

Joan Peeler frowned, pouring tea through a wicker strainer into a chipped cup. "Why don't the other girls complain?"

"They're afraid of a worse placement. She says if we complain she'll send us to Mac."

Joan put her strainer down. "If what you say is true and we can prove it, she can have her license revoked."

I imagined how it would really play. Joan started her investigation, got transferred to the San Gabriel Valley, and I lost my chance to have a young caseworker who still got excited about her clients. "That could take a long time. I need out now."

"But what about the other children? Don't you care what happens to them?" Joan Peeler's eyes were large and disappointed in me, ringed in dark liner outside the lids.

I thought of the other girls, quiet Micaela, Lina, little Kiki Torrez. They were as hungry as I was. And the girls who came after us, girls who right now didn't even know the word *foster*, what about them? I should want to close Amelia down. But it was hard for me to picture those girls. All I knew was, I was starving and I had to get myself out of there. I felt terrible that I would want to save myself and not them. It wasn't how I wanted to think of myself. But at bottom, I knew they'd do the same. No one was going to worry about me if they had a chance to get out. I'd feel the wind as they hit the door. "I've stopped having my period," I said. "I eat out of the trash. Don't ask me to wait." Reverend Thomas said that in hell, the sinners were indifferent to the suffering of others, it was part of damnation. I hadn't understood that until now.

She bought me another pastry, and I made a sketch of her

on the back of one of her papers, drew her hair a little less stringy, overlooked the zit on her chin, spaced her gray eyes a bit better. I dated it and gave it to her. A year ago I would have felt a panic at being thought heartless. Now I just wanted to eat regularly.

JOAN PEELER said she had never come across a kid like me, she wanted to have me tested. I spent a couple of days filling out forms with a fat black pencil. *Sheep is to horse as ostrich is to what*. I'd been through this before, when we came back from Europe and they thought I was retarded. I wasn't tempted to draw pictures on the computer cards this time. Joan said the results were significant. I should be going to a special school, I should be challenged, I was beyond tenth grade, I should be in college already.

She started visiting me weekly, sometimes twice a week, taking me out for a good meal on the county. Fried chicken, pork chops. Half-pound hamburgers at restaurants where all the waiters were actors. They brought us extra onion rings and sides of cole slaw.

During these meals, Joan Peeler told me about herself. She was really a screenwriter, social work was just her day job. *Screenwriter*. I imagined my mother's sneer. Joan was writing a screenplay about her experiences as a caseworker for DCS. "You wouldn't believe the things I've seen. It's incredible." Her boyfriend, Marsh, was also a screenwriter; he worked for Kinko's Copies. They had a white dog named Casper. She wanted to win my trust so I would tell her things about my life to include in her screenplay. Research, she called it. She was

227

hip, working for the county, she knew where it was at, I could tell her anything.

It was a game. She wanted me to strip myself bare, I lifted my long sleeve to the elbow, let her see a few of my dogbite scars. I hated her and needed her. Joan Peeler never ate a stick of margarine. She never begged for quarters in a liquor store parking lot to make a phone call. I felt like I was trading pieces of myself for hamburgers. Strips of my thigh to bait the hook. While we talked, I sketched naked Carnival dancers wearing elaborate masks.

16

JOAN PEELER found me a new placement. The girls pointedly ignored me as Joan helped me carry my stuff out to her red dented Karmann Ghia with bumper stickers that said, Love Your Mother, Move to the Light, Friends Don't Let Friends Vote Republican. Silvana sniffed that it was because I was white, I got special treatment. Maybe she was right. She probably was. It wasn't fair at all. It wasn't. But that March day, one of those perfect March days in L.A. when every photographer in town was out scrambling for shots of the city with a bluebird sky and white-capped mountains and hundred-mile views, I didn't care why. All I cared was that I was leaving.

There was snow on Baldy, and you could see every palm tree on Wilshire Boulevard five miles away. Joan Peeler played a Talking Heads tape for the drive.

"You'll like these people, Astrid," she said as we drove west on Melrose, past body shops and pupuserias. "Ron and Claire Richards. She's an actress and he does something with television."

"Do they have kids?" I asked. Hoping they didn't. No more

babysitting, or 99-cent gifts when the two-year-old gets a ride-in Barbie car.

"No. In fact, they're looking to adopt."

That was a new one, something I never considered. Adoption. The word rattled in my head like rocks in an oatmeal box. I didn't know what to think. We passed Paramount Studios, the big triple-arched gate, parking kiosk, people riding around on fat-tired bicycles. The longing in her eyes. "Next year, I'll be in there," Joan said. Sometimes I didn't know who was younger, her or me.

I handled the word *adoption* in my mind like it was radioactive, saw my mother's face, pulpy and blind in sunken-cheeked fury.

Joan drove through the strip of funky Melrose shops west of La Brea, with shops of used boots and toys for grown-ups, turned south onto a quiet side street, into an old neighborhood of stucco bungalows and full-growth sycamores with chalky white trunks and leaves like hands. We parked in front of one, and I followed Joan to the door. An enamel plaque under the doorbell read *The Richards* in script. Joan rang the doorbell.

The woman who answered the door reminded me of Audrey Hepburn. Dark hair, long neck, wide radiant smile, about thirty. Her cheeks were flushed as she waved us in. "I'm Claire. We've been waiting for you." She had an old-fashioned kind of voice, velvety, her words completely enunciated, *ing* instead of *in'*, the *t* crisp, precise.

Joan carried my suitcase. I had my mother's books and Uncle Ray's box, my Olivia things in a bag.

"Here, let me help you," the woman said, taking the bag, setting it on the coffee table. "Put that down anywhere."

I put my things next to the table, looked around the low-ceilinged living room painted a pinkish white, its floor stripped to reddish pine planks. I liked it already. There was a painting over the fireplace, a jellyfish on a dark blue background, penetrated with fine bright lines. Art, something painted by hand. I couldn't believe it. Someone bought a piece of art. And a wall of books with worn spines, CDs, records, and tapes. The free-form couch along two walls looked comfortable, a blue, red, and purple woven design, reading lamp in the center. I was afraid to breathe. This couldn't be right, it couldn't be for me. She was going to change her mind.

"There are just a few things we need to go over," Joan said, sitting down on the couch, opening her briefcase. "Astrid, could you excuse us?"

"Make yourself at home," Claire Richards said to me, smiling, reaching out in a gesture of gift. "Please, look around."

She sat down with Joan, who opened my file, but she kept smiling at me, too much, like she was worried what I'd think of her and her home. I wished I could tell her she had nothing to worry about.

I went into the kitchen. It was small, tiled red and white, with a pearly-topped table and chrome chairs. A real *Leave It to Beaver* kitchen, decorated with a salt and pepper shaker collection. Betty Boops and porcelain cows and sets of cacti. It was a kitchen to drink cocoa in, to play checkers. I was afraid of how much I wanted this.

I walked out into the small backyard, bright with wide flowerbeds and pots on a wooden deck, a weeping Chinese elm. There was a flying goose windmill, and red poinsettia grew against the house's white wall in the sun. Kitsch, I heard my mother's voice in my ear. But it wasn't, it was charming. Claire Richards was charming, with her wide love-me smile. Her bedroom, which backed up to the deck through open French doors, was charming. The quilt on the low pine double bed, the armoire, the hope chest, and the rag rug.

As I moved back into the hall, I could see them, heads together over the coffee table, looking at my file. "She's had an incredibly hard time of it," Joan Peeler was telling my new foster mother. "She was shot at one foster home . . ."

Claire Richards shook her head in disbelief, that anyone could be so awful as to shoot a child.

The bathroom would be my favorite room, I could tell that already. Tiled aqua and rose, the original twenties ceramic, a frosted glass enclosure on the tub, a swan swimming between cattails. There was something deeply familiar about the swan. Had we lived somewhere with swan etched glass like this? Bottles and soaps and candles nestled on the bath tray that stretched between the two sides of the tub. I opened containers and smelled and rubbed things on my arms. Luckily the scars were fading, Claire Richards wouldn't have to see the glaring red weals, she seemed the sensitive type.

They were still discussing my case as I moved to the front bedroom. "She's very bright, as I've said, but she's missed a lot of school — all the moving, you understand —"

"Maybe some tutoring," Claire Richards said.

My room. Soft pine twin beds, in case of sleepovers. Thin, old-fashioned patchwork quilts, real handmade quilts edged in eyelet lace. Calico half curtains, more eyelet. Pine desk, bookcase. A Dürer etching of a rabbit in a neat pinewood frame. It looked scared, every hair plain. Waiting to see what would happen. I sat down on the bed. I couldn't picture myself filling this room, inhabiting it, imposing my personality here.

Joan and I said our tearful good-byes, complete with hugs.

"Well," Claire Richards said brightly after the social worker had gone. I was sitting next to her on the free-form couch. She clutched her hands around her knees, smiled. "Here you are." Her teeth were the blue-white of skim milk, translucent. I wished I could put her at ease. Although it was her house, she was more nervous than I was. "Did you see your room? I left it plain so you could put your own things up. Make it yours."

I wanted to tell her I wasn't what she expected. I was different, she might not want me. "I like the Dürer."

She laughed, a short burst, clapped her hands together. "Oh, I think we're going to get along fine. I'm only sorry Ron couldn't be here. My husband. He's in Nova Scotia shooting this week, he won't be back until next Wednesday. But what can you do. Would you like some tea? Or a Coke? I bought Coke, I didn't know what you'd drink. We also have juice, or I could make you a smoothie —"

"Tea is fine," I said.

I NEVER SPENT more time with anyone than I spent with Claire Richards the week that followed. I could tell she'd never been around kids. She took me with her to the dry cleaner's, the bank, like she was afraid to leave me alone for a moment, as if I were five and not fifteen.

For a week, we ate out of paper cartons and jars with foreign writing on the labels from the Chalet Gourmet. Soft runny wedges of cheese, crusty baguettes, wrinkly Greek olives.

Dark red proscuitto and honeydew melon, rose-scented diamonds of baklava. She didn't eat much, but urged me to finish the roast beef, the grapefruit sweet as an orange. After three months with Cruella, I didn't need urging.

We sat over our living room picnics and I told her stories about my mother, about the homes, avoiding anything too ugly, too extreme. I knew how to do this. I told her about my mother, but only the good things. I wasn't a complainer, I wouldn't end up saying bad things about you, Claire Richards.

She showed me her photo albums and scrapbooks. I didn't recognize her in the pictures. She was very shy, I could hardly imagine her in front of an audience, but I saw from her albums that in character, she didn't even resemble her normal self. She sang, she danced, she wept on her knees with a veil over her head. She laughed in a low-cut blouse, a sword in her hand.

"That's *Threepenny Opera*," she said. "We did it at Yale."

She was Lady Macbeth, before that the daughter in *'Night, Mother*. Catherine in *Suddenly, Last Summer*.

She didn't act much anymore. She slid her garnet heart pendant along its chain, tucked it under her ripe lower lip. "I get so tired of it. You spend hours getting ready, drag yourself to the call, where they look at you for two seconds and decide you're too ethnic. Too classic. Too something."

"Too ethnic?" Her wide pale forehead, her glossy hair.

"It means brunette." She smiled. One front tooth was crooked, it crossed just slightly over the other one. "Too small means breasts. Classic means old. It's not a very nice business, I'm afraid. I still go out, but it's an exercise in futility."

I wiped the last of the Boursin cheese out of the container with my finger. "Why do it then?"

234

"What, and give up show business?" She laughed so easily, when she was happy, but also when she was sad.

THE NEW Beverly Cinema was right around the corner from her house. They were playing *King of Hearts* and *Children of Paradise*, and we bought a giant popcorn and laughed and cried and laughed at each other crying. I used to go there all the time with my mother, but the movies were different. She didn't like weepy films. She liked to quote D. H. Lawrence: "Sentimentalism is the working off on yourself of feelings you haven't really got." Hers were grim European films — Antonioni, Bertolucci, Bergman — films where everybody died or wished they had. Claire's movies were lovely dreams. I wanted to crawl inside them, live in them, a pretty mad girl in a tutu. Gluttonous, we went back and saw them again the next night. My heart felt like a balloon that was filling too full, and I panicked. I might get the bends, the way scuba divers did when they surfaced too fast.

At night I lay awake in my bed with the white eyelet ruffle, looking at the Dürer rabbit. It was bound to turn wrong. Joan Peeler was going to tell me it was just a mistake, that they'd changed their minds, they wanted a three-year-old. They'd decided to wait another couple of years. I worried about Claire's husband. I didn't want him to come home, take her away from me. I wanted it to always be like it was, the two of us in the living room eating pâté de foie gras and strawberries for dinner and listening to Debussy records, talking about our lives. She wanted to know all about me, what I was like, who I was. I worried, there wasn't really much to tell. I had no preferences. I ate anything, wore anything, sat where you told me, slept where you said. I was infinitely adaptable. Claire wanted to know things like, did I like coconut soap or green apple? I didn't know. "No, you have to decide," she said.

So I became a user of green apple soap, of chamomile shampoo. I preferred to have the window open when I slept. I liked my meat rare. I had a favorite color, ultramarine blue, a favorite number, nine. But sometimes I suspected Claire was looking for more than there was to me.

"What was the best day of your life?" she asked me one afternoon as we lay on the free-form couch, her head on one armrest, mine on the other. Judy Garland sang on the stereo, "My Funny Valentine."

"Today," I said.

"No." She laughed, throwing her napkin at me. "From before."

I tried to remember, but it was like looking for buried coins in the sand. I kept turning things over, cutting myself on rusty cans, broken beer bottles hidden there, but eventually I found an old coin, brushed it off. I could read the date, the country of origin.

"It was when we were living in Amsterdam. A tall thin house by the canal. There was a steep twisted staircase, and I was always afraid of falling." Dark green canal water and rijsttafel. Water rats as big as opossums. The thick smell of hashish in the coffeehouses. My mother always stoned.

"I remember, it was a sunny day, and we ate sandwiches of raw hamburger and onions, standing up at a corner café, and my mother sang this cowboy song: 'Whoopee ti yi yo, git along little dogies.'" It was the only memory I had of Amsterdam being sunny.

Claire laughed, a sound like bells, drew her knees up to her chin and wrapped her arms around them, gazing at me in a way I could have bottled and stored like a great wine.

"We sat in the sun overlooking the canal, and she said, 'Look, Astrid, watch this.' And she waved at the people passing by on a glass sightseeing boat. And all the passengers waved back. They thought we were Dutch, see, welcoming them to our city. That was my best day." The sun and the herring gulls and all those people waving, thinking we were from there, that we belonged.

At the other end of the couch, Claire sighed, unfolding her legs, smiling nostalgically. She didn't see who I had been then, a thin, lonely child, warmed by the mistaken thought that I belonged. She saw only the childish fun.

"You've been everywhere, haven't you."

I had, but it hadn't done me much good.

THE DAY Ron was expected home from Nova Scotia, Claire threw out all the take-out packages, cleaned the kitchen, and did three loads of laundry. The house was fragrant with cooking, and Emmylou Harris sang something about bandits in Mexico. Claire had rubber gloves on, she was pulling meat off a chicken that was still hot, wearing a red-and-white-checked apron and lipstick. "I'm making paella, what do you think of that?"

It made me anxious. I liked the way it was, we'd settled into a routine, and now it was being thrown off by the part I didn't yet know, the part that could change everything for me. Already I resented her husband, and I hadn't even met him. But I vacuumed the living room, helped her make their bed with fresh sheets printed with falling roses, red and white. "Red and white are the marriage colors," Claire explained.

She opened the French doors to the garden, blooming vibrantly in the April sun. Her hands lingered and smoothed the white quilt. I knew she wanted to be in this bed with him, making love with him. I secretly hoped he would miss his plane, get into an accident on the way to the airport. I was unnerved by her tremulous anticipation. She reminded me of a certain kind of rose she grew in the garden, called Pristine. It was white with a trace of pink around the outside, and when you picked it, the petals all fell off.

I didn't know why he had to come back now. I was having such a good time. I'd never been such a source of interest. I certainly didn't want to share this with some husband, some Ed on the couch. Even an Uncle Ray would upset the wonderful balance.

At about six, his car pulled up in the driveway, a small silver Alfa Romeo. He got out, slung a hanging bag over his shoulder, removed a duffel and an aluminum briefcase, the gray of his hair catching the late sun. I stood uneasily on the porch as she ran to him. They kissed, and I had to look away. Didn't she know how easily this could go bad, wasn't she afraid?

WE ATE PAELLA outside on the patio under a string of lights shaped like chili peppers, Emmylou singing in the background, the sweetheart of the rodeo. Mosquitoes whined. Claire lit citronella candles, and Ron told us about the assignment he'd gone to Halifax to film, a story about a haunted bar. He was a segment producer on a show about the weird and occult.

Evidently the ghost nearly smothered a customer to death last year in the men's room.

"It took us three hours to get him back in there. Even with the film crew, he almost chickened out. He knew it was going to try to finish him off."

"What would you have done if it had?" Claire asked.

Ron stretched his legs out on the bench in front of him, hands clasped behind his head. "I'd have sicced the Tidy Bowl man on it."

"Very funny." Her face was the shape of a perfect candy-box heart, but there was a haze of mistrust over her features.

"I could try Vanish."

As they joked, I tried to see what Claire found so great about him. He was attractive but not stunning — medium height, trim, small features, closely shaven. He brushed his steel-gray hair back without a part. He wore rimless glasses and his cheeks were rosy for a man's. Hazel eyes, hands smooth with trimmed nails, smooth wedding band. Everything about Ron was smooth, calm, underplayed. He told a story, but it didn't matter if we liked it or not, not like Barry, looking for applause. He didn't overwhelm you. He didn't seem to need anything.

She took his plate, scraped the scraps onto hers, stacked it underneath, reaching for mine. "If you don't watch out, you could be the one to vanish." She said it lightly, but the timing was off.

"The La Brea Vortex," he said.

The phone rang and Ron went through the open French doors to answer it. We saw him lie down on the white quilt, pick at his toenails as he talked. Claire stopped clearing the table, and her face blurred, resolved, blurred. She stood at the picnic table fiddling with the plates, with the scraps and silverware, trying to hear what he was saying.

He hung up and came back to the table. Her shadows swept back by his sun.

"Work?" Claire asked, as if it made no difference.

"Jeffrey wanted to come over and talk about a script. I said no." He reached out and took her hand. I couldn't stand to see how she flushed with pleasure.

Now he remembered that I was still there, playing with some saffron rice from the paella on the tabletop, making an orange spiral. "We've got some catching up to do." He was so smooth. I could imagine him getting some lonely Ouija board reader to confess her conversations with the dead husband on camera, holding her gnarled hand in his smooth one, the smooth gold wedding band, his calm voice saying, "Go on."

She talked some about what we'd been doing, that she'd signed me up at Fairfax High, that we'd gone to the movies and a jazz concert at the art museum. "Astrid's quite an artist," she said. "Show him what you've been doing."

Claire had bought me a set of Pelikan watercolors in a big black case, a book of thick-textured paper. I'd been painting the garden, the droop of the Chinese elm, the poinsettias against the white wall. Spires of delphinium, blush of roses. Copies of the Dürer rabbit. Claire practicing ballet in the living room. Claire with a glass of white wine. Claire, her hair up in a turbaned towel. I didn't want to show them to Ron. They were too revealing.

"Show him," Claire said. "They're beautiful."

It irked me that she wanted me to show him. I thought they

were something between us, from me to her. I didn't know him. Why did she want me to? Maybe to prove they'd made the right decision in taking me. Maybe to show what a good job she was doing with me.

I went and got the big pad, handed it to Ron, and then went out in the dark garden and kicked the heads off the stray Mexican evening primroses that crept into the lawn. I heard him turning the pages. I couldn't watch.

"Look at this." He laughed. "And this. She's a natural. They're terrific," he called out to me in the dark. I kept kicking the heads off the primroses.

"She's embarrassed," Claire said. "Don't be embarrassed, Astrid. You have a gift. How many people can say that?"

The only one I knew was behind bars.

A cricket or night bird was making squeaky sounds like a hamster going around a wheel. On the patio, under the chili lights, Claire described making the paella, as if it were a Keystone comedy, working up an enthusiasm that made my stomach ache. I looked at Ron, in his white shirt washed with a trace of pink-orange from the lights, laughing along with her. His arms crossed behind his head, his pleasant face laughing, his clean foot in its sandal perched on his jean-covered knee. Why don't you go away, Ron? There were witch doctors waiting to be interviewed, tortilla miracles to be documented. But the sound of her laughter was sticky as sap, the smell of night-blooming jasmine soft as a milk bath.

"Astrid, are you still there?" Claire called out to me, peering into the darkness.

"Just thinking," I said, pulling a sprig of mint from under the hose bib, crushing it in my hand. Thinking that tonight they would lie together in the pine bed with the rose sheets, and I would be alone again. Women always put men first. That's how everything got so screwed up.

AFTER MY WEEK alone with Claire, I reluctantly returned to school, to finish out tenth grade at Fairfax High. I was happy enough not to have to go back to Hollywood, where they had seen me eating out of the garbage. This was a whole new start. At Fairfax I was blissfully invisible again. I came home from school each day to find Claire waiting for me with a sandwich and a glass of iced tea, a smile, questions. At first it seemed weird and unnecessary. I had never come home to someone waiting for me before, someone looking forward to the sound of my key in the door, not even when I was a child. It felt like she was going to accuse me of something, but that wasn't it. She wanted to know about my composition on Edgar Allan Poe and my illustrations on the chambers of the heart and the circulation of the blood. She was sympathetic when I got a D on an algebra test.

She asked about the other kids, but I didn't have much to tell. At the best of times, I was never very sociable. School was a job, I did it and left. I had no intention of joining the Spanish club or Students Against Drunk Driving. I even passed by the stoner crowd without a glance. I had Claire now, waiting for me. She was all I needed.

"Did you have a nice day at school?" she'd ask, drawing up a chair at the little red-and-white kitchen table.

She had some mistaken notion that Fairfax was like high school where she grew up in Connecticut, despite the clear presence of metal detectors at every entrance. I didn't tell her about the free-for-alls on the school yard, muggings on the bus. A girl burned a cigarette hole into the back of another girl's shirt at nutrition, right in front of me, looking at me, as if daring me to stop her. I saw a boy being threatened with a knife in the hallway outside my Spanish class. Girls talked about their abortions in gym class. Claire didn't need to know about that. I wanted the world to be beautiful for her. I wanted things to work out. I always had a great day, no matter what.

ON SATURDAY, Ron mowed the lawn, cutting the heads off the primroses, and then settled into reading some scripts. We had lox and bagels for breakfast, and Claire went to her ballet class. I sat with my paints next to Ron at the table. I was getting used to him. He didn't try to be any friendlier than I wanted.

"How does Claire seem to you?" he asked all of a sudden. He looked at me over the tops of his glasses like an old man.

"Fine," I said.

But I had some idea what he was talking about. Claire paced at night, I heard her bare feet on the floorboards. She talked as if silence would crush her if she didn't prop it up with a steady stream of sound. She cried easily. She took me to the observatory and started crying in the star show. The April constellations.

"You have my pager number, you know. You can always reach me."

I kept painting the way the poinsettia looked against the white wall of the house. Like a shotgun blast.

*

CLAIRE PUSHED back the muslin curtain, glanced out at the street. She was waiting for Ron. It was still light out, moving toward summer, a six o'clock honeyed twilight.

"I think Ron is having an affair," she said.

I was surprised. Not at the thought — I knew the reason she would stop talking when he was on the phone, the way she would gently probe him to discover his whereabouts. But that she would say it aloud indicated a progression of her doubts.

I thought about Ron. His smoothness. Sure, he could get women anytime he wanted. But he worried too much about Claire. If he was messing around, why would he care? And he worked hard, long hours, always came home tired. He wasn't that young. I didn't think he had the energy.

"He's just working," I said.

Claire peered out into the street from behind the curtain. "So he says."

"HAVE YOU seen my keys?" Ron asked. "I've looked everywhere for them."

"Take mine," Claire said. "I can have another set made."

"Yeah, but it bugs me that I'm losing things. They've got to be around here somewhere."

He took Claire's keys, but it bothered him. He was a highly organized man.

One day, I saw Claire take a pen from Ron's inside jacket pocket, slip it into her jeans.

"Have you seen my Cross pen?" he asked a few days later.

"No," she said.

He frowned at me. "Did you take it, Astrid? Tell me the

truth, I won't be upset. It's just things are disappearing and it's driving me crazy. I'm not accusing you of stealing them, but did you borrow it and not put it back?"

I didn't know what to say. I didn't want to rat on Claire, but I didn't want him thinking I was stealing from him either. I would do anything not to lose this placement. "I didn't take it, really. I wouldn't."

"I believe you," he said, running his hand through his silver hair. "I must be getting senile."

"Maybe it's poltergeists," Claire said.

When Claire went out for an audition, I searched the house methodically. Under their bed I found a box painted red and white and decorated with pieces of broken mirror. Inside, it was also red, and full of the things that he'd been missing — an army knife, a watch, his stapler, scissors, keys, nail clippers. There was a Polaroid of them laughing, and two Polaroids glued together face-to-face, I couldn't pry them apart. A magnet hung from the lid of the box, and a steel plate was glued to the bottom. I could feel the tug of the magnet as I replaced the lid.

17

I FINISHED the tenth grade at the end of June. I did incredibly well, considering. C in algebra, it was a mercy grade, they never give out D's as final grades in honors classes. But with Claire's nightly help, I got A's in English and history, world art and biology, even Spanish. If she had asked me to go out for football, I would have done that too. To celebrate, Ron took us to Musso and Frank, a restaurant right on Hollywood Boulevard. I'd never noticed it before. Just down from the last apartment I lived in with my mother.

We parked in back and walked down the stairs with their polished brass railings, past the old-fashioned kitchen. We could see the chefs cooking. It smelled like stew, or meat loaf, the way time should smell, solid and nourishing. We walked single file past the scarred wooden counter, people eating steaks and chops and reading *Variety*, warmed by the grill fires, served by old men waiters in green-and-red jackets. It was a time warp, flash frozen in 1927. I liked it, it made me feel safe.

We were seated in the back room. Ron knew people. He introduced us — "my wife, Claire," and for a moment I thought he was going to introduce me as their daughter. But it was "and our friend Astrid." I beat back the sharpness of my disappointment with the thought that Marvel wouldn't have bothered to introduce me at all, and Amelia, well, we were lucky to get fed.

I drank my Shirley Temple and Claire pointed out movie stars in excited whispers. They didn't look very glamorous in real life. Smaller than you'd think, dressed plainly, just eating dinner. Jason Robards and another man sat across from us with two bored kids, the men talking business, the kids making bread balls and throwing them at each other.

Claire and Ron split a bottle of wine, and Claire gave me sips from her glass. She touched Ron constantly, his hair, arm, shoulder. I was jealous. I wanted her all to myself. I was aware it wasn't normal, normal daughters didn't get jealous of their fathers. They wished both their parents would disappear.

Ron took something from his pocket, concealed in his smooth hand. "For a job well done," he said.

He put it on my plate. It was a red velvet box, shaped like a heart. I opened it. Inside was a faceted lavender jewel on a gold chain. "Every girl needs a little jewelry," he said.

Claire clipped it around my neck. "Amethyst is a great healer," she whispered as she put it on me, kissing me on the cheek. "Only good times now." Ron leaned forward and I let him kiss me too.

I felt tears coming. They surprised me.

The food arrived and I watched them while we ate, Claire's dark glossy hair falling against her cheek, her large soft eyes. Ron's smooth man's face. I pretended that they were really my parents. The steak and the wine went to my head, and I imagined being the child of Claire and Ron Richards. Who was I, the real Astrid Richards? Doing well in school, of course I was going to college. I listened as they laughed, something about their days at Yale together, though I knew Ron was married to somebody else then, that he dumped his wife for Claire. I imagined myself at Yale, knee-deep in crisp fall leaves, in a thick camel's hair coat. I sat in dark paneled lecture halls looking at slides of Da Vinci. I was going to study in Tuscany my junior year. On Parents' Day, Claire and Ron came to visit, Claire wearing her pearls. She showed me where her dorm was.

I touched the amethyst around my neck. *Only good times now . . .*

RON WAS GONE most of the summer. He came home and she did his laundry and cooked too much food. He made phone calls, worked on his laptop computer, had meetings, checked his messages, and then he was gone again.

It threw Claire when he came and then went so soon, but at least she didn't pace at night anymore. She worked in her garden almost every day, wearing gloves and an enormous straw Chinese hat. Tending her tomatoes. She'd planted four different kinds — yellow and red cherry, Romas for spaghetti sauce, Beefsteaks big as a baby's head. We faithfully watched a TV show on Saturday mornings that told her how to grow things. She staked the tall delphiniums, debudded the roses for the biggest flowers. She weeded every day, and watered at dusk, filling the air with the scent of wet hot earth. Her peaked hat moved in the beds like a floating Balinese temple.

Sometimes I helped her, but mostly I sat under the Chinese elm and drew. She sang songs she learned when she was my age, "Are You Going to Scarborough Fair?" and "John Barleycorn Must Die." Her voice was trained, supple as leather, precise as a knife thrower's blade. Singing or talking, it had the same graceful quality, and an accent I thought at first was English, but then realized was the old-fashioned American of a thirties movie, a person who could get away with saying "grand." Too classic, they told her when she went out on auditions. It didn't mean old. It meant too beautiful for the times, when anything that lasted longer than six months was considered passé. I loved to listen to her sing, or tell me stories about her childhood in suburban Connecticut, it sounded like heaven to me.

When she left to audition, or go to ballet class, I liked to go into her bedroom, brush my hair with her silver brush, touch the clothes in her closet, shaped cotton dresses simple as vases, watercolor silks. On her dresser, I unstoppered the L'Air du Temps in the frosted glass bottle, two doves nestled together, and touched the scent to my wrists, behind my ears. Time's Air. I looked at myself in the mirror over her vanity. My hair gleamed the color of dull unbleached silk, brushed back from an off-center part, revealing the hair slightly curly at the hairline. Claire and her hairdresser said the bangs had to go. I never knew they didn't suit me before. I turned my face from side to side. The scars had all but disappeared. I could pass for beautiful.

Around my neck, the amethyst glinted. Before, I would have hidden it in the toe of a sock crammed into a shoe in the closet. But here, we wore our jewelry. We deserved it. "When a woman has jewelry, she wears it," Claire had explained. I had jewelry now. I was a girl with jewelry.

I tried on Claire's double strand of pearls in the mirror, ran the smooth, lustrous beads through my fingers, touched the coral rose of the clasp. The pearls weren't really white, they were a warm oyster beige, with little knots in between so if they broke, you only lost one. I wished my life could be like that, knotted up so that even if something broke, the whole thing wouldn't come apart.

"Dinner at eight? That would be grand," I said to myself in the mirror, like Katharine Hepburn, my fingers looped in the pearls.

Claire had a picture of me on her bureau, next to one of her and Ron, in a sterling silver frame. Nobody had ever framed a picture of me and set it on the dresser. I took the hem of my T-shirt, huffed on the glass and shined it. She had taken it a couple of weeks before, at the beach. I was squinting into the camera, laughing at something she said, my hair paler than the sand. She didn't frame the one I took of her, covered from head to toe in a long beach wrap, Chinese hat, and sunglasses. She looked like the Invisible Man. She only disrobed to go into the water, wading out to her thighs. She didn't like to swim.

"I know it's ridiculous," she said, "but I keep thinking I'm going to be sucked out to sea."

It wasn't the only thing she was afraid of.

She was afraid of spiders and supermarkets and sitting with her back to the door. "Bad chi," she said. She hated the color purple, and the numbers four and especially eight. She detested crowds and the nosy lady next door, Mrs. Kromach. I thought I was afraid of things, but Claire was way ahead of me. She joked about her fears, but it was the kind of joke where you knew people thought it was ridiculous, and you pretended you thought so too, but underneath you were completely serious. "Actors are always superstitious," she said.

She did my numerology. I was a 50, which was the same as a 32. I had the power to sway the masses. She was a 36, which was the same as a 27, the Scepter. A number of courage and power. She used to be a 22 before she was married, a 4. Very bad. "So you see, Ron saved my life." She laughed uneasily.

I couldn't imagine ever having, or wanting to have, the power to sway the masses, but if it made her feel good, I figured, what was the harm. I helped her out with projects meant to boost good chi. One day we bought square mirrors and I actually climbed to the roof of the house to put them on the red tiles, facing Mrs. Kromach's house. "So her bad chi will bounce back on her, the old bag."

There was a rose trellis over the front path, and she didn't like people who wouldn't go through it. Only goodness and love can pass through a rose arch, she said. She was uneasy if someone came in the back door. She wouldn't let me wear black. The first time I did, she told me, "Black belongs to Saturn, he's unfriendly to children."

I took off her pearls and put them back in the case under the scarves in her top left drawer. She kept most of her jewelry in a paper bag in the freezer, where she thought burglars wouldn't find it. But the pearls couldn't take being frozen, they had to stay warm.

In the right two drawers were her silk things, in light mid-tones, champagne and shell pink and ice blue, slips and nightgowns, bras and panties that matched. Everything folded and tucked with sachets. Below that, T-shirts in neat stacks, a white stack and a colored pile, celadon, mauve, taupe. To the left, shorts and light sweaters. Shawls on the bottom. Her winter clothes lay folded and sealed in zippered cases at the top of the closet.

This instinct to order and rituals was one of the things I liked best about Claire, her calendars and rules. She knew when it was time to put winter clothes away. I loved that. Her sense of order, graceful and eccentric, little secrets women knew, lingerie bags and matching underwear. She threw out my Starr underthings, full of holes, and bought me all new ones at a department store, discussing the fit of bras with the elderly saleslady. I wanted satin and lace, black and emerald green, but Claire gently overruled me. I pretended she was my mother and whined a bit before giving in.

CLAIRE HAD new photographs taken, actor's head shots. We went to Hollywood to pick them up from a shop on Cahuenga. In photographs, she looked different, focused, animated. In person she was thin, dreamy, as full of odd angles as a Picasso mademoiselle. The photographer, an old Armenian man with a sleepy eye, thought I should have photographs too. "She could model," he said to Claire. "I've seen worse."

My hand instinctively rose to touch the scars on my jaw. Couldn't he see how ugly I was?

Claire smiled, stroked my hair. "Would you like that?"

"No," I said, low, so the photographer wouldn't hear me.

"We'll keep it in mind," Claire said.

On the way back to the car in the heat of a pigeon-wing-pale afternoon, we passed an old hippie man with gray hair and a green army surplus bag strapped to his chest, asking people for money. Passersby shouldered his outstretched paper cup aside and crossed the street. He wasn't menacing enough for this line of work. I thought of myself panhandling in the liquor store parking lot, but it wasn't the same. I wasn't an alkie, a drug addict. I was only fifteen. He'd done it to himself.

"Come on," he said. "Help a guy out."

I was ready to cross, to escape this scarecrow of a man, but Claire looked over at him. She didn't know how to ignore people.

"Can you spare some change, lady? Anything'll help."

The light changed, but Claire wasn't paying attention. She was digging in her purse, emptying out her change. She never learned about street people, that if you showed them the least little kindness, they'd latch onto you like castor seeds. Claire only saw how thin he was, the limp where he must have been hit by a car while panhandling between traffic lights. My mother would have offered to shove him out in front of a bus, but Claire cared. She believed in the commonality of the soul.

The hippie man pocketed the money. "You're a real human being, lady. Most people won't look a man in the eye when he's down." He gave me an accusing look. "I don't care if a guy gives me something, I just want him to look me in the eye, you know what I'm saying?"

"I do," Claire said, in her voice that was cool water and soft hands.

"I worked steady all my life, but I pulled my back out, see. I never drank on the job. I never did."

"I'm sure you didn't." The stoplight turned red again. I

was ready to pull Claire out into traffic. Everywhere we went, people ended up telling her their sad stories. They could see she was too polite to just walk away. He came closer. She was probably the first normal person who'd listened to him for days.

"Unemployment only lasts so long," he said. I could smell him. Either he'd pissed on himself or someone else had done the honors. "Nobody gives a shit."

"Some people do," Claire said. The late afternoon sun was turning her dark hair red around the edges.

"You're a real human being," he said. "They're out of style now, though. Machines, that's what they want." He was breathing right into her face, but she was too sweet to turn her head. She didn't want to offend him. They always seemed to know that about her. "I mean, how many people they need to fry burgers?"

"Not enough. Or maybe too many." She smiled, insecure, shoving her windblown hair out of her face.

The light turned green, but we were going nowhere. Stalled in the stream at Sunset and Cahuenga. People walked around us like we were a hole in the sidewalk.

He stepped closer again, lowered his voice confidentially. "Do you think of me as a man?" He stuck his tongue through the slot of a missing tooth.

She flushed, shrugged her shoulders, embarrassed. Of course she didn't. I wanted to shove him off the curb.

"Women used to like me a lot. While I was working."

I could see the tension on her face, she wanted to back away, but she didn't want to hurt his feelings. She was twisting the bag of eight-by-ten glossies she'd just paid two hundred dollars for. A black Corvette went by, trailing rap music.

"You're a nice lady, but you wouldn't take your clothes off for me, would you."

She was bending her photographs, her sensitive face quivering with contradiction. "I don't . . ." she mumbled.

"I don't blame you. But you wouldn't." He looked so sad.

I took her arm. "Claire, we have to go now."

But she was too caught up in the homeless man who was pulling a mind trip on her. He had her snared.

"I miss women," he said. "The way they smelled. I miss that. Like you, whatever you've got on."

She wore her L'Air du Temps, out of place as a wildflower in a war zone. I was amazed he could detect her fragrance through his own stench.

But I knew what he meant. I loved the way she smelled too. I liked to sit on her bed as she combed and French-braided my hair. I could sit there as long as she wanted, just breathing the air where she was.

"Thank you," she whispered. That was Claire, afraid of hurting anyone's feelings, even this sad old bum.

"Can I smell your hair?" he asked.

She went pale. She had no boundaries. He could do anything, she wouldn't know how to stop him.

"Don't be scared," he said, holding up his hands, the nails like horn. "Look at all these people. I won't touch you."

She swallowed and nodded, closed her eyes as the man came close, lifted a section of her dark hair gently on the tips of his fingers, like it was a flower, and breathed in the scent. She shampooed with rosemary and cloves. The smile on his face.

"Thank you," he whispered, and backed away without turning around, leaving her standing at Cahuenga and Sunset, her eyes closed, clutching her bag of photographs of a different person entirely.

CLAIRE TOOK ME to see the Kandinsky show at the art museum. I'd never liked abstract art. My mother and her friends could go wild over a canvas that was just black and white pinstripes, or a big red square. I liked art that was of something. Cézanne card players, Van Gogh's boots. I liked tiny Mughal miniatures, and ink-brushed Japanese crows and cattails and cranes.

But if Claire wanted to see Kandinsky, we'd go see him.

I felt better when I got to the museum, the familiar plaza, the fountains, the muted lighting, the softened voices. The way Starr felt in church, that's how I felt at the art museum, both safe and elevated. Kandinsky wasn't all that abstract, I could still see the Russian cities with their turbaned towers, and horsemen three abreast with spears, cannons, and ladies in long gowns with high headdresses. Pure colors, like the illustrations in a picture book.

In the next room, the pictures were dissolving.

"Can't you feel the movement?" Claire said, pointing out a big angle on the canvas, the tip facing right, the fan left. The edge of her hands following the lines. "It's like an arrow."

The guard watched her excited hands, too close to the painting for his liking. "Miss?"

She flushed and apologized, like an A student who'd overslept once in her life. She pulled me back to sit on a bench, where she was safe to gesticulate. I tried to let myself feel it, the way Claire did. Things that weren't there, that might not be there.

"See," she said, quietly, keeping her eye on the guard. "The yellow comes toward you, the blue moves away. The yellow expands, the blue contracts."

The red, the yellow, this well of dark green — expanding, contracting, still pools with bleeding edges, an angle like a fist. A boy and a girl, arms around each other's shoulders, drifted past the pictures, like they were passing shopwindows.

"And see how he takes the edge away from the frame, making an asymmetrical edge?" She pointed to the lemon ribbon curving the left side.

I had heard people say things like this in museums, and had always thought they were just trying to impress their friends. But this was Claire, and I knew she really wanted me to understand. I stared at the painting, the angle, the ribbon. So much going on in Kandinsky, it was like the frames were having trouble keeping the pictures inside.

In another gallery, Claire stopped in front of a bunch of pencil sketches. Lines on paper, angles and circles, like pickup sticks and tiddlywinks. Like what you'd doodle while you were talking on the telephone.

"See this angle?" She pointed at a sharp angle in pencil, and then gestured over to the massive composition that all the sketches and oil studies led up to. "See it?" The angle dominated the canvas.

She drew my attention to various elements of the pencil sketches, circles, arcs, and I found them in the finished composition, in vibrant red, and a deep graded blue. He had all the elements right from the start. Each sketch held its own part of the idea, like a series of keys that you had to put all together to make the safe open. If I could stack them and hold them to the light, I would see the form of the completed composition. I stared, dumbfounded at the vision.

We walked arm in arm through the show, pointing out to each other details that recurred, the abstracted horsemen, the towers, the different kinds of angles, the color changing as a form crossed another form. Mainly, it was the sense of order, vision retained over time, that brought me to my knees.

I sat on a bench and took out my sketch pad, tried to draw the basic forms. Acute angles, arcs, like the movement of a clock. It was impossible. I needed color, I needed ink and a brush. I didn't know what I needed.

"Imagine the work to assemble all this in one place," Claire said. "The years of convincing people to lend their artworks."

I imagined Kandinsky's mind, spread out all over the world, and then gathered together. Everyone having only a piece of the puzzle. Only in a show like this could you see the complete picture, stack the pieces up, hold them to the light, see how it all fit together. It made me hopeful, like someday my life would make sense too, if I could just hold all the pieces together at the same time.

We went back twice a week for the rest of the summer. Claire bought me oil pastels so I could work in color without making the guards nervous. We would spend all day in a single room, looking at one picture. I had never done that before. A composition from 1913 presaged the First World War. "He was very sensitive. He could tell it was coming," Claire said. The blackness, the cannons, wild, a mood so violent and dark, of course he had to invent abstraction.

The return to Russia. The exuberance of the avant-garde, but the darkening suspicion that it was coming to a close, even as it was flowering. On to the Bauhaus in the twenties. Straight lines, geometric forms. You didn't let yourself go in times like that. You tried to find some underlying structure. I understood him perfectly. Finally, the move to Paris. Pinks and blues and lavenders. Organic forms again, for the first time in years. What a relief Paris must have been, the color, the ability to be soft again.

I wondered how I would paint our times. Shiny cars and wounded flesh, denim blue and zigzagged dog teeth, bits of broken mirror, fire and orange moons and garnet hearts.

IN THE FALL I signed up for honors classes again. Claire made me think it was worth trying. Of course you took the honors classes. Of course you wore your jewelry. Of course you signed up for art classes at the museum. Of course.

In the empty studio in the basement of the art museum, we waited for the teacher, Ms. Tricia Day. My palms sweated onto the portfolio case Claire had bought me. She wanted to sign me up for an adult class in painting. There were teen courses, in photography, fabric art, video. But no painting. "We'll go talk to the teacher," she said.

A woman came in. Small, middle-aged, with cropped gray hair. She wore khaki pants and black horn-rimmed glasses. She looked at us wearily, an overeager mother and her spoiled kid, asking for special treatment. I was embarrassed just being there, but Claire was surprisingly businesslike. Ms. Day went through my portfolio briskly, her eyes moving in sharp lines over the surfaces. The realistic things, Claire lying on the couch, poinsettias, and the L.A. Kandinskys. "Where have you studied?"

I shook my head. "Nowhere."

She finished the portfolio and handed it back to Claire. "Okay. We'll give it a try."

Every Tuesday night, Claire brought me to the museum, went home, and then returned three hours later to pick me up. I felt guilty for her willingness to do things for me, like I was using her. I heard my mother saying, "Don't be absurd. She wants to be used." But I didn't want to be like that. I wanted to be like Claire. Who but Claire would make sure I had art class, would give up a Tuesday night for me?

In art class, I learned to build a support, stretch canvas, gesso it smooth. Ms. Day had us experiment with color, with strokes. The stroke of the brush was the evidence of the gesture of your arm. A record of your existence, the quality of your personality, your touch, pressure, the authority of your movement. We painted still lifes. Flowers, books. Some of the ladies in class painted only tiny flowers. Ms. Day told them to paint bigger but they were too embarrassed. I painted flowers big as pizzas, strawberries magnified to a series of green triangles on a red ground, the patterns of the seeds. Ms. Day was spartan in her praise, blunt in her criticism. Every class there was somebody crying. My mother would have liked her. I liked her too.

I carefully edited what I wrote to my mother. Hello, how are you, how's the writing. I wrote about grades, gardening, art class, the smell of the Santa Anas and the scorched landscape, the blues of November, shortening of days. *Strate A's, home-come queen.* I sent her small drawings, watercolors the size of postcards, she didn't have much space. She loved the Kandinsky period, and my new work. I sent her a series of pencil drawings on onionskin paper. It was a self-portrait, but layered, a line here, a line there, one at a time, for her to figure out — she had to layer to get the whole thing. I didn't lay it out for her anymore. She had to work for it.

MY MOTHER WROTE that she had poems in *Kenyon Review* and in the all-poetry issue of *Zyzzyva*. I asked Claire if we could get them, and she took me up to Book Soup on the Strip, bought them both for me. There was a long poem about running in prison, that was a big part of her day. When she wasn't writing she was running the track, fifty, a hundred miles a week. She wore out her shoes every four months, and sometimes they'd give her new ones and sometimes they wouldn't. I had an idea.

I Xeroxed ten copies of the poem, and used them as the background for drawings. I sat at the table in the red-and-white kitchen and drew in oil pastel on top of her words, the feeling of running, of senseless, circular activity. Like her mind.

The rains had begun, they whispered outside the steamed kitchen window. Claire sat next to me with a cup of mint tea. "Tell me about her."

There was something that kept me from talking much about my mother to Claire. She was curious, like everyone else, my counselors at school, Ray, Joan Peeler, the editors of small literary journals. Poets in prison, the sheer paradox. I didn't know what to say. She murdered a man. She was my mother. I didn't know if I was like her or not. Mostly, I didn't want to talk about her. I wanted Claire to be something separate from my mother, I wanted them to be on different pages, and only I could hold them up to the light together.

Claire read the running poem again. "I love this line, *the back stretch, twenty years. A clock without hands.* Life in prison, it's unimaginable. *Three years gone, the beaten dirt around.* She must be so brave. How can she stand it?"

"She's never where she is," I said. "She's only inside her head."

"That must be wonderful." Claire stroked the side of the mug like the cheek of a child. "I wish I could do that."

I was glad she couldn't. Things touched Claire. Maybe too much, but at least they touched her. She couldn't twist things around in her mind, make the ends come out right. I looked at my mother's poem in *Kenyon*. So interesting that she was always the heroine, the outlaw, one against the rest. Never the villain.

"It's the difference between a true artist and everybody else." Claire sighed. "They can remake the world."

"You're an artist," I said.

"An actress," she said. "Not even that."

I'd seen a couple of Claire's movies now. She was transparent, heartbreaking. I would be afraid to be so vulnerable. I'd spent the last three years trying to build up some kind of a skin, so I wouldn't drip with blood every time I brushed up against something. She was naked, she peeled herself daily. In one film, she played a professor's wife, trembling, in pearls. In another, an eighteenth-century woman, a cast-off lover, in a convent. "You're a terrific actress," I said.

Claire shrugged, read the other poem, about a fight in prison. "I like your mother's violence. Her strength. How I admire that."

I dipped a small sumi brush into a bottle of ink, and in a few

262

strokes I inked in arcs and lines, a black spot. Her violence. Claire, what did you know about violence? My mother's strength? Well, she wasn't strong enough to avoid being the background of my art. Just the background. Her words just my canvas.

ONE SLUGGISHLY warm and hazy day, as I came home from school, Claire met me at the rose arch. "I got a part!" she called out before I was even through it.

She threw her head back and bared her throat to the weak winter sun, laughter bursting upward like a geyser. Hugging me, kissing me. She tried calling Ron in Russia, in the Urals, where he was covering a research convention for telekinetics. She couldn't reach him. Even that didn't take the sparkle from the air. She opened a bottle of Tattinger champagne, kept cold in the refrigerator for a special occasion. It came flooding out all over the glasses and the table, foaming down to the floor. We toasted the new job.

It wasn't a big part, but it was tricky. She played a character's elegant but drunken wife at a dinner party, in a long gown and diamonds. A lot of drinking and eating, she had to remember when to do what, so it would all cut together. "Always somebody's lonely wife," she sighed. "What is this, typecasting?"

She got the part because the director was a friend of Ron's, and the actress who was supposed to play the lonely wife, the director's ex-wife's sister, broke her collarbone at the last minute and they needed someone about the same height and coloring who could wear the strapless dress.

"At least I'm talking to the protagonist," she explained. "They can't cut the scene."

It was a small role, just five lines, a woman who shows up dead two scenes later. I helped her rehearse it, playing the hero. The hard part, she explained, was that she had to eat and drink during the scene, while she was talking. She had it down after the second try, but insisted on doing it over and over again. She was very particular to remember which word she paused and drank the wine on, exactly when she raised her fork, with which hand and how high. "Eating scenes are the worst," she explained. "Everything has to match." We rehearsed the part for a week. She was so serious about five lines. I didn't realize actors were so perfectionistic. I'd always thought they just went on and did it.

On the day of the shoot, she had a six a.m. makeup call. She told me not to get up, but I got up anyway. I sat with her as she made herself a smoothie, added protein powder, spirulina, brewer's yeast, vitamin E and C. She was very pale, and silent. Concentrating. She did a breathing exercise called Breathing Monkeys, singing Chinese syllables on both the exhale and the inhale. The exhaled tones were low and resonant, but the inhaled ones were weird, high and wailing. It was called chi gong, she said it kept her calm.

I gave her a quick hug as she was leaving. She'd taught me never to say "good luck." "Break a leg" was what you said to actors. "Break a leg!" I called after her, and cringed to see her trip on a sprinkler head.

I raced home after school, eager to hear how the shoot had

gone, and especially to hear about Harold McCann — the English star playing Guy — but she wasn't back yet. I did all my homework, even read ahead in English and history. By six it was dark, and not a call, not a clue. I hoped she hadn't gotten into an accident, she was so nervous this morning. But she probably went out for a drink with the other actors afterward, or dinner or something. Still, it wasn't like her not to call. She called if she was so much as running late at the market.

I fixed dinner, meat loaf and cornbread, a salad, and kept thinking, by the time it was ready she'd be home. At twenty after eight, I heard her car in the driveway. I met her at the door. "I made dinner," I said.

Her eye makeup in circles around her eyes. She ran past me, made for the bathroom. I heard her throwing up.

"Claire?"

She came out, lay down on the couch, covered her eyes with the back of her arm. I took her shoes off. "Can I get you something? Aspirin? Seven-Up?"

She started crying, deep harsh moans, turned her head away from me.

I got her some Tylenol and a glass of soda, watched as she took it in sips. "Vinegar. On a washcloth." She fell back onto the cushions. "White vinegar. Wring it out." Her voice hoarse as sandpaper. "And turn out the lights."

I turned off the lamps, soaked a washcloth in vinegar, wrung it out, brought it to her. I didn't dare ask what had happened.

"Seventeen takes," she said, placing the washcloth over her forehead and eyes. "Do you know how long that is? A hundred people waiting for you? I will never, ever act again."

I held her hand, sat on the floor by her prone figure in the dark room filled with vinegar fumes. I didn't know what to say. It was like watching someone you loved step on a land mine, all the parts flying around. You don't know what to do with the pieces.

"Put on Leonard Cohen," she whispered. "The first album, with 'The Sisters of Mercy.' "

I found the album, the one with Cohen's beaky face on the front, a saint rising from flames on the back, put it on. I sat by her, pressed her hand hard against my cheek. His sad singsong voice droning plaintively about the Sisters of Mercy, how he hoped you'd run into them too.

After a while she stopped crying, I think she fell asleep.

I'd never cared about someone so much that I could feel their pain before. It made me sick, that they could do something like that to Claire, and I wasn't there, to tell her, Quit, you don't have to do this. "I love you, Claire," I said softly.

I WENT TO art class one evening, and we waited for Ms. Day, but she didn't show up. One of the old lady students drove me home. I opened the door, hung with a Christmas wreath with little candied pears and porcelain doves, expecting to find Claire in the living room, reading one of her magazines and listening to music, but she wasn't there.

I found her sitting on my bed, cross-legged, reading my mother's papers. Letters from prison, poet's journals, personal papers, all fanned out around her. She looked pale, absorbed, biting the nail of her ring finger. I didn't know what I was supposed to do. I was outraged, I was scared. She shouldn't have been reading those things. I needed to keep them separate. I didn't want her to have anything to do with my mother, anything I couldn't control. And now she'd gone and opened the box. Like Pandora. Letting out all the evil. They were always so fascinated by Ingrid Magnussen. I felt myself retreating again, into her shadow. These were my things. Not even mine. I trusted her.

"What are you doing?"

She jumped, throwing the notebook she was reading into the air. Her mouth opened to explain, then closed. Opened again. No sound came. When she was upset, she couldn't say a thing. She tried gathering the offending materials with trembling hands, but they came in too many shapes, they scattered under her awkward clutchings. Defeated, she let them fall, closed her eyes, covered her face with her hands. She reminded me of Caitlin, who thought we couldn't see her if she couldn't see us. "Don't hate me," she said.

"Why, Claire? I would have shown you if you had asked."

I started to collect the notebooks, rice paper bound in string, Italian marbleized notebooks, Amsterdam school copybooks, smooth-bound, leather-bound, tied with shoelaces. My mother's journals, my absence written in the margins. None of this was about me. Even the letters. Only her.

"I was depressed. You were gone. She seemed so strong."

She was looking for a role model? I almost had to laugh. Claire admiring my mother made me want to slap her. Wake up! I wanted to scream. Ingrid Magnussen could damage you just passing by on the way to the bathroom.

And now she'd read the letters. She knew that I'd refused to discuss her with my mother. I imagined how it must have hurt her. Now I wished I'd thrown them out, not lugged them around like a curse. Ingrid Magnussen. How could I explain? I didn't want my mother to know about you, Claire. You're the one good thing that ever happened to me. I didn't want to take any chances. How my mother would hate you. She doesn't want me to be happy, Claire. She liked it that I hated Marvel. It made her feel close to me. An artist doesn't need to be happy, she said. If I were happy, I wouldn't need her, she meant. I might forget her. And she was right. I just might.

She scolded me in those letters. *What do I care about a 98 on a spelling test? Your flower garden. You're so boring, I don't even recognize you. Who are these people you're living with now? What are you really thinking?* But I never told her a thing.

"You want to know about my mother?" I took a gray ribboned notebook, opened it, and handed it to Claire. "Here. Read it."

She took her hands down, her eyes puffy and red, her nose running. She hiccupped and took it from me. I didn't have to look over her shoulder. I knew what it said.

Spread a malicious rumor.

Let a beloved old person's dog out of the yard.

Suggest suicide to a severely depressed person.

"What is this?" she asked.

Tell a child it isn't very attractive or bright.

Put Drano in glassine folded papers and leave them on street-corners.

Throw handfuls of useless foreign coins into a beggar's cup, and make sure they thank you profusely. "God bless you, miss."

"It's not real, though," Claire said. "It's not like she actually does these things."

I only shrugged. How could Claire understand a woman like my mother? She would write these lists for hours, laughing until tears flowed.

Claire looked at me hungrily, pleading. How could I stay angry with her? My mother had no idea what my favorite food was, where I'd live if I could live anywhere in the world. Claire was the one who discovered me. She knew I'd want to live in Big Sur, in a cabin with a woodstove and a spring, that I liked green apple soap, that *Boris Godunov* was my favorite opera, that I was afraid of milk. She helped me pack the papers back into the box, shut it, and put it under the bed.

18

RON AND CLAIRE were fighting again in their room. I could hear it as I lay in my bed, the rabbit crouching on my wall, his ears erect and trembling. Claire wanted Ron to quit his job, find something to do that didn't involve cattle mutilations or witchcraft in the Pueblos.

"What do you want me to do, wash dishes?" It was rare to hear Ron raise his voice. But he was tired, just back from Russia, he hadn't expected a fight. Usually it was a home-cooked meal and kisses and clean sheets. "I'm earning a living. It's just a job, Claire. Jesus, sometimes I just don't know what goes on in your head."

But it was a lie. What Ron did was peddle fear. There was quite a market, it seemed. Everywhere, people were frightened. Threatening shapes lurked at the edges of vision, in the next car, at the ATM, maybe waiting for them in the hall with a .38. There was poison in supermarket toothpaste. Ebola, hepatitis C. Husbands disappeared on the way to the liquor store. Children showed up dead in ditches without their hands. The picture was pulled away from the frame, the outlines were gone. People wanted monsters and ghosts and voices from beyond the grave. Something foreign, intentional, not senseless and familiar as a kid getting shot for his leather jacket.

That's what Ron supplied. Fear in a frame. Aliens are always preferable to confused, violent acts. It was a career steeped in cynicism, pumped through with hypocrisy.

Her voice in reply was like bending sheet metal.

But I could understand him word for word. "What, you think I come off a fourteen-hour day, jetlagged, at some spoon-bending convention in Yakutsk, ready to party? Hey, wow, bring on the bimbos! Maybe you should try getting some work, and remember what it's like to be wiped out at the end of a day."

I felt his words burn her flesh like a lash. I tried to hear what she was saying, but her voice faded to a murmur. Claire couldn't defend herself, she curled up like a leaf under a glass.

"Astrid doesn't need you waiting with the milk and the cookies. Jesus, Claire! She's a young woman. I think she'd like spending a few hours by herself. Maybe make some friends of her own if you'd give her a chance."

But I did need her, Ron. Nobody ever waited for me when I got home from school — and never milk. He didn't even know that much. I mattered to her. Couldn't he understand what that meant to me, and to her? If he cared, he would never say such things to her. How dare he pretend that he loved her. I cracked open my door to see if I could hear her, but she must have been whispering.

"Of course they stopped calling. Gloria said she called and called and you never picked up. Of course they gave up."

Now all I could hear was her crying. She cried the way

children do, sobbing, hiccupping, nose running. And the soothing tones of his voice.

I could picture him, taking her in his arms, rocking her against his chest, stroking her hair, and she'd let him, that was the worst part of it. And they'd make love, and she'd fall asleep, thinking he was so kind, after all, he must love her. It would be all better. That was how he did it. Hurt her, and then made it all better. I hated him. He came home, upset her, when he was just going to leave her again.

A LETTER CAME in the mail, from my mother. I started to open it when I realized it wasn't for me. It was addressed to Claire. What was my mother doing writing to Claire? I never told her about Claire. Should I give it to her? I decided I couldn't take the chance. My mother might say anything. Might threaten her, might lie, or frighten her. I could always say I opened it by accident. I took it into my room, slitted it open.

> *Dear Claire,*
>
> *Yes, I think it would be marvelous if you'd visit. It's been so long since I've seen Astrid, I don't know if I'd recognize her — and I'm always delighted to meet my loyal readers. I will put you on my visitors list — you've never been convicted of a felony, have you?*
>
> *Just teasing.*
>
> *Your friend,*
> *Ingrid.*

The idea that they corresponded filled me with a sickening dread. *Your friend, Ingrid.* She must have written after I'd caught her reading in my room at Christmastime. I felt betrayed, helpless, anxious. I would have confronted her with it, but I'd have had to admit I'd opened her mail. So I tore up the letter and burned it in my wastebasket. Hopefully she would just be depressed that my mother never wrote back, and give up.

IT WAS FEBRUARY, a gray morning so overcast we couldn't see the Hollywood Hills from our yard. We were going to visit my mother. Claire had set it up. She put on a miniskirt, turtleneck, and tights, all in mahogany brown, frowned in the mirror. "Maybe jeans would be better."

"No denim," I said.

The idea of this meeting was almost too much to bear. I could only lose. My mother could hurt her. Or she could win her over. I didn't know which was worse. Claire was mine, someone who loved me. Why did my mother have to get in the middle? But that was my mother, she always had to be the center of attention, everything had to be about her.

I hadn't seen her since Starr. Marvel refused to let the van people take me, she thought the less I saw her the better. I looked in the mirror, imagining what my mother would think of me now. The scars on my face were just the start. I'd been through a few things since then. I wouldn't know how to be with her now, I was too big to hide in her silences. And now I had Claire to worry about.

I touched my hand to my forehead and told Claire, "I think I'm coming down with something."

"Stage fright," she said, smoothing the skirt with the palms of her hands. "I'm having a bit myself."

I had second thoughts about my clothes too, a long skirt and Doc Martens, thick socks, a crocheted sweater with a lace collar from Fred Segal, where all trendy young Hollywood shopped. My mother was going to hate it. But I had nothing to change into, all my clothes were like that now.

We drove east for an hour. Claire chatted nervously. She never could stand a silence. I looked out the windows, sucked a peppermint for carsickness, nestled into my thick Irish sweater. Gradually, the suburbs thinned out, replaced by lumberyards and fields, the smell of manure, and long, fog-clad views framed by lines of windbreak eucalyptus. CYA, the men's prison. It had been more than two years since I'd last come this way, a very different girl in pink shoes. I even recognized the little market. Coke, 12 pack, $2.49. "Turn here."

We drove back along the same blacktop road to the CIW, the steam stack and the water tower, the guard tower that marked the edge of the prison. We parked in the visitors lot.

Claire took a deep breath. "This doesn't look so bad."

The crows cawed aggressively in the ficus trees. It was freezing cold. I pulled my sweater down over my hands. We passed through the guard tower. Claire brought a book for my mother, *Tender Is the Night*. Fitzgerald, Claire's favorite, but the guards wouldn't let her bring it in. My boots set off the metal detector. I had to take them off for the guards to search. The jangle of keys, the slam of the gate, walkie-talkies, these were the sounds of visiting my mother.

We sat at a picnic table under the blue overhang. I watched the gate where my mother would come in, but Claire was looking the wrong way, toward Reception, where the new prisoners milled around or pushed brooms — they volunteered to sweep, they were so bored. Most were young, one or two over twenty-five. Their dead-looking faces wished us nothing good.

Claire shivered. She was trying to be brave. "Why are they staring at us like that?"

I opened my hand, examined the lines in the palm, my fate. Life would be hard. "Don't look at them."

It was cold, but now I was sweating, waiting for my mother. Who knew, maybe they would become friends. Maybe my mother wasn't playing a game, or not too ugly a one. Claire could keep her in postage, and she would be a nice character witness someday.

I saw my mother, waiting while the CO opened the gate. Her hair was long again, forming a pale scarf across the front of her blue dress, down one breast. She hesitated, she was as nervous as I was. So beautiful. She always surprised me with her beauty. Even when she had just been away for a night, I'd see her and catch my breath. She was thinner than the last time I'd seen her, all the excess flesh had been burned away. Her eyes had become even brighter, I could feel them from the gate. She was very upright, muscular, and tan. She looked less like a Lorelei now, more like an assassin from *Blade Runner*. She strode up, smiling, but I felt the uncertainty in her hands, stiff on my shoulders. We looked into each other's eyes, and I was astonished to find that we were the same height. Her eyes were searching within me, trying to find something to recognize. They made me suddenly shy, embarrassed of my fancy clothes, even of Claire. I was ashamed of the idea that I could escape her, even of wanting to. Now she knew me. She hugged me, and held her hand out to Claire.

"Welcome to Valhalla," she said, shaking Claire's hand.

I tried to imagine how my mother must be feeling right then, meeting the woman I'd been living with, a woman I liked so much I hadn't written anything about her. Now my mother could see how beautiful she was, how sensitive, the child's mouth, the heart-shaped face, the delicacy of her neck, her freshly cut hair.

Claire smiled with relief that my mother had made the first move. She didn't understand the nature of poisons.

My mother sat down next to me, put her hand over mine, but it wasn't so large anymore. Our hands were growing into the same shape. She saw that too, held her palm to mine. She looked older than the last time I saw her, lines etching into her tanned face, around the eyes and thin mouth. Or maybe it was just in comparison to Claire. She was spare, dense, sharp, steel to Claire's wax. I prayed to a God I didn't believe in to please let this be over soon.

"It's not at all what I thought," Claire said.

"It doesn't really exist," my mother said, waving her hand in an elegant gesture. "It's an illusion."

"You said that in your poem." A new poem, in *Iowa Review*. About a woman turning into a bird, the pain of the new feathers coming in. "It was exquisite."

I winced at her old-fashioned, actressy diction. I could imagine my mother mocking her later to her cellblock sisters. But I couldn't protect Claire now. It was too late. I saw that the perennial hint of irony in the corners of my mother's lips had now been etched into a permanent line, the tattoo of a gesture.

My mother crossed her legs, tanned and muscular as carved oak, bare under her blue dress, white sneakers. "My daughter says you're an actress." She wore no sweater in the cold grayness of the morning. The fog suited her, I smelled the sea on her, although we were a hundred miles from any ocean.

Claire twisted her wedding ring, it was loose on her thin fingers. "To tell you the truth, my career's a disaster. I botched my last job so badly, I'll probably never work again."

Why did she always have to tell the truth? I should have told her, certain people should always be lied to.

My mother instinctively felt for the crack in Claire's personal history, like a rock climber in fog sensing fingerholds in a cliff face. "Nerves?" she said kindly.

Claire leaned closer to my mother, eager to share confidences. "It was a nightmare," she said, and began to describe the awful day.

Overhead the clouds roiled and clotted, like dysentery, and I felt sick. Claire was afraid of so many things, she only went thigh-deep into the ocean because she was afraid of being swept under. So why couldn't she feel the undertow? My mother's smile, so kind-looking. There's a riptide here, Claire. Lifeguards have had to rescue stronger swimmers than you.

"They treat actors so badly," my mother said.

"I've had it." Claire slid her garnet heart pendant along its chain, tucked it under her lip. "No more. Dragging myself to auditions, just to have them look at me for two seconds and decide I'm too ethnic for orange juice, too classic for TV moms."

My mother's profile sharp against the chinchilla sky. You

277

could have drawn a straight line using the edge of her nose. "What are you, all of thirty?"

"Thirty-five next month." The truth, the whole truth, and nothing but the truth. She would be the witness from hell. She couldn't resist the urge to lie down and bare her breast to the lance. "That's why Astrid and I get along. Scorpio and Pisces understand one another." She winked at me across the table.

My mother didn't like that we understood each other, Claire and I. I could tell by the way she was pulling my hair. The crows cawed and flapped their dull, glossy wings. But she smiled at Claire. "Astrid and I never understood each other. Aquarius and Scorpio. She's so secretive, haven't you found that? I never knew what she was thinking."

"I wasn't thinking anything," I said.

"She opens up," Claire said cheerfully. "We talk all the time. I had her chart done. It's very well balanced. Her name is lucky too." The ease with which Claire knelt at the block, stretched her neck out, still chattering away.

"She hasn't been very lucky so far," my mother said, almost purring. "But maybe her luck is changing." Couldn't Claire smell the oleanders cooking down, the slight bitter edge of the toxin?

"We just adore her," Claire said, and for a moment I saw her as my mother saw her. Actressy, naive, ridiculous. No, I wanted to say, stop, don't judge her based on this. She doesn't audition well. You don't know her at all. Claire just kept talking, unaware of what was going on. "She's doing wonderfully well, she's on the honor roll this year. We're trying to keep that old grade point average up." She made a half-circle gesture

278

with her fist, a Girl Scout gesture, hearty and optimistic. *The old grade point average.* I was mortified and I didn't want to be. When would my mother have worked with me, hour after hour, to raise the old grade point average? I wanted to wrap Claire in a blanket the way you do with someone who's on fire, and roll her in the grass to save her.

My mother leaned toward Claire, her blue eyes snapping like blue fire. "Put a pyramid over her desk. They say it improves memory," she said with a straight face.

"My memory's fine," I said.

But Claire was intrigued. Already my mother had found a weak spot, and I was sure would soon find more. And Claire didn't realize for a moment that my mother was jerking her chain. Such innocence. "A pyramid. I hadn't thought of that. I practice feng shui, though. You know, where you put the furniture and all." Claire beamed, thinking my mother was a kindred soul, rearranging the furniture for good energy, talking to houseplants.

I wanted to change the conversation before she started talking about Mrs. Kromach and the mirrors on the roof. I wished she'd glued a mirror right to her forehead. "We live right near the big photo labs on La Brea," I interjected. "Off Willoughby."

My mother continued as if I hadn't spoken. "And your husband is even in the business. The paranormal, I mean." Those ironic commas in the corners of her mouth. "You've got the inside scoop." She stretched her arms over her head, I could imagine the little pops up and down her spine. "You should tell him, his show is very popular in here."

She rested her arm on my shoulder. I discreetly shrugged it

off. I might have to be her audience, but I wasn't her co-conspirator.

Claire didn't even notice. She giggled, zipping her garnet heart on its thin chain. She reminded me of the tarot card where the boy is looking up at the sun as he is about to walk off a cliff. "Actually, he thinks it's just a big joke. He doesn't believe in the supernatural."

"You'd think that would be dangerous in his line of work." My mother tapped on the orange plastic of the picnic table. I could see her mind winding out, leaping ahead. I wanted to throw something in there, stop the machine.

"I told him just that," Claire said, leaning forward, dark eyes shining. "They had a ghost that almost killed someone this fall." Then she stopped, unsure, thinking she'd made a gaffe, talking about murder in front of my mother. I could read her skin like a newspaper.

"You don't worry about him?"

Claire was grateful my mother had let her little faux pas gently slide by. She didn't see, my mother had hold of what she really wanted. "Oh, Ingrid, if you only knew. I don't think people should fool around with things they don't believe in. Ghosts are real, even if you don't believe in them."

Oh, we knew about ghosts, my mother and I. They take their revenge. But rather than admit that, my mother quoted Shakespeare. *"There are more things in heaven and earth, Horatio, than are dreamt of in your philosophy."*

Claire clapped her hands in delight, that someone else had quoted the Bard for a change. Ron's friends always missed her references.

My mother flicked her long hair back, draped her arm around me again. "It's like not believing in electricity just because you can't see it." Her bright blue assassin's eyes smiled at Claire. I knew what she was thinking. *Can't you see what an idiot this woman is, Astrid? How could you prefer her to me?*

"Absolutely," Claire said.

"I don't believe in electricity, either," I said. "Or Hamlet. He's just a construct. A figment of some writer's imagination."

My mother ignored me. "Does he have to travel a good deal, your husband? What's his name again? Ron?" She wrapped a strand of my hair around her little finger, keeping me in check.

"He's always gone," Claire admitted. "He wasn't even home for Christmas." She was playing with that garnet heart again, sliding it up and down the chain.

"It must be lonely for you," my mother said. Sadly. So sympathetic. I wished I could get up and run away, but I would never leave Claire here alone with her.

"It used to be," Claire said. "But now I have Astrid."

"Such a wonderful girl." My mother stroked the side of my face with her work-roughened finger, deliberately scraping my skin. I was a traitor. I had betrayed my master. She knew why I'd kept Claire in the background. Because I loved her, and she loved me. Because I had the family I should have had all this time, the family my mother never thought was important, could never give me. "Astrid, do you mind letting us talk for a moment alone? Some grown-up things."

I looked from her to my foster mother. Claire smiled. "Go ahead. Just for a minute." Like I was a kid who had to be encouraged to get into the sandbox. She didn't know how long a minute could be, what might happen in a minute.

I got up reluctantly and went over to the fence closest to the road, ran my fingertips over the bark of a tree. Overhead, a crow stared down at me with its soulless gaze, squawked in a voice that was almost human, as if it was trying to tell me something. "Piss off," I said. I was getting as bad as Claire, listening to birds.

I watched them, leaning toward each other over the table. My mother tanned and towheaded, in blue, Claire pale and dark, in brown. It was surreal, Claire here with my mother, at an orange picnic table at Frontera. Like a dream where I was naked and standing in line at the student store. I just forgot to get dressed. I was dreaming this, I told myself, and I could wake up.

Claire pressed her palm to her forehead, like she was taking her temperature. My mother took Claire's other thin hand between her large ones. My mother was talking without stopping, low, reasonable, I'd seen her hypnotize a cat this way. Claire was upset. What was she telling her? I didn't care what my mother's game was. Her time was up. We were leaving, she was staying. She couldn't screw this up for me, no matter what she said.

They both looked up as I rejoined them. My mother glared at me, then veiled it with a smile, patted Claire's hand. "You just remember what I told you."

Claire said nothing. Serious now. All her giggles had vanished, her pleasure at finding another person who quoted Shakespeare. She stood up, pale fingernails propped on the tabletop. "I'll meet you at the car," she said.

My mother and I watched her go, her long legs in their matte brown, the quietness of her movements. My mother had taken all the electricity away, the liveliness, the charm. She scooped her out, the way the Chinese used to cut open the skull of a living monkey and eat its brains with a spoon.

"What did you tell her?"

My mother leaned back on the bench, folding her arms behind her head. Yawned luxuriously, like a cat. "I hear she's having trouble with her husband." She smiled, sensually, rubbing the blond down on her forearms. "It's not you, is it? I know you have an attraction to older men."

"No, it's not me." She couldn't play with me the way she played with Claire. "You stay out of it."

I'd never dared speak to her that way before. If she were not stuck here at Frontera, I would never have had the nerve. But I would be leaving and she would be staying, and in that fact there was a strength I would never have found if she were out.

I could see it startled her to have me oppose her. It angered her that I felt I could, but she was controlled, I could see her switch gears. She gave me a smile of slow irony. "Your mommy just wants to help, precious," she said, licking her words like a cat lapping cream. "I have to do what I can for my new friend."

We both watched Claire out past the cyclone fencing, as she walked to the Saab, distracted. She bumped into the fender of a station wagon. "Just leave her alone."

"Oh, but it's fun," my mother said, bored with the pretense. She always preferred to bring me behind the scenes. "Easy, but fun. Like drowning kittens. And in my current situation, I have to take my fun where I can. What I want to know is, how could you stand to live with Poor Claire? Did you know there was an entire order, the Poor Claires? I would imagine it's a terrible bore. Keeping up the old grade point average and whatnot. Pathetic."

"She's a genuinely nice person," I said, turning away from her. "You wouldn't know about that."

My mother snorted. "God forbid, the nice disease. I would have thought you'd outgrown fairy tales."

I kept my back to her. "Don't screw it up for me."

"Who, me?" My mother was laughing at me. "What could I do? I'm a poor prisoner. A little bird with a broken wing."

I turned around. "You don't know what it's been like." I bent over her, one knee on the bench beside her. "If you love me, you'll help me."

She smiled, slow and treacherous. "Help you, darling? I'd rather see you in the worst kind of foster hell than with a woman like that." She reached up to push a lock of hair away from my face, and I jerked away. She grabbed my wrist, forcing me to look at her. Now she was dead serious. What was under the games was pure will. I was terrified to struggle. "What are you going to learn from a woman like that?" she said. "How to pine artistically? Twenty-seven names for tears?" A guard made a motion toward us, and she quickly dropped my wrist.

She stood and kissed me on the cheek, embraced me lightly. We were the same height but I could feel how strong she was, she was like the cables that held up bridges. She hissed in my ear, "All I can say is, keep your bags packed."

*

CLAIRE STARED out at the road. A tear slipped from her over-filled eyes. *Twenty-seven names for tears*. But no, that wasn't my thought. I refused to be brainwashed. This was Claire. I put my hand on her shoulder as she made the turn onto the rural highway. She smiled and patted it with her small, cold one. "I think I did well with your mom, don't you?"

"You did," I told her, gazing out the window so I wouldn't have to lie to her face. "She really liked you."

A tear rolled down her cheek, and I brushed it away with the back of my hand. "What did she say to you?"

Claire shook her head, sighed. She started the windshield wipers, though it was only a mist, turned them off when they started squeaking on the dry glass. "She said I was right about Ron. That he was having an affair. I knew it anyway. She just confirmed it."

"How would she know," I said angrily. "For God's sake, Claire, she just met you."

"All the signs are there." She sniffled, wiped her nose on her hand. "I just didn't want to see them." But then she smiled. "Don't concern yourself. We'll work it out."

I SAT AT MY DESK under the ridiculous pyramid, drawing my self-portrait, looking in a hand mirror. I was doing it in pen, not glancing down, trying not to lift the pen from the paper. One line. The squarish jaw, the fat unsmiling lips, the round reproachful eyes. Broad Danish nose, mane of pale hair. I drew myself until I could make a good likeness even with my eyes closed, until I'd memorized the pattern of the movement in my hand, in my arm, the gesture of my face, until I could see my face on the wall. I'm not you, Mother. I'm not.

Claire was supposed to go to an audition. She had told Ron she would, but she had me call in and say she was sick. She was soaking in the bathtub with her lavender oil and a chunk of amethyst, trying to soothe her jagged edges. Ron was supposed to be home on Friday, but something came up. His trips home were handholds for her, so she could swing from one square on the calendar to the next. When he said he was going to come home and didn't, she swung forward and grasped thin air, fell.

I intercepted a letter from prison from my mother to Claire. In it, my mother advised a love potion to put in his food, but everything in the formula she sent looked poisonous to me. I drew a picture over her letter, a series of serpentine curves speared by an angle, put it in a new envelope and sent it back to her.

In the living room, Claire played her Leonard Cohen. Suzanne taking her down to the place by the river.

I kept drawing my face.

19

By April, the desert had already sucked spring from the air like blotting paper. The Hollywood Hills rose unnaturally clear, as if we were looking at them through binoculars. The new leaves were wilting in the heat that left us sweating and dispirited in the house with the blinds down.

Claire brought out the jewelry she kept in the freezer and dumped it onto her bed, a pirate's treasure, deliciously icy. Freezing strands of green jade beads with jeweled clasps, a pendant of amber enclosing a fossilized fern. I pressed it, cold, to my cheek. I draped an antique crystal bracelet down the part in my hair, let it lap on my forehead like a cool tongue.

"That was my great-aunt Priscilla's," Claire said. "She wore it to her presentation ball at the Waldorf-Astoria, just before the Great War." She lay on her back in her underwear, her hair dark with sweat, a smoky topaz bracelet across her forehead intersected by an intricate gold chain that came to rest on the tip of her nose. She was painfully thin, with sharp hipbones and ribs stark as a carved wooden Christ. I could see her beauty mark above the line of her panties. "She was a field nurse at Ypres. A very brave woman."

Every bracelet, every bead, had a story. I plucked an onyx ring from the pile between us on the bed, rectangular, its black slick surface pierced by a tiny diamond. I slipped it on, but it was tiny, only fit my smallest finger, above the knuckle. "Whose was this?" I held it out so she could see it without moving her head.

"Great-grandmother Matilde. A quintessential Parisienne."

Its owner dead a hundred years, perhaps, but still she made me feel large and ill bred. I imagined jet-black hair, curls, a sharp tongue. Her black eyes would have caught my least awkwardness. She would have disapproved of me, my gawky arms and legs, I would have been too large for her little chairs and tiny gold-rimmed porcelain cups, a moose among antelope. I gave it to Claire, who slipped it right on.

The garnet choker, icy around my neck, was a wedding present from her mill-owning Manchester great-grandfather to his wife, Beatrice. The gold jaguar with emerald eyes I balanced on my knee was brought back from Brazil in the twenties by her father's aunt Geraldine Woods, who danced with Isadora Duncan. I was wearing Claire's family album. Maternal grandmothers and paternal great-aunts, women in emerald taffeta, velvet and garnets. Time, place, and personality locked into stone and silver filigree.

In comparison to this, my past was smoke, a story my mother once told me and later denied. No onyxes for me, no aquamarines memorializing the lives of my ancestors. I had only their eyes, their hands, the shape of a nose, a nostalgia for snowfall and carved wood.

Claire dripped a gold necklace over one closed eye socket, jade beads in the other. She spoke carefully, nothing slid off.

"They used to bury people like this. Mouths full of jewels and a gold coin over each eye. Fare for the ferryman." She drizzled her coral necklace into the well of her navel, and her pearl double strand, between her breasts. After a minute, she picked up the pearls, opened her mouth and let the strand drop in, closed her lips over the shiny eggs. Her mother had given her the pearls when she married, though she didn't want her to marry a Jew. When Claire told me, she expected me to be horrified, but I'd lived with Marvel Turlock, Amelia Ramos. Prejudice was hardly a surprise. The only thing I wondered was why would she give her pearls.

Claire lay still, pretending to be dead. A jeweled corpse in her pink lace lingerie, covered with a fine drizzle of sweat. I wasn't sure I liked this new game. Through the French doors, in the foot of space showing under the blinds, I could see the garden, left wild this spring. Claire didn't garden anymore, no pruning and weeding under her Chinese peaked hat. She didn't stake the flowers, and now they bloomed ragged, the second-year glads tilting to one side, Mexican evening primroses annexing the unmowed lawn.

Ron was away again, twice in one month, this time in Andalusia taping a piece about Gypsies. Out combing the world for what was most bizarre, racking up frequent flier miles. If he wanted to see something weird and uncanny, he should have just walked into his own bedroom and seen his wife lying on the bed in her pink lace panties and bra, covered in jade and pearls, pretending she was dead. Underneath the

bed, the voodoo box, magnets and clippers and pens, sealed
Polaroid photographs, conjured him home.

Suddenly, she was gagging on the pearls. She sat up, retching. The jewels fell from her body. She pulled the strand of
pearls from her mouth, catching it in her hand. She was so
pale, her mouth seemed unnaturally red by comparison, and
she had dark circles under her eyes. She slumped over the cluster of lustrous eggs, wet with spit, on the edge of the bed with
her back to me, her spine threaded like jade.

She reached back for my hand, her nails dirty, tips small and
sensitive as a child's, the rings incongruous as gumball machine
prizes. I took her hand. She brought my hand around to her
face, pressing its back against her wet cheek. She was burning
up. I rested my face on her shoulder, her back was like fire.
"Ron'll be back soon," I tried to reassure her.

She nodded, head heavy on her slender neck, like one of her
drooping tulips, the knobs of her spine like a diamondback's
rattle. "It's so hot already. What will I do when summer
comes?"

She was all skin and nerves, no substance, no weight. She
was her own skin kite, stretched before dry violent winds.

"We should go to the beach," I suggested.

She shook her head, fast, as if a fly had landed on her. "It's
not that."

I was sitting on one of the jewels, it was digging into my
hip. I freed one of my hands and reached under myself, pulled
it out. It was an aquamarine, big as an almond in the shell.
Aquamarines grew with emeralds, Claire told me. But emeralds
were fragile and always broke into smaller pieces, while aquamarines were stronger, grew huge crystals without any trouble,

so they weren't worth as much. It was the emerald that didn't break that was the really valuable thing.

I handed her the ice-blue stone, the color of my mother's eyes. She put it on her forefinger, where it hung like a doorknob on a rope. She gazed into it. "This belonged to my mother. My father got it for her to celebrate an around-the-world cruise." She took it off. "It was too big for her too."

Next door, Mrs. Kromach's parrot whistled the same three notes in an ascending scale, three and a half notes apart. An ice-cream truck rolled down the street, playing "Pop Goes the Weasel." Claire lay down on her back so she could look at me, one hand behind her head. She was very beautiful, even now, her dark hair loose around her shoulders, wet at the hairline, her dark eyebrows arched and glossy, her small breasts curved in pink lace.

"If you were going to kill yourself, how would you do it?" she asked.

I turned onto my stomach, sorted through the jewelry. I tried on a gold bangle. It wouldn't fit over my hand. I thought of my suicides, the way I would run my death through my fingers like jet beads. "I wouldn't."

She laced an Indian silver necklace onto her flat stomach, strands of hairlike tubes making metal into a fluid like mercury. "Well, say you wanted to."

"It's against my religion." Sweat trickled down between my breasts, pooled in my navel.

"What religion is that?"

"I'm a survivalist."

She wouldn't allow that. I wasn't playing. It was against the rules. "Just say you did. Say you were very old and had a horrible incurable cancer."

"I'd get lots of Demerol and wait it out." I was not going to discuss suicide with Claire. It was on my mother's list of anti-social acts. I wasn't going to tell her the surest way, the bone cancer boy's plan, injecting an air bubble into your vein and letting it move through your blood like a pearl. I was sure her aunt Priscilla used that once or twice on the battlefield when the morphine ran out. Then there was a load of cyanide at the back of the tongue, the way they did it to cats. It was very fast. When you committed suicide, you didn't want something slow. Someone could walk in, someone could save you.

Claire clasped her hand to one knee, rocked a little, up and down her spine. "You know how I'd do it?"

She was pulling me down that road and I wasn't going to go there. "Let's go to the beach, okay? It's so hot, it's making us crazy."

She didn't even hear me. Her eyes looked dreamy, like someone in love. "I'd gas myself. That's the way. They say it's just like going to sleep."

She reminded me of a woman lying down in snow. Just lying down for a little while, she was so tired. She'd been walking so long, she just wanted to rest, and it wasn't as cold as she thought. She was so sleepy. It was the surrender she wanted. To stop fighting the storm and the enveloping night, to lie down in whiteness and sleep. I understood. I used to dream that I was skin-diving down a coral wall. Euphoria set in as the nitrogen built up in my bloodstream, and the only direction was down into darkness and forgetting.

I had to wake her up. Slap her face, march her around, feed

her black coffee. I told her about the Japanese sailor adrift for four days when he killed himself. "They found him twenty minutes later. He was still warm."

We heard the hum of someone running a lawn mower down the street. The sweetness of jasmine took the rest of the air. She sighed, filling out ribs sharp as the blades of the mower. "But how long can a person float, looking at an empty horizon? How long do you drift before you call it quits?"

What answer could I give her? I'd been doing it for years. She was my life raft, my turtle. I lay down, put my head on her shoulder. She smelled of sweat and L'Air du Temps, but now dusty blue, as if her melancholy had stained the perfume.

"Anything can happen," I said.

She kissed me on the mouth. Her mouth tasted like iced coffee and cardamom, and I was overwhelmed by the taste, her hot skin and the smell of unwashed hair. I was confused, but not unwilling. I would have let her do anything to me.

She dropped back onto the pillow, her arm over her eyes. I raised up on one elbow. I didn't know what to say.

"I feel so unreal," she said.

She turned over, her back to me, her garnet heart pendant stuck to the back of her shoulder. Her dirty hair was heavy as a bunch of black grapes, and her waist and hip curved like a pale guitar. She picked up the strand of pearls and lowered it in a spiral on the bedspread, but when she moved it slid in toward her body, spoiling the design. She picked it up, tried again, like a girl picking petals off daisies, trying to get the right answer.

"If only I had a child," she said.

I felt a twang on a rarely played string. I was well aware I was the instead-baby, a stand-in for what she really wanted. If

293

she had a baby, she wouldn't need me. But a baby was out of the question. She was so thin, she was starving herself. I'd caught her vomiting after we ate.

"I was pregnant once, at Yale. It never occurred to me that was the only baby I'd ever have."

The whine of the lawn mower filled the silence. I would have liked to say something encouraging, but I couldn't think of anything. I plucked the heart off her back. Her thinness belied her spoken desire. She'd lost so much weight she could wear my clothes now. She did when I was at school. I came home sometimes and certain outfits were warm, smelling of L'Air du Temps. I pictured her in my clothes, certain things she favored, a plaid skirt, a skinny top. Standing in the mirror, imagining she was sixteen, a junior in high school. She did a perfect imitation of me, the gawky teenager. Crossing her legs the way I did, twining them and tucking the foot behind the calf. Starting with a shrug before I talked, dismissing what I was about to say in advance. My uneasy smile, that flashed and disappeared in a second. She tried me on like my clothes. But it wasn't me she wanted to be, it was just sixteen.

I watched the garden under the blinds, the long shadows cast by the cypress, the palm, across the textured green. If she were sixteen, what? She wouldn't have made the mistakes she's made? Maybe she would choose better? Maybe she wouldn't have to choose at all, she could just stay sixteen. But she was trying on the wrong person's clothes. I wasn't anyone she'd want to be. She was too fragile to be me, it would crush her, like the pressure of a deep wall dive.

Mostly she lay here like this, thinking about Ron, when would he come home, was there another woman? Worrying about luck and evil influences, while wearing talismans of her family past, women who did something with their lives, made something of themselves, or at least got dressed every day, women who never kissed a sixteen-year-old foster daughter because they felt unreal, never let the weeds grow in their gardens because it was too hot to pull them.

I wanted to tell her not to entertain despair like this. Despair wasn't a guest, you didn't play its favorite music, find it a comfortable chair. Despair was the enemy. It frightened me for Claire to bare her needs so openly. If a person needed something badly, it was my experience that it would surely be taken away. I didn't need to put mirrors on the roof to know that.

IT WAS A RELIEF when Ron came home. She got up, took a shower, cleaned the house. She made food, too much of it, and put on red lipstick. She took off Leonard Cohen and put on Teddy Wilson's big band, sang along to "Basin Street Blues." Ron made love with her at night, sometimes even in the afternoon. Neither of them made much noise, but I could hear the quiet laughter behind their closed door.

Early one morning, when Claire was still sleeping, I heard him on the phone in the living room. He was talking to a woman, I sensed it immediately when I came in, the way he smiled as he talked in his striped pajama bottoms — wrapping the phone cord around his smooth fingers. He laughed at something she said. "Flounder. Whatever. Cod."

He started when he saw me in the doorway. The blood bleached out of his rosy cheeks, then returned, deeper. He ran his hand through his hair so that the paler strips sprang back under his touch. He talked a bit more, arrangements, flights, hotels, he scribbled on a scrap of paper in his open briefcase. I didn't move. He hung up the phone.

He stood up, hiking his pajama bottoms. "We're going to Reykjavík. Hot springs with documented healing powers."

"Take Claire with you," I said.

He threw the paper into his briefcase, shut it, locked it. "I'd be working all the time. You know Claire. She'd sit in the motel and cook herself into some morbid fantasy. It'd be a nightmare."

Reluctantly, I saw his point. Whether he stayed out of town as much as he could to screw around, or just to avoid dealing with Claire, or even on the off-chance he was what he claimed to be, just a tired husband trying to make a living, it would be a disaster to bring Claire along if he couldn't spend time with her. She couldn't just wander around by herself, see the sights. She'd sit in the hotel and wonder what he was doing, which woman it was. Torturing herself.

But it didn't let him off the hook. He was her husband. He was responsible. I didn't like the way he talked to that woman on the phone in Claire's own house. I could imagine him with a woman in a dark restaurant, seducing her with that same smooth voice.

I leaned in the doorway, in case he decided to try to go back to bed and pretend nothing had happened. I wanted to make him understand that she needed him. His duty was here. "She told me how she would kill herself if she wanted to."

That got his attention, made him stumble a bit in his smoothness, a man tripping over a crack in the sidewalk, an actor who'd forgotten his lines. He brushed back his hair, playing for time. "What did she say?"

"She said she'd gas herself."

He sat down, closed his eyes, put his hands over them, the smooth fingertips meeting over his nose. Suddenly I felt sorry for him too. I only wanted to get his attention, make him realize he couldn't simply fly off and pretend everything was normal around her. He couldn't leave her all to me.

"Do you think she's just talking?" he asked, fear in his hazel eyes.

He was asking me? He was the one with the answers. The man with the firm grip on reality, the one who told us when to get up and when to go to bed, what channel we were watching, what we thought about nuclear testing and welfare reform. He was the one who held the world securely in his smooth hands like a big basketball. I stared at him helplessly, horrified that he didn't know whether or not Claire would kill herself. He was her husband. Who was I, some kid they'd taken in.

I couldn't help but picture Claire lying on the bed, clad in her jewels, pearls welled in her mouth. What she had given up to be with Ron. The way she cried at night, arms pressed tight around her, bent almost double, like a person with stomach cramps. But no, she still waited for me to come from school, she wouldn't want me to find her dead. "She misses you."

"It's almost summer hiatus," Ron said. "We'll go somewhere. Really get away, just the three of us. Camping in Yellowstone, something like that. What do you think?"

The three of us, riding horses, hiking, sitting around the campfire, memorizing the stars. No phone, no fax, no laptop computer. No parties, meetings, friends coming by with a script. Ron all to herself. That would be something to look forward to. She wouldn't want to miss camping with Ron. "She'd like that," I finally said. Though I thought I'd believe it when I saw it. He was a great reneger.

"I know it hasn't been easy for you." He put his hand on my shoulder. Smooth. There was heat in his hand, it warmed my whole shoulder. For a moment I wondered what it would feel like to make love to Ron. His bare chest so close I could stroke it, the gray hairs, the quarter-sized nipples. He smelled good, Monsieur Givenchy. His voice, not too deep, sandy and calming. But then I remembered, this was the man who was causing all the problems, who didn't know how to love Claire. He was cheating on her, I could feel it in his body. He had the world, all Claire had was him. But I couldn't help liking his hand on my shoulder, the look in his eyes. Trying not to react to his masculine presence, solidity in his blue pajama bottoms. *She's a young woman,* he told Claire. It was just part of his act, the appreciation thing. I bet he did it with all the lonely spoonbenders. I stepped away, so his arm dropped. "You better come through," I told him.

20

IN JUNE, true to his promise, Ron rented a cabin in Oregon. No phone, no electricity, he even left his computer at home. In the forests of the Cascades, we fished in high green rubber boots to our waists. He showed me the fly reel, how to cast like a delicate spell, the glistening steelhead trout like secrets you could pluck from the water. Claire pored over bird books, wildflower guides, intent on naming, as if the names gave life to the forms. When she identified one, she was as proud as if she herself created the meadowlark, the maidenhair fern. Or we'd sit in the big meadow, propped up each by our own tree, and Ron played cowboy songs on his harmonica, "Red River Valley" and "Yellow Rose of Texas."

I thought of my mother in Amsterdam, singing *Whoopee ti yi yo, git along little dogies*. Explaining to me that a dogie was a calf that had lost its mother. *It's your misfortune and none of my own*. Ron was from New York, I wondered where he learned songs like that. TV probably. I saw how he looked at me when I sketched by the riverbank, but did nothing to encourage it. I could live without Ron, but not without Claire.

When it rained, he and Claire walked together down the trails cushioned in pine needles, the ferns smelling like licorice. At night we played Monopoly and Scrabble, three-handed blackjack, charades. Claire and Ron did routines from *Streetcar Named Desire*, *Picnic*. I could see what it was like when they were first together. His admiration for her. That's what she needed to remember, how he was the one who wanted her.

I'd never spent so much time with Ron before. It started to irritate me, how he was always the one running the show. When he got up, he woke me and Claire up. But when we got up first, we crept around, because Ron was still sleeping. *A man's world*. It bothered me, the way it was Ron who decided the day's activity, whether it was a good day for fishing or hiking or a trip out to the coast. Ron who said when we needed to go to the store and when we could get by another day, whether we took slickers or sweaters or bought firewood. I'd never had a father and now I didn't want one.

But Claire looked healthy again. She didn't throw up anymore. Her coloring grew vivid. She made gallons of soup in a big cast-iron pot, while Ron grilled fish over the open fire. We had pancakes in the morning, or eggs and bacon. Ron smiled, crunching bacon strips. "Poison, poison. And such small portions" — the punch line of a joke they had. Thick sandwiches in our backpacks for lunch, ham and salami, whole tomatoes, smoky cheese.

Claire complained that she couldn't fit into her jeans anymore, but Ron hugged her around the thighs and tried to bite them. "I like you fat. Enormous. Rubenesque."

"Liar." She laughed, swatting at him.

I dangled my line in the McKenzie, where the sun glittered on the surface between the trees, and the shapes of fish darted deeper, where the trees laid their shadows across the moving water. Upriver, Ron cast and reeled, but I didn't really care if I caught anything. Claire walked along the bank singing to herself, in a fluid, effortless soprano, *Oh Shenandoah, I long to hear you* . . . She picked wildflowers, which she pressed between layers of cardboard when we got back to the cabin. I felt at home there, the silence, the spectrum of green under a resonant sky ringed by the tall fingers of Jefferson pine and Douglas fir, a sky you could expect to see drifting with dragons and angels. A sky like a window in a portrait of a Renaissance cardinal. The music of flowing water and the resinous perfume of the evergreens.

I cast and reeled, my back warm in the sun, stared into my shadow in the water where it formed a dark window in the reflections. I could see down to the bottom with the stones and the fishes, the shapes moving toward the fly.

Suddenly the reel sang and the line zipped out. I panicked. "I got one!" I screamed up to Ron. "What do I do?"

"Let him go, until he stops running," Ron yelled downriver to me.

The reel still turned, but finally slowed.

"Now bring him back to you."

I reeled, feeling the weight of the fish, he was stronger than I thought, or the drag of the current on him. I dug my heels in and pulled, watched the long flexible rod bend in a whip curve. Then the line went slack. "He's gone!"

"Reel!" Ron yelled as he came wading downriver, carefully, step by step. He had the net out. "He's coming back this way."

I reeled like mad and sure enough, the line turned, he was swimming back upriver. I held my breath, I could not have anticipated my excitement at lowering my line into a river and having a living fish take the fly. Having something alive where I'd come in empty-handed.

"Play him out," Ron said.

I let the line spool away. The fish ran upstream. I shrieked with laughter as I stumbled into a hole and my waders filled with icy water. Ron pulled me up, steadied me. "You want me to land it for you?" Already reaching for my pole.

"No," I said, jerking it from him. It was my fish. Nobody was going to take this fish away from me. I felt as if I'd caught it on my own flesh, line from my clothes. I needed this fish.

Claire came to watch. She sat on the bank and drew her knees up to her chin. "Be careful," she said.

The fish made three more passes before Ron thought it was tired enough to bring in. "Reel him in now, reel him in."

My arm ached from the reeling, but my heart leapt as he broke from the water, gleaming liquid silver, two feet long. He was still thrashing wildly.

"Hold on to him, don't lose him now," Ron said, coming for the fish with his net.

I wouldn't lose this fish if it dragged me all the way to Coos Bay. Enough had slipped through my hands already.

Ron netted him and together we walked to the bank. Ron scrambled up the side, holding the giant thrashing fish in the net.

"It's so alive," Claire said. "Throw it back, Astrid."

"Are you kidding? Her first fish? Bop him," he said, handing me a hammer. "On the head."

The fish flopped on the grass, trying to jump back into the water.

"Quick, or we'll lose him."

"Astrid, don't." Claire looked at me with her tenderest wildflower expression.

I took the hammer and whacked the fish in the head. Claire turned away. I knew what she was thinking, that I was siding with Ron, with the world and its harshness. But I wanted that fish. I took out the hook and held it up, and Ron took a picture of me like that. Claire wouldn't talk to me for the rest of the afternoon, but I felt like a real kid, and I didn't want to feel guilty about it.

I HATED THAT we had to go back to L.A. Now Claire had to share Ron with phone calls and faxes and too many people. Our house was full of projects and options, scripts in turn-around, industry rumors, notes in *Variety*. Ron's friends didn't know how to talk to me. The women ignored me and the men were too interested, they stood too close, they leaned in door-ways and told me I was beautiful, was I thinking of acting?

I stayed close to Claire, but it made me nervous to watch her wait on these people, these indifferent strangers, chilling their white wine, making pesto, taking another trip to Chalet Gourmet. Ron said not to bother, they could order pizza, bring in El Pollo Loco, but Claire said she could never serve guests out of cardboard containers. She didn't get it. They didn't see themselves as her guests. To them she was just a wife, an out-of-work actress, a drudge. There were so many pretty women that summer, in sundresses and bikini tops, sarongs, I knew she was trying to figure out which one was Ron's Circe.

Finally, she went on Prozac, but it gave her too much

energy. She couldn't sit down, and she started to drink to even out the effects. Ron didn't like it because she said things that she thought were funny but nobody else laughed. She was like a woman in a film that was badly dubbed, either too fast or too slow. She bungled the punch lines.

IN SEPTEMBER, in wind and ashes, I started the twelfth grade at Fairfax, and Ron went back to work. Now Claire couldn't find enough to do in the husbandless house. She scrubbed floors, cleaned windows, rearranged the furniture. One day she gave all her clothes away to Goodwill. Without sedatives, she was up all night, filing magazine clippings, dusting books. She had headaches, and believed someone was listening in on the phone. She swore she could hear the click before she hung up. She made me listen.

"Do you hear it?" she asked, her dark eyes glittering.

"Maybe," I said, not wanting her to be all alone in her night. "I can't really tell."

IN OCTOBER the heat gave way to the blue afternoon haze of true autumn, hand-shaped leaves of the sycamores showed orange against the dusty white trunks, and a red-gold blush lay on the hills. One day I came home from school and found Claire staring at herself in her round vanity mirror in her room, her silver brush forgotten in her hand. "My face is uneven, have you noticed? My nose is off-center." She turned her head to the side, examined the profile, puffed out her cheeks and pushed her imagined off-center nose to the right, mashed the tip down. "I hate pointed noses. Your mother has Garbo's nose, did you ever notice that? If I had mine done, I'd want one like that."

She wasn't talking about noses. Claire was just tired of seeing her own face in the mirror, it was a code of her failings. There was something missing, but it wasn't what she thought. She fretted that her hairline was receding, that she was going to end up looking like Edgar Allan Poe. Her fearful gaze magnified the incomplete tops of her ears, shrank her small lips.

"Small teeth mean bad luck," she said, showing them to me in the mirror. "Short life." Her teeth were barley beads, pearl-like and gleaming. But her eyes had grown increasingly deep. I could hardly see the lids anymore, and her sharp bones once again made bridges in her face, a Rodin sculptured bronze head, merciless in its paring down.

As we got into December, Claire cheered up. She loved the holidays. She was reading magazines with pictures of Christmas in England, in Paris, in Taos, New Mexico. She wanted to do everything. "Let's have a perfect Christmas," she said.

We wired a wreath in eucalyptus and pomegranates we dipped into melted wax. She bought boxes of Christmas cards, soft handmade paper with lace and golden stars. *Swan Lake* played on the classical station. We sewed garlands of tiny chili peppers, stuck cloves into tangerines, tied them with velvet the color of brandy. She bought me a red velvet dress with a white lace collar and cuffs at Jessica McClintock in Beverly Hills. Perfect, she said.

It scared me when she said perfect. Perfect was always too much to ask.

*

RON CAME HOME until after New Year's. She waited for him, so we could all buy the tree together, like a real family. In the car, she described just what she wanted. Symmetrical, soft-needled, six feet at least. The tree man tried to help but gave up after pulling out and untwining dozens of trees.

"I don't get any of this," Ron said, watching Claire's desperate search. "Jesus grew up in Bethlehem. High desert. We should be buying an olive, a date palm. A frigging Jerusalem artichoke."

I walked along the side with the spray-painted trees, some in white like a starched chemical snowfall, others painted gold, pink, red, even black. The black tree, about three feet high, looked like it had been burnt. I wondered who would want a black tree, but I knew someone would. There was no limit to the ways in which people could be strange. Someone would buy it as a joke, a belated Halloween, to decorate with plastic skulls and tiny guillotines. Or it would become someone's Yuletide political statement. Or someone would take it just for the pleasure of making their kids cry.

The smell of the trees was like Oregon. If only we could be back there right now, a soft rain falling, in the cabin, the woodstove. I joined Claire, where she was agonizing over a tree that was almost right, except for a bit of a gap in the branches on one side. She pointed it out with anxious hands. I assured her she could keep it to the wall, nobody would ever notice it.

"That's not the point," she said. "If something is wrong, you can't just turn it to the wall."

I knew what she meant, but convinced her to take it anyway.

At home, Claire instructed Ron in the hanging of lights. Originally she wanted candles, but Ron drew the line there. We wound strings of chilies and popcorn round and around, while Ron watched a big soccer game on TV. Mexico playing Argentina. He wouldn't turn it off so Claire could have Christmas carols. *A man's world.* He could barely pull himself away long enough to put the gold angel on top.

Claire turned out the room lights and we sat and watched the tree in the dark, while Mexico overran South America.

THE MORNING of Christmas Eve, Ron got a call about a vision of the Virgin Mary seen in Bayou St. Louis. He had to go film it. They had a big fight and Claire locked herself in their room. In the kitchen, I was polishing the silver, a job I'd learned to do very well. We were going to have dinner with crystal and linens. I had my new Christmas dress from Jessica McClintock. Claire had already stuffed the goose, and picked up a real English trifle from Chalet Gourmet. We had tickets for the midnight *Messiah* at the Hollywood Bowl.

We didn't go. I ate ham sandwiches and watched *It's a Wonderful Life.* Claire came out and threw the goose in the trash. She poured herself small glasses of sherry, one after the other, and watched TV with me, crying on and off in the plaid bathrobe Ron had given her as an early Christmas present. I had a glass or two of the sweet liquor to keep her company, it was no worse than cough syrup. She finally took a couple of sleeping pills and passed out on the couch. She snored like a mower in high grass.

She slept through most of Christmas morning, then woke with a terrible headache at noon. We didn't talk about Ron, but she wouldn't touch the presents he left for her. I got a real fisherman sweater, a new set of acrylic paints, a big book of Japanese woodcuts, and silk pajamas like something Myrna Loy would wear in a *Thin Man* movie.

My present was small compared with the ones Ron bought her. "Here, open something."

"I don't want anything," she said from under her washcloth soaked in vinegar.

"I made it for you."

She pushed aside the washcloth, and despite the pain in her temples, slipped off the raffia ties, and opened the marbled paper wrapping I had made myself. Inside was a portrait of her, in a round wooden frame. She started to cry, then ran to the bathroom and threw up. I could hear her gagging. I picked up the picture, in charcoal, traced her high rounded forehead, the slope of fine bones, the sharp chin, arched brows.

"Claire?" I said through the bathroom door.

I heard water running and tried the door. It wasn't locked. She sat on the edge of the tub in her red plaid bathrobe, pale as winter, hand over her mouth, eyes turned toward the windows. She was blinking back tears and wouldn't look at me. She seemed to be collapsing at the center, one arm wrapped around her waist, as if keeping herself from breaking in two.

I didn't know what to do when she was like this. I gazed down at the tiles, salmon pink, counted the shiny squares. Twenty-four from tub to heater. Thirty from the door to the sink. A decorative motif was the color of cherry cough drops, punctuated with almond cuneiform script. The frosted glass shower door swan bowed its head.

"I should never drink." She washed her mouth out in the sink, cupping water in her palm. "It just makes things worse."

She wiped her hands and face on a towel, took my hand. "Now I've ruined your Christmas."

I made her lie down on the couch, opened my new paints, spread colors on a plate, and painted a sheet of thick paper half black, half red, and made flames like the back of the Leonard Cohen album. The woman on the radio sang "Ave Maria." "What does *Ave* mean?"

"Bird," she said.

The woman's voice was a bird, flying in a hot wind, battered by the effort. I painted it in the fire, black.

WHEN RON came home from New Orleans, Claire didn't get up from the couch. She didn't clean up, shop, cook, change the sheets, put on lipstick, or try to make it better. She lay in her red bathrobe on the couch, sherry bottle right by her hand, she'd been sipping steadily all day long, eating cinnamon toast and leaving the crusts, listening to opera. That's what she craved. Hysterical loves and inevitable betrayals. The women all ended up stabbing themselves, drinking poison, bitten by snakes.

"For Christ's sake, at least get dressed," Ron said. "Astrid shouldn't have to see this."

I wished he wouldn't use me as a reason. Why couldn't he say, I'm worried about you, I love you, you need to see someone?

"Astrid, do I embarrass you?" Claire asked. If she were sober, she would never have put me on the spot like that.

"No," I said. But it did, when they passed me back and forth like a side dish at dinner.

"She says I don't embarrass her."

Ron said, "You embarrass me."

Claire nodded, drunk against the armrest of the couch in the blinking Christmas lights. She raised one thin philosophical finger. "Now we're getting somewhere. Tell me, Ron, have I always embarrassed you? Or is this a recent development?" She had a funny way of talking when she was drinking, of lipping her words, top over bottom, like Sandy Dennis in *Who's Afraid of Virginia Woolf?*

On the stereo, the soprano launched into her big aria before she did herself in, *Madame Butterfly* or *Aida*, I can't remember which. Claire closed her eyes, tried to lose herself in the singing. Ron turned off the CD.

"Claire, I had to go. It's what I do," Ron explained, standing over her, his palms out, as if he were singing. "I'm sorry it was Christmas, but it was a Christmas story. I couldn't wait until February, now could I."

"It's what you do," she said in the flat voice I hated.

He pointed with that smooth clean finger. "Don't."

I wished she'd bite it, break it off, but instead she glanced down, finished her drink and put the sherry glass on the table, carefully, and nestled down under the mohair blanket. She was always cold now. "Did she go with you? The blond, what's-her-bimbo, Cindy. Kimmie."

"Oh this." He turned away, starting picking things up, dirty Kleenexes, empty glasses, dishtowel, bowl. I didn't help him. I sat on the couch with Claire, wishing he'd leave us alone. "Christ I'm tired of your paranoia. I should have an affair, just to give you some basis. At least then I'd get the fun along with the crap."

Claire watched him with heavy-lidded eyes, red-rimmed

from crying. "She doesn't embarrass you, though. It doesn't embarrass you to be running around with her."

He reached down to pick up her empty glass. "Blah, blah, blah."

Before I realized what was happening, she sprang to her feet and slapped him across the face. I was glad, she'd needed to do that for months. But then, instead of telling him so, she sagged back to the couch, hands flopped on her knees, and started to cry in hiccupy sobs. It took all her strength just to slap him. I felt both sorry and disgusted.

"Excuse us, will you?" Ron asked me.

I looked at Claire, to see if she wanted me to stay, be a witness. But she was just sobbing, her face uncovered.

"Please," he said, more firmly.

I went back to my room, closed the door, then opened it slightly when they started talking again.

"You promised," he said. "If we got a child."

"I can't help it," she said.

"I didn't think so," he said. "She really should go, then."

I strained my ears for the sound of her voice, but I couldn't hear her reply. Why didn't she say something? I wished I could see her, but his back blocked my view as he stood over her. I tried to imagine her face. She was drunk, her skin stained and rubbery. What was in her eyes? Hatred? Pleading? Confusion? I waited for her to defend me, something, but she didn't respond.

"It isn't working out," he continued.

What struck me was not so much that he could talk about sending me back, like a dog you got from the pound when it dug up the yard and ruined the carpets. It was the reasonableness of his tone, caring but detached, like a doctor. It was the only reasonable thing, the voice said. It just wasn't working out.

"Maybe you're the one who's not working out," she said, reaching for the sherry bottle as she said it. He knocked it from her hand. It went flying, I heard it hit and roll on the pine floor.

"I can't stand your poses," he said. "Who are you supposed to be now, the wounded matriarch? Christ, she takes care of you. That wasn't the idea."

He was lying. That was exactly the idea. He got me to take care of her, keep an eye on her, keep her company while he was away. Why didn't she say it? She didn't know how to defy him.

"You can't take her away," was all she said. "Where would she go?"

It was the wrong question, Claire.

"She'll have a place, I'm sure," Ron said. "But look at you. You're falling apart. Again. You promised, but here we are. And I'm supposed to drop everything and put you back together again. Well, I'm warning you, if I have to pick up the pieces again, you're going to give up something too." Still the reasonable voice. He was making it all her fault.

"You take everything away," she sobbed. "You leave me with nothing."

He turned away from her, and now I could see his face, the disgust. "God, you're such a bad actress," he said. "I'd almost forgotten."

When he stepped out of my line of sight, I saw her, hands around her ears, her knees under her chin, she was rocking back and forth, saying, "Do you have to take everything? Do you have to have it all?"

"Maybe you need some time," he said. "Think it over."

I heard his footsteps, closed the door before he caught me spying on them. I heard him pass down the hall.

I peeked out the door, she was back lying on the couch. She pulled the mohair blanket up over her head. I could hear her moaning.

I closed the door and sat on my bed, helpless. It was my mother all over again. Why did they do this? I'd been taking care of Claire for almost two years. I was the one she told everything. I was the one who worried, submitted to her rituals, calmed her fears, while he was off chasing poltergeists and Virgin Mary apparitions. How could he send me away now? I opened the door, determined to talk to him, to tell him he couldn't, when he came out of the bedroom with his hanging bag over his shoulder, his briefcase in his hand. His eyes caught mine, but they slid closed like steel doors as he swung past me out into the living room.

I didn't think Claire could get any paler, but when she saw Ron with those bags, she turned powder white. She scrambled from the couch, the blanket fell to the floor. Her bathrobe was all twisted around, I could see her underwear. "Don't go." She grabbed onto his corduroy jacket. "You can't leave me. I love you."

He inhaled, and for a moment I thought he was going to change his mind, but then his eyebrows pressed down on his eyes, and he turned, breaking her hold. "Work it out."

"Ron, please." She grabbed for him again but she was too drunk, she missed and fell onto her knees. "Please."

I went back to my room and lay facedown on the bed. I couldn't stand to watch her crawl after him, grabbing onto his legs, begging, staggering after him out the door, in her red Christmas bathrobe all falling open. I could hear her outside now, weeping, promising she'd be good, promising him everything. The slam of his car door, the engine starting up, the unwinding ascending note of the Alfa backing out as she continued to plead. I imagined Mrs. Kromach peering out from behind her powder-blue curtains, Mr. Levi staring in amazement from under his Hasidic brim.

Claire came back in, calling me. I put the pillow over my head. *Weakling*, I thought. *Traitor*. She was in front of my door, but I didn't answer. She would give me up for him, she would do anything to have him. Just like before, my mother and Barry. "Please, Astrid," she begged me through the door, but I wouldn't listen. *This sickness would never happen to me.*

Finally she went to her room, closed the door, and I hated her for crawling after him and hated myself for my disgust, for knowing just how Ron felt. I lay there on my bed, hating all of us, listening to her cry, she'd done nothing but for a week. *Twenty-seven names for tears.*

I heard Leonard Cohen start up, asking if she heard her master sing. The circular repetition of an overwhelming question. I wanted to seal myself up, while I still had something of my own that I hadn't given to Claire. I had to pull back or I would be torn away, like a scarf closed in a car door.

How I despised her weakness. Just like my mother said I would. It repelled me. I would have fought for her, but Claire couldn't even stand up for herself. I couldn't save us both. On my desk was the picture of me and the steelhead trout from summer. Ron had it framed. I looked so happy. I should have known it wouldn't last. Nothing lasts. Didn't I know that by now? *Keep your bags packed*, my mother said. And me with less than a year to go, with college dangling before me.

But then I remembered how Claire took me to Cal Arts to see if I wanted to apply there, even got me the application. How she made me take honors classes, helped me with the homework, drove me to the museum every Tuesday night. If I had a future at all, it was only because she gave it to me. But then I saw her crawling again, begging, and was repelled afresh. Astrid help me. Astrid pick up the pieces. How could I? I was counting on her too much. I had to start facing that.

I read for a while in a book about Kandinsky, tried out some of his ideas about form and tension. How the tension in a line increased as it approached the edge. I tried not to listen as the Leonard Cohen cycled around. She must have fallen asleep by now. Let her sleep it off.

I drew until it got dark, then turned on the light and spun the pyramid that hung over my desk, the ridiculous pyramid my mother had sold Claire on. When I closed the Kandinsky book, I couldn't help noticing the inscription. *To Astrid, with all my love, Claire.*

It went through me like a current, shorting out my childish resentment. If I had anything good, it was only because of Claire. If I could think of myself as worthwhile for a second, it was because Claire made me think so. If I could contemplate a future at all, it was because she believed there was one. Claire had given me back the world. And what was I doing now that she needed me? Rolling up my windows, loading in supplies, unreeling the barbed wire.

I got up and went to her room. "Claire?" I called through the closed door. I tried the door but it was locked. She never locked the door, except when they were having sex. I knocked. "Claire, are you okay?"

I heard her say something, but I couldn't make it out.

"Claire, open up." I jiggled the doorhandle.

Then I heard what it was she was saying. "Sorry. So sorry. I'm just so goddamned sorry."

"Open up, please, Claire. I want to talk to you."

"Go away, Astrid." Her voice was almost unrecognizably drunk. I was surprised. I thought she'd be sobering up or passed out by now. "Take my advice. Stay away from all broken people." I heard her sobbing dryly, almost retching, almost laughing, it became a sort of hum through the door.

I almost said, you're not broken, you're just going through something. But I couldn't. She knew. There was something terribly wrong with her, all the way inside. She was like a big diamond with a dead spot in the middle. I was supposed to breathe life into that dead spot, but it hadn't worked. She was going to call Ron wherever it was he went, and say, you're right, send her back. I can't live without you.

"You can't send me back," I said through the door.

"Your mother was right," she said, slurring the words. I heard things crash to the floor. "I am a fool. I can't even stand myself." My mother. Making everything worse. I'd sent back all the letters I could find, but there must have been others.

I sat down on the floor. I felt like an accident victim, holding on to my falling-out insides. Suddenly, I was overwhelmed with the urge to go back to my room, fall into bed, under the clean sheets, and sleep. But I fought it, tried to think of something to say through the door. "She doesn't know you."

I heard the squeak of her bed, she was up, staggered to the

door. "He's not coming back, Astrid." She was right on the other side. Her voice fell from standing height to sitting as she spoke through the crack. "He's going to divorce me."

I hoped he would. Then she might have a chance, the two of us, taking it slow, no more Ron coming home, trailing fear, selling hope, leaving her on Christmas, arriving home just when she was getting used to him being gone. It would be fine. No more pretending, holding our breaths, listening in as he talked on the phone. "Claire, you know, it wouldn't be the worst thing."

She laughed woozily. "Seventeen years old. Tell me, baby, what is the worst thing?"

The wood grain of the door was a maze I followed with my fingernail. I was about to say, try having your mother in prison, and the one person you love and trust is going off her rocker. Try being in the best place you ever had and they were talking about sending you back.

But then again, I would not have wanted to be Claire. I would have rather been myself, even my mother, imprisoned for life, full of her own impotent ferocity, than be Claire, worried about burglars and rapists and small teeth mean bad luck and my eyes don't match and don't kill the fish and does my husband still love me, did he ever, or did he just think I was someone else, and I can't pretend anymore.

I wanted to hold her close, but something inside was pushing her away. This was Claire, who loves you, I reminded myself, but I couldn't feel it right now. She couldn't even take care of herself, and I felt myself drifting off. I felt her reaching for my hand, she wanted to come in. I didn't think I could save her anymore. The maze trail I was following dead-ended in a

317

peacock eye. "My mother would say the worst thing is losing your self-respect."

I heard her start to cry again. Sharp, painful hiccups I felt in my own throat. She banged on the door with her fist, or maybe it was her head. I couldn't stand it, I had to back down into lies.

"Claire, you know he'll be back. He loves you, don't worry."

I didn't care if he came back or not. He wanted to send me away, and for that I hoped he wrecked his classic Alfa that matched his gray hair.

"If I knew what self-respect was," I heard her say, "then maybe I'd know if I'd lost it."

I was so sleepy. I couldn't keep my eyes open. I leaned my head against the door. Out in the living room, the lights on the Christmas tree flashed on and off, the needles scattered on the unopened presents.

"You want something to eat?"

She didn't want anything.

"I'm just getting something to eat. I'll be back in a second."

I made myself a ham sandwich. The Christmas tree needles were all over the floor. They crunched underfoot. The sherry bottle was gone, she must have taken it with her. She was going to have the hangover of a lifetime. She had left my portrait on the coffee table. I took it into my room, propped it on the desk. I looked into her deep gaze, I could hear her asking me, what do you want, croissant or brioche? Where would you go if you could go anywhere in the world? I traced my finger over her high rounded forehead, like a Gothic Madonna. I went back to her door, knocked.

"Claire, let me in."

I heard the squeak of the bedsprings as she turned over, the effort it took to get up, stumble the three steps to the door. She fumbled with the lock. I opened the door and she fell back into bed, still wearing that red bathrobe. She pawed her way under the covers like a blind burrowing animal. Thank God, she wasn't crying anymore, she was ready to pass out. I turned off Leonard Cohen.

"I'm so cold," she mumbled. "Come in with me."

I got in, clothes and all. She put her cold feet on mine, her head on my shoulder. The sheets smelled of sherry and dirty hair and L'Air du Temps.

"Stay with me, promise. Don't leave."

I held her cold hands, rested my head against hers as she fell asleep. I watched her in the light of the bedside lamp, which was always on now. Her mouth was open, she snored heavily. I told myself, things will turn out all right. Ron would come home or he wouldn't, and we'd just go on together. He wouldn't really send me away. He just didn't want to see how damaged she was. As long as she didn't show him, that was all he asked for. A good show.

➤

21

CLAIRE WAS STILL SLEEPING when I woke up. I got up, careful not to disturb her, and went out to the kitchen. I poured myself some cereal. It was very bright, quiet, a pure crystalline light. I was glad Ron was gone. If he were here, there would have been phone calls, the whine of the coffee grinder, Claire might be up making breakfast with her smile painted on. I decided to stay in my silk pajamas a while longer. I got my new paints out and painted the way the light looked on the bare wood floor, the yellow tray of sunlight, the way it climbed the curtains. I loved when it was like this. I recalled days just like this when I was young, playing in a patch of sunlight when my mother slept in. A laundry basket over my head, squares of light. I remembered exactly how the sun looked and felt on the back of my hand.

After a while, I checked on Claire. She was still asleep. The room was dark gray, no morning light penetrated the west-facing French doors covered with blinds. It smelled stale. She had one hand flung across the top of the pillow. Her mouth was open, but she wasn't snoring now.

"Claire?" I put my face right in hers. She smelled of sherry and something metallic. She didn't move. I put my hand on her shoulder, shook her gently. "Claire?" She didn't do anything. The hair stood up on my neck and arms. I couldn't hear her breathing. "Claire?" I shook her again, but her head flopped like Owen's giraffe's. "Claire, wake up." I lifted her by her shoulders and dropped her. "Claire!" I yelled at her, hoping she would open her eyes, that she would put her hand to her head and tell me not to shout, I was giving her a headache. It was impossible. She was playing a trick, pretending. "Claire!" I screamed into her sleeping face, pumping my hands on her chest, listening for her breath. Nothing.

I searched the bedside table, the floor. On the far side, I found the pills on the floor, along with the empty sherry bottle. It was what I'd heard falling when we were talking through the door. The pill bottle was open, the pills spilled out, small pink tablets. Butalan, the label said. For Insomnia. Do Not Take With Alcohol. Do Not Operate Machinery.

The sounds I was making were no longer even screams. I wanted to throw something into the fat ugly eye of God. I threw the Kleenex box. The brass bell. I knocked the bedside light off the nightstand. I pulled the magnet box from under the bed and threw it across the room. Ron's keys and pens and clippers fell out, the Polaroids. For what? I ripped the blinds off the French doors, and the room blinked bright. I took a high-heeled shoe from the foot of the bed and smashed through the windowpanes with it, cut my hand, couldn't feel it. I took her silver-backed hairbrush and threw it overhand like a baseball into the round mirror. I took the phone and beat the receiver against the headboard until it came apart in my hands, leaving dents in the soft pine.

I was exhausted and couldn't find anything more to throw. I sat back down on the bed and took her hand. It was so cold. I put it against my hot wet cheek, trying to warm it up, I smoothed her dark hair away from her face.

If only I had known, Claire. My beautiful fucked-up Claire. I lay my head on her chest where there was no heartbeat. My face next to hers on the flowered pillow, breathing in her breath that was no longer breath. She was so pale. Cold. I held her cold hands, slightly chapped, the wedding ring that was too big. Turned them over, kissed the cold palms, my hot lips on the lines. How she used to worry about those lines. One ran from the edge of the hand and crossed the line of life. Fatal accident, she said it meant. I rubbed the line with my thumb, slick with tears.

Fatal accident. That thought was almost unbearable, but possible. Maybe she hadn't meant to do it. Claire wouldn't have planned it like this. She hadn't even washed her hair. She would have prepared, everything would have been perfect. She would have written a note, explaining everything two or five ways. Maybe all she wanted was to sleep.

I laughed, bitter as nightshade. Maybe it was just an accident. What wasn't an accident. Who wasn't.

I picked up the squarish white bottle still half full of pills. Butabarbitol sodium, 100 mg. It practically glowed in my hands. The worst always happened. Why did I keep forgetting that? Now I saw this was not just a bottle, it was a door. You climbed through the round neck of the bottle and came out somewhere else entirely. You could escape. Cash in your chips.

I looked deep into the jar of pink pills. I knew how to do this. You took them slowly. Not like in the movies, where they took them by the handful. You'd just puke them up. The trick was to take one, wait a few minutes, take the next. Have some sherry. One by one. In a couple of hours, you passed out, and it was done.

The house was still. I heard the tick of the clock on the bedside table. A car drove past in the street. Fresh air came through the broken windows. She lay with her mouth open on the flowered pillow in her red bathrobe in the brightness of the morning. I rubbed my cheek against the wool of her robe, the robe Ron got her, she hadn't taken it off for days. God, I hated that bathrobe, its cheery red plaid. It was always too bright. He never really knew her.

I put the lid back on the pills and dropped them on the bed. I had to get rid of that robe before anything. It was the least I could do. I pulled down the covers. The robe was all twisted around, bunched up in the back. I opened the belt and pulled her out of it, how thin she was, how light, her ribs were individually displayed. I laid her back down, careful, careful, I could hardly look at her. Like Christ in her shell-pink underwear. In her dresser I found a soft mauve angora sweater. This was more Claire, the soft color, the plush wool. I put my face into it, hungry for softness, let it soak up my tears. I sat her up. It was hard, I had to lean her against me, overwhelmed by the scent of perfume and her hair. I could hardly breathe, but somehow I pulled the sweater over her head, somehow threaded her arms through, pulled the softness down over her bony shoulder blades. I sat and hugged her, pressing my face to her neck.

I arranged her on the pillow like a princess in a fairy tale, in a glass coffin, a kiss should awaken her. But it didn't work. I closed her mouth, smoothed the sheets and blankets, found the silver brush in the debris and brushed her hair. I found it comforting, I had done this for her when she was alive. She never even said good-bye. The day my mother left, she didn't look back either.

I knew I should call Ron. But I didn't want to share her with him. I wanted her all to myself for just a little while more. When Ron arrived, I would lose Claire for the last time. He didn't know her, he could bloody well wait.

I couldn't get it out of my head, I was right there when she died. If only I'd woken up. If only I'd imagined what could happen. My mother always told me I had no imagination. Claire called me and I didn't go to her. Wouldn't even open my door. I had told her the worst thing was to lose your self-respect. How could I have told her such a thing? Christ, that wasn't the worst thing, not by a long shot.

Outside in the garden, the grass was uncut but very green in the clear winter sun. The Chinese elm wept like a willow. The bulbs were done, but the roses bloomed furiously, the red hallucinatory glow of Mr. Lincoln, the pale blush of Pristine. The ground underneath was pooled with red and white petals. In here, the room was steeped in L'Air du Temps from the bottle I'd shattered. I picked up the top, the frosted birds. Now they looked like something to decorate a headstone.

In a drawer, I found the book of pressed flowers she made from the gleanings of our walks on the McKenzie that summer. How happy she'd been in her Chinese hat, tied under the chin, canvas bag full of discoveries. Here they were, labeled in her round feminine hand, pressed on pages tied together with taupe grosgrain ribbon, *Lady's Slipper, Dogwood, Wild Rose, Rhododendron* with their threadlike stamens.

What do you want, Astrid? What do you think? No one would ever ask me that again. I stroked her hair, her dark eyebrows, her eyelids, the delicate formation of cheekbone and eye socket and temple and brow, the sharpness of chin like a drop of water upside down. If only I'd gone to her right away. If only I hadn't made her wait. I should never have left her alone with our disgust, Ron's and mine. It was the one thing she couldn't stand, to be left alone.

At ten o'clock, the mail came. At eleven, Mrs. Kromach practiced her electric organ next door, her parrot squawking along. I knew her entire repertoire. "Zip-a-Dee-Doo-Dah." "There's No Business Like Show Business." "Chattanooga Choo Choo." She liked state songs: "Gary, Indiana." "Iowa Stubborn." "California, Here I Come." "Everything's Up to Date in Kansas City." She made the same mistakes every time. "She's doing it to drive us crazy," Claire would say. "She knows how to play those songs." She'd never have to hear it anymore

At noon, a leaf blower droned in the air. At one, the Orthodox nursery school let out. I heard the high-pitched voices on the street, the cheerful querulousness of the Hasidic neighbor women in their guttural languages. How they frightened you, Claire, those simple women in their long skirts with their infinite broods, arrogant sons and big oafish daughters, strong enough to lift a truck but timid in gaggles with bows in their hair. You always thought they were trying to hex you. You made me paint my hand blue and print it on the white stucco above the doorbell, a spell against the evil eye.

My knee touched hers, recoiled. Her leg was stiff. She was far away now, she was passing through the seven mortal coils, going up to God. I ran my fingers down the pretty, pointed nose, along the smooth forehead, the slight indentation at the temple where no pulse fluttered. She never seemed more complete, more sure of herself. Not trying to please anyone anymore.

She loved me, but she didn't know me now.

From 1:45 to 4:15 the phone rang five times. She missed her hair appointment with Emile. Two hang-ups. Ron's friends were meeting for drinks at Cava. MCI wanted to give the Richardses a break on their phone bill. Each time the phone rang, I somehow expected her to jerk awake and answer it. She could never stand not answering the phone. Even when she knew it wouldn't be for her. It might be a job, though she'd stopped going out on auditions. It might be a friend, though she had no friends. She could get involved in long winding conversations with boiler room operators, Red Carpet Realty, Gold Star Construction.

I couldn't understand how she could be gone. What would happen to the way she had of opening a jar like an orchestra percussionist hitting a triangle, a single precise gesture? The reddish highlights in her hair in the summertime. Her aunt who served at Ypres. I was the one who had them now, like an armload of butterflies. Who else knew she put mirrors on the roof, or that her favorite movies were *Dr. Zhivago* and *Breakfast at Tiffany's*, that her favorite color was indigo blue? Her lucky number was two. The foods she could never eat were coconut and marzipan.

I remembered the day she took me to Cal Arts. I was intimidated by the students, they seemed pretentious for people with funny haircuts, and their work was ugly. It cost ten thousand dollars a year to go there. "Don't think about money," Claire said. "This is the place, unless you think you want to go east." We'd sent in the application in November. I had to forget all that now.

I sat cross-legged next to her on the bed, counted the pills in the jar. For Insomnia. There were still plenty. More than enough, and the last person who would ever think about me was gone. My mother? She just wanted possession. She thought if she could kill Claire, she would get me back, so she could erase me some more. I felt the pull of that dark circle, the neck of the bottle. It was a rabbit hole, I could jump down it and pull it in after me. *You never knew when help might come.* But I knew. It came and I turned my back, I let it go down. I pushed my savior out of the life raft. I panicked. Now I reaped my despair.

I sat with the jar in my hand, watching that winter sky's blush, weak pink strained through blue haze, coming through the angle-pruned branches and weeping boughs of the elm. Sunset came so early now. She loved this time of day, loved feeling beautifully melancholy and sitting under the elm, looking up into its branches, dark against the sky.

In the end, I didn't take the pills. It seemed too grandiose, a big gesture, fraudulent. I didn't deserve to forget that I had turned my back on her. Oblivion wiped the books clean. It was too easy. I was the keeper of the butterflies now. Instead, I dialed Ron's pager, added the 999 that meant emergency. I sat back down and waited.

*

RON SAT NEXT TO ME on the bed, his shoulders sagging like an old horse's back and his face pressed into his hands, as if he could not look at one more thing. "You were supposed to watch her," he said.

"You were the one who left."

He gasped, and broke into long, shuddering sobs. I never thought I would feel sorry for Ron, but I did. I put my hand on his shoulder, and he pressed his hand over mine. It occurred to me I could make him feel better. I could stroke his hair, and say, *It's not your fault. She had problems we couldn't have helped, no matter what we did.* That's what Claire would have done. I could have made him love me. Maybe he would keep me.

He held my hand and stared down at her silk slippers beside the bed. "I've been afraid of this for years."

He pressed my hand to his cheek. I could feel his tears spill over the back, seeping between my fingers. Claire would have felt sorry for him if she weren't dead. "I loved her so much," he said. "I wasn't a saint, but I loved her. You don't know."

He looked up at me with his red-rimmed eyes, waiting for me to deliver my lines. *I know you did, Ron.* Claire would say it. I could feel Olivia too, pressing me. He could take care of me. *A man's world.*

But I couldn't bring myself to do it. Claire was dead. What did it matter if he loved her or not?

I pulled my hand away and got up, started picking up some of the things I'd thrown on the floor. There was his Cross pen. I tossed it in his lap. "She had it all the time," I said. "You didn't know her at all."

He bent his head, touched her dark hair that I had brushed,

ran his hand down her mauve angora sleeve. "You can still stay," he said. "Don't worry about that."

I thought it was what I'd wanted to hear. But now that he said it, I knew I'd feel better out on Sunset Boulevard with the other runaways, asleep on a piss quilt on the steps of the homeless church, eating out of the trash at Two Guys from Italy. I couldn't stay here without Claire. I could never say the lines he wanted, paint on my prettiest smile, listen for his car in the driveway. My face in the vanity mirror was sharp and jagged. He was reaching out to me, but my face was beyond reaching.

I turned away and looked out at the night and our reflection in the broken French doors: me in my silk pajamas, Ron on the bed, Claire on the pillow, bathed in the bed's lampside glow, for once utterly indifferent.

"Why couldn't you just have loved her more?" I said.

His hand dropped down. He shook his head. Nobody knew why. Nobody ever knew why.

IT TOOK LONGER to pack than when I left Amelia's. There were all the new clothes Claire gave me, the books, the little Dürer rabbit. I took everything. I only had one suitcase, so I packed the rest in shopping bags. It took seven bags to pack it all. I went into the kitchen, reached into the jewelry bag, and took the aquamarine ring that was always too big for her, and her mother too. But it fit me fine.

It was almost midnight when a caseworker came in a minivan, a middle-aged white woman in jeans and pearl earrings. Joan Peeler had left DCS last year to work in development at Fox. Ron helped me carry my things out to the van. "I'm sorry," he said as I climbed in. He fumbled for his wallet, pressed some money on me. Two hundred-dollar bills. My mother would have thrown them in his face, but I took them.

I watched the house, the way it got smaller in the back window of the van as we drove off in the moonless night, the end of what might have been. A little Hollywood bungalow beyond the huge white trunks of the sycamores. I didn't give a damn what happened to me now.

22

MacLaren Children's Center was in a way a relief. The worst had happened. The waiting was over.

I lay in my narrow bed, low to the ground. Except for the two changes of clothes in the pressboard drawers beneath the mattress, all my things were in storage. My skin burned. I'd been deloused and still stank of coal-tar soap. Everyone was asleep but the girls in the hall, girls who had to be watched, the suicide girls, the epileptics, the uncontrollables. It was finally quiet.

Now I found it easy to imagine my mother in her bunk at Frontera. We weren't so different after all. The same block walls, linoleum floors, the shadows of pines against the outside lights, and the sleeping shapes of my roommates under their thin thermal blankets. It was too hot in here, but I didn't open the window. Claire was dead. Who cared if it was too hot.

I stroked the furry ends of my short hair with one palm. I was glad I'd cut it off. A gang of girls jumped me twice, once in the Big Field, once coming back from the gym, because someone's boyfriend thought I was looking good. I didn't want to be pretty. I lay fingering the bruises blooming on my cheek, shading from purple to green, watching the shadows of the pines behind the curtain, dancing in the wind like Balinese shadow puppets behind a screen, moving to gamelan music.

I had gotten a call from Ron yesterday morning. He was taking her ashes back to Connecticut, and offered to pay for my ticket if I wanted to come with him. I didn't want to see Claire delivered back to her family, more people who didn't know her. I couldn't stand around like a stranger through the eulogy. *She kissed me on the lips*, I would have told them.

"You didn't know her at all," I told Ron. She didn't want to be cremated, she wanted to be buried with her pearls in her mouth, a jewel over each eye. Ron never knew what she wanted, he always thought he knew best. *You were supposed to watch her.* He knew she was suicidal when he took me in. That's why I was hired. I was the suicide watch. Not the baby after all.

The pine shadows moved across my blanket, the wall behind me. People were just like that. We couldn't even see each other, just the shadows moving, pushed by unseen winds. What difference did it make if I was here or somewhere else. I couldn't keep her alive.

A girl out in the hall groaned. One of my roommates turned over, mumbled into her blanket. All the bad dreams. This was exactly where I belonged. For once I didn't feel out of place. Even with my mother, I was always holding my breath, waiting for something to happen, for her not to come home, for some disaster. Ron never should have trusted me with Claire. She should have gotten a little kid, someone to stay alive for.

She should have realized I was a bad luck person, she should never have thought I was someone to count on. I was more like my mother than I'd ever believed. And even that thought didn't frighten me anymore.

THE NEXT DAY I met a boy in the art room, Paul Trout. He had lank hair and bad skin, and his hands moved without him. He was like me, he couldn't sit without drawing something. When I passed him on my way to the sink, I looked over his shoulder. His black pen and felt-tip drawings were like something you'd see in a comic book. Women in black leather with big breasts and high heels, brandishing guns the size of fire hoses. Men with bulging crotches and knives. Weird graffiti-like mandalas with yin-yangs and dragons, and finned cars from the fifties.

He stared at me all the time. I felt his eyes while I painted. But it didn't bother me, Paul Trout's intense, blinkless stare. It wasn't like the boys in the senior classroom, their stares like a raid, moist, groping, more than a little hostile. This was an artist's stare, attentive to detail, taking in the truth without preconceptions. It was a stare that didn't turn away when I stared back, but was startled to find itself returned.

When he came around behind me to use the wastebasket, he watched me paint. I didn't try to cover up. Let him look. It was Claire on the bed in her mauve sweater, the dark figure of Ron in the doorway. The whole thing bathed in red ambulance lights. Lots of diagonals. It was hard to paint well, the brushes were plastic, the poster paint dried fast and powdery. I mixed colors on the back of a pie pan.

333

"That's really good," he said.

I didn't need him to tell me it was good. I'd been making art all my life, before I could talk, and after, when I could, but didn't choose to.

"Nobody here can paint," he said. "I hate jungles."

He meant the hallways. All the hallways at Mac were painted with murals of jungles, elephants and palm trees, acres of foliage, African villages with conelike thatched huts. The rendering was naive, Rousseau with none of the menace or mystery, but it wasn't done by the kids. We weren't allowed to paint the halls. Instead, they'd hired some kind of children's book illustrator, some wallpaper designer. They probably thought our art would be too ugly, too upsetting. They didn't know, most of the kids would have done exactly what the hall artist did. Peaceable kingdoms in which nothing bad ever happened. Soaring eagles and playful lions and African nymphs carrying water, flowers without sexual parts.

"This is the fourth time I've been here," Paul Trout said.

It was why I'd never seen him except in the art room. If you came back on purpose, ran away from your placement, you lost your privileges, your coed nights. But I understood why they came back. It wasn't that bad here at Mac. If it weren't for the violence, the other kids, I could understand how someone could see it almost as paradise. But you couldn't have this many damaged people in one place without it becoming like any other cellblock or psych ward. They could paint the halls all they wanted, the nightmare was still real. No matter how green the lawn or bright the hallway murals or how good the art was on the twelve-foot perimeter wall, no matter how kind the cottage teams and the caseworkers were, how many celebrity barbeques they had or swimming pools they put in, it was still the last resort for children damaged in so many ways, it was miraculous we could still sit down to dinner, laugh at TV, drop into sleep.

Paul Trout wasn't the only returnee. There were lots of them. It was safer in here, there were rules and regular meals, professional care. Mac was a floor you could not fall below. I supposed the ex-cons who kept going back to prison felt the same way.

"You cut off your hair," he said. "Why'd you do that? It was pretty."

"Attracted attention," I said.

"I thought girls liked that."

I smiled, felt the bitter aftertaste in my mouth. This boy might know a lot about cruelty and waste, but he didn't know a thing about beauty. How could he? He was used to that skin, people turning away, not seeing the fire in his lucid brown eyes. I could tell, he imagined beauty, attention, would feel like love.

"Sometimes it hurts more than it helps," I said.

"You're beautiful anyway," he said, going back to his drawing. "There's not much you can do about that."

I painted Claire's dark hair, layering blue and then brown, blending in the highlights, catching the red. "It doesn't mean anything. Only to other people."

"You say that like it's nothing."

"It is." What was beauty unless you intended to use it, like a hammer, or a key? It was just something for other people to use and admire, or envy, despise. To nail their dreams onto like a picture hanger on a blank wall. And so many girls saying, use me, dream me.

335

"You've never been ugly." The boy looked down at his hand filling the blank spaces in a science fiction scene. "Women treat you like you're a disease they might catch. And if in a weak moment they let you touch them, they make you pay." His mouth closed, then opened to say more, but closed without saying a word. He'd said too much. His mouth turned down. "Someone like you, you wouldn't let me touch you, would you."

Where did he get the idea he was ugly? Bad skin could happen to anyone. "I don't let anyone touch me," I finally said.

I painted in the pharmacy jar of butabarbitol sodium on the rag rug by her bed, the tiny pills spilling out. Bright pink against the dark rug.

"Why not?"

Why not? Because I was tired of men. Hanging in doorways, standing too close, their smell of beer or fifteen-year-old whiskey. Men who didn't come to the emergency room with you, men who left on Christmas Eve. Men who slammed the security gates, who made you love them and then changed their minds. Forests of boys, their ragged shrubs full of eyes following you, grabbing your breasts, waving their money, eyes already knocking you down, taking what they felt was theirs.

Because I could still see a woman in a red bathrobe crawling in the street. A woman on a roof in the wind, mute and strange. Women with pills, with knives, women dyeing their hair. Women painting doorknobs with poison for love, making dinners too large to eat, firing into a child's room at close range. It was a play and I knew how it ended, I didn't want to audition for any of the roles. It was no game, no casual thrill. It was three-bullet Russian roulette.

I painted a mirror on the wall opposite Claire's dresser where there was no mirror, and in the red-tinted darkness, my own staring image, with long pale hair, in the crimson velvet Christmas dress I never got a chance to wear. The me that died with her. I painted a crimson ribbon around my neck. It made my neck look slashed.

"Are you gay?" Paul Trout asked me.

I shrugged. Maybe that would be better. I thought back to how I felt when Olivia danced with me, and the time Claire kissed me on the lips. I didn't know. People just wanted to be loved. That was the thing about words, they were clear and specific — *chair, eye, stone* — but when you talked about feelings, words were too stiff, they were this and not that, they couldn't include all the meanings. In defining, they always left something out. I thought of my mother's lovers, Jeremy and Jesus and Mark, narrow-waisted young men with clear eyes and voices like slipper satin across your bare chest. I thought how beautiful Claire was, dancing in her own living room, jeté, pas de bourée, how I loved her. I looked up at him, "Does it matter?"

"Doesn't anything matter to you?"

"Survival," I said, but even that sounded untrue now. "I guess."

"That's not much."

I painted a butterfly in Claire's room. Swallowtail. Another, cabbage white. "I haven't gotten any farther than that."

WE WALKED the Big Field together when he got his privileges back. The girls called him my boyfriend, but it was just another word, it didn't quite capture the truth. Paul Trout was the only person I'd met there I could talk to. He wanted to see me on the outside, asked for an address, a phone number, someplace he could reach me, but I didn't know where I'd be, and I couldn't trust my mother to forward anything. Anyway, I'd decided not to give her my new address. I didn't want anything more to do with her. He gave me the name of a comic book shop in Hollywood, said he'd check there, wherever he was. "Just mark the letters *Hold for Paul Trout*."

I was sorry when he got his placement, to a group home in Pomona. He was the first kid I'd really enjoyed spending time with since my days with Davey, the first one who could remotely understand what I had been through. We were just getting to know each other, and now he was gone. I had to get used to that. Everybody left you eventually. He gave me one of his drawings to remember him by. It was me as a superhero, in a tight white T-shirt and ragged shorts, my body clearly the subject of much observation and thought. I'd just vanquished a biker archvillain, my Doc Marten bootheel planted on his bloody bare chest, a smoking gun in my hand. I shot him through the heart. *I don't let anyone touch me* was printed over my head.

OUTSIDE the junior boys' cottage a few days after Paul left, I sat at an orange picnic table, waiting for my interview. I ran my hand through my chopped hair, let the winter sun warm my scalp. The families weren't supposed to be shopping, it was supposed to be a "getting to know you" visit, but it was an audition and everyone knew it. I wasn't worried. I didn't want to get placed. I'd rather stay here until I was eighteen. Paul was right, there was lots worse than Mac. I didn't want to get involved with anybody ever again. But nobody got to stay.

At a table under the big pines, another interview was taking place, a sibling set. They were always the worst. The cute little brother in the woman's lap, the older brother, past cute, pubescent, downy-lipped, standing off to the right, hands in his pockets. They only wanted the little one. Big brother was trying to convince them how responsible he was, how he'd help take care of the little guy, carry the trash, mow the lawn. I could barely watch it.

I had my first interview on Tuesday. Bill and Ann Greenway from Downey. They'd been foster parents for years. They just had one go back to her birth parents. They'd had her three years. Bill wiped his mouth with the back of his hand as he told it, Ann blinking back tears. I studied my shoes, white Keds, blue stripes down the sides, oversized lace holes. One thing in my favor, I wasn't going back to my mother anytime soon.

I didn't say much. I didn't even want to look at them. I could get to like them. I liked them already. Their kindnesses made small sucking noises at me, like water in the bathtub. It would be easy to let them take me home. I could see their house, bright and comfortable, on a street of tract houses but nice, maybe two-story. Pictures of kids on the tables, old swing set in the backyard. The sunny high school, even their church sounded inviting, nobody got fanatic there, or worried too much about sin or damnation. I bet they called their minister by his first name.

I could have gone with them, Ann and Bill Greenway of

Downey. But with them, I might forget things. All the butterflies might fly away. Pressed wildflowers and Bach in the morning, dark hair on the pillow, pearls. *Aida* and Leonard Cohen, Mrs. Kromach and picnics in the living room, pâté and caviar. In Downey, it wouldn't matter that I knew about Kandinsky and Ypres and the French names for the turns in ballet. I might forget black thread through skin, a .38 bullet crashing through bone, the smell of new houses and the way my mother looked when they handcuffed her, the odd tenderness with which the burly cop held his hand over her head so she wouldn't hit it getting into the squad car. With Ann and Bill Greenway of Downey, they would dim, fade away. Amsterdam and Eduardo's hotel, tea at the Beverly Wilshire and the way Claire stood trembling when that bum smelled her hair. I would never again look at homeless kids in doorways off Sunset and see my own face staring back.

"You'll like it with us, Astrid," Ann said, her clean white hand on my arm.

She smelled of Jergens hand lotion, a pallid pink sweetness, not L'Air du Temps or Ma Griffe or my mother's secretive violets, a scent which for chemical reasons could only be smelled for a moment at a time. *Which do you like better, tarragon or thyme?* All that was a dream, you couldn't hold on, you couldn't depend on frosted glass birds and Debussy.

I looked at Bill and Ann, their well-meaning faces, sturdy shoes, no hard questions. Bill's graying blond crew cut, his silver-rimmed glasses, Ann's snip-and-curl beauty shop hair. This was attainable, solid and homely and indestructible as indoor-outdoor carpeting. I should have been grabbing it. But I found myself pulling away from her hand.

It wasn't that I didn't believe them. I believed everything they said, they were a salvation, a solution to my most basic lack. But I recalled a morning years ago in a boxy church in Tujunga, the fluorescent lights, chipped folding chairs. Starr charmed as a snake while Reverend Thomas explained damnation. The damned could be saved, he said, anytime. But they refused to give up their sins. Though they suffered endlessly, they would not give them up, even for salvation, perfect divine love.

I hadn't understood at the time. If sinners were so unhappy, why would they prefer their suffering? But now I knew why. Without my wounds, who was I? My scars were my face, my past was my life. It wasn't like I didn't know where all this remembering got you, all that hunger for beauty and astonishing cruelty and ever-present loss. But I knew I would never go to Bill with a troubling personal matter, a boy who liked me too much, a teacher who scolded unfairly. I had already seen more of the world, its beauty and misery and sheer surprise, than they could hope or fear to perceive.

But I knew one more thing. That people who denied who they were or where they had been were in the greatest danger. They were blind sleepwalkers on tightropes, fingers scoring thin air. So I let them go, got up and walked away, knowing I'd given up something I could never get back. Not Ann and Bill Greenway, but some illusion I'd had, that I could be saved, start again.

So now I sat at the tables again, waiting for my next interview. I saw her, a skinny brunette in dark glasses, she was taking a shortcut across the wet lawn, sinking into the just-watered turf in high heels, not caring she was ripping up the grass. Her silver earrings flashed in the January sun like fishing lures. Her sweater fell off one shoulder, revealing a black bra strap. She lost a shoe, the earth sucking it right off her foot. She hopped back on one leg, and mashed her bare foot angrily in. I knew already, I'd be going with her.

23

HER NAME was Rena Grushenka. In a week, she took me home in her whitewashed Econoline van with the Grateful Dead sticker in the back window, the red and blue halves of the skull divided down the middle like a bad headache. It was cold, raining, sky a smother of dull gray. I liked how she laid rubber in the parking lot. Watching the wall and wire of Mac dropping away out the window, I tried not to think too much about what lay ahead. We wandered through a maze of suburban neighborhood, looking for the freeway, and I concentrated on memorizing the way I had come — the white house with the dovecote, the green shutters, the mailbox, an Oriental pierced-concrete wall streaked with rain. High-voltage wires stretched between steel towers like giants holding jump ropes into the distance.

Rena lit a black cigarette and offered me one. "Russian Sobranie. Best in world."

I took it, lit it with her disposable lighter, and studied my new mother. Her coal-black hair, completely matte, was a hole in the charcoal afternoon. High breasts pushed into a savage cleavage framed in a black crocheted sweater unbuttoned to the fourth button. Her dream-catcher earrings touched her shoulders, and I couldn't imagine what kind of dreams might lodge there. When she'd found the freeway, she shoved a tape into the cassette deck, an old Elton John. "Like a candle in the wind," she sang in a deep throaty voice flavored with Russian soft consonants, hands on the big steering wheel grubby and full of rings, the nails chipped red.

Butterflies suddenly filled the cab of the van — swallowtails, monarchs, buckeyes, cabbage whites — the fluttering wings of my too many feelings, too many memories, I didn't know how Rena could see through the windshield for the heartbeat gossamer of their wings.

It was less than a year, I told myself. Eighteen and out. I would graduate, get a job, my life would be my own. This was just a place to live rent-free until I could decide what the next act was going to be. Forget college, that wasn't going to happen for me, so why set myself up. I sure wasn't going to let myself get disappointed again. *I never let anyone touch me.* Damn straight.

I concentrated on the shapes of the downtown towers as they emerged from the gloom, tops in the clouds, a half-remembered dream. We turned north on the 5, following train tracks around downtown, County Hospital, the warehouse area around the brewery, where the artists lived in their studios — we'd been to parties there, my mother and I, a lifetime ago, so long it seemed like someone else's memory, a song I'd heard once in a dream.

Rena turned off at Stadium Way, and there were no houses now, just tangled green freewayside foliage and concrete. We

344

paralleled the 5 for a while, then passed underneath, into a little neighborhood like an island below sea level, the freeway a wall on our left. On the right, through the rain-smeared windshield, street after street rolled by, each posted No Outlet. I saw cramped front yards, and laundry hanging wet on lines and over fences in front of Spanish cottages and tiny Craftsman bungalows, bars on all the windows. I saw macramé plant holders hanging from porches, children's toys in bare-dirt front lawns, and enormous oleanders. Frogtown, the graffiti proclaimed.

We pulled up in front of a glum cocoa-brown Spanish bungalow with heavy plasterwork, dark windows, and a patchy lawn surrounded by a chain-link fence. On one side, the neighbors had a boat in the driveway that was bigger than their house. On the other was a plumbing contractor. It was exactly where I belonged, a girl who could turn away from the one good thing in her life.

"No place like home," said Rena Grushenka. I couldn't tell if she was being ironic or not.

She didn't help me carry my things. I took the most important bags — art supplies, the Dürer rabbit with Ron's money hidden behind the frame — and followed her up the cracked path to the splintered porch. A white cat dashed in when Rena opened the door. "Sasha, you bad boy," she said. "Out screwing."

It took a moment to adjust to the darkness inside the small house. Furniture was my first impression, jumbled together like in a thrift store. Too many lamps, none lit. A dark-haired plump girl lay on a green figured velvet sofa watching TV. She pushed the white cat away when it jumped in her lap. She glanced up at me, wasn't impressed, went back to her show.

"Yvonne," Rena said. "She got more stuff. You help."

"You," Yvonne said.

"Hey, what I say you? Lazy cow."

"*Chingao,* talk about lazy." But she pushed herself up from the too-soft couch, and I saw she was pregnant. Her dark eyes under the skimpy cover of half-moon plucked eyebrows met mine. "Have you ever came to the wrong place," she said.

Rena snorted. "What you think is right place? You tell me, we all go."

The girl gave her the finger, took a sweatshirt from the old-fashioned hatstand, lazily pulled the hood over her hair. "Come on."

We went back out into the rain, a fine drizzle now, and she took two bags, I took two more. "I'm Astrid," I said.

"Yeah, so?"

We took the stuff to a room down a hall, across from the kitchen. Two beds, both unmade. "That one's yours," Yvonne said, dumping my bags onto it. "Don't touch my stuff or I'll kill you." She turned and left me alone.

It was a mess without precedence. Clothes on the beds, the desk, piled up against the walls, pouring out the open closet. I'd never seen so many clothes. And hair magazines, photonovelas in shreds. Over her bed, Yvonne had pictures torn out of magazines, girls and boys holding hands, riding bareback on the beach. On the dresser, a Chinese paper horse with trappings of silky red fringe and gold foil guarded a bright yellow portable radio, a fancy makeup kit with twenty shades of eye shadow, and a picture of a young TV actor in a two-dollar frame.

I gathered the stuff off my bed, a wet towel, pair of overalls, pink sweatshirt, a dirty plate, and tried to decide which would be less offensive, throwing them on the floor or the other bed. The floor, I decided. In the dresser, though, she'd left two drawers empty, and there were a half-dozen free hangers in the closet.

I ordered my clothes into neat piles in my drawers, hung the best things, made the bed. There was no room for the rest. *Don't touch my stuff or I'll kill you*, she'd said. I'd spoken exactly those words myself. Now I remembered my room at Claire's, seeing it for the first time and wondering how I would ever fill it up. She'd given me too much, I couldn't hold on. I deserved this. I arranged my things in the shopping bags and slid them under the metal frame of the old-fashioned bed, all my artifacts. All the people I had been. It was like a graveyard under there. I hung the cartoon that Paul Trout had made of me over my bed. *I never let anyone touch me.* I wondered where he was now, whether I would ever hear from him again. Whether someone would love him someday, show him what beauty meant.

After I'd unpacked, I crossed the narrow hall to the kitchen, where Rena sat with another girl, her dark-rooted hair dyed magenta. Each had an open Heineken bottle and they shared a filthy glass ashtray. The counters were all dirty dishes and takeout debris. "Astrid. This is other one, Niki." Rena turned to the magenta-haired girl.

This girl sized me up more carefully than the pregnant girl. Brown eyes weighed me to the tenth of an ounce, patted me down, checked the seams of my clothing. "Who hit you?"

I shrugged. "Some girls at Mac. It's going away."

Niki sat back in her mismatched dinette chair, skinny arms behind her head. "Sisters don't like white girls messing with their men." Tilted her head back to sip from her beer, but didn't take her eyes off me. "They give you that haircut too?"

"What, you're Hawaii 5-0?" Rena said. "Leave her be." She got up and fished another beer out of the battered refrigerator, covered with stickers from rock bands. A glimpse of the interior didn't look promising. Beer, takeout cartons, some lunch meat. Rena held a beer up. "Want one?"

I took it. I was here now. We drank beer, we smoked black cigarettes. I wondered what else we did on Ripple Street.

Rena searched for something in the cabinets, opening and slamming the chipped beige doors. There wasn't anything but a bunch of dusty old pots, odd glasses and plates. "You eat chips I buy?"

"Yvonne," Niki said, drinking her beer.

"Eat for two," Rena said.

Niki and Rena went off somewhere in the van. Yvonne lay on one side, asleep on the couch, sucking her thumb. The white cat curled against her back. There was an empty bag of Doritos on the table. The TV was still on, local news. A helicopter crash on the 10. People crying, reporters interviewing them on the shoulder of the freeway. Blood and confusion.

I went out onto the porch. The rain had stopped, the earth smelled damp and green. Two girls my age walked by with their kids, one on a tricycle, the other in a pink baby carriage. They stared at me, plucked eyebrows rendering their faces expressionless. A powder-blue American car from the sixties, somebody's pride and joy, all shining chrome and white upholstery, roared by, the engine deep and explosive, and we watched it rise to the top of Ripple Street.

A crack opened in the clouds to the west, and a golden light washed over the distant hills. Down here, the street was dark already, it would get dark early here, the hillside across the freeway blocked the light, but there was sunlight at the high end of the street and on the hills, gilding the domes of the observatory, which perched on the edge of the mountain like a cathedral.

I walked toward the light, past businesses and little houses advertising child care, two-story fourplexes with wooden stairs and banana trees and corn growing in the yard, the Dolly Madison bakery. An electronics shop. A movie prop outlet, Cadillac Jack's, a Conestoga wagon in its fenced lot. Salazar Mazda repair shop on the corner, where Fletcher Drive crossed the river.

From the bridge, the view opened to the river, warmed in the last light like a gift, streaming between bruised gray clouds. The river ran under the road, heading for Long Beach. I rested my arms on the damp concrete railing and looked north toward the hills and the park. The water flowed through its big concrete embankments, the bottom covered with decades of silt and boulders and trees. It was returning to its wild state despite the massive sloped shore, a secret river. A tall white bird fished among the rocks, standing on one leg like in a Japanese woodcut. Fifty views of the L.A. River.

A horn honked and a man shouted "Give me a piece of that" out of a car window. But it didn't matter, nobody could stop on the bridge anyway. I wondered if Claire was here, if she could see me. I wished she could see this crane, the river bottom. It was beautiful and I didn't deserve it, but I couldn't help lifting my face to the last golden light.

*

THE NEXT DAY Rena woke us before dawn. I was dreaming I was drowning, a shipwreck in the North Atlantic, it was just as well to wake up. The room was still dark, and freezing cold. "Workers of the world, arise," Rena said, banishing our dreams with the smoke of her black cigarette. "You got nothing to lose but Visa Card, Happy Meal, Kotex with Wings." She turned on the light.

Yvonne groaned in the other bed, picked up a shoe and threw it half heartedly at Rena. "Fuckin' Thursday."

We dressed with our backs to each other. Yvonne's heavy breasts and lush thighs were startling in their beauty. I saw Matisse in her lines, I saw Renoir. She was only my age, but by comparison I had the body of a child.

"Gonna report that *puta* to the INS. Kick her ass back to Russia." She pawed through the piles of clothes, pulled out a turtleneck, sniffed it, threw it back. I stumbled down the hall to wash my face, brush my teeth. When I came out, she was already in the kitchen, pouring coffee into a battered Thermos, stuffing handfuls of saltines in a bag.

In the cold darkness, clouds of white vapor escaped from the tailpipe of the Ford panel van, ghostly in its whitewash, which didn't entirely conceal the gray bondo underneath. In the big captain's chair, Rena Grushenka smoked a black Sobranie with a gold tip and sipped coffee from a Winchell's slotted cup. Rolling Stones played on the tape deck. Her high-heeled boots tapped time on the dash.

Yvonne and I climbed into the back and closed the doors. It was dark and smelled of moldy carpet squares. We huddled together on the ripped-out carseat against the far wall. Niki got in the front and Rena slammed the three-on-the-tree shift into place. "Find 'em, don't grind 'em." Niki lit a Marlboro, coughed wetly and spat out the window.

"I quit smokin' for the baby, but what's the damn point," Yvonne said.

Rena found first, and we lurched into the stillness of Ripple Street. The orange streetlights illuminated the quiet neighborhood, the air perfumed caramel and vanilla by the night shift at the Dolly Madison bakery. I could hear the trucks pulling up to the loading bays as we ascended from the river bottom. A deep truck horn honked, and Rena fluffed her tangled black hair. Even at five in the morning, her shirt was already unbuttoned, her cleavage heightened severely by a Fredericks push-up bra. She sang along with the tape in her good alto voice, about how some girls give you diamonds, some girls Cadillacs. Her Jagger impersonation was impressive.

We turned left on Fletcher, past the Mazda repair and the Star Strip, our van rattling like cans in the moist darkness. We went under the 5 and crossed Riverside Drive, fragrant with hamburgers from Rick's. She turned left at the Astro coffee shop, its parking lot half-full of police cars. She spat three times out the window as we passed by.

Then we began to climb, up into a neighborhood of narrow streets, houses crowded along steep slopes wall to wall, stucco duplexes and nondescript boxes, occasionally an old Spanish-style. Stairs on the uphill side, carports on the downhill. I knelt between the captain's seats for the view. I could see the whole river valley from here — headlights of cars on the 5 and the 2, the sleeping hills of Glassell Park and Elysian Heights dotted with lights. Vacant lots full of wild fennel, ferny and licorice-smelling in the dewy darkness. The smell mingled with the mold of the van and cigarettes and the reek of leftover alcohol. Rena flicked her cigarette out the window.

Yvonne snapped on the interior light and flipped through a water-bloated *Seventeen* magazine. The blond girl on the cover smiled bravely, although clearly dismayed to have found herself in such circumstances. I looked at the magazine over her shoulder. I could never figure out where they found all those happy, pimpleless teens. Yvonne paused at a picture of a girl and a boy riding a fat horse bareback on the beach. "Did you ever ride a horse?"

"No. I went to the racetrack once." Medea's Pride at five-to-one. His hand on her waist. "You?"

"I been on the pony ride at Griffith Park," Yvonne said.

"Over there," Rena pointed.

A gray texturecoat house had black plastic bags plumped next to the trash. Rena stopped and Niki jumped out, cut the tab of one with a pocketknife. "Clothes." She and Yvonne handed the bags up to me in the back. They were heavier than I'd thought, must have had appliances in the bottom. Yvonne lifted them easily, she was strong as a man. Niki swung the bags, a practiced move.

"I'm so tired," Yvonne said, as we started off again. "I hate my life." She filled the coffee cup, gulped it down, filled it again and handed it to me. It was instant, hot and too strong.

Behind the wheel, Rena dragged on her cigarette, she held it like a pencil. "I told you get rid. What you need baby? Cow."

Rena Grushenka. Rock music and American slang both twenty years out of date, discount Stoli from Bargain Circus. She trained her black magpie eyes on the curb with its neatly arrayed trash cans and recycling bins. She could see in the dark with those eyes. This morning she wore a necklace of silver milagros, arms, hands, and legs. You were supposed to pin them to the velvet skirts of the Virgin to pray, but to Rena they were just pawned body parts.

"Hey, turnip people," she called out the window as we squeezed past an old Cadillac double-parked, a Mexican couple emptying somebody's recycling. Bagged cans and bottles crammed their trunk and backseat. *"Dobro utro, kulaks."* She laughed with her mouth wide open, her gold inlays glinting.

They stared at us without expression as we clattered by.

Rena sang along with Mick in her thick accent, tapping on the blue steering wheel with the inside of her ring, craning her neck in and out like a chicken. She had a deep voice, a good ear.

Niki yawned and stretched in the other captain's chair. "I need a ride back to work sometime to pick up my truck. Werner took me to his place last night." She grinned her lop-toothed smile.

Rena sipped from her Winchell's cup. "The knackwurst."

"Four times," Niki said. "I can hardly walk." Werner, supposedly a German rock promoter, came to the Bavarian Gardens, where Niki worked three nights a week, though she wasn't twenty-one. She had a fake ID from one of Rena's friends.

"You should bring knackwurst. I got to meet."

"Fat chance of that," Niki said. "He gets one look at you bitches, he'll be on the first plane back to Frankfurt."

"You're just afraid he'll see you're a man," Yvonne said.

Their talk went on like this, ceaseless as waves. I leaned on my forearms against the oxidized blue console between the front seats. Before me lay a collage of debris, like a forest floor:

empty black Sobranie packages, fliers in Spanish, a little brush full of black hair, a key ring with a blue rubber coin purse, the kind you squeeze on the sides and the mouth opens up. I played with it, making it sing along to the tape.

The sunrise was a pale rubbing along the eastern horizon, gray-white clouds like scumbled pastels, a sponge-painted sky. Gradually, the manmade features of the landscape receded — the train yards, freeway, houses, and roads — until all that remained was blue hills backlit by dawn light, red over the ridgeline. It was a set for a western movie. I could almost see the arms of giant saguaro, the scurry of coyote and kit fox. The Great Basin, Valley of Smoke. I held my breath. I wished it could always be like this, no people, no city, just rising sun and blue hills.

But the sun cleared the ridge, returning the 2 and the 5, early traffic moving downtown, truck drivers heading to Bakersfield, thinking about pancakes, and us in the van on garbage day.

We continued to sift the city's flotsam, rescuing a wine rack and a couple of broken cane-bottom chairs. We took on an aluminum walker, a box of musty books, and a full recycling bin of Rolling Rock empties that sharpened the mold smell in the back. I pocketed a book about Buddhism, and one called *My Antonia*.

I liked these winding streets and hillside spills of bougainvillea, the long flights of stairs. We drove by the house where Anaïs Nin lived, and I had no one to point it out to. My mother used to like to drive by the places famous writers lived in L.A. — Henry Miller, Thomas Mann, Isherwood, Huxley. I remembered this particular view of the lake, the Chinese mailbox. We had all her books. I liked their titles — *Ladders to Fire, House of Incest* — and her face on the covers, the false eyelashes, her storybook hair coiled and twisted. There was a picture of her with her head in a birdcage. But who was left to care?

We stopped for doughnuts, startling a convention of parking lot pigeons that rose in a great flickering wheel of dark and light grays, taking the stale morning sun on their wings, the freshness already bled from the air. Yvonne stayed in the van, reading her magazine. The girl at the counter at Winchell's rubbed sleep from her eyes as Rena, Niki, and I came into the shop. Rena bent over the glass case in her cherry-red pants, giving an on-purpose bust-and-rump show for the homeless men and mental patients from the nearby board and care, cruelly flaunting what they couldn't have, and I couldn't help thinking of Claire when the bum smelled her hair. We ordered our doughnuts, jelly-filled, custard, glazed. Rena had the girl refill her coffee cup.

Outside, a man squatted by the door, in his arms a tray of ladybugs in plastic bubbles.

"Ladybug," he half sang. "Laaaady-bug."

He was a small man, wiry, of indeterminate age, his face weathered, his black beard and long ponytail shot with gray. Unlike most street people, he didn't seem drunk or insane.

Rena and Niki ignored him, but I stopped to look at the red specks crawling in the bubble. What was the harm in being polite. Anyway, I'd never seen anyone selling ladybugs as a profession.

"Eats the aphids in your garden," he said.

"We don't have a garden," I said.

He smiled. His teeth were gray but not rotten. "Take one anyway. They're lucky."

I gave him a dollar and he handed me the ladybugs in their plastic bubble, the kind rings and trolls came in in the twenty-five-cent gumball machines.

In the van we lingered over our fried dough and caffeine. Flakes of sugar fell on our clothes. The worst thing about Ripple Street was the food. We ate takeout every night. At Rena's, nobody cooked. She didn't even own a recipe book. Her battered recycle bin pans were coated with dust. Four women in one house and nobody knew how to do anything, no one wanted to. We just called Tiny Thai. For people who would stop for empty beer bottles, we pissed all our money away.

As we drove to the other side of the lake, I turned my plastic bubble over, slowly, watching the ladybugs run to stay upright. They were healthier than you'd think. Caught this morning. I imagined the ladybug man's patient blue eyes searching the dewy fennel for the red dots.

Throw it back, Claire had said. *It's so alive.*

But they were lucky, that's what the ladybug man said.

From between the captain's seats, I could see Silver Lake in its nest of hills reflecting the cloudless sky. It reminded me of a place in Switzerland I went once with my mother. A mountain dropping right down into the lake, the town on the slope. There were camellias and palm trees and tall narrow shutters, and it had started to snow as we ate lunch. Snow on the pink camellias.

Now we were on the good side of the lake. We gazed longingly at the big houses, Spanish, Cape Cod, New Orleans, in a morning scented bready-sweet from the big carob trees. Imagining what it would be to be so real. "That one's mine," Yvonne said, pointing to the half-Tudor with the brick driveway. Niki liked a modern one, all glass, you could see the fifties-style lamps against the ceiling, a Calder mobile. "I don't want any junk in my house," she said. "I want it stripped. Chrome and black leather."

As we switchbacked up the hill, we passed a house where someone was practicing the piano before work. It was a Spanish-style place, white with a tile roof and a live oak in the tiny front yard behind a wrought iron fence. It looked so safe, something that could hold beauty like a pool glinting with trout.

Rena noticed me watching it pass. "You think they don't got problem?" Rena said. "Everybody got problem. You got me, they got insurance, house payment, Preparation H." She smiled, baring the part between her two upper teeth. "We are the free birds. They want to be us."

We stopped before a house perched way on top of the hill, they had stuff at the curb. I jumped down, got the baby gate, the high chair with blue food-mottled pads, the playpen and the bouncer seat. Yvonne's eyes turned dark when she saw what I was handing her. Her high color bleached to beige, her mouth pressed together. She grabbed the chair and threw it in the back, more roughly than necessary.

She curled up on the carseat when we were moving again, picked up her *Seventeen* and turned pages, her hands trembling. She closed the magazine and stared at the girl on the cover, a girl who had never been pregnant, never had a social worker or a filling. Yvonne stroked the water-wavy cover. I could tell, she wanted to know what that girl knew, feel how she felt, to be so beautiful, wanted, confident. Like people touching the statue of a saint.

"You think I'd look good blond?" Yvonne held the cover up next to her face.

"It's never done me much good," I said, rotating the ladybugs, making them run.

I saw Claire's face on the banks of the McKenzie, pleading with me to let the fish go. It was the least I could do. I would have to make my own luck anyway. I leaned out behind Niki and opened the bubble into the wind.

IT WAS quarter to eight when we pulled up in front of Marshall High. My eighth school in five years. The front building was faced with elaborate brick, but temporary trailers flanked it on every side. Yvonne lowered her head over the magazine, embarrassed to be seen. She had just dropped out of school this winter.

"Hey," Rena called to me as I got out of the van. She leaned across Niki, holding out a couple of folded bills. "Money makes world go around."

I took the money and thought of Amelia as I shoved it in my pocket. "Thanks."

Niki sneered at the kids sitting on the wall, finishing their cigarettes before class. "School sucks. Why don't you blow it off? Rena doesn't care."

I shrugged. "I've only got one more semester," I said. But truthfully, I was afraid to have one less thing in my life.

24

I SAT UP in bed at one in the morning, cotton stuffed in my ears, as Rena and the comrades partied down in the living room. Just now, they were wailing along to an old Who record cranked so loud I could feel it right through the floor. This was why Rena liked it down here among contractors and bakeries and sheet metal shops. You could make all the noise you wanted. I was learning, everything on Ripple Street was rock 'n' roll. Niki sang with three different bands, and Rena's personal soundtrack consisted of all the big seventies rock she'd first heard on black market tapes in Magnitogorsk. I tried to recall the melodies of Debussy, the gamelan, Miles Davis, but the Who bass line pounded it right out of my head.

To me this rock was just more faceless sex in a man's world, up against a concrete wall behind bathrooms. Give me a Satie tone poem like light on a Monet haystack, or Brazilian Astrud like a Matisse line. Let me lie down in a half-shuttered room in the south of France with Matisse and the soft flutter of heavy-feathered white doves, their mild calls. Only a little time, Henri, before Picasso will come with his big boots. We should take our afternoon.

I missed beauty. The Tujunga night with too many stars, Claire's neck as she bent over me, checking my homework. My mother, swimming underwater in the pool in Hollywood, the melody of her words. All gone now. This was my life, the way it was. *Loneliness is the human condition, get used to it.*

Across the room, Yvonne's bed was empty, she had left with someone at about eleven to go to a party across the river. I sat up in bed, drawing by lamplight, chasing an indigo line of oil pastel on violet paper with a whispery silver. It was a boat, a dark canoe, on the shore of a moonless sea. There was no one in the boat, no oars, no sail. It made me think of the sunless seas of Kublai Khan and also of my mother's Vikings sending their dead out on boats.

I blew on my hands, rubbed them together. The furnace wasn't working, Rena still hadn't fixed it. We just wore sweaters all the time. "Cold?" she said. "In California? You joke." They weren't feeling it, out there braying to the records, drinking Hunter's Brandy, some high-octane Russian specialty that tasted like vodka flavored with nails.

I looked around the cramped, crowded room, like the stockroom of a Goodwill store. I imagined what my mother would say if she could see who I was now, her burning little artist. Just another used item in Rena's thrift shop. You like that lamp with the bubbled green base? Name a price. How about the oil painting of the fat-cheeked peasant woman with the orange kerchief? For you, ten dollars. A bouquet of beaded flowers? Talk to Rena, she'd let you have it for seven-fifty. We had a furry Oriental rug, and a solid oak table, only slightly tilted, along with five unmatched chairs, special today. We had an enormous tiki salad set, and a complete *Encyclopædia Britannica* from 1962. We had three matted white cats, cathair over everything, cat smell. All this, and an old-fashioned hi-fi in a fruitwood cabinet and a stack of records from the seventies higher than Bowie's platform shoes.

And our clothes, Mother, how do you like our clothes? Polyester tops and lavender hiphuggers, yellow shirts with industrial zippers. Clothes floated around from closet to closet until we were bored, then we sold them and bought something else. You wouldn't recognize the girl I've become. My hair is growing out, I found a pair of Jackie O sunglasses and I wear them all the time.

My clothes are gone, the rich orphan clothes from Fred Segal and Barney's New York. Rena made me sell them. I'm sure you'd approve. We were unloading in the parking lot of Natalia's Nails one Saturday. I was arranging coffee mugs when I saw Rena pulling my clothes out of a black plastic garbage bag. My French blue tweed jacket, my Betsey Johnson halter dress, my Myrna Loy pajamas. Hanging them on hangers on the rolling rack.

I snatched them off the rack, stood there shaking. She had gone through my drawers, my closet. "These are mine."

Rena ignored me, shook out a rose-and-gray long skirt, pinned it to a hanger. "Why you need? Dressed best at Marshall High School? Maybe Tiny Thai, Trader Joe? Maybe *Melrose Place* call for you to be star?" She bent and took out an armful of my Fred Segal T-shirts, dumped them into my arms. "Here." She put a roll of tape and a marker on top. "You name price, you keep money, *ladno*?" She kept pulling my things out of plastic garbage bags, hanging them up. Dove-gray high-waisted pants with an Edwardian jacket, a charcoal velvet collar. White shirt with ruffled front. My Jessica McClintock dress with the white cutwork collar.

"Not that," I said. "Come on, have a heart."

Rena squinted at me, blowing a strand of her matte black hair out of her face, exasperated. "You get good price for that. What you saving it for, tea with little Tsarevich Alexei? They shot him 1918." She took the dress out of the bag, shook it and hung it back up. "Is fact."

I stood there, my arms full of the silky T-shirts. Egyptian cotton. Sour pliers squeezed my throat, juicing it like a lemon. She couldn't make me sell my clothes. That witch.

But I couldn't stop the thought that, really, what exactly was I saving them for? When would I ever need a two-hundred-dollar Jessica McClintock dress again? It was a roast-goose-with-chestnuts dress, Puccini at the Music Center, gold rims on china. I looked at Rena in her shiny red blouse, unbuttoned to the third button, high heels, and jeans. Niki, setting up kitchen appliances, magenta hair and black polyester. Yvonne, round as a watermelon in her purple baby doll dress with a swirl pattern from the sixties, sadly arranging the baby furniture, posing a worn teddy bear in the high chair.

Why couldn't anybody ever hang on to anything? You never believed in sentiment, Mother, you saved only your own words, one picture of my grandmother and one of your 4-H cow. Only Claire could hold memory. It was the present that she couldn't sort out.

"Someone gave it to me," I finally said to Rena.

"So?" Rena looked up from her hangers. "You're lucky, someone gave to you. Now you sell, get money out."

I stood there, sullen, my arms still full of T-shirts.

"You want car?" Rena said. "Artist college? You think I don't know? How you think you pay? So this dress. Pretty dress. Someone gave. But money is . . ." She stopped, struggling to find the words, what money was. Finally, she threw her hands up. "*Money*. You want remember, so just remember."

So I did it. I marked a price on my crimson velvet dream. I marked it high, hoping it wouldn't sell. I marked them all high. But they sold. As the sun got warm, the hard bargainers left and the couples came, lazily, arm in arm, old people out for a stroll, young people. The T-shirts, the pants, the jackets went. But by afternoon, the crimson dress was still unsold. People kept asking Rena if it was really one hundred dollars.

"What she say," Rena replied in her deep voice, implying helplessness.

"It's a Jessica McClintock," I said defensively. "Never been worn." My mistake, for anticipating there would be a future, that the dream would just go on and on.

I could still remember how I looked in it when I tried it on at the store in Beverly Hills. I looked innocent, like somebody's daughter, somebody's real daughter. A girl who was cared for. A girl in that dress wasn't a girl who had a beer and a cigarette for lunch, who lay down for the father on carpet pads in an unfinished house. It wasn't a dress that knew how to make a living if it had to, that had to worry about its teeth and whether its mother would come home. When I showed it to Claire, she made me turn for her like a ballerina on a music box, her hands

363

clapped to her mouth, pride flowing from her like tears. She believed I was that girl. And for a moment, so did I.

All day, I helped them on with it, slid the satin lining over their sweaty shoulders, zipped it up as far as it would go without straining. After the fifth woman had tried it on, I started not caring so much. At about three, a group of girls came around, and one of them kept looking at the red dress, holding it up to herself. "Can I try this on?"

I took the plastic off, slid the dress down her arms, over the pale downy hair, pulled it along her body, zipped the back as she held up her dark ponytail. It looked just right on her. As it had never looked on me. I'd never seen the girl before. She didn't go to Marshall. She probably went to Immaculate Heart or the French School. A cared-for girl, someone's daughter. I held it for her as she went to the 7-Eleven to call her mother. Fifteen minutes later, an attractive older woman showed up in a butter-yellow Mercedes, black linen slacks, suede moccasins with horse bit buckles. I helped the girl into the dress again, and the woman gave me the hundred, a single crisp bill. They were going to a cousin's wedding in New York. The dress would be perfect. I could tell from the mother's expression that she knew exactly what it was worth.

We went on until five, then started breaking it down, loading up the van and Niki's pickup truck. All my things had sold. I sat on the fender of the van and counted my money. I'd made over four hundred dollars.

"See, not so bad," Rena said, balancing a box of plates on her hip. "How much you get?"

I mumbled it, ashamed, but also a little proud. It was the first money I'd ever earned.

"Good. Give me hundred." She held out her hand.

"What for?"

She snapped her fingers, extended her hand again.

"No way." I held the money behind my back.

Her black eyes sparkled with bad temper. "What, you think you sell all by yourself on streetcorner? You pay me, I pay Natalia, Natalia pays landlord, what you think? Everybody pay somebody."

"You said I could keep it."

"After pay me."

"For Christ's sake," Niki said, looking up from where she was arranging cheap clothes on a blanket on the ground. "Go ahead and pay her. You have to."

I shook my head no.

Rena shifted the box to the other hip, and when she spoke, her voice was harsh. "Listen to me, *devushka*. I pay, you pay. Just business. When was last time you had three hundred dollars in your hand? So how I hurt you?"

How could I tell her? What about my feelings, I wanted to say, except what was the point? With her it was all just money, and things that could be traded for money. She'd stolen something from me, and even got me to do the selling for her. I couldn't help wondering what you would do, Mother. It didn't apply. I couldn't imagine you at the mercy of Rena Grushenka, in the parking lot of Natalia's Nails, selling your clothes, crying over a dress. I didn't know what else to do, so I held out the hundred, the red dress hundred, and she snatched it from my hand like a dog bite.

But as I sat in bed, listening to the noise and laughter and occasional crash from the living room, I knew that even you had to pay someone now, for your pot and your inks and the good kind of tampons, dental floss and vitamin C. But you would come up with a compelling reason, a theory, a philosophy. You'd make it noble, heroic. You'd write a poem about it, "The Red Dress." I could never do that.

Out in the living room, someone put on an old Zeppelin album. I could hear them singing along in their thick accents, the churning of Jimmy Page's guitar. It was four in the morning and I could smell melting candle wax, dripping in great pools on the tables and windowsills. I didn't need Claire's candle magic book to see *burning house* written there. It was why I slept in my clothes, kept my shoes by the bed, money in my wallet, most important things in a bag by the window.

You'd think they'd try to get some sleep — the next day we were going to the flea market at Fairfax High, to sell our sambo statuettes made of bottlecaps, trays painted with botanical nightmares, never-worn baby clothes, and all the moldy *Reader's Digest*s. But I could tell, they wouldn't sleep until Monday. I hoped I wouldn't see anyone I knew.

I turned over the page, started another canoe. Silver on black. The door opened, Rena's friend Misha stumbled in, posed, playing air guitar along with Jimmy, his plump red lips like an enormous infant's. He was practically drooling. "I come to see you, *maya liubov. Krasivaya devushka.*"

"Go away, Misha."

He staggered over to my bed, sat down next to me. "Don't be cruel," he sang, like Elvis, and bent to drool on my neck.

"Leave me alone." I tried to shove him off, but he was too big and loose, I couldn't find anything solid to push against.

"Don't worry," he said. "I don't do nothing." He lay down

366

on the bed next to me, spread out like a stain. The alcohol reek was a miasma, it reminded me that there were snakes that stunned their prey with their breath. "I am only so lonesome."

I called for help, but no one could hear me over the music. Misha was heavy, he rested his head on my shoulder, slobbering on my neck. His weepy blue eyes so close, one heavy arm around me.

I hit him, but it was no use, he was too drunk, my fist bounced off his flesh, he couldn't feel anything. "Misha, get off me."

"You're so beautiful girl," he said, trying to kiss me. He smelled of vodka and something greasy, someone must have brought a bucket of chicken.

My knife was just under my pillow. I didn't want to stab Misha, I knew him. I'd listened to him play bottleneck guitar. He had a dog named Chernobyl, he wanted to move to Chicago and be a blues guitarist, except he didn't like cold weather. Rena gave him this haircut, the bangs slightly crooked. He wasn't a bad man, but he was kissing my closed mouth, one hand groping under the blanket, though I was fully dressed. His fumbling hand found nothing but vintage polyester.

"Love me a little," he begged in my ear. "Love me, *devushka*, for we all going to die."

Finally, I got a knee up and when he shifted I hit him with my drawing board and slid out of bed.

In the living room, most of the people were gone. Natalia was dancing by herself in front of the stereo, a bottle of Bargain Circus Stoli clutched by the neck in one hand. Georgi was passed out in the black armchair, his head leaning against its fuzzy arm, a white cat curled in his lap. A cane chair was knocked over, a big ashtray lay facedown on the floor. A puddle of something glistened on the scarred leathertop coffee table.

Rena and her boyfriend, Sergei, lay on the green velvet couch, and he was doing it to her with his fingers. Her shoes were still on, her skirt. His shirt was open, he had a medallion on a chain that hung down. I hated to barge in, but then again, Misha was her friend. She was responsible.

"Rena," I said. "Misha's trying to get in bed with me."

Four drunken eyes gazed up at me, two black, two blue. It took them a moment to focus. Sergei whispered something to her in Russian and she laughed. "Misha won't do nothing. Hit him on head with something," Rena said.

Sergei was watching me as he kneaded her thigh, bit her neck. He looked like a white tiger devouring a kill.

When I went back into my room, Misha had passed out. He had a bloody cut on his head from where I hit him. He was snoring, holding my pillow like it was me. He wasn't waking up anytime soon. I went to sleep in Yvonne's empty bed. The stereo stopped at five, and I got a restless hour or two of sleep, dreaming of animals rummaging through the garbage. I was awakened by a man pissing in the bathroom across the hall without closing the door, a stream that seemed to last for about five minutes. He didn't flush. Then the stereo came back on, the Who again. *Who are you?* the band sang. I tried to remember, but I really couldn't say.

25

WE SAT IN THE KITCHEN on a dreary Saturday, sewing leather bags for crystals. It was Rena's latest moneymaking idea. Niki played demo tapes of the different bands Werner booked, but they all sounded the same, skinny white kid rage, out-of-control guitars. She was looking for a new band. "This one's all right, don't you think? Fuck!" She jabbed the needle into a finger, stuck it into her lipstick-blackened mouth. "This sewing's for shit. What does she think we are, some fucking elves?"

We were smoking hash under glass while we worked. I let the smoke fill up under the little shot glass that Niki stole from the Bavarian Gardens, it had an upside-down Johnnie Walker printed on it. I put my mouth down to the edge, picked up a corner of the glass, and sucked the thick hash fumes into my lungs. Yvonne didn't smoke, she said it was bad for the baby.

"What difference does it make?" Niki said, putting a chunk of hash on the pin for herself. "It's not like you're going to keep it."

The corners of her mouth turned down. "You think that

way, I don't want you taking me to baby class," Yvonne said. "Astrid'll take me."

I started coughing. I tried to do Butterfly McQueen from the childbirth scene in *Gone with the Wind*. "I don't know nothin' 'bout birthin' no babies," but I couldn't get my voice to go high enough. I thought of Michael, he always did Butterfly better than me. I missed him.

"At least you have good thoughts," Yvonne said.

Childbirth. I shuddered. "I'm not even eighteen."

"That's okay, they don't serve liquor," Niki said, throwing a finished bag on the pile. She picked up another one that was all cut out and ready for sewing.

Stoned, I traced a rising smoke pattern into a scrap of leather with an X-acto blade. I was good at this, better than my mother used to be. I could do a crow, a cat. I could do a cat in three cuts. I did a baby with a curl on its forehead and tossed it to Yvonne.

The door banged open behind us, letting in a rush of cold air. Rena came in with a roll of dark green suede tucked under her arm. "Georgi sell whole thing, trade for lamp," she grinned proudly. "Nice, huh?" Then her gaze landed on me, etching designs into the leather. "What, you crazy?" She grabbed the doeskin away from me, thumped the back of my head with the heel of her hand. "Pothead stupid girl. You think is cheap?" Then she noticed the design and frowned, her lower lip pouted out. She held the scrap up to the light. "Not bad." She tossed it back to me. "I think it sell. Do all bags. We make money on this."

I nodded. I blew whatever I made on art supplies and food and going in with Niki on dope. College had already vanished, disappearing like a boat into fog. At Claire's, I'd begun to think of my life as a series of Kandinsky pencil sketches, meaningless by themselves, but arranged together they would begin to form an elegant composition. I even thought I had seen the shape of the future in them. But now I had lost too many pieces. They had returned to a handful of pine needles on a forest floor, unreadable.

Sergei came in carrying a bag, his cheeks flushed pink in his handsome, wide, un-Californian face. He unloaded two bottles of vodka, put one in the freezer, set the other on the counter, and took down two green glasses. He sniffed the air. "Mmm, dinner."

"So who invites you?" Rena said, hopping up to sit on the counter, unscrewing the cap of the vodka. She poured three fingers into each glass.

"Oh, these girls not starve Sergei," he said. He opened the oven, peered in at the bubbling dish I was making for Yvonne, a broccoli-and-cheese casserole, to build her up for the baby. She'd been stunned to watch me put the ingredients together, she hadn't realized you could cook without a box with instructions. Sergei bathed his face in the smell and the heat of the oven.

I cut a tiger into a leather scrap, reminding myself that Sergei was just Rena with a better facade. Handsome as a Cossack, a milky Slavic blond with sleepy blue eyes that caught every movement. By profession, a thief. Rena occasionally moved merchandise for him, a truckload of leather couches, racks of women's coats, a shipment of stuffed animals from Singapore, small appliances from Israel. Around here, he was a constant sexual fact. He left the bathroom door open while he

371

shaved in the nude, did a hundred push-ups every morning, his milky white skin veined with blue. If he saw you were watching he'd add a clap to show off. Those wide shoulders, the neat waist. When Sergei was in the room, I never knew what to do with my hands, with my mouth.

I looked over at Yvonne across the table, bent over piles of little bags and leather scraps, sewing, patient as a girl in a fairy tale. Any other girl would be sewing the ruffles on her prom gown, or knitting baby shoes. Now I felt bad about making fun of her earlier. "Sure, I'll go to baby class with you," I said. "If you think I'll be any use."

She smiled down at her sewing, ducking her head. She didn't like to show her bad teeth. "It's no sweat. I do all the work. All you gotta do is hold the towel."

"Huff 'n' puff," Niki said. "Bunch of beachballs blowing it out the wrong end. A real laugh riot. You'll see." Niki broke off another chunk of hash, put it on the pin. She lit it and watched the smoke fill the glass like a genie in a lamp. When she took the hit, she broke into a coughing fit even worse than mine.

"None for me?" Sergei asked, pointing at the shot glass.

"Fuck you, Sergei," Niki said. "When did you ever buy us any?"

But she put a little out for him anyway, and I tried to ignore the way he looked right at me as he stooped to put his lips where mine had been. But I felt my face burn right up to the hairline.

We all ate, except Rena, who smoked and drank vodka. As soon as she left the room for a moment, Sergei leaned over, broad white hands folded before him. "So, when we make love, *devushka*?"

"You sleazebag," Niki said, pointing her fork at him. "I ought to tell Rena."

"Anyway, Astrid's got a boyfriend," Yvonne said. "An artist. He lives in New York."

I'd told her all about Paul Trout. I'd finally picked up his letters from Yellow Brick Road in Hollywood, on the same street where I pulled the knife on the girl who thought I was Wendy. Niki took me there after school, on the way to meeting some guys who needed a singer. I felt bad I hadn't written to him before, I'd thought of it many times, but I was afraid. Chances were he never looked back. On the drive into Hollywood, I looked nervously at the envelope, marked *Hold for Paul Trout*. The hope implied. It was a mistake already. I thought of a song Rena played that I hated like death, "Love the One You're With." It was the tune life kept forcing on me, and yet there I was, hope fluttering like a bird in my hand.

The shop was tiny, more crowded even than Rena's. Comic books everywhere. Niki and I leafed through the stacks. Some of the comics were jokey, like Zippy the Pinhead and old Mr. Natural. Others were dark and expressionist, Sam Spade meets Murnau. There were racks of homemade magazines full of bad poets. Comics in Japanese, many of them pornographic. Tongue-in-cheek stories of career girls and supermodels drawn in the Lichtenstein pop style. A Jewish rodent trapped in a Blackshirt paranoid nightmare. They sold everything from the standard DCs to locally drawn, Xeroxed, staple-spined 'zines. While Niki read a gangster girl tale, I went to the counter, told myself there'd be nothing for me.

A skinny guy in a burgundy bowling shirt doodled on the counter, pale arms covered with tattoos. I cleared my throat until he looked up. His eyes were pot-hazed. "I'm a friend of Paul Trout's. Did he leave anything for me?"

He smiled a little shyly, wiping his nose on the back of his hand. "He went to New York, didn't you hear?" He rummaged under the counter and came up with two letters, the envelopes so heavily illustrated you could barely see the Yellow Brick Road address. The outside was marked *Hold for Astrid Magnussen*.

"No return address?"

"He moves a lot. Don't be surprised."

I left one for Paul, illustrating my life on Ripple Street. Trashpicking, our living room. I didn't know what else to do with it. He was gone.

In the corner booth at the rock 'n' roll Denny's on Sunset, I sat with Niki as she negotiated with the boys from the band, two bleached blonds and a hyperactive brunette — the drummer, I knew without asking. I was afraid to open the letters. Instead, I sketched some of the other customers. Goth girls in black tights and black ratted hair, conspiring over Diet Pepsis and double orders of onion rings. On the other side, two aging rockers in leather and studs ate their burgers; one was talking on a cell phone. It was like some kind of era-by-era fashion layout, Mohawks and ducktails and dreadlocks, polyester and platforms.

"I'm not paying to play with twelve other bands. What, are you retarded?" Niki was saying. "They're supposed to pay you, not the other way around." I sketched the blond bass player as he guiltily tongued his chin stud from the inside. The brunette spasmodically tapped on the water glasses with his knife. "You gotta play where they pay. Where you from anyway, Fresno?"

"But it's like the Roxy, you know?" the taller blond said. He was obviously the spokesman, the eloquent one. Lead guitar. "The *Roxy*. It's like the . . ."

"The Roxy," the other blond said.

I finally worked up the nerve to open the first letter, slitting the beautiful envelope with the Denny's dinner knife. Inside was a series of ink drawings done in Paul's unmistakable comic book style, bold blacks and whites: Paul, walking lonely comic book streets. Paul, sitting at a Nighthawks café. He sees a blond girl on the street with short chopped-up hair and follows her, only to have her turn out to be somebody else. *Would he ever see her again?* the last caption read, as he drew at his desk, the wall covered with pictures of me.

The second envelope held a comic strip story of a prison break, three boys blasting their way out through steel doors with rocket launchers. They steal a car, the signs say Leaving L.A. They tear across the desert in the night. Next there's a street sign in broken mosaic, it says St. Marks Place. Angular hipsters in black pass a doorway, 143. The Statue of Liberty in the background wears shades, it's reading a comic book.

I folded the drawings, slipped them back into the envelope decorated with lightning bolts, stars, and a girl on a white horse in a comic book sky. *Hold for Astrid Magnussen.* If only I'd known that he would.

And now it was too late. I looked at Sergei across the table in Rena's kitchen. He could care less about my boyfriend in New York. He didn't even care about his girlfriend in the next room. He was just like one of Rena's white cats — eat, sleep, and fornicate. Since the night I'd seen them together on the couch, he was always watching me with his hint of a grin, as if there were some secret we shared. "So how is your boyfriend?" he asked. "Big? Is he big?"

Niki laughed. "He's huge, Sergei. Haven't you heard of him? Moby Dick."

Olivia had told me all about men like Sergei. Hard men with blue veins in their sculpted white arms, heavy-lidded blue eyes and narrow waists. You could make a deal with a man like that. A man who knew what he wanted. I kept my eyes on my broccoli and cheese.

"You get tired of waiting," he said. "You come see me."

"What if you're no good?" I said, making the other girls laugh.

"Only worry you fall in love Sergei," he said, his voice like a hand between my legs.

MY LATEST CASEWORKER, Mrs. Luanne Davis, was a middle-aged black woman in a white blouse tied in a bow at the neck and relaxed hair in a pageboy. I spotted her right off when I arrived at the McDonald's on Sunset after school. I ordered a burger and fries and a Coke, and for once, the screaming of children in the ball pit didn't bother me. I'd gone to Playland the night before with Niki, where she sang with one of Werner's bands, Freeze. I carried her microphone stand, which made me a roadie, so I didn't need an ID. Niki was the only one who could sing. She had a purring, ironical voice, she sang the way Anne Sexton read poetry. But everyone else screamed, and nobody could play, and I was still half-deaf from it.

The social worker passed a wad of letters across the sticky table to me. Such potential for damage, I didn't even want to pick them up. I hated the sight of them, my mother's handwriting, the crabbed lines I could see through the blue airmail envelopes. She could get seven pages per stamp, and each thin sheet weighed more than the night. They were like a kelp forest, they cast a weird green light, you could get lost there, become tangled and drown. I had not written to her since Claire died.

Sipping her black coffee with Sweet'n Low, Mrs. Luanne Davis spoke slowly, overenunciating in light of my temporary deafness. "You really should write her. She's in segregation. It can't be easy."

"I didn't put her there," I said, still eyeing the letters like Portuguese man-of-wars floating on the innocent sea.

She frowned. She had lines between her eyebrows from frowning at girls like me, girls who didn't believe anybody could love them, least of all their dangerous parents. "I can't tell you how few children I have whose parents write. They'd be thrilled to death."

"Yeah, I'm super lucky," I said, but I dutifully put them in my pack.

I finished my food, watching the kids jump off the net onto one small boy who couldn't find his feet in the ball pit. Over and over they jumped onto him, laughing while he screamed. His teenaged mother was too busy talking to her friend to help him. Finally, she yelled something at the other kids, but she didn't get up or do anything to protect her son. When she turned back to her friend, our eyes met. It was Kiki Torrez. We made no sign that we knew each other, we just looked a little longer than a casual glance, and then she went on talking to her friend. And I thought, prisoners probably traded just that glance, when they met on the outside.

When I got home, Yvonne was in front of the TV on the figured green velvet couch, watching a talk show for teenagers. "This is the mother," she told me, not taking her eyes from the screen. "She gave up the daughter when she was sixteen. They never saw each other before this second." Big child's tears dripped down her face.

I didn't know how she could stand to watch this, it was as phony as an ad. I couldn't help thinking of the adopted mother who'd raised the girl, how sick it must make her feel to see her carefully raised daughter in the arms of a stranger, applauded by the talk show audience. But I knew Yvonne was imagining herself coming back into her baby's life twenty years from now, slim, confident, dressed in a blue suit with high heels and perfect hair, her grown child embracing her, forgiving her everything. And what were the chances of that.

I sat down next to Yvonne and looked through my mother's letters, opened one.

Dear Astrid,

    Why don't you write? You cannot possibly hold me responsible for Claire Richards's suicide. That woman was born to overdose. I told you the first time I saw her. Believe me, she's better off now.

    On the other hand, I am writing from Ad Seg, prison within a prison. This is what is left of my world, an 8x8 cell shared with Lunaria Irolo, a woman as mad as her name.

    During the day, the crows caw, dissonant and querulous, a perfect imitation of the damned. Of course, nothing that sings would alight near this place. No, we are left

quite alone with our unholy crows and the long-distance
cries of the gulls.

   The buzz and slam of the gates reverberate in this great
hollow chamber, roll across poured cement floors to where
we crouch behind a chain-link fence, behind the slitted
doors, plotting murder, plotting revenge. I am behind
the fence, they say. They handcuff us even to shower. Well
they should.

I liked that idea, my mother behind the fence, handcuffed.
She couldn't hurt me from there.

   From the slitted window in the door, I can see the COs
at their desks in the middle of the unit. Our janitors of
penitence, eating doughnuts. Keys glitter important at their
waists. It's the keys I watch. I am hypnotized by keys, thick
fistfuls of them, I can taste their acid galvanization, more
precious than wisdom.

   Yesterday, Sgt. Brown decided my half hour in the
shower counts as part of the hour I'm permitted out of my
cell each day. I remember when I had hoped he would be a
reasonable man, black, slender, well-spoken. But I should
have known. His deep voice seems not to issue from his
meager frame, it's as artificial as a preacher's, steeped in
an overblown sense of his own importance, the Cerberus of
our concrete Inferno.

   In my extensive leisure time, I am practicing astral pro-
tection. As Lunaria's voice drones on, I rise from my bunk
and fly out across the fields, following the freeway west
until I can see the downtown towers. I have touched the

mosaics of the Central Library's glazed pyramid. I have seen the ancient carp glistening orange, pimento, dappled silver, and black in the koi ponds of the New Otani. I ride updrafts around the Bonaventure's neat cylinders, its glass elevators ricocheting between floors. Do you remember the time we ate at the top, went once around in the revolving bar? You wouldn't get near the windows, you screamed that the space was pulling you out. We had to move to a booth in the center, remember? You know the mistrust of heights is the mistrust of self, you don't know whether you're going to jump.

And I see you, walking in alleys, sitting in vacant lots crowded with weeds, Queen Anne's lace dotted with rain. You think you cannot bear losing that weakling, Claire. Remember, there's only one virtue, Astrid. The Romans were right. One can bear anything. The pain we cannot bear will kill us outright.

Mother.

But I didn't believe her for a second. Long ago, she told me that to slash each other to ribbons in battle each day and be put back together each night was the Vikings' idea of heaven. Eternal slaughter, that was the thing. You were never killed outright. It was like the eagle feeding on your liver by day and having it grow back, only more fun.

26

—

THE TRAINS ACROSS the river rolled on iron wheels, making a soothing percussion in the night. On our side, back by the bakery, a boy was playing electric guitar. He couldn't sleep either, the sound of the trains stirred him. His guitar bore his longing up into the darkness like sparks, a music profound in its objectless desire, beautiful beyond solace or solution.

In the other bed, Yvonne was restless. The maple frame groaned under her weight when she turned. She had eight weeks to go and I couldn't imagine her getting any larger. The swell of her belly rose above the plane of sheet in a smooth volcanic dome, a Mount Saint Helens, Popocatépetl, ready for eruption. Time was moving in the room, in the music of the trains, ratchet by ratchet, a train so vast it needed three locomotives to roll its bulk through the night. Where did the trains go, Mother? Were we there yet?

Sometimes I imagined I had a father who worked nights for the railroad. A signalman for the Southern Pacific who wore heavy fireproof gloves big as oars, and wiped sweat from his forehead with a massive forearm. If I had a father who worked nights for the railroad, I might have had a mother who would listen for the click of the door when he came home, and I would hear her quiet voice, their muffled laughter through the thin walls of the house. How soft their voices would be, and sweet, like pigeons brooding under a bridge.

If I were a poet, that's what I'd write about. People who worked in the middle of the night. Men who loaded trains, emergency room nurses with their gentle hands. Night clerks in hotels, cabdrivers on graveyard, waitresses in all-night coffee shops. They knew the world, how precious it was when a person remembered your name, the comfort of a rhetorical question, "How's it going, how's the kids?" They knew how long the night was. They knew the sound life made as it left. It rattled, like a slamming screen door in the wind. Night workers lived without illusions, they wiped dreams off counters, they loaded freight. They headed back to the airport for one last fare.

Under the bed, a darker current wove itself into the night. My mother's unread letters, fluid with lies, shifted and heaved, like the debris of an enormous shipwreck that continued to be washed ashore years after the liner went down. I would allow no more words. From now on, I only wanted things that could be touched, tasted, the scent of new houses, the buzz of wires before rain. A river flowing in moonlight, trees growing out of concrete, scraps of brocade in a fifty-cent bin, red geraniums on a sweatshop window ledge. Give me the way rooftops of stucco apartments piled up forms in the afternoon like late surf, something without a spin, not a self-portrait in water and wind. Give me the boy playing electric guitar, my foster home bed at the end of Ripple Street, and the shape of Yvonne and her baby that was coming. She was the hills of California under mustard and green, tawny as lions in summer.

Across the room, Yvonne cried out. Her pillow fell on the floor. I got it for her. It was spongy with sweat. She sweated so much at night, I sometimes had to help her change the sheets. I put the pillow behind her dark hair, pushed the soaked strands from her face. She was hot as a steaming load of wet laundry. The guitar unraveled a song I could only occasionally recognize as "So You Want to Be a Rock and Roll Star."

"Astrid," Yvonne whispered.

"Listen," I said. "Someone's playing guitar."

"I had the worst dream," she mumbled. "People kept stealing my stuff. They took my horse."

Her felted paper horse, white with gold paper trappings and red silk fringe, sat on the dresser, front leg raised, neck curved into an arch that echoed the frightened curve of her eyebrows.

"It's still there," I said, putting my hand on her cheek. I knew it would feel cool on her hot skin. My mother used to do this when I was sick, I suddenly remembered, and for a moment I could feel it distinctly, the touch of her cool hands.

Yvonne lifted her head to see the horse still prancing in the moonlight, then lay back on the pillow. "I wish this was over."

I knew what Rena would say. *The sooner the better*. A few months ago, I'd have gone her one further. I would have thought, what was the difference? When she gave birth to the baby, once it had been given away, there would always be something more to lose, a boyfriend, a home, a job, sickness, more babies, days and nights rolling over each other in an ocean that was always the same. Why hurry disaster?

But now I had seen her sitting cross-legged on her bed whispering to her belly, telling it how great the world was going to be, that there were horses and birthdays, white cats and ice cream. Even if Yvonne wouldn't be there for roller skates and the first day of school, it had to count for something. She had it now, that sweetness, that dream. "Yeah, when it's time, you'll think it's too soon," I said.

Yvonne held my hand to her hot forehead. "You're always cool. You don't sweat at all. Oh, the baby's moving," she whispered. "You want to feel it?"

She shoved up her T-shirt and I put my hand on her bare belly, round and hot as rising dough, to feel the odd distortions of the baby's movements against my palm. Her smile was lopsided, divided, delight warring with what she knew was coming.

"I think it's a girl," she whispered. "The other one was a girl."

She talked about her babies only late at night when we were alone. Rena wouldn't let her talk about them, she told her not to think about them. But Yvonne needed to talk. The father of this one, Ezequiel, drove a pickup truck. They had met at Griffith Park, and she fell in love when he put her on the merry-go-round.

I tried to think of something to say. "She's got a good kick. Maybe she'll be a ballerina, *ese*."

The simple melody line of the electric guitar bounced off

the hills and fed in through the window, and the mound of Yvonne's stomach danced in time, the tiny bumps of hands and feet.

"I want her to do Girl Scouts. You're gonna do Girl Scouts, *mija*," she said to the mound. She looked back up at me. "Did you ever do it?"

I shook my head.

"I always wanted to," she said, tracing figure eights on the damp sheet. "But I couldn't ask. My mom would've laughed her head off. 'Your big ass in the damn Girl Scouts?'"

We sat there for the longest time, not saying anything. Hoping her daughter would have all the good things. The guitarist had quieted down, he was playing "Michelle." My mother loved that song. She could sing it in French.

Yvonne dozed off, and I went back to bed, thinking of my mother's cool hands on my face in the heat of a fever, the way she would wrap me in sheets soaked in ice water, eucalyptus, and cloves. *I am your home,* she'd once said, and it was still true.

I crawled under the bed, pulled out the sack of her letters, some packets thin as a promise, others fat like white koi. The bag was heavy, it exhaled the scent of her violets. I got up silently, not to wake Yvonne, and slipped out of the room, shutting the door tightly behind me.

In the living room, on the green couch, I turned on the beaded lamp that made everything look like a Toulouse-Lautrec painting. I lifted handfuls of letters onto the coffee table. I hated my mother but I craved her. I wanted to understand how she could fill my world with such beauty, and could also say, that woman was born to OD.

385

The battered tomcat stalked along the back of the couch, cautiously climbed onto me. I let it curl up under my heart, heavy and warm and purring like a truck in low gear.

Dear Astrid,

It's three in the morning, we've just had fourth count. In Ad Seg, the lights burn all night, fluorescent and stark on gray block walls just wide enough for the bed and the toilet. Still no letter from you. Only Sister Lunaria's sexual litany. It runs day and night from the bottom bunk, like shifts of Tibetan monks praying the world into being. This evening, the exegesis has centered upon the Book of Raul, her last boyfriend. How worshipfully she describes the size and configuration of his member, the prismatic catalog of his erotic response.

Sex is the last thing I think about here. Freedom is my only concern. I ponder the configuration of molecules in the walls. I meditate upon the nature of matter, a prevalence of void within the whirling electron rodeo. I try to vibrate between the packets of quanta, phasing at precisely the opposite wavelength, so that eventually I will exist in between the pulses, and matter will become wholly permeable. Someday, I will walk right through these walls.

"Gonzales is giving it to Vicki Manolo over on Simmons A," quoth Lunaria. "He's hung like a horse. When he sits down it's like he's got a baseball bat in there."

The inmates like Gonzales. He takes the trouble to flirt, wears cologne, his hands are clean as white calla. She is masturbating, imagining enormous penises, she's coupling with horses, with bulls, she's positively Jovian in her fantasies, while I stare up at the pinpricks in the acoustical tiles and listen to the nightbreath of the prison.

These days, I hear everything. I hear the click of the cards in guard tower 1, not poker, sounds like gin rummy, listen to their sad admissions of hemorrhoids and domestic suspicions. The old ladies in the honor cottage, Miller, snore with their dentures in a glass. I hear the rats in Culinary. A woman screams in the SCU, she hears the rats too, but doesn't understand they're not in her bed. Restraints are quickly applied.

In the dormitories of Reception, I hear murmured threats as they shake down a new girl. She's soft, a check kiter, she wasn't prepared to be here. They take everything she has left to take. "Pussy," they say after they're through.

The rest of the prison sleeps fitfully, rocked in dreams made vivid by captivity. I know what they're dreaming. I read them like novels, it's better than Joyce. They're dreaming of men who beat them, a backhand, unsubtle kick to the groin. Men who clench their teeth before striking, they hiss, "Look what you're making me do." The women cringe even in sleep, under the stares of men's eyeballs roadmapped with veins, popped with rage, the whites the color of mayonnaise left out for a week. One wonders how they could even see to deliver their blows. But women's fear is a magnet. I hope you don't know this. It draws the fist, the hands of men, hard as God's.

Others are luckier. They dream of men with gentle hands, eloquent with tenderness, fingers that brushed along a cheek, that outlined open lips in the lovers' braille. Hands that sculpted sweetness from sullen flesh, that traced breast and ignited hips, opening, kneading. Flesh becomes bread in the heat of those hands, braided and rising.

Some dream of crime, guns and money. Vials of dreams that disappeared like late snow. I am there. I see the face of a surprised ARCO attendant just at the moment it spreads into a collage of bright blood and bone.

I lie down in the cherished apartment, its white carpet, garbage disposal, dishwasher, security parking. I too cheat the old couple out of their savings and celebrate over a bottle of Mumm's and Sevruga on toast. I carefully take a sliding glass door off the track of a two-story house in Mar Vista. I buy a fur coat at Saks with a stolen American Express credit card. It's the best Russian sable, golden as brandy.

Best are the freedom dreams. Steering wheels so real in the hand, the spring of the accelerator, gas tanks marked FULL. Wind through open windows, we don't use the air conditioner, we suck in the live air going by. We take the freeways, using the fast lanes, watch for signs saying San Francisco, New Orleans. We pass trucks on great interstates, truck drivers blowing their airhorns. We drink sodas at gas stations, eat burgers rare at roadside cafés, order extra everything. We listen to country music stations, we pick up Tijuana, Chicago, Atlanta, GA, and sleep in motels where the clerk never even looks up, just takes the money.

On Barneburg B, my cellmate Lydia Guzman dreams of walking on Whittier Blvd. in summertime, a rush of roughly cut drugs throbbing salsa down her thighs slick with ten-dollar nylons. She stuns the vatos with her slow

haunch-dripping stride, her skirt impossibly tight. Her
laughter tastes like burnt sunshine, cactus, and the worm.

But most of all, we dream of children. The touch of
small hands, glinty rows of seed pearl teeth. We are al-
ways losing our children. In parking lots, in the market, on
the bus. We turn and call. Shawanda, we call, Luz, Astrid.
How could we lose you, we were being so careful. We only
looked away for a moment. Arms full of packages, we
stand alone on the sidewalk and someone has taken our
children.

Mother.

They could lock her up, but they couldn't prevent the transformation of the world in her mind. This was what Claire
never understood. The act by which my mother put her face on
the world. There were crimes that were too subtle to be effec-
tively prosecuted.

I sat up and the white cat flowed off me like milk. I folded
the letter and put it back in its envelope, threw it onto the
crowded coffee table. She didn't fool me. I was the soft girl in
Reception. She'd rob me of everything I had left to take. I
would not be seduced by the music of her words. I could
always tell the ragged truth from an elegant lie.

Nobody took me away, Mother. My hand never slipped
from your grasp. That wasn't how it went down. I was more
like a car you'd parked while drunk, then couldn't remember
where you'd left it. You looked away for seventeen years and
when you looked back, I was a woman you didn't recognize. So
now I was supposed to feel pity for you and those other women
who'd lost their own children during a holdup, a murder, a

fiesta of greed? Save your poet's sympathy and find some better believer. Just because a poet said something didn't mean it was true, only that it sounded good. Someday I'd read it all in a poem for the *New Yorker*.

Yes, I was tattooed, just as she'd said. Every inch of my skin was penetrated and stained. I was the original painted lady, a Japanese gangster, a walking art gallery. Hold me up to the light, read my bright wounds. If I had warned Barry I might have stopped her. But she had already claimed me. I wiped my tears, dried my hands on the white cat, and reached for another handful of glass to rub on my skin. Another letter full of agitated goings-on, dramas, and fantasies. I skimmed down the page.

Somewhere in Ad Seg, a woman is crying. She's been crying all night. I've been trying to find her, but at last, I realize, she's not here at all. It's you. Stop crying, Astrid. I forbid it. You have to be strong. I'm in your room, Astrid, do you feel me? You share it with a girl, I see her too, her lank hair, her thin arched eyebrows. She sleeps well, but not you. You sit up in bed with the yellow chenille spread — God, where did she find that thing, your new foster mother? My mother had one just like it.

I see you cradling your bare knees, forehead pressed against them. Crickets stroke their legs like pool players lining up shots. Stop crying, do you hear me? Who do you think you are? What am I doing here, except to show you how a woman is stronger than that?

It's such a liability to love another person, but in here, it's like playing catch with grenades. The lifers tell me to

390

forget you, do easy time. "You can make a life here," they say. "Choose a mate, find new children." Sometimes it's so awful, I think that they're right. I should forget you. Sometimes I wish you were dead, so I would know you were safe.

A woman in my unit gave her children heroin from the time they were small, so she'd always know where they were. They're all in jail, alive. She likes it that way. If I thought I'd be here forever, I would forget you. I'd have to. It sickens me to think of you out there, picking up wounds while I spin in this cellblock, impotent as a genie in a lamp. Astrid, stop crying, damn you!

I will get out, Astrid, I promise you that. I will win an appeal, I will walk through the walls, I will fly away like a white crow.

Mother.

Yes, I was crying. These words like bombs she sealed up and had delivered, leaving me ragged and bloody weeks later. You imagine you can see me, Mother? All you could ever see was your own face in a mirror.

You always said I knew nothing, but that was the place to begin. I would never claim to know what women in prison dreamed about, or the rights of beauty, or what the night's magic held. If I thought for a second I did, I'd never have the chance to find out, to see it whole, to watch it emerge and reveal itself. I don't have to put my face on every cloud, be the protagonist of every random event.

Who am I, Mother? I'm not you. That's why you wish I were dead. You can't shape me anymore. I am the uncontrolled element, the random act, I am forward movement in time. You think you can see me? Then tell me, who am I? You don't know. I am nothing like you. My nose is different, flat at the bridge, not sharp as a fold in rice paper. My eyes aren't ice blue, tinted with your peculiar mix of beauty and cruelty. They are dark as bruises on the inside of an arm, they never smile. You forbid me to cry? I'm no longer yours to command. You used to say I had no imagination. If by that you meant I could feel shame, and remorse, you were right. I can't remake the world just by willing it so. I don't know how to believe my own lies. It takes a certain kind of genius.

I went out on the front porch, the splintered boards under my bare feet. The wind carried the steady noise of traffic on the 5 and barking dogs, the pop of gunfire a block or two off in a night tinged red from the sodium vapor streetlights, it was bleeding. *We were the ones who sacked Rome,* she said on that long-ago night on the rooftop under the raven's-eye moon. *Don't forget who you are.*

How could I ever forget. I was her ghost daughter, sitting at empty tables with crayons and pens while she worked on a poem, a girl malleable as white clay. Someone to shape, instruct in the ways of being her. She was always shaping me. She showed me an orange, a cluster of pine needles, a faceted quartz, and made me describe them to her. I couldn't have been more than three or four. My words, that's what she wanted. "What's this?" she kept asking. "What's this?" But how could I tell her? She'd taken all the words.

The smell of vanilla wafers saturated the night air, and the wind clicked through the palms like thoughts through my sleepless mind. Who am I? I am a girl you didn't know, Mother.

The silent girl in the back row of the schoolroom, drawing in notebooks. Remember how they didn't know if I even spoke English when we came back to the States? They tested me to find out if I was retarded or deaf. But you never asked why. You never thought, maybe I should have left Astrid some words.

I thought of Yvonne in our room, asleep, thumb in mouth, wrapped around her baby like a top. "I can see her," you said. You could never see her, Mother. Not if you stood in that room all night. You could only see her plucked eyebrows, her bad teeth, the books that she read with fainting women on the covers. You could never recognize the kindness in that girl, the depth of her needs, how desperately she wanted to belong, that's why she was pregnant again. You could judge her as you judged everything else, inferior, but you could never see her. Things weren't real to you. They were just raw material for you to reshape to tell a story you liked better. You could never just listen to a boy play guitar, you'd have to turn it into a poem, make it all about you.

I went back inside, spread all her letters out on Rena's wobble-legged kitchen table, letters from Starr's and from Marvel's, letters from Amelia's and Claire's and these last bitter installments. There were enough to drown me forever. The ink of her writing was a fungus, a malignant spell on birch bark, a twisted rune. I picked up the scissors and began cutting, snapping the strings of her words, uncoupling her complicated train of thought car by car. She couldn't stop me now. I refused to see through her eyes any longer.

Carefully, I chose words and phrases from the pile, laid them out on the gray-and-white linoleum tabletop and began to arrange them in lines. Gray dawn was straining peaches by the time I was done.

> It sickens me to think of you
> a prevalence of void
> unholy
> immovable
> damned. gifts.
> an overblown sense of his own importance.
> I wish you were dead

> forget about you.
> crow
> florid with
> fantasies
> it's so awful
> a perfect imitation

> a liability to love
> forget you
> Ingrid Magnussen

> quite alone
> masturbating
> rot
> disappointment
> grotesque

> Your arms cradle
> poisons

garbage
grenades

Loneliness
long-distance cries
forever
never
response.

take everything
feel me?
the human condition

Stop
plotting murder
penitence
Cultivate it

you
forbid
appeal
rage
impotent
it's too
important
I
cringe

fuck
you

insane
person
dissonant and querulous

my
gas tanks marked FULL

I glued them to sheets of paper. I give them back to you. Your own little slaves. Oh my God, they're in revolt. It's Spartacus, Rome is burning. Now sack it, Mother. Take what you can before it all burns to ash.

—

27

THE CRYSTALLINE DAYS of March, that rarest of seasons, came like a benediction, regal and scented with cedar and pine. Needle-cold winds rinsed every impurity from the air, so clear you could see the mountain ranges all the way to Riverside, crisp and defined as a paint-by-the-numbers kit, windclouds pluming off their powdered flanks like a PBS show about Everest. The news said snowline was down to four thousand feet. These were ultramarine days, trimmed in ermine, and the nights showed all their ten thousand stars, gleaming overhead like a proof, a calculus woven on the warp and weft of certain fundamental truths.

How clear it was without my mother behind my eyes. I was reborn, a Siamese twin who had finally been separated from its hated, cumbersome double. I woke early, expectant as a small child, to a world washed clean of my mother's poisonous fog, her milky miasmas. This sparkling blue, this March, would be my metaphor, my insignia, like Mary's robe, blue edged with ermine, midnight with diamonds. Who would I be now that I had taken myself back, to be Astrid Magnussen, finally, alone.

Dear Astrid,

Bravo! Though your letter as poetry leaves something to be desired, at least it indicates a spark, a capacity for fire which I never would have believed you possessed. But really, you cannot think you will cut yourself free of me so easily. I live in you, in your bones, the delicate coils of your mind. I made you. I formed the thoughts you find, the moods you carry. Your blood whispers my name. Even in rebellion, you are mine.

You want my penitence, demand my shame? Why would you want me to be less than I am, so you could find it easier to dismiss me? I'd rather you think me grotesque, florid with fantasy.

I'm out of segregation, thank you for asking. Waiting for me on my restoration to Barneburg B was, among other missives, a letter from Harper's. *Oh the praise, a jailhouse Plath! (Although I am no suicide, no baked poetess with my head among the potatoes.)*

Do not give up on me so soon, Astrid. There are people who are interested in my case. I will not molder here like the Man in the Iron Mask. This is the millennium. Anything can happen. And if I had to be wrongly imprisoned to be noticed by Harper's — *well . . . you could almost say it was worth it.*

And to think, when I was out, a good day was a hand-written rejection from Dog Breath Review.

They're taking a long poem on bird themes — the prison crows, migratory geese, I even used the doves, re-member them? On St. Andrew's Place. Of course you do. You remember everything. You were afraid of the ruined dovecote, wouldn't go out into the yard until I'd prodded among the clumps of ivy to scare off snakes.

You were always frightened of the wrong thing. I found the fact that the doves returned, though the chicken wire had long since given way to ivy, a far more troubling prospect.

You want to write me off? Try. Just realize when you're cutting off the plank upon which you stand, which end of it is nailed to the ship.

I will survive, but will you? I have a following — I call them my children. Young pierced artists avid with admiration, they make their pilgrimage here from Fontana and Long Beach, Sonoma and San Bernardino, they come from as far away as Vancouver, B.C. And if I can say so, they are much more to my taste than trembling actresses with two-carat wedding bands. They claim a network of renegade feminists, lesbians, practitioners of Wicca and performance artists up and down the West Coast, a sort of Underground Goddess Train. They're ready to help me any way that they can; they are willing to forgive me anything. Why aren't you?

Your loving mother,
Masturbating Rot Crow

P.S. I have a surprise for you. I've just met with my new attorney, Susan D. Valeris. Recognize the name? Attorney for the feminine damned? The one in the black curls, red lips like those chattering windup teeth? She's come to exploit my martyrdom. I don't begrudge her. There's more than enough for everyone.

I stood in the doorway, watching the clouds rise from the mountains. They would not let her out. She killed a man, he was only thirty-two. Why should it matter that she was a poet, a jailhouse Plath? A man was dead because of her. He wasn't perfect, he was selfish, a flawed person, so what. She would do it again, next time with even less reason. Look at what she did to Claire. I could not believe any attorney would consider representing her.

No, she was making this up. Trying to snare me, trip me up, stuff me back in her sack. It wasn't going to work, not anymore. I had freed myself from her strange womb, I would not be lured back. Let her wrap her new children in fantasy, conspire with them under the ficuses in the visitors yard. I knew exactly what there was to be frightened about. They had no idea there were snakes in the ivy.

IN FOURTH-PERIOD American history at Marshall High School, we were studying the Civil War. In the overcrowded classroom, students sat on windowsills and the bookcases in the back. The heat in the classroom wasn't working and Mr. Delgado wore a thick green sweater someone knitted for him. He wrote on the board, backhand, the word *Gettysburg*, as I tried to capture the rough weave of the sweater and his awkward stance on my lined notebook paper. Then I turned to my history book, open on the desk, with its photograph of the great battlefield.

I'd examined it at home under a magnifying glass. You couldn't see it without the glass, but the bodies in the photograph had no shoes, no guns, no uniforms. They lay on the short grass in their socks and their white eyes gazed at the clouded-over sky and you couldn't tell which side they were on. The landscape ended behind a row of trees in the distance like a stage. The war had moved on, there was nothing left but the dead.

In three days of battle, 150,000 men fought at Gettysburg. There were fifty thousand casualties. I struggled with the enormity of that. One in three dead, wounded, or missing. Like a giant hole ripped in the fabric of existence. Claire died, Barry died, but seven thousand died at Gettysburg. How could God watch them pass without weeping? How could he have allowed the sun to rise on Gettysburg?

I remembered my mother and I once visited a battlefield in France. We took a train north, a long ride. My mother wore blue, there was a woman with thick black hair and a man in a worn leather jacket with us. We ate ham and oranges on the train. There were stains inside the oranges, they were bleeding. At the station, we bought poppies, and took a taxi out of town. The car stopped at the edge of an enormous field. It was cold, the brown grass bent down in the wind. White stones dotted the plain and I remembered how empty it was, and the wind passed right through my thin coat. Where is it? I asked. *Ici*, the man said, stroking his blond mustache. White plaster in his hair.

I stared at the short rippling grass, but I couldn't picture the soldiers there dying, the roar of cannons, it was so quiet, so very empty, and the poppy in my hand throbbed red like a heart. They took pictures of each other against the yellow-gray sky. The woman gave me a chocolate in a gold wrapper on the way home.

I could still taste that chocolate, feel the poppy red in my hand. And the man. *Etienne*. The light came down from a skylight into his studio, glass honeycombed with chicken wire. It was always cold there. The floor was gray concrete. There was an old gray couch bolstered with newspapers, and everything was covered with white dust from the plaster he used making his statues, plaster covering wire and rags. I played with a wooden sculptor's doll there, posing it while my mother posed.

So much white. Her body, and the plaster, and the dust, we were white as bakers. The old space heater he placed near her stool didn't do much but buzz and throw out the smell of burned hair. He played French rock 'n' roll. I could still feel how cold it was. He had a skeleton hanging from a hook that I could make dance.

She sent me down to the store for a bottle of milk. *Une bouteille du lait*, I rehearsed as I walked. I didn't want to go but she made me. The milk came in a bottle with a bright foil lid. I got lost on the way back. I wandered in circles, too frightened to cry, holding the milk in the gathering dusk. Finally I was too tired to walk, and sat down on the steps of an apartment house by the rows of buttons, darkened except where the fingers touched, there it was bright. A glass door with a curved handle. Smell of French cigarettes, car exhaust. Flannel trouserlegs went by, nylons and high heels, woolen coats. I was hungry but I was afraid to open the milk, afraid she would be angry.

Suddenly I saw the blank windows of my dream.

Où est ta maman? the nylons asked, the trouserlegs asked. *Elle revient*, I said, but I didn't believe it.

My mother jumped out of a taxi in her Afghan coat with the embroidery and the curly wool trim. She screamed at me, grabbed me. The bottle slipped from my hands. The way the milk looked on the sidewalk. Shiny white, with sharp pieces of glass.

ON THE WAY home from school, I copied the battlefield photograph and sent it to her with four cut-out words, loose in an envelope:

WHO   REALLY

ARE   YOU

I SAT ON the rag rug in my room after dinner, cutting old magazine covers into shadow puppets with the X-acto and sewing them onto bamboo skewers I'd saved from Tiny Thai. They were mythical figures, half-animal, half-human — the Monkey King, the antlered man who was sacrificed each year to fertilize the crops, wise centaur Chiron and cowheaded Isis, Medusa and the Minotaur, the Goat Man and the White Crow Woman and the Fox Mistress with her latest moneymaking scheme. Even sad Daedalus and his feathered boy.

I was sewing the Minotaur's arm to his body when there was a soft knock on the door. Musk, the smell of something stolen. Sergei leaned against the doorjamb, his muscled arms folded, in a crisp white shirt and jeans, a gold watch like a ship's clock on his wrist. His eyes flicking around the room, taking in the clutter — clothes piled in boxes, my bags of full sketch pads and finished drawings, the flowered curtains fading to pastel. His glance took in everything, but not like an artist's, seeing form, seeing shadow. This gaze was professional, wordlessly estimating the possibilities, how hard it would be to get what he wanted through the window and out to the truck. Nothing that he saw was worth bothering about. Threadbare carpet, old beds, Yvonne's paper horse, a paperweight with glitter instead of snow that said Universal Studios Tour. He shook his head. "A dog should not live here," he said. "Astrid. What you going to do?"

I tied the Minotaur's arm to the skewer, held it in front of the lamp, made it go up and down, miming his words. *"A dog should not live here,"* I said, imitating his heavy accent. "Children, yes. But dogs no. No dogs." The Minotaur pointed at him. "What you got against dogs?"

"Play with dolls." He smiled. "Sometimes you are woman, sometimes little girl."

I put the Minotaur in a can with the others, a bouquet of paper demigods and monsters. "Rena's not here. She's out getting loaded with Natalia."

"Who say I come to see Rena?" Sergei peeled himself away from his doorjamb and came in, casually, just wandering, innocent as a shoplifter. He picked things up and put them down exactly where they had been, and he never made a sound. I couldn't stop watching him. It was as if one of my animal-men had come to life, as if I had summoned him. How many times had I thought of just this moment, Sergei come a-calling, like a cat yowling on the back fence for you. I emitted some civetlike female stink, a distinct perfume of sexual wanting, that he had followed to find me here in the dark.

Sergei picked up Yvonne's paperweight and shook it, watched the glitter fall. Out in the living room, the TV was on, Yvonne absorbed in some trendy nighttime drama about hip young people wearing clothes from Fred Segal, with good haircuts and more stylish problems than hers. He stuck a finger in Yvonne's eyeshadow tray, traced some on his eyelids. "What you think?" he smiled, cocking his head, looking at himself, smoothing his blond hair back with one hand, vain as a woman. He watched me in the mirror.

He had wide sleepy eyelids, the silver suited them. He looked like a prince in ballet, but his scent was distinctly animal, he filled the room with his musk. I'd once stolen a T-shirt of his, for just that smell. I wondered if he ever found out.

"Astrid." He sat on the edge of my bed, put his thick rope-veined arm along the back of my headboard. You didn't even hear the springs squeak when he sat. "Why you avoid me?"

I started to cut a mermaid with long, art nouveau hair from the cover of an old *Scientific American*. "You're her boyfriend. I like living here. Therefore, I avoid you."

That purring cat voice. "Who tells her? Me? You?" he said. "I know you a little, Astrid *krasavitza*. Not such good girl. People think, but not what I see."

"What do you see?" I asked. Curious as to what bizarre distortions my image had undergone in the translation within the sewer system of Sergei's mind.

"You see me, you like. I feel you watch but then look away. Maybe afraid you get like her, *da?*" He jerked his head toward the front of the house, Yvonne, gesturing a big belly. "You don't trust. I never give you baby."

As if that were it. I was afraid, but not of that. I knew if I ever let him touch me, I would not be able to stop. I remembered the day my mother and her friends went to drink at the revolving bar on top of the Bonaventure Hotel, and I was pulled toward the windows, the nothingness was pulling me out. I felt that feeling every time I was in a room with Sergei, that sliding toward a fall.

"Maybe I like Rena," I said, making tiny cuts down the mermaid's tail for scales. "Women don't like it much when you screw around with their lovers."

His smile wiped his face like a mop. "Don't worry Rena." He laughed, a rumbling laugh that came from beneath the neat belt, the tight jeans. "She don't own thing long. She like to trade. Sergei today, somebody tomorrow. Hi, bye, don't forget hat. But for you, something else. Look."

He pulled something out of his shirt pocket. It caught my eye like a firefly. It was a necklace, a diamond on a silvery chain. "I find this lying in street. You want?"

He was trying to buy me off with a stolen necklace? I had to laugh. Found it in the street. In someone's nightstand, more likely. Or around her throat even, how could I know? *I take the sliding glass door off the track of a two-story house in Mar Vista.* A child-molester offering you candy, a ride in his car. So this was how someone like Sergei seduced a woman he wanted. Where just his smell and voice and the blue ropes of vein in his arms was enough, those sleepy blue eyes now sparkling under silver lids, that criminal smile.

He pulled a sad face. "Astrid. Beauty girl. This is gift from my heart."

Sergei's heart. That empty corridor, that unaired room. *Sentimentalism is the working off on yourself of feelings you haven't really got.* If I were a good girl, I would be insulted, I would kick him out. I would ignore his smile, and shape of him inside his jeans. But he knew me. He smelled my desire.

I felt myself slipping toward the windows, pulled by thin air.

He hooked the chain around my neck. Then he took my hand and put it on his groin, warm, I could feel him getting hard under my hand. It was obscene, and it excited me to feel him there, a man I wanted like falling. He leaned down and kissed me the way I wanted to be kissed, hard and tasting of last night's booze-up. He unzipped my polyester shirt, pulled it over my head, took my skirt off and threw it onto Yvonne's bed. His hands waking me up, I'd been sleeping, I hadn't even known it, it had been so long.

Then he stopped, and I opened my eyes. He was looking at my scars. Tracing the Morse code of dog bite on my arms and legs with his fingertips, then the bullet scars, shoulder, chest, and hip, measuring their depth with his thumb, calculating their age and severity. "Who does this to you?"

How could I begin to explain who did it to me. I would have to start with the date of my birth. I glanced at the door, still open, we could hear the TV. "Is this an exhibition or what?"

He shut it noiselessly, unbuttoned his shirt and hung it on the chair, pulled off his pants. His body white as milk, blue-veined, it was frightening, lean and dense as marble. It took my breath away. How could anybody confuse truth with beauty, I thought as I looked at him. Truth came with sunken eyes, bony or scarred, decayed. Its teeth were bad, its hair gray and unkempt. While beauty was empty as a gourd, vain as a para-keet. But it had power. It smelled of musk and oranges and made you close your eyes in a prayer.

He knew how to touch me, knew what I liked. I wasn't sur-prised. I was a bad girl, lying down for the father again. His mouth on my breasts, his hands over my bottom, up between my legs. There was no poetry about us humping on the yellow chenille bedspread on the floor. He hauled me into the positions he liked, my legs over his shoulders, riding me like a Cossack. Standing up with his arms linked to hold my weight as he thrust into me. I saw us in the closet mirror. I was surprised to see how little I resembled myself, with my lidded eyes, my sexual smile, not Astrid, not Ingrid, nobody I ever saw before, with my big bottom and long legs around him, how long I was, how white.

Dear Astrid,

A girl from Contemporary Literature *came to interview me. She wanted to know all about me. We talked for hours; everything I told her was a lie. We are larger than biography, my darling. If anyone should know this it's you. After all, what is the biography of the spirit? You were an artist's daughter. You had beauty and wonder, you received genius with your toddler's applesauce, with your goodnight kiss. Then you had plastic Jesus and a middle-aged lover with seven fingers, you were held hostage in turquoise, you were the pampered daughter of a shadow. Now you are on Ripple Street, where you send me pictures of dead men and make bad poems out of my words, you want to know who I am?*

Who am I? I am who I say I am and tomorrow someone else entirely. You are too nostalgic, you want memory to secure you, console you. The past is a bore. What matters is only oneself and what one creates from what one has learned. Imagination uses what it needs and discards the rest — where you want to erect a museum.

Don't hoard the past, Astrid. Don't cherish anything.
Burn it. The artist is the phoenix who burns to emerge.

Mother.

I SEPARATED our dirty clothes at the Fletcher coin op, colors from lights, cold from hot. I liked doing laundry, the sorting, dropping the coins, the soothing smell of detergent and dryers, rumble of the machines, the snap of cotton and denim as the women folded their clothes, their fresh sheets. Children played games with their mothers' laundry baskets, wearing them like cages, sitting in them like boats. I wanted to sit in one too, pretend I was sailing.

My mother hated any chore, especially the ones that had to be performed in public. She waited until all our clothes were dirty, and sometimes washed our underwear in the sink, so we could put it off another few days. When we finally could not get away with it one day more, we'd quickly load our wash in the machines and then leave, go take in a movie, look at some books. Each time, we'd come back to find it wet, thrown out on top of the washers or on the folding tables. I hated it that people handled our things. Everybody else could stay and watch their laundry, why couldn't we? "Because we're not everybody," my mother would say. "We're not even remotely like everybody."

Except even she had dirty laundry.

When the loads of laundry were dry, the sheets bleached back to sanity, I drove home in Niki's truck, she let me borrow it for special occasions, like when she was too drunk to drive, or I was washing her clothes. I parked in the driveway. There were two girls I'd never seen before sitting on Rena's front

409

steps. White girls, fresh faces, no makeup. One wore a vintage-style dress with little flowers, her sandy hair in a bun with a chopstick stuck in it. The dark one had on jeans and a pink cotton turtleneck. Black clean shoulder-length hair. Her little nipples poked at the front of the pink cotton.

The vintage-dress girl stood up, squinting into the sun, her eyes the same gray as her dress, freckles. She smiled uncertainly when I got out of the truck. "Are you Astrid Magnussen?" she asked.

I hauled a garbage bag full of folded clothes out of the passenger seat, lifted another from the bed in the back. "Who wants to know?"

"I'm Hannah," she said. "This is Julie."

The other girl smiled too, but not as widely.

I never saw them before. They sure didn't go to Marshall, and they were too young to be social workers. "Yeah, and?"

Hannah, pink-cheeked with embarrassment, looked over at dark-haired Julie for encouragement. Suddenly, I became aware of what I must seem like to them. Hard, street. My eyeliner, my black polyester shirt, my heavy black boots, my cascade of silver earrings, hoops from pinkie-sized to softball. Niki and Yvonne had pierced my ears one day when they were bored. I let them do it. It pleased them to shape me. I'd learned, whatever you hung from my earlobes or put on my back, I was insoluble, like sand in water. Stir me up, I always came to rest on the bottom.

"We just came to meet you, to see, you know, if there was anything we could do," Hannah said.

"We know your mother," Julie said. She had a deeper voice, calmer. "We visit with her in Corona."

Her children. Her new children. Stainless as snowdrops.

Bright and newborn. Amnesiac. I had been in foster care almost six years now, I had starved, wept, begged, my body was a battlefield, my spirit scarred and cratered as a city under siege, and now I was being replaced by something unmutilated, something intact?

"We're at Pitzer College, out in Pomona. We studied her in Women's Studies. We visit her every week. She knows so much about everything, she's really incredible. Every time we go she just blows us away."

What was my mother thinking, sending these college girls? Was she trying to grind me into talc, flour for some bitter bread? Was this the ultimate punishment for my refusal to forget? "What does she want from me?"

"Oh, no," Hannah said. "She didn't send us. We came on our own. But we told her we'd send you a copy of the interview, you know?" She held up a magazine she had rolled in her hands, blushed deeply. In a way, I envied that blush. I couldn't blush like that anymore. I felt old, gnawed pliant and unrecognizable as a shoe given to a dog. "And then we thought, you know, now that we knew where you lived, we could —" She smiled helplessly.

"We thought we'd come and see if we could help you or something," Julie said.

I saw that I scared them. They thought my mother's daughter would be something else, something more like them. Something gentle, wide-open. That was a riot. My mother didn't scare them, but I did.

"Is that it?" I asked, holding out my hand for the magazine.

Hannah tried to straighten out the curl of the magazine on her flowered knee. My mother's face on the cover, behind chicken wire, on the phone in the seclusion room. She must have done something, usually you get to be at the picnic tables. She looked beautiful, smiling, her teeth still perfect, the only lifer at Frontera with perfect teeth, but her eyes looked weary. *Contemporary Literature*.

I sat down next to Julie on the splintered front steps. Hannah took a seat a step down, her dress flowing in a curve like an Isadora Duncan dance step. I opened the piece, flipped through it. My mother's gestures, flat of palm to forehead, elbow on the ledge. Head against the window, eyes downcast. *We are larger than biography*. "What do you talk about with her?" I asked.

"Poetry." Hannah shrugged. "What we're reading. Music, all kinds of things. She sometimes talks about something she saw on the news. Stuff you wouldn't even think twice about, but she gets some take on it that's just incredible."

The transformation of the world.

"She talks about you," Julie said.

That was a surprise. "What's she say about me?"

"That you're in a, you know. Home. She feels terrible about what's happened," Hannah said. "For you most of all."

I looked at these girls, college girls, with their fresh make-upless faces, trusting, caring. And I felt the gap between us, all the things I wouldn't be because I was who I was. I was graduating in two months, but I wasn't going to Pitzer, that was for sure. I was the old child, the past that had to be burned away, so my mother, the phoenix, could emerge once again, a golden bird rising from ash. I tried to see my mother through their eyes. The beautiful imprisoned poetic soul, the suffering genius. Did my mother suffer? I forced myself to imagine it.

412

She certainly suffered when Barry kicked her out of his house that day, after sleeping with her. But when she killed him, the suffering was somehow redeemed. Was she suffering now? I really couldn't say.

"So you thought you'd come out and what?" I asked. "Adopt me?"

I laughed but they didn't. I'd grown too hard, maybe I was more like my mother than I thought.

Julie gave Hannah a "told you so" look. I could see this had been the sandy girl's idea. "Yeah, well, sort of. If you wanted."

Their sincerity so unexpected, their sympathies so misplaced. "You don't think she killed him, do you," I said.

Hannah shook her head, quickly. "It's all been a terrible mistake. A nightmare. She talks all about it in the interview."

I was sure she had. She was always at her best with an audience. "Something you should know," I told her. "She did kill him."

Hannah stared at me. Julie's gaze fled to her friend. They were shocked. Julie stepped protectively toward her gauzy friend, and I felt suddenly cruel, like I'd told small children there was no tooth fairy, that it was just their mom sneaking into their room after they went to bed. But they weren't small children, they were women, they were admiring someone they didn't know the first thing about. Look at the hag Truth for once, college girl.

"That's not true," Hannah said. Shook her head, shook it again, as if she could clear my words out of it. "It isn't." She was asking me to tell her it wasn't.

"I was there," I told her. "I saw her mix up the medicine. She's not what she seems."

413

"She's still a great poet," Julie said.

"Yes," I say. "A killer and a poet."

Hannah played with a button on the front of her gray dress, and it popped off in her hand. She stared at it in her palm, her face stained red as beet borscht. "She must have had her reasons. Maybe he was beating her."

"He wasn't beating her," I said. I put my hands on my knees and pushed myself into a standing position. I felt suddenly very tired. Maybe there was still some stash in Niki's room.

Julie looked up at me, brown eyes serious and calm. I would have thought her more sensible than Hannah, less likely to have been taken in by my mother's spell. "Why'd she do it, then?"

"Why do people kill people who leave them?" I said. "Because they feel hurt and angry and they can't stand that feeling."

"I've felt that way," Hannah said. The lowering light of the sun was touching the curly escaped ends of her hair, making a frizzy halo around her fair head.

"But you didn't kill anyone," I said.

"I wanted to."

I looked at her, twisting the hem of her vintage dress with the small flowers, the front gapping open where the button fell off, her stomach was rosy. "Sure. Maybe you even fantasized about how you would do it. You didn't do it. There's a huge difference."

A mockingbird sang in the yucca tree next door, a spill of liquid sound.

"Maybe not so big a difference," Julie said. "Some people are just more impulsive than others."

I slapped the magazine against the leg of my jeans. They were going to justify her some way. Protect the Goddess Beauty no matter what. *They are willing to forgive me anything.* "Look, thanks for coming, but I have to go in."

"I wrote my number on the back of the magazine," Hannah said, rising. "Call if you, you know. Want to."

Her new children. I stood on the porch and watched them go back to their car. Julie was driving. It was a green Olds station wagon, vintage, so big it had skylights. It made a ringing sound as she drove away. I took the magazine and threw it in the trash. Trying to pass her lies off, like some elderly Salome hiding behind her veils. I could have told her children a thing or two about my mother. I could have told them they would never find the woman inside that shimmering cloth, smelling of mold and violets. There were always more veils underneath. They would have to tear them away like cobwebs, fiercely, and more would come as fast as they stripped them away. Eventually, she would spin them into her silk like flies, to digest at her leisure, and shroud her face again, a moon in a cloud.

28

—

NIKI TORE OFF a square of the acid and put it on my tongue, then one for her. It came on small sheets of paper printed with pink flamingos on motorcycles. We sat on the porch, looking at the wreck of the neighbor's old Riviera parked up on blocks. The weather was heating up, hazing over, tepid as bathwater, moist as a wet sock. I felt nothing at all. "Maybe we should take another one." If I was going to do it, I wanted to make sure I'd get off. Yvonne thought we were crazy to mess with our heads this way, but I was just crazy enough now. Susan D. Valeris had called me three times already. I stopped answering the phone, told Rena to hang up on anyone asking for me.

"It takes a while," Niki said. "You'll know when it happens. Believe me, you won't sleep through it."

Nothing happened for almost an hour, I was sure the stuff was no good, but then it came on, all at once, like an elevator. Niki laughed and waved her hand in front of my face, the fingers leaving trails behind them. "High enough now?"

My skin felt hot and prickly, like I'd broken out in a rash, but my skin looked the same. It was the sky that had suddenly changed. It had gone blank. Blank as a cataract, an enormous white eye. I felt anxious under that terrible empty sky. It was as if God had gone senile and blind. Maybe he did not want to see anymore. That made sense. All around us, everything was the way it usually was, only unbearably so. I tried never to think about how ugly it was here. I tried to find the one beautiful thing.

But on this drug, I found I couldn't shut it out, focus down. It was terrifying. I was overwhelmed by the sordid and abandoned, growing like a hellish garden, the splintered step, the four dead cars in the neighbor's weedy lot, rusting back to earth, the iron fence of the prop outlet topped with razor wire, the broken glass in the street. It occurred to me that we lived exactly at the bottom of L.A., the place where people dumped stolen cars and set them on fire. The place where everything drifting came to rest. I felt sick, my skin burned. There was a metal taste in my mouth as if I'd chewed foil. In the street, I noticed a dead bird, smashed flat, surrounded by its soft feathers.

I was afraid to tell Niki I was scared, it occurred to me if I named it, I might start screaming. I might never stop.

The whole world had been reduced to this, lifeless debris. And we were just more of the city's detritus, like the bird, the abandoned shopping carts, the wrecked Riviera. I could feel the hum of the high power lines, the insidious radiation mutating our cells. Nobody cared about the people down here. We were at the end of civilization, where it had given up out of senility and exhaustion. And we were what was left, Niki and I, like cockroaches after the end of the world, scuttling through the ruins, fighting over scraps of the dead corpse. Like my dream of my mother's melted face. I was afraid to ask if my face was melting. I didn't want to call attention to it.

"You okay?" Niki had hold of a handful of my hair at the nape of my neck, pulled gently.

I shook my head, infinitesimally, I couldn't even be sure whether I had done it or just thought I had. I was afraid to do more.

"Don't worry," she said. "You're just coming on."

She was turning into a jack-in-the-box, a Raggedy Ann. I had to hold on to the fact that I knew her, it was only a trick of my mind. This was Niki, I kept telling myself. I knew her. Abandoned at six by her mother at a Thrifty drugstore in Alhambra, Niki always counted the house, assessed the odds, worked out percentages. I liked to watch her when she was getting ready for work, with her starched Bavarian waitress costume on, looking like Heidi in a Warhol film. Even if I did not recognize her, I knew her. I had to hang on to that.

I was sweating, cracking up like the decades-old paving job in the smeared linoleum sun.

"Can we get out of here?" I whispered, trembling, nauseated. "I hate this. I mean, really."

"Just tell me where," she said. Her eyes looked strange, black and buttony, like a doll's.

IN THE COOL HUSH of the Impressionist rooms at the County Art Museum, the world was restored to me, in all its color and light and form. How had I forgotten? Nothing could happen to me here. This was the port, the outpost of the true world, where there could still be art, and beauty, and memory. How many times had I walked here with Claire, with my mother. Niki had never been here before. The two of us walked past fishing boats rocking at anchor, luminescent lemony gold white skies shading to rose, foreground reflections in the watery street.

We stopped before a painting where a woman was reading a book in a garden in the shade at the edge of a park. Her dress of white linen edged in blue rustled when she turned the pages. Such a delicious blue-green, the picture smelled like mint, the grass deep as ferns. I saw us in the picture, Niki in trailing white, myself in dotted swiss. We walked out to the woman slowly, she was ready to pour our tea. I was here in the gallery, but I was also walking through the damp grass, my hem stained with green, the breeze through the thin cloth of my dress.

The acid came on in waves, we rocked as we stood before the paintings from the force of the drug. But I wasn't frightened anymore. I knew where I was. I was with Niki in the true world.

"This is out-fucking-rageous," she whispered, holding my hand.

Some of the paintings opened up, like windows, like doors, while others remained just painted canvas. I could reach in to Cézanne's peaches and cherries on a rich white crumpled tablecloth, pick up a peach and put it back on the plate. I understood Cézanne. "Look how you see the cherries from above, but the peaches from the side," I said.

"They look like cherry bombs," Niki said, gathering her fingers together and then flicking them out wide. The lively stems of the cherries flicked out like firecrackers.

"Your eyes want to make it normal but it won't go," I said.

I imagined painting the picture, I could see exactly what order he did what.

The owlman sidled over and hunched his shoulders. "No touch."

"Yodo," Niki said under her breath, and we moved away to the next painting.

I felt I could have painted all the paintings myself. The acid kept coming on and coming on, I didn't know how much higher I could get. It wasn't at all like the Percodans — stoned, stupid, escape. This was higher than high. Two-hundredth floor, five-hundredth floor. Van Gogh's night sky.

We stopped to get something to drink at the museum café. I knew exactly where I was, in the same building as the auditorium, my old classroom just downstairs. My own personal playground. I got into the drink dispenser, I played the opening of the "Sleeping Beauty Waltz" with the different soft drinks. "What am I playing?" I asked her.

"Be cool," Niki said.

I tried to be cool, but it was too funny. When it was time to pay, I couldn't remember about the money, how it worked. The cashier looked like a tapioca pudding. She wouldn't look at us. She said some numbers and I pulled out my money, but I didn't know what to do with it. I held it open on my hand and let her pick the right combination from the palm. *"Danke, chorisho, guten tag, Arigato,"* I said. *"Dar es Salaam."* Hoping she'd think we were just foreigners.

"Dar es Salaam," Niki said as we took seats on the plaza.

This was exactly how I should have been as a child, joyful, light as a toy balloon. Niki and I sat in the shade and drank our drinks, watched the people go by, noticing how much they looked like certain animals. There was a gnu, and a lion, and a secretary bird. Tapir and a curly-haired yak. When had I ever laughed like this before?

After we were done, Niki said we should go use the bathroom.

"I don't have to," I said.

"You won't know until it's too late," Niki said. "Come on."

We walked back into the building, found the doors with the ridiculous stick figures in pants or skirt. The ridiculous way we thought *male*, *female*, as pants or skirt. Suddenly, the whole sexual universe and its conventions seemed fantastic, contrived.

"Don't look in the mirror," Niki said. "Look at your shoes."

It was dark gray tile, bad light, dirty floor. I felt the fear return. A metallic taste in my mouth. An old lady in a tan pantsuit, tan face, tan hair, tan shoes, a yellow belt, came out of one of the stalls, stared at us. "She looks like a grilled cheese sandwich," I said.

"My friend's sick," Niki said, trying not to laugh out loud. She pushed me into the handicapped toilet, closed the door behind us. She had to unzip my pants and put me on the pot like I was two years old. I couldn't go, it was too funny.

"Shut up and go," Niki said.

I swung my legs. It really felt like I was two. "Make tinkle for Annie," I said. And I let go. I really had to, after all. The sound made me laugh. "I love you, Niki," I said.

"I love you too," she said.

But on the way out I caught a glimpse of myself in the mirror. I looked very red-faced, my eyes black as a magpie's, hair tangled. I looked feral. It scared me. Niki hurried me out.

We were in the Contemporary wing. I never went there. When I came with my mother, she would stand me in front of a Rothko, a blue-and-red square, and explain it to me for an hour. I never did get it. Now Niki and I stood in front of it, in the same space I stood when I was young, and watched the three zones of color throb, pulse, and other tones emerge, a tomato, a garnet, purple. The red advanced, the blue retreated, just like Kandinsky said. It was a door and we walked in.

Loss. That's what was in there. Grief, sorrow, wordless and unfathomable. Not what I felt this morning, septic, panicked. This was distilled. Niki put her arm around my waist, I put mine around hers. We stood and mourned. I could imagine how Jesus felt, his pity for all of humanity, how impossible it was, how admirable. The painting was Casals, a requiem. My mother and me, Niki and Yvonne, Paul and Davey and Claire, everybody. How vast was a human being's capacity for suffering. The only thing you could do was stand in awe of it. It wasn't a question of survival at all. It was the fullness of it, how much could you hold, how much could you care.

We walked out into the sunshine, gravely, like people after a funeral.

I took Niki into the Permanent Collection, I had to see the goddesses now. In the Indian rooms lived the rest of the ancient equation. Ripe figures dancing, making love, sleeping, sitting on lotuses, their hands in their characteristic mudras. Shiva danced in his bronze frame of fire. Indian raga music played softly in the background. We found a stone Boddhisattva, in his mustache and fine jewels. He had been through the door that Rothko painted, and held both that and the dance. He had come out the other side. We sat on the bench and allowed his heart to enter us. Other people came through but they didn't stay. Their eyes flickered on us, and they moved away. They were like flies to a stone. We couldn't even see them.

IT TOOK a long time to come down. We sat with Yvonne for a while, watching TV, but it seemed incomprehensible. The room swirled with color and motion, and she was staring at tiny heads in a box. The lamps were more interesting. I drew the way the air filled with perfect six-sided snowflakes. I could make them fall and make them go back up again. Sergei came into the room, he looked just like the white cat that followed him in. He talked to us about something, but his mind was a goldfish bowl. The skirts and pants thing.

Suddenly I couldn't stand to be inside our cramped, ugly house, with Sergei and his goldfish, its mouth opening and closing stupidly. I took some paper and watercolors onto the porch and painted wet on wet, streaks that became Blakean figures in sunrise, and dancers under the sea. Niki came out and smoked and looked at the rings around the streetlights. Later Rena and Natalia shared their Stoli with us, but it didn't do a thing. Rena was the fox woman and Natalia an Arabian horse with a dish face. They spoke Russian and we understood every word they said.

By three in the morning, I was getting awfully tired of snowflakes and the way the walls were breathing. *Make tinkle for Annie.* That's what I couldn't stop thinking about. At first, I thought, maybe it was really make tinkle for Mommy, but when I heard it in my head, it was always the same. Make tinkle

for Annie. Who was Annie, and why do I make tinkle for her?
I was trembling, my nerves shot, as Yvonne lay sleeping on her
tidefoam and the snowflakes fell in our room. Annie, who are
you, and where is Mommy? Yellow, was all I could get, yellow
sunlight, and a white swan, a warm smell like laundry.

IN THE MORNING, I cut out words from the funny section of
the paper:

WHO IS ANNIE

29

⁓

As I had promised, I accompanied Yvonne to baby class at Waite Memorial Hospital. I held her tennis balls, her towel. I couldn't seem to take it seriously. I didn't know if it was the aftermath of the acid, but everything seemed funny. The plastic doll we handled looked like a space alien. The young couples seemed like big children, playing a game, the pregnancy game. These girls couldn't really be pregnant, they had pillows shoved up underneath their baby doll dresses. I liked the feeling of all the baby things, even washing the doll and diapering it with the Mickey Mouse diaper.

Yvonne pretended she was my sister-in-law, and that her husband, my brother, was in the army. Patrick, she liked the name. A TV actor. "I got a letter from Patrick, did I tell you?" she told me during the break, while we all drank sweet juice from tiny paper cups, ate ginger snaps. "My husband," she told the couple next to her. "He's getting sent to, you know —"

"Dar es Salaam," I said.

"I miss him, don't you?"

"Not that much," I said. "He's way older than me." I

imagined a big blond man who brought me dolls from his different tours. Heidi dolls, dope hidden up their skirts.

"He sent me five hundred dollars for the layette," she said. "Made me promise not to go to yard sales. He wants everything brand-new. It's a waste of money, but if that's what he wants . . ."

This was fun. I was never a little girl playing games with other little girls, dolly mommy daddy games.

They showed her how to hold the baby to her breast, holding the breast in one hand. She suckled the plastic child. I had to laugh.

"Shhh," Yvonne said, cuddling the space alien, stroking its indented head. "Such a pretty little baby. Don't you listen to that bad girl laughing, *mija*. You're my baby, yes you are."

Later, Yvonne lay on the orange mat, blowing and counting, and I put the tennis balls under her back, switched to the rolled towels. I held the watch and timed her contractions, I breathed with her, we both hyperventilated. She wasn't nervous. "Don't worry," Yvonne said, smiling up at me, her belly like a giant South Sea Island pearl in a cocktail ring. "I been through this before."

They explained about the epidural and drugs, but no one there was going to have drugs. They all wanted the natural experience. It all seemed wrapped in plastic, unreal, like stewardesses on planes demonstrating the seat belts and the pattern for orderly disembarkation in case of crash at sea, the people taking a glance at the cards in the seat pocket in front of them. Sure, they thought, no problem. A peek at the nearest exit and then they were ready for in-flight service, peanuts and a movie.

*

RENA SOAKED UP the fierce April sun in her black macramé bikini, drinking a tumbler of vodka and Fresca, she called it a Russian Margarita. The men from the plumbing contractor next door loitered by the low chain-link fence, sucking their teeth at her. She pretended she didn't notice, but slowly applied Tropic Tan to the tops of her breasts, stroked down her arms, while the workmen grabbed their crotches and called out suggestions in Spanish. The metal chaise was half-collapsed beneath her, we were lulled by the sound of the rusty sprinkler watering the lawn of crabgrass and dandelions.

"You're going to get skin cancer," I said.

She rolled her bottom lip out. "We're dead long time, kiddo." She liked to say these American words, knowing how they sounded in her mouth. She lifted her Russian Margarita, drank. *"Nazdaroviye."*

It meant to your health, but she didn't care about that. She lit a black cigarette, let the smoke rise in arabesques.

I was sitting on an old lawn chair in the shade of the big oleander, sketching Rena as she soaked up the blistering UV rays. She sprayed herself with a small bottle filled with ice water, and the men watching over the chain-link fence shuddered. You could see the shape of her nipples through the knitted fabric. She smiled to herself.

This is what she loved, to make a few plumber's grunts come in their pants. A sale, a Russian Margarita, a quickie in the bathroom with Sergei, that was as far into the future as she cared to look. I admired her confidence. Skin cancer, lung cancer, men, furniture, junk, something would always come along. It was good for me to be around her now. I could not afford to think about the future.

I had only two months until graduation, and then a short fall off the edge of the world. At night, I dreamed of my mother, she was always leaving. I dreamed I missed a ride out to New York for art school, I lost an invitation to a party with Paul Trout. I stayed up and looked through my stack of twelve-year-old *ArtNews*es I'd found on trash day, studied the photographs of the women artists, their tangled hair, gray, long brown, stringy blond. Amy Ayres, Sandal McInnes, Nicholette Reis. I wanted to be them. Amy, with her curly gray hair and her wrinkled T-shirt, posing in front of her huge abstract of curved cones and cylinders. Amy, how can I be you? I read your article, but I can't find the clue. Your middle-class parents, your sick father. Your art teacher in high school created a scholarship for you. At Marshall I didn't even have art.

I gazed down at my drawing of Rena, dotted with water from the sprinkler. Really, I didn't even like drawings. When I went to the museum, I looked at paintings, sculptures, anything but lines on a piece of paper. It was just that my hand needed something to do, my eye needed a reason to shape the space between Rena and the sprinkler she had running and her wobbly-legged table of rusted white diamond mesh that held one drink and an ashtray. I liked the way the tabletop echoed the black diamonds of her bikini and the chain-link fence, how the curve of her tumbler was the same as the curve of her raised thigh and the taller man's arm draped over the fence, and leaves on the banana tree at the Casados' house across the street.

If I didn't draw, what reason would there be for the way the light fell on the scallop of tiles on the Casados' roof, and the lumpy tufts of lawn, the delicate braids of green foxtails soon to go brown, and the way the sky seemed to squash everything flat to the earth like an enormous foot? I'd have to get pregnant, or drink, to blur it all out, except for myself very large in the foreground.

Luckily I wasn't in the classes where they talked about college. I was in the classes where they told us about condoms and bringing guns to school. Claire signed me up for all the honors classes, but I couldn't hold on. If she were alive, I might have tried, followed up, asked for a scholarship, I would know what to do. Now all that was slipping away.

On the other hand, I still went to school, did the work, took the tests. I was going to graduate, for all that meant. Niki thought I was an idiot. Who would know if I went or not, who would care? But it was still something to do. I went and drew the chair legs, the way they looked like the legs of water striders. I could spend an hour exaggerating the perspective of all the desks diminishing toward the blackboard, the backs of heads, necks, hair. Yolanda Collins sat in front of me in math class. I could gaze at the back of her head all period long, the layers of tiny braids laced together in designs intricate as Persian rugs, sometimes with beads or cord woven in.

I looked down at the pad in my hands. At least I had this diamond-shaped pattern, the trapezoid of the gate. Wasn't that enough? Did there have to be more?

I looked at Rena, slathering on her Tropic Tan, baking to medium-well in the blistering sun, happy as a cupcake in frilled paper. "Rena, you ever wonder why people get out of bed in the morning? Why do they bother? Why not just drink turpentine?"

Rena turned her head to the side, shaded her eyes with her

429

hand, glanced at me, then went back to sunny-side up. "You are Russian I think. A Russian always ask, what is meaning of life." She pulled a long, depressed face. "What is meaning of life, *maya liubov*? Is our bad weather. Here is California, Astrid darling. You don't ask meaning. Too bad Akhmatova, but we got beach volleyball, sports car, tummy tuck. Don't worry, be happy. Buy something."

She smiled to herself, arms down at her sides, eyes closed, glistening on her chaise lounge like bacon frying in a pan. Small beads of water clung to the tiny hairs of her upper lip, pooled between her breasts. Maybe she was the lucky one, I thought, a woman who had divested herself of both future and past. No dreams, no standards, a woman who smoked and drank and slept with men like Sergei, men who were spiritually what came up out of the sewers when it rained. I could learn from her. Rena Grushenka didn't worry about her teeth, didn't take vitamin C. She ate salt on everything and was always drunk by three. She certainly didn't feel sick because she wasn't going to college and making something of her life. She lay in the sun and gave the workmen hard-ons while she could.

"You get boyfriend, you stop worry," she said.

I didn't want to tell her I had a boyfriend. Hers.

She turned on her side, her large nippled breast falling out of her bikini top to the workmen's vociferous approval. She hiked her top up, which called forth more excitement. She ignored it all, rested her head on her hand. "I been thinking. Everybody has license plate frame from dealer. Van Nuys Toyota, We're Number 1. I think, we buy license plate frame, you paint nice, we get maybe ten, fifteen dollars. Cost us dollar."

"What's my cut?" I derived a perverse satisfaction in knowing the right moment to say it. I had arrived on Ripple Street, the paradise of my despair.

THE DARK GREEN Jaguar sedan parked in front of the plumbing contractor should have tipped me off, but I didn't put it together until I saw her in the living room, the explosion of black curls, her bright red lipstick I recognized from the news. She wore a white-trimmed navy blue Chanel suit that might even have been real. She was sitting on the green couch, writing a check. Rena was talking to her, smoking, laughing, her gold inlays glinting in her mouth. I wanted to run out the door. Only a morbid interest kept me in the room. What could she possibly have to say to me?

"She like the salad set." Rena looked at me. "She buy for friend collect Tiki everything."

"It's the latest," said the woman, handing the yellow check to Rena. "Tiki restaurants, mai tais, Trader Vic's, you name it." Her voice was higher than you'd think, girlish for a lawyer's.

She stood and held out her hand to me, short red nails garish against her white skin. She was shorter than I was. She wore a good, green-scented perfume, a hint of citrus, almost like a man's aftershave. She had on a gold necklace thick as a bike chain, with a square-cut emerald embedded in it. Her teeth were unnaturally white. "Susan D. Valeris."

I shook her hand. It was very small and dry. She wore a wide wedding band on her forefinger, and an onyx intaglio signet on the pinky of the other hand.

"You mind if Astrid and I . . . ?" she asked Rena, wagging her wedding-banded finger between the two of us. Eeny meeny miney mo.

"It's not problem," Rena said, looking at the check again, putting it in her pocket. "You can stay, see if there's anything else you like. Everything for sale."

When we were alone, Susan D. gestured to the green couch for me to sit down. I didn't. It was my house, I didn't have to follow instruction. "How much did you give her?"

"Doesn't matter," the lawyer said, taking her seat again. "The point is, you've been avoiding my calls." To my surprise, she pulled a pack of cigarettes from her Hermès Kelly bag, which I recognized from my Olivia days to be strictly genuine. "Mind if I smoke?"

I shook my head. She lit up with a gold lighter. Cartier — the gold pleats. "Cigarette?" she offered. I shook my head. She put the pack and the lighter down on the cluttered table, exhaled into the afternoon light. "I don't know why I never got around to quitting," she said.

"All the prisoners smoke," I said. "You can offer them a cigarette."

She nodded. "Your mother said you were bright. I think it was an underestimation." She looked around the crowded living room, the bentwood hatrack and the hi-fi and the records, the beaded lamp and the fringed lamp and the poodle lamp with the milk glass shade, the peasant woman with the orange scarf, and the rest of the artifacts in Rena's thrift shop. A white cat jumped into her lap and she quickly stood up, brushed off her navy suit. "Nice place you got here," she said, and sat back down, glancing for the location of the hairy interloper. "Looking forward to graduation? Making your plans for the future?"

I let my bookbag drop onto the dusty upholstered armchair, sending a cloud of motes up into the stuffy air. "Thought I might become a criminal lawyer," I said. "That or a hooker. Maybe a garbage collector."

She made no parry, kept her mind on her purpose. "May I ask why you haven't returned my calls?"

I leaned against the wall, watching her quick, confident movements. "Go ahead and ask," I said.

She put her slim red leather briefcase on her lap and opened it, removed a folder and a yellow legal pad. "Your mother said you might be difficult," she said. "That you blame her for what's happened." Susan gazed into my eyes, as if she got a point for every second of eye contact she could maintain. I could see her practicing in front of a mirror when she was in law school.

I waited to hear the rest of the story they'd concocted.

"I know you've been through a terrible ordeal," she said. She looked down at the file. "Six foster homes, MacLaren Hall. The suicide of your foster mother, Claire Richards, was it? Your mother said you were close to her. It must have been devastating."

I felt the wave of anger rise through me. Claire's death was mine. She had no right to handle it, to bring it up and somehow relate it to my mother's case. But maybe this too was a tactic. To get it all out in the open to begin with, so I wouldn't be sullen, withholding my feelings about Claire, difficult to draw out. An aggressive opening at chess. I saw that she knew just what she was doing. Going for the sore spot right away. "Did you ask your client about her involvement with that?"

"Surely you don't blame your mother for the death of a woman she only met once," Susan said, as if there was no question about the absurdity of such a statement. "She's not a sorcerer, is she?" She settled back on the couch, took a drag on her cigarette, watching me through the smoke, evaluating my reaction.

Now I was scared. The two of them could really pull this off. I saw how easily this bouquet of oleander and nightshade could be twisted around into a laurel wreath. "But I do blame her, Susan."

"Tell me," she said, holding the cigarette in the left hand, making some notes on the yellow pad with the right.

"My mother did everything she could do to get Claire out of my life," I said. "Claire was fragile and my mother knew exactly where to push."

Susan took a drag, squinted against the smoke. "And why would she do that?"

I pushed away from the wall and went over to the hatrack. I didn't want to look at her anymore, or rather, have her looking at me, sizing me up. I put on an old hat and watched her in the mirror. "Because Claire loved me." It was a straw hat with a net veil, I pulled the veil over my eyes.

"You felt she was jealous," Susan said in a motherly way, spewing smoke into the air, an octopus spraying ink.

I adjusted the veil, then tilted the brim of the hat. "She was extremely jealous. Claire was nice to me, and I loved her. She couldn't stand that. Not that she ever paid attention to me when she had the chance, but when someone else did, she couldn't take it."

Susan leaned forward, elbows on knees, eyes lifted to the rough, cottage-cheese ceiling, and I could hear her brain clicking, a mechanical readjustment, tapping and turning what I had just told her, searching for the advantage. "But what mother wouldn't be jealous," she said. "Of a daughter growing fond of a foster mother. Honestly speaking." She flicked her ash into the beanbag ashtray, shaping the cherry on the bottom.

I turned to her, looking at her through the veil, glad she couldn't see the fear in my eyes. "Honestly speaking, she killed Claire. She shoved her over the cliff, okay? Maybe she can't be prosecuted for it, but don't try to sell me this new and improved spin. She killed Claire and she killed Barry. Let's just get on with it."

Susan sighed and put her pen down. She took another hit of her cigarette and ground it out in the ashtray. "You're a tough nut, aren't you."

"You're the one who wants to let a murderer go free," I said. I took off the hat and threw it on the chair, scaring the white cat, who ran out of the room.

"She was denied due process. It's in the record," Susan said, striking the edge of her hand into the other palm. I could see her in court, her hands translating her for the hearing impaired. "The public defender didn't even raise a sweat in her defense." The accusing finger, red-tipped. "She was drugged, my God, she could barely speak. It's in the file, the dose and everything. Nobody said a word. The prosecution's case was completely circumstantial." Hands palm down, crossed and cut outward, like a baseball ref's "safe." She was building momentum, but I'd heard enough.

"So what's in it for you?" I interrupted, in as dry and unimpressed a voice as I could register.

"Justice has not been served," she said firmly. I could see her on the steps of the courthouse, performing for the TV crews.

"But it has," I said. "Blindly, and maybe even by mistake, but it has been served. Rare, I know. A modern miracle."

Susan slumped to the back of the couch, as if my comments had drained her of all her righteous vigor. A car with the radio up loud, spewing ranchero music, cruised by and Susan quickly turned to look out the window at the dark green Jaguar parked in front. When she was satisfied that it was still there, gleaming by the curb, she returned to me. Slowly, and wearily. "Astrid, when young people are so cynical, it makes me despair for the future of this country."

It was the funniest thing I'd heard all day. I had to laugh. I didn't find much funny these days, but this definitely was bizarre by anyone's standards.

Suddenly the weariness disappeared like the courthouse righteousness before it. Now I was looking at a cold and clever strategist, not so very unlike Ingrid Magnussen herself. "Barry Kolker could have died of heart failure," Susan said calmly. "The autopsy was not conclusive. He was overweight, and a drug user, was he not?"

"Whatever you say." *The truth is whatever I say it is.* "Look, you want me to lie for her. Let's go on from there and see if we have anything to talk about."

Susan slowly smiled in her red lipstick, pushing her black curls back from her face with one hand, her lashes very black against her white face. As if a bit ashamed of herself, but also

436

somewhat relieved that she did not have to sell me as hard as she thought she might.

"Let's go for a drive," she said.

BEHIND the tinted windows of her Jaguar, I nestled into the smell of leather and money. It wrapped around me like fur. She had the jazz station from Long Beach on the radio, a free-form West Coast piece with a flute and an electric guitar. We rose out of Ripple Street, past the unlicensed day care and the bakery and the trompe l'oeil of Clearwater in silence, made the left on Fletcher, left on Glendale, right onto Silverlake Boulevard, and drove around the lake for a while. Gulls bobbed on the blue-green water. The drought had exposed a huge concrete collar around the lake, but in the sealed world of the Jaguar, it was sixty-eight degrees. Such a pleasure to be in a rich woman's car. Now a new song filled the rarified atmosphere, I immediately recognized it. Oliver Nelson, "Stolen Moments."

I closed my eyes and imagined I was with Olivia and not my mother's lawyer. Her bare arms, her profile, scarf tied Kelly-style around her head and throat. That precious moment. All the more so for being unreal, gone in an instant, something to savor like perfume on the wind, piano played in a passing house in the afternoon. I hung on to it as Susan parked on the far side of the lake, where we could see the blue-green water, dotted with white, the picturesque hillside beyond. She turned the music down, but you could still hear Nelson's trumpet.

"I want you to ask yourself, what's she guilty of?" Susan asked, turning toward me from the driver's seat. "I mean, in your mind. Really. Murder, or being a lousy mother? Of not being there for you when you needed her."

I looked at the little woman, her black curls maybe one shade too black, her eyes a little mascara-smudged from the heat. The weariness was an act, but also the truth. Like so many things, the words hopelessly imprecise. I wished I had something to draw her with. She was in the process of becoming a caricature of herself. Not yet, now she was merely recognizable. But in five years, ten, she would only look like herself at a distance. Up close she would be drawn and frightened. "Honestly, aren't you just trying to punish her for being a crappy parent, and not for the alleged murder?" She cracked her window with the electric button, snapped in the car's lighter, and reached into her bag for her cigarettes. "What was Barry Kolker to you anyway, some boyfriend of your mother's. She had a number of boyfriends. You couldn't have been that attached."

"He's dead," I said. "You're accusing me of being cynical?"

She put a cigarette in her mouth and the lighter popped out. She lit it, filling the car with smoke. She exhaled up toward the slit in the window. "No, it's not Kolker. You're angry with her for abandoning you. Naturally. You've led six difficult years, and like a child, you point to the almighty mother. It's her fault. The idea that she too is a victim would never occur to you."

Out the window, in the unairconditioned part of reality, a very red-faced jogger trotted by us, dragging a tired setter on a leash. "Is that what you'll say if I tell the truth at her trial?"

We watched her plodding down the sidewalk, the dog trying to sniff at the plants as they went by. "Something like

438

that," she said, the first honest thing I'd heard her say since I'd shaken her small hand. She sighed and flicked ash out the window. Some blew back in. She brushed it off her suit. "Astrid. She may not have been some TV mom, Barbara Billingsley with her apron and pearls, but she loves you. More than you can imagine. Right now she really needs your faith in her. You should hear her, talking about you, how she worries about you, how much she wants to be with you again."

I thought again about my imaginary trip with her, the sight of her, the magic of her speech. Now I was not so sure, maybe it was true. I wanted to ask this woman what my mother said about me. I wanted to hear her tell me what my mother thought about me, but I didn't dare leave her that opening. Bobby Fischer had taught me better than that. "She'd say anything to get out."

"Talk to her. I can set it up. Just listen to what she has to say, Astrid," Susan urged. "Six years is a long time. People do change."

My moment's uncertainty faded. I knew exactly how far Ingrid Magnussen had changed. I had her letters. I'd read them, page by page, swimming across the red tide. I knew all about her tenderness and motherly concern. Me and the white cat. But now there was something that had changed. What had changed was that for the first time in my life, my mother needed something from me, something I had the power to give or withhold, and not the other way around. I opened up the air-flow vent and let the air-conditioning kiss my face.

My mother needed me. It sank in, what that meant, how incredible it was. If I went on the stand and said she did it, told about our trip to Tijuana, about the pounds of oleander and

439

jimson weed and belladonna she'd boiled down in the kitchen, she'd never get out. And if I lied, said Barry was superparanoid, he'd developed a complex about her, he was crazy, about how she'd been so drugged when I saw her at Sybil Brand she hadn't even recognized me, she might win an appeal, get a new trial, she could be out walking around before I was twenty-one.

Reverend Thomas would not have approved of the emotion that filled me now, its sweetness was irresistible. I had her own knife to her throat. I could ask for something, I could make demands. What's in it for me, that's what I'd learned to ask, unapologetically, in my time with Rena. What's my cut. I could put a price tag on my soul. Now I just had to figure out what I could sell it for.

"Okay," I said. "Set it up."

Susan took a last drag of her cigarette, threw it out the window, then raised the glass. Now she was all business. "Anything you want in the meantime, some spending money?"

I hated this woman. What I had been through the last six years meant nothing to her. I was simply one more brick in the structure she was erecting, I had just slipped into place. She didn't believe my mother was innocent. She only cared that there would be cameras on the courthouse steps. And her name, Susan D. Valeris, under her moving red lips. The publicity would be worth plenty.

"I'll take a couple hundred," I said.

I WALKED ALONG the river in the last afternoon light, my hands in my pockets, Baldy all pink in the east with reflected sunset, Susan's money crumpled in my fist. I strolled north, past the contractor's lot and the bakery loading bays, the sculptor's yard at the end of Clearwater Street, painted trompe l'oeil like a little French village. A dog rushed the fence and the wide planks jerked as the animal struck it, barking and growling. Over the fence through the razor wire, shapes in bronze, balanced inside big metal hoops like Shiva, turned slowly in the wind. I found a chunk of concrete broken loose from the embankment and threw it into the river. It fell among the willows, and a flurry of whistling wings rose from cover, brown wading birds. It was happening again. I was being drawn back into her world, into her shadow, just when I was starting to feel free.

I coughed the dry hacking cough I'd had all spring, from smoking pot and the perennial mold at Rena's. I dashed down the slope to the water, squatted and touched the current with my fingertips. Cold, real. Water from mountains. I put it between my eyes, the third eye spot. Help me, River.

And what if she did get out? If she came walking up to the house on Ripple Street, if she said, "I'm back. Pack up, Astrid, we're leaving." Could I resist her? I pictured her, in the white shirt and jeans they let her change into when they arrested her. "Let's go," she said. I saw us standing on the porch at Rena's, staring at each other, but nothing beyond that.

Was she still in my bones, in my every thought?

I squatted by the water as it flowed over the tumbled rocks, thought how far must they have come to have settled in this concrete channel, the stream clear and melodious, the smell of fresh water. I didn't want to think about my mother anymore. It made me tired. I'd rather think about the way the willows and the cottonwoods and palms broke their way through the concrete, growing right out of the flood control channel, how the river struggled to reestablish itself. A little silt was carried down, settled. A seed dropped into it, sprouted. Little roots shot downward. The next thing you had trees, shrubs, birds.

My mother once wrote a poem about rivers. They were women, she wrote. Starting out small girls, tiny streams decorated with wildflowers. Then they were torrents, gouging paths through sheer granite, flinging themselves off cliffs, fearless and irresistible. Later, they grew fat and serviceable, broad slow curves carrying commerce and sewage, but in their unconscious depths catfish gorged, grew the size of barges, and in the hundred-year storms, they rose up, forgetting the promises they made, the wedding vows, and drowned everything for miles around. Finally, they gave out, birth-emptied, malarial, into a fan of swamp that met the sea.

But this river was none of these things. It flowed serene and ignored past fences spray-painted 18th Street, Roscos, Frogtown, alive despite everything, guarding the secrets of survival. This river was a girl like me.

A makeshift tent sat on a small island in the middle of the miniature forest, its blue plastic tarp startling amid the grays and greens. The here-and-now Hiltons, Barry used to call them. I knew whose it was. A tall, thin Vietnam vet in khakis and camouflage, I'd seen him around early in the mornings, the thin thread of smoke from his small coffee-can stove. I'd seen him in front of the Spanish market on Glendale Boulevard, the boarded-up side, playing poker with his friends in the long shadows of afternoon.

Wild mustard flowered on the cracked banks, and I picked a bouquet for Yvonne. What was a weed, anyway. A plant

442

nobody planted? A seed escaped from a traveler's coat, something that didn't belong? Was it something that grew better than what should have been there? Wasn't it just a word, *weed*, trailing its judgments. *Useless, without value. Unwanted.*

Well, anyone could buy a green Jaguar, find beauty in a Japanese screen two thousand years old. I would rather be a connoisseur of neglected rivers and flowering mustard and the flush of iridescent pink on an intersection pigeon's charcoal neck. I thought of the vet, warming dinner over a can, and the old woman feeding her pigeons in the intersection behind the Kentucky Fried Chicken. And what about the ladybug man, the blue of his eyes over gray threaded black? There were me and Yvonne, Niki and Paul Trout, maybe even Sergei or Susan D. Valeris, why not? What were any of us but a handful of weeds. Who was to say what our value was? What was the value of four Vietnam vets playing poker every afternoon in front of the Spanish market on Glendale Boulevard, making their moves with a greasy deck missing a queen and a five? Maybe the world depended on them, maybe they were the Fates, or the Graces. Cézanne would have drawn them in charcoal. Van Gogh would have painted himself among them.

BUT THAT NIGHT I dreamed the old dream again, of gray Paris streets and the maze of stone, the bricked blind windows. This time there were doors of glass with curved art nouveau handles, they were all locked. I knew I had to find my mother. It was getting dark, dark figures lurked in the cellar entrances. I rang all the buzzers to the apartments. Women came to the door, looking like her, smiling, some even called my name. But none of them was her.

I knew she was in there, I banged on the door, screamed for her to let me in. The door buzzed to admit me, but just as I pushed it in, I saw her leaving from the courtyard gate, a passenger in a small red car, wearing her curly Afghan coat and big sunglasses over her blind eyes, she was leaning back in the seat and laughing. I ran after her, crying, begging.

Yvonne shook me awake. She took my head in her lap, and her long brown hair draped over us like a shawl. Her belly was warm and firm as a bolster. Through the strands of her hair wove the colored strands of light I still saw, cast by a kid's carousel bedside lamp I'd scavenged on trash day. "We get all the bad dreams, *ese*," she said, stroking my wet cheek with the palm of her hand. "We got to leave some for somebody else."

30

THE MATERNITY WARD of Waite Memorial Hospital reminded me of all the schools I'd ever gone to. Sand-textured walls painted the color of old teeth, lockers in the hall, linoleum floors dark and light brown, acoustic tiles packed with string. Only the screaming up and down the halls was different. It scared me. I didn't belong here, I thought, as I followed Yvonne down the corridor. I should be going to third period, learning something distant and cerebral, safely tucked between book covers. In life, anything could happen.

I brought all the things we'd learned to use in baby class, the tennis balls, the rolled-up towels, the watch, but Yvonne didn't want to do it, puff and count, lie on the tennis balls. All she wanted was to suck on the white terry cloth and let me wipe her face with ice, sing to her in my tuneless voice. I sang songs from musicals I used to watch with Michael — *Camelot*, *My Fair Lady*. I sang to her, "Oh Shenandoah, I long to hear you," that Claire had once sung on the banks of the McKenzie. While all around us, through the curtains, women screamed in their narrow labor beds, cursing, groaning, and calling for their mothers in ten languages. It sounded like the laboratories of the Inquisition.

Rena didn't stay long. She drove us there, dropped us off, signed the papers. Whenever I started liking her, something like this happened.

"Mama," Yvonne whimpered, tears rolling down her face. She squeezed my arm as another contraction came. We'd been here for nine hours, through two shifts of nurses. My arm was bruised from hand to shoulder. "Don't leave me," she said.

"I won't." I fed her some of the ice chips they let her have. They wouldn't let her drink anything, in case she had to have anesthesia. They didn't want her puking into the mask. She puked anyway. I held the small plastic kidney-shaped pan up under her chin. The fluorescent light accused us.

The nurse looked up at the monitor, stuck her fingers up Yvonne to check her dilation. She was still eight centimeters. Ten was full dilation, and they told us over and over again there wasn't much they could do until then. Now was what they called transition, the worst time. Yvonne wore a white T-shirt and green kneesocks, face yellow and slick with sweat, her hair dirty and tangled. I wiped the stringy vomit from her lips.

"Sing me a song," Yvonne said through her cracked lips.

"If ever I should leave you," I sang into her spiraled ear, pierced all the way up. "It wouldn't be in summer . . ."

Yvonne looked huge in the tiny bed. The fetal monitor was strapped to her belly, but I refused to look at the TV screen. I watched her face. She reminded me of a Francis Bacon painting, fading in and out of her resemblance to anything human, struggling to resist disappearing into an undifferentiated world of pain. I brushed her hair out of her face, made braids again.

446

Women's bravery, I thought as I worked on her hair from bottom to top, untangling the black mass. I would never be able to go through this. The pain came in waves, in sheets, starting in her belly and extending outward, a flower of pain blooming through her body, a jagged steel lotus.

I couldn't stop thinking about the body, what a hard fact it was. That philosopher who said we think, therefore we are, should have spent an hour in the maternity ward of Waite Memorial Hospital. He'd have had to change his whole philosophy.

The mind was so thin, barely a spiderweb, with all its fine thoughts, aspirations, and beliefs in its own importance. Watch how easily it unravels, evaporates under the first lick of pain. Gasping on the bed, Yvonne bordered on the unrecognizable, disintegrating into a ripe collection of nerves, fibers, sacs, and waters and the ancient clock in the blood. Compared to this eternal body, the individual was a smoke, a cloud. The body was the only reality. I hurt, therefore I am.

The nurse came in, looked up at the monitor, checked Yvonne's contractions, blood pressure, her movements crisp and authoritative. The last shift we'd had Connie Hwang, we'd trusted her, she smiled and touched Yvonne gently with her plump hands. But this one, Melinda Meek, snapped at Yvonne for whining. "You'll be fine," she said. "You've done this before." She scared me with her efficiency, her bony fingers. I could tell she knew we were foster children, that Yvonne wouldn't keep the baby. She'd already decided we were irresponsible and deserved every bit of our suffering. I could see her as a correctional officer. Now I wished my mother were here. She would know how to get rid of Melinda Meek. Even in transition she would spit in Melinda's stingy face, threaten to strangle her in the cord of the fetal monitor.

"It hurts," Yvonne said.

"Nobody said it was a picnic," Melinda said. "You've got to breathe."

Yvonne tried, gasped and blew, she wanted everyone to like her, even this sour-faced nurse.

"Can't you just give her something?" I said.

"She's doing fine," Melinda said crisply, her triangular eyes a veiled threat.

"Cheap-ass motherfuckers," the woman said on the other side of the white shower curtains. "Don't give poor people no damn drugs."

"Please," Yvonne said, clutching at Melinda's white jacket. "I beg of you."

The nurse efficiently peeled back Yvonne's hand, patted it firmly onto her belly. "You're already eight centimeters. It's almost over."

Yvonne sobbed softly, rhythmically, hopelessly, too tired to even cry. I rubbed her stomach.

Nobody ever talked about what a struggle this all was. I could see why women used to die in childbirth. They didn't catch some kind of microbe, or even hemorrhage. They just gave up. They stopped caring whether or not the baby came. They knew if they didn't die, they'd be going through it again the next year, and the next. I could understand how a woman might just stop trying, like a tired swimmer, let her head go under, the water fill her lungs. I slowly massaged Yvonne's neck, her shoulders, I wouldn't let her go under. She sucked ice through threadbare white terry. If my mother were here, she'd have made Melinda Meek cough up the drugs, sure enough.

"*Mamacita, ay*," Yvonne wailed.

I didn't know why she would call for her mother. She hated her mother. She hadn't seen her in six years, since the day she locked Yvonne and her brother and sisters in their apartment in Burbank to go out and party, and never came back. Yvonne said she let her boyfriends run a train on her when she was eleven. I didn't even know what that meant. Gang bang, she said. And still she called out, *Mama*.

It wasn't just Yvonne. All down the ward, they called for their mothers. *Mommy, ma, mom, mama*. Even with husbands at their sides, they called out for mama. Nine hours ago, when we came in, a woman with a voice like a lye bath alternately screamed at her husband and called for her mother. A grown woman sobbing like a child. *Mommy* . . . I was embarrassed for her. Now I knew better.

I held on to Yvonne's hands, and I imagined my mother, seventeen years ago, giving birth to me. Did she call for her mother? I imagined her screaming at my father, calling him worthless, a liar, useless, until he went out for a beer, leaving her alone with the landlady on a cold November morning. She had me at home, she'd never liked doctors. I could imagine how her screams and curses must have pierced the quiet of the walk street in Venice Beach, startling a kid going by on a skateboard, while the landlady smoked hash and rifled her purse. But did she call out, *Mami, help me*?

I thought of her mother, the one picture I had, the little I knew. Karin Thorvald, who may or may not have been a distant relation of King Olaf of Norway, classical actress and drunk, who could recite Shakespeare by heart while feeding the chickens and who drowned in the cow pond when my mother was thirteen. I couldn't imagine her calling out for anyone.

But then I realized, they didn't mean their own mothers. Not those weak women, those victims. Drug addicts, shopaholics, cookie bakers. They didn't mean the women who let them down, who failed to help them into womanhood, women who let their boyfriends run a train on them. Bingers and purgers, women smiling into mirrors, women in girdles, women on barstools. Not those women with their complaints and their magazines, controlling women, women who asked, what's in it for me? Not the women watching TV while they made dinner, women who dyed their hair blond behind closed doors trying to look twenty-three. They didn't mean the mothers washing dishes wishing they'd never married, the ones in the ER, saying they fell down the stairs, not the ones in prison saying loneliness is the human condition, get used to it.

They wanted the real mother, the blood mother, the great womb, mother of a fierce compassion, a woman large enough to hold all the pain, to carry it away. What we needed was someone who bled, someone deep and rich as a field, a wide-hipped mother, awesome, immense, women like huge soft couches, mothers coursing with blood, mothers big enough, wide enough, for us to hide in, to sink down to the bottom of, mothers who would breathe for us when we could not breathe anymore, who would fight for us, who would kill for us, die for us.

Yvonne was sitting up, holding her breath, eyes bulging out. It was the thing she should not do.

"Breathe," I said in her ear. "Please, Yvonne, try."

She tried to breathe, a couple of shallow inhalations, but it hurt too much. She flopped back down on the narrow bed, too tired to go on. All she could do was grip my hand and cry. And I thought of the way the baby was linked to her, as she was linked to her mother, and her mother, all the way back, inside and inside, knit into a chain of disaster that brought her to this bed, this day. And not only her. I wondered what my own inheritance was going to be.

"I wish I was dead," Yvonne said into the pillowcase with the flowers I'd brought from home.

THE BABY CAME four hours later. A girl, born 5:32 P.M. A Gemini. We went home the next day. Rena picked us up at the hospital's front loop. She refused to come in. We stopped at the observation window in Neonatal, but the baby was already gone. Rena wouldn't let Yvonne take the baby home even for a few weeks.

"Better just walk away," Rena had said. "You get attach, a loser game."

She was right, I thought, as I pushed Yvonne's wheelchair to the exit, though her motives cared nothing for Yvonne, she just didn't want to become a foster grandma. She never had any kids, never wanted any. *What's in it for me?* "Babies make me sick," she was always telling Yvonne. "Eat, shit, cry. You think you keep, think again."

In the hospital driveway, Niki got out of the van, gave Yvonne a bunch of balloons, hugged her. We helped her into the back. She was still tired, she could barely walk. There was a pinched nerve in her left leg, and stitches where the doctor cut her. She smelled sour, like old blood. She looked like she just got hit by a car. Rena didn't even look at her.

I sat with her in the back on the ripped-out carseat. Yvonne leaned against me, her head on my shoulder. "Sing 'Michelle,'" she whispered.

I held her hand, pressed my other hand against her forehead the way she liked, and sang softly in my tuneless voice as we bounced and clattered along, heading for home. *"Michelle, ma belle."* The song seemed to soothe her. She rested her head against my shoulder and quietly sucked her thumb.

WEEKS WENT BY, and there was no call from Susan to let me know when I would see my mother. Now that she'd won my complicity, I heard no more about it. Not in May, not in June. I sat by the river's edge, watching the white egrets and brown wading birds fish in the current. It was my graduation day over at Marshall High School, but I saw no reason to attend. Even if she were out, my mother would never have come. Ceremonies not of her own invention didn't interest her. I would rather just let it pass quietly, like a middle-aged woman's birthday.

The truth was, I was scared, so scared I was afraid to even mention it, like the morning I did the acid. It was a fear that could open its mouth and swallow me whole, like a hammerhead shark in five feet of water. I didn't know what happened now. I wasn't headed to Yale or art school, I was going nowhere. I was painting license plate frames, I was sleeping with a thief, he said I could move in with him anytime. Maybe I'd learn to pick locks, hijack a truck. Why should my mother have a monopoly on crime?

I sat by the water, watching it flow, and the egrets preen, their button eyes, thinking about what Mr. Delgado had said in our last class. He said the reason we studied history was to find out why things were the way they were, how we got here. He said you could do anything you wanted to people who didn't know their history. That was the way a totalitarian system worked.

Who was I, really? I was the sole occupant of my mother's totalitarian state, my own personal history rewritten to fit the story she was telling that day. There were so many missing pieces. I was starting to find some of them, working my way upriver, collecting a secret cache of broken memories in a shoebox. There was a swan in it, a white wooden swan with long black nares, like the swan on Claire's frosted shower doors. I sat on the swan and made tinkle for Annie. There were white tile squares on the floor, that I played making shapes out of as I sat there, flowers and houses. They were perfect six-sided hexagonals and they all fit together. Also a yellow kitchen linoleum with a paint-spatter design, red and black, and laundry baskets. That laundry feeling, the smell of dryer. Yellow sunlight through a roll-down blind. My finger through the round pull.

But who was Annie? A friend? A babysitter? And why had she potty-trained me instead of my mother? I wanted to know what was behind the swan and the yellow linoleum. There were other children there, I remembered that, watching them going to school. And a box full of crayons. Did we live with her, or had she left me there?

And Klaus, the silhouette that was my father. *We are larger than biography*. Where did that leave me? I wanted to know how they met, fell in love, why they split up. Their time together was a battleground full of white stones, grass grown over the trenches, a war I lost everything in and had no way to know what happened. I wanted to know about our traveling years, why we could never go home.

I lay back on the sloped embankment and looked up. It was the best place to look at the sky. The concrete banks blocked out its fuzzy flat edges, where you saw the smog and the haze, and you just got the good part, the center, a perfect bowl of infinite blue. I let myself fall upward into that ultramarine. Not a pale, arctic morning like my mother's eyes, this blue was tender, warm, merciful, without white, pure chroma, a Raphael sky. When you didn't see the horizon, you could almost believe it was a bowl. The roundness of it hypnotized me.

I heard someone's steps coming toward me. It was Yvonne. Her heavy tread, long hair like a sheet of water. I lay back down. She sat next to me.

"Lie down, look at this great sky."

She lay down next to me, her hands folded across her stomach the way she did when she was pregnant, though the baby was gone. She was quiet, smaller than usual, like a leaf shrinking. A flight of pigeons raced across the rich curved surface of the sky, their wings beating white and gray in unison, like a semaphore. I wondered if they knew where they were going when they flew like that.

I squeezed her hand. It was like holding my own hand. Her lips were pouty, chapped. It was like we were floating here in the sky, cut off from future and past. Why couldn't that be enough. A flight of pigeons should be enough. Something without a story. Maybe I should set aside my broken string of beads, my shoeboxes of memories. No matter how much I dug, it was only a story, and not enough. Why couldn't it just be a heron. No story, just a bird with long thin legs.

If I could just stop time. The river and the sky.

"You ever think of killing yourself?" Yvonne said.

"Some people say that when you come back, you pick up just where you left off." I took Yvonne's arm in mine. Her skin was so soft. Her T-shirt smelled of despair, like metal and rain.

"I thought it was your graduation today, *ese*," she said.

"What's the point," I said. "Marching across the stage like ducks in a shooting gallery."

Yvonne sighed. "If I was you, I'd be proud."

I smiled. "If you were me, you'd be me. Whoever the hell that is."

Mrs. Luanne Davis suggested applying to City College, I could transfer anytime, but I'd already lost faith. A future wasn't something I could forge by myself out of all these broken pieces I had, like Siegfried's sword in the old story. The future was a white fog into which I would vanish, unmarked by the flourish of rustling taffeta blue and gold. No mother to guide me.

I imagined the lies the valedictorian was telling them right now. About the *exciting future that lies ahead*. I wish she'd tell them the truth: *Half of you have gone as far in life as you're ever going to. Look around. It's all downhill from here. The rest of us will go a bit further, a steady job, a trip to Hawaii, or a move to Phoenix, Arizona, but out of fifteen hundred how many will do anything truly worthwhile, write a play, paint a painting that will hang in a gallery, find a cure for herpes? Two of us, maybe three?*

And how many will find true love? About the same. And enlightenment? Maybe one. The rest of us will make compromises, find excuses, someone or something to blame, and hold that over our hearts like a pendant on a chain.

I was crying. I knew I could have done better, I could have made arrangements, I could have followed up, found someone to help me. At this moment my classmates were going up for their awards, National Merit, Junior State. How did I get so lost? Mother, why did you let my hand slip from yours on the bus, your arms so full of packages? I felt like time was a great sea, and I was floating on the back of a turtle, and no sails broke the horizon.

"So funny, you know," Yvonne said. "I was sure I was going to hate you. When you came, I thought, who needs this gringa, listen to her, who she thinks she is, Princess Diana? That's what I say to Niki. This is all we need, girlfriend. But now, you know, we did. Need you."

I squeezed her hand. I had Yvonne, I had Niki. I had this Raphael sky. I had five hundred dollars and an aquamarine from a dead woman and a future in salvage. What more could a girl want.

THAT SUMMER we flogged our stuff at swap meets from Ontario to Santa Fe Springs. Rena got a deal on zebra-striped contact paper, so I zebra-striped barstools, bathroom scales, shoebox "storage units." I striped the hospital potty chair, the walker, for the zingy seniors. The cats hid.

"Display," was Rena's new catchword. "We have to have display."

Our dinette set already went, striped and varnished. She got four hundred dollars for it, gave me a hundred. She said I could stay as long as I wanted, pay room and board like Niki. She meant it as a compliment, but it scared me to death.

At the Fairfax High swap meet, we had a blue plastic tarp stretched over our booth, so the ladies could come in and look at our clothes without having sunstroke. They were like fish, nibbling along the reef, and we were the morays, waiting patiently for them to come closer.

"Benito wants me to move in," Yvonne said when Rena was busy with a customer, adjusting a hat on the woman, telling her how great it looked.

"You're not going to," Niki said.

Yvonne smiled dreamily.

She was in love again. I saw no reason to dissuade her. These days, I had given up trying to understand what was right or wrong, what mattered or didn't. "He seems like a nice guy," I said.

"How many people ask you to come share their life?" Yvonne said.

"People who want a steady screw," Niki said. "Laundry and dishes."

I shared a mug of Russian Sports Mix with Yvonne, a weak brew of vodka and Gatorade that Rena drank all day long.

Rena brought a sunburned woman over to meet me, hoisted the striped American Tourister hardsider onto the folding table.

"This is our artist," Rena said, lighting one of her black sobranies. "Astrid Magnussen. You remember name. Someday that suitcase worth millions."

457

The woman smiled and shook my hand. I tried not to breathe Sports Mix on her. Rena handed me a permanent marker with a flourish, and I signed my name along the bottom edge of the suitcase. Sometimes being with Rena was like doing acid. The artist. The Buddhist book I'd found on trash day said you accrued virtue just by doing a good job with whatever you were doing, completely applying yourself to the task at hand. I looked at the zebra bar and barstools, the suitcase disappearing with the sunburned woman. They looked good. I liked making them. Maybe if that was all I did my entire life, wasn't that good enough? The Buddhists thought it shouldn't matter whether it's contact paper or Zen calligraphy, brain surgery or literature. In the Tao, they were of equal value, if they were done in the same spirit.

"Lazy girls," Rena said. "You have to talk to customer. Work up sale."

She saw a young man in shorts and Top-Siders looking at the barstools, turned on her smile and went out to hook him. She saw those Top-Siders fifty feet off.

Niki finished her mug of Gatorade cocktail, made a face, poured some more while Rena had her hands full. "The things we do for a high."

"When are you going?" I asked Yvonne.

"Tomorrow," she whispered, half-hiding behind her curtain of smooth hair.

I stroked her hair back with my hand, tucked it behind her small, multipierced ear. She looked up at me and smiled, and hugged her. She burst into tears. "I don't know, Astrid, do you think I should? You always know what to do."

I laughed, caught unaware. I squatted down by her seat on a rickety director's chair. "Me? I know less than nothing."

"I thought you didn't lie," she said, smiling, holding her hand in front of her mouth, a habit to conceal her bad teeth. Maybe Benito would marry her. Maybe he would take her to the dentist. Maybe he would hold her in the night and love her. Who was to say he wouldn't?

"I'm going to miss you," I said.

She nodded, couldn't talk, crying while she was smiling. "God, I must look like such a mess." She swiped at her mascara that was running down her cheeks.

"You look like Miss America," I said, hugging her. It was what women said. "You know, when they put the crown on? And she's crying and laughing and taking her walk."

That made her laugh. She liked Miss America. We watched it and got stoned and she took some dusty silk flowers Rena had lying around and walked up and down the living room, waving the mechanical beauty queen wave.

"If we get married, you can be maid of honor," she said.

I saw the cake in her eyes, the little bride and groom on top, the icing like lace, layer after layer, and a dress like the cake, white flowers glued to the car and everybody honking as they drove away.

"I'll be there," I said. Imagining the wedding party, not a soul over eighteen, each one planning a life along the course of the lyrics of popular songs. It made me sad to think of it.

"You'll get back together with your boyfriend," she said, as if to soften the blow. "Don't worry. He'll wait for you."

"Sure," I said. But I knew, nobody waited for anybody.

*

THE NEXT NIGHT, Yvonne packed a few clothes, her horse, and her radio, but she left the picture of the TV actor in his frame on the dresser. Rena gave her some money, rolled up in a rubber band. We all waited on the front porch with her until Benito came by in his primer-gray Cutlass. Then she was gone.

31

ON THE ANVIL OF AUGUST, the city lay paralyzed, stunned into stupidity by the heat. The sidewalks shrank under the sun. It was a landscape of total surrender. The air was chlorinated, thick and hostile, like the atmosphere of a dead planet. But in the front yard, the big oleander bloomed like a wedding bouquet, a sky full of pinwheel stars. It made me think of my mother.

There was still no call from Susan. Many times, I'd wanted to call her and demand a meeting. But I knew better. This was a chess game. First the urgency, then the waiting. I would not run down the street after her, begging. I would develop my pieces and secure my defenses.

I woke up very early now, to catch a few breaths of cool air before the heat set in. I stood on the porch and gazed at the giant oleander. It was old, it had a trunk like a tree. You just had to roast a marshmallow on one twig and you were dead. She'd boiled pounds of it to make the brew of Barry's death. I wondered why it had to be so poisonous. Oleanders could live through anything, they could stand heat, drought, neglect, and put out thousands of waxy blooms. So what did they need poison for? Couldn't they just be bitter? They weren't like rattlesnakes, they didn't even eat what they killed. The way she boiled it down, distilled it, like her hatred. Maybe it was a poison in the soil, something about L.A., the hatred, the callousness, something we didn't want to think about, that the plant concentrated in its tissues. Maybe it wasn't a source of poison, but just another victim.

By eight it was already too hot to be outside. I went back inside to make Tasha's lunch. She was the new girl in Yvonne's bed, thirteen, going to King Junior High, D track, summer term. Grave, silent, she had a vertical scar on her upper lip just healing. She flinched if people moved too fast near her.

"You'll do great," I said, making her celery with peanut butter in the creases and a Granny Smith apple. "I'll be watching."

I drove her to school in Niki's truck, let her off in front of Thomas Starr King Junior High, watched her go in scared and small, her backpack hanging with key chains. I felt helpless to prevent her life from taking its likely direction. Could a person save another person? She turned to wave at me. I waved back. I didn't drive off until she was inside.

Dear Astrid,

It's been six years today. Six years since I walked through the gates of this peculiar finishing school. Like Dante: Nel mezzo del cammin di nostra vita. / Mi ritrovai per una selva oscura. / Che la diritta via era smarrita. *The third day over 110. Yesterday an inmate slit another woman's throat with a bent can. Lydia tore up a*

poem I wrote about a man I saw once, a snake tattoo disap-
pearing into his jeans. I made her tape it together again,
but you can't imagine the strain. Aside from you, I think
this is the longest relationship I've ever had. She's sure I
love her, though it's nothing of the kind. She adores those
poems of mine that refer to her, thinks it's a public declar-
ation.

Love. I would ban the word from the vocabulary. Such
imprecision. Love, which love, what love? Sentiment, fan-
tasy, longing, lust? Obsession, devouring need? Perhaps
the only love that is accurate without qualification is the
love of a very young child. Afterward, she too becomes a
person, and thus compromised. "Do you love me?" you
asked in the dark of your narrow bed. "Do you love me
Mommy?"

"Of course," I told you. "Now go to sleep."

Love is a bedtime story, a teddy bear, familiar, one eye
missing.

"Do you love me, carita?" Lydia says, twisting my
arm, forcing my face into the rough horsehair blanket,
biting my neck. "Say it, you bitch."

Love is a toy, a token, a scented handkerchief.

"Tell me you love me," Barry said.

"I love you," I said. "I love you, I love you."

Love is a check, that can be forged, that can be cashed.
Love is a payment that comes due.

Lydia lies on her side on my bunk, the curve of her hip
the crest of a wave in shallow water, turquoise, Playa del
Carmen, Martinique. Leafing through a new
Celebridades. I bought her a subscription. She says it

makes her feel part of the world. I can't see getting excited about movies I won't see, political issues of the day fail to move me, they have nothing to say within the deep prison stillness.

Time has taken on an utterly different quality for me. What difference does a year make? In a perverse way, I pity the women who are still a part of time, trapped by it, how many months, how many days. I have been cut free, I move among centuries. Writers send me books — Joseph Brodsky, Marianne Moore, Pound. I think maybe I will study Chinese.

"You ever go to Guanajuato?" Lydia asks. "All the big stars going there now."

Guanajuato, Astrid. Do you remember? I know you do. We went with Alejandro the painter, as distinguished from Alejandro the poet. From San Miguel. My Spanish wasn't good enough to determine the quality of the poet's oeuvre, but Alejandro the painter was very bad indeed. He should not have created at all. He should have simply sat on a stool and charged one to look at him. And so shy, he could never look in my eyes until after he'd finished speaking. Instead, he'd talk to my hand, the arch of my foot, the curve of my calf. Only after he had stopped could he look into my eyes. He trembled when we made love, the faint smell of geraniums.

But he was never shy with you, was he? You had such long conversations — conspiring, head to head. I felt ex-cluded. He was the one who taught you to draw. He would draw for you, and then you would draw after him. La mesa, la botilla, las mujeres. I tried to teach you poetry, but *you were always so obstinate. Why would you never learn anything from me?*

I wish we'd never left Guanajuato.

Mother.

Alejandro the painter. Watching the line flow from his fingers, the movements of his arm. Was he a bad painter? It never occurred to me, as it never occurred to me that she could have felt excluded. She was beautiful there, she wore a white dress, and the buildings were ochre and yellow, her sandals crisscrossed like a Roman's up her leg. I traced the white X's when she took them off. The hotel with screens and scrollwork around the door, the rooms open to the tiled walkway. You could hear what everybody was saying. When she smoked a joint she had to blow it out the balcony doors. It was a strange room, ochre, taller than it was square. She liked it, said there was room to think. And the bands of mariachis competed in the street below, the sound of concerts every night, from our beds under the netting.

"So?" Rena said. "Is she getting out?"

"No," I said.

Driving up from San Miguel de Allende in his toy-sized Citroën car, his shirt very white against his copper skin. Was she admitting she made a mistake? If only she could admit it. *Confess.* I might lie for her then, talk to her lawyer, take the stand and swear beyond a shadow of a doubt that she never. Perhaps this was as close as she would get to admitting a thing.

I wished we had stayed in Guanajuato too.

*

THEN NIKI moved out. She was joining a Toronto band, it was one of Werner's. "Come with me," she said as she loaded her pickup. I handed her a suitcase, zebra-striped. We both smiled, checked each other for tears. She left me some addresses and phone numbers, but I knew I wouldn't be using them. I had to face this, that people left and you didn't see them again.

Within a week, Rena moved two new girls into Niki's room, Shana and Raquel, twelve and fourteen. Shana had epilepsy, and Raquel couldn't read, it was her second time in seventh grade. More broken children for Rena Grushenka's discount salvage yard.

SEPTEMBER came with its skirts of fire. Fire up on the Angeles Crest. Fire in Malibu, Altadena. Fire all along the San Gabriels, in the San Gorgonio wilderness, fire was a flaming hoop the city would have to jump through to reach the blues of October. In Frogtown, we had three shootings in one week — a holdup at the ARCO station, a lost motorist caught on a dead-end street in a Van Gogh midnight, a woman shot by her out-of-work electrician husband during a domestic dispute.

It was in the furnace of oleander time that Susan finally called. "I had a trial," she explained. "But we're back on track. I've scheduled you a visit, day after tomorrow."

I was tempted to balk, tell her I wasn't available, make things difficult, but in the end I agreed. I was as ready as I would ever be.

So on a morning already surrendered to the scourging wind

466

and punishing heat, Camille Barron, Susan's assistant, came for me, and we took the long drive out to Corona. In the visitors yard, we sat at an orange picnic table under the shade structure, drinking cold cans of soda from the pop machine, wiping them across our foreheads, pressing them to our cheeks. Waiting for my mother. Sweat dripped between my breasts, down my back. Camille looked wilted but stoic in her beige sheath, her fashionable short haircut limp and sweaty around the edges. She didn't bother to talk to me, she was only the errand girl. "Here she comes," Camille said.

My mother waited for the CO to unlock the gate. She still looked wonderful, thin and wiry, her pale hair twisted up in the back with a pencil stuck in it. A year and a half. I stood up. She walked over to us, warily, squinting in the sun, wisps of her hair blowing in the wind like smoke. Her tanned skin was more lined since I'd seen her last. She was getting that leathery look, like a white settler in Kenya. But she hadn't changed as much as I had.

She stopped when she got under the overhang, and I didn't move, I wanted her to see who I was now. My acid green shirt with the industrial zipper, my eyes ringed in heavy black shadow and liner, my ears with their octave of earrings. My woman's legs in a swap meet skirt, that Sergei loved to put over his shoulders, my hips, my full breasts. High wedgie shoes borrowed from Rena for the occasion. Not the pink girl with the prom shoes, not the rich orphan. I was Rena's girl now. I could pass for any girl heading to just where my mother was. But not the soft girl, the check kiter. She would not take anything from me. Not anymore.

For the first time when I visited, she didn't smile. I could see

467

shock on her face, and I was glad of it. Her lawyer's assistant looked between the two of us, uninterested, then got up and went inside the cooler concrete of the visitors shelter, leaving us alone.

My mother reached out and took my hand. I let her. "When I get out, I'll make it up to you," she said. "Even in two or three years, you'll still need a mother, won't you?"

She was holding my hand, she was a foot away from me. I stared at her. It was as if some alien was speaking through her. What kind of a routine was this?

"Who said you're getting out?" I said.

My mother dropped my hand, stepped back a pace. The look in her eyes faded the aquamarine to robin's egg.

"I just said I'd talk to you. I didn't say I'd do it. I've got a deal to make."

Now robin's egg turned to ash.

"What deal?" she asked, leaning against a post, her arms folded across the front of her denim dress, the very same dress she wore when I saw her last, now two shades lighter blue.

"A trade," I said. "Do you want to sit here or under the trees?"

She turned and led me to her favorite place in the visitors yard, under the white-trunked ficus trees looking out at the road, her back to Reception, the farthest point from the first lookout tower. We sat on the dry, summer-battered grass, it scored my bare legs.

She sat gracefully, her legs to one side, like a girl in a meadow. I was larger than her now, but not as graceful, not beautiful, but present, solid as a hunk of marble before it's been carved. I let her watch me in profile. I couldn't look at her while I spoke. I was not hard enough, I knew I would be thrown by her bitter surprise.

"Here's the deal," I said. "There are certain things I want to know. You tell me, and I'll do what you want me to do."

My mother picked one of the dandelions out of the grass, blew the tufts from the head. "Or what."

"Or I tell the truth and you can rot in here till you die," I said.

I heard the grass rustle as she changed her position. When I looked, she was lying on her back, examining the stem from which the plumes had been blown. "Susan can discredit your testimony any number of ways."

"You need me," I said. "You know it. Whatever she says."

"I hate this look, by the way," she said. "You're a Sunset Boulevard motel, a fifteen-dollar blow job in a parked car."

"I can look however you want," I said. "I'll wear kneesocks if you like." She was twirling the dandelion between her palms. "I'm the one who can tell them it was Barry's paranoid fixation. That he hounded you. I can say he had threatened to commit suicide, fake it to look like you did it, to punish you for leaving him." Her blurred features behind the chicken-wire glass. "I'm the one who knows how fucked up you were at Sybil Brand. When I came to see you that day, you didn't even recognize me." It still made me sick to think of it.

"If I submit to this examination." She flicked the dandelion stem away.

"Yes."

She kicked off her two-hole tennis shoes and ran her feet through the grass. She stretched her legs out in front of her and propped herself on her elbows, like she was at the beach. She

469

gazed at her feet, tapping them together at the ball. "You used to have a certain delicacy about you. A transparency. You've become heavy, opaque."

"Who was my father?" I asked.

"A man." Watching her bare toes, clicking together.

"Klaus Anders, no middle name," I said, picking at a scab on the web of my hand. "Painter. Age forty. Born, Copenhagen, Denmark. How did you meet?"

"In Venice Beach." She was still watching her feet. "At one of those parties that last all summer long. He had the drugs."

"You looked just like brother and sister," I said.

"He was much older than I," she said. She rolled over onto her belly. "He was forty, a painter of biomorphic abstractions. It was already passé by that time." She parted the grass like short hair. "He was always passé. His ideas, his enthusiasms. Mediocre. I don't know what I saw in him."

"Don't say you don't know, that's crap," I said.

She sighed. I was making her tired. So what. "It was a long time ago, Astrid. Several lifetimes at least. I'm not the same person."

"Liar," I said. "You're exactly the same."

She was silent. I had never called her a name before.

"You're still such a child, aren't you," she said. I could tell she was struggling for composure. Another person wouldn't have been able to see it, but I could tell in the way the skin around her eyes seemed to grow thinner, her nose a millimeter more sharp. "You've taken my propaganda for truth."

"So set me straight," I said. "What was it you saw in him."

"Comfort probably. He was easy. Very physical. He made friends easily. He called everybody 'pal.'" She smiled slightly, still looking down at the grass she was parting, like going through a file. "Big and easy. He asked nothing of me."

Yes, I believed that. A man who wanted something from her would never have been attractive. It had to be her desire, her fire. "Then what?"

She plucked a handful of grass, threw it away. "Do we have to do this? It's such an old newsreel."

"I want to see it," I said.

"He painted, he got loaded more than he painted. He went to the beach. He was mediocre. There's just not much to say. It's not that he was going nowhere, it's that he'd already arrived."

"And then you got pregnant."

She cut me a killing look. "I didn't 'get pregnant,' I'll leave that for your illiterate friends. I decided I would have you. 'Decision' being the operative word." She let her hair down, shook the grass out of it. It was raw silk in the filtered light. "Whatever fantasy you might have spun for yourself, an accident you were not. A mistake, maybe, but not an accident."

A woman's mistakes . . . "Why him? Why then?"

"I needed someone, didn't I? He was handsome, good-natured. He wasn't averse to the idea. Voilà."

"Did you love him?"

"I don't want to talk about love, that semantic rat's nest." She unbent her long, slim legs and stood, brushing her skirt off. She leaned against the tree trunk, one foot up on the white flesh, crossed her arms to steady herself. "We had a rather heated sexual relationship. One overlooks many things." Over her head, a woman had scratched Mona '76 in the white wood.

I looked up at her, my mother, this woman I had known and

471

never really knew, this woman always on the verge of disap
pearance. I would not let her get away from me now. "You
worshipped him. I read it in your journal."

"'Worship' is not quite the word we're looking for here,"
she said, watching the road. "Worship assumes a spiritua
dimension. I'm looking for a term with an earthier connota
tion."

"Then I was born."

"Then you were born."

I imagined him and her, the blonds, him with that wid
laughing mouth, probably stoned out of his mind, her, com
fortable, in the curve of his heavy arm. "Did he love me?"

She laughed, the commas of irony framing her mouth. "H
was rather a child himself, I'm afraid. He loved you the way
boy loves a pet turtle, or a road race set. He could take you t
the beach and play with you for hours, lifting you up and dow
in the surf. Or he could stick you in the playpen and leave th
house to go out drinking with his friends, when he was sup
posed to be baby-sitting. One day I came home and there ha
been a fire. His turpentine-soaked rags and brushes had caugl
fire, the house went up in about five minutes. He was nowhei
around. Evidently your crib sheet had already scorched. It wa
a miracle you weren't burned alive. A neighbor heard yo
screaming."

I tried to remember, the playpen, the fire. I could distinctl
remember the smell of turpentine, a smell I'd always loved. Bı
the smell of fire, that pervasive odor of danger, I'd alway
associated with my mother.

"That was the end of our idyll de Venice Beach. I was tire
of his mediocrity, his excuses. I was making what little monε

we had, he was living off me, we had no home anymore. I told him it was over. He was ready, believe me, there were no tears on that score. And so ends the saga of Ingrid and Klaus."

But all I could think of was the big man lifting me in and out of the surf. I could almost remember it. The feeling of the waves on my feet, bubbling like laughter. The smell of the sea, and the roar. "Did he ever try to see me, as I grew up?"

"Why do you want to know all this useless history?" she snapped, pushing away from the tree. She squatted so she could look me in the eye. Sweat beaded her forehead. "It's just going to hurt you, Astrid. I wanted to protect you from all this. For twelve years, I stood between you and these senseless artifacts of someone else's past."

"My past," I said.

"My God, you were a baby," she said, standing up again, smoothing the line of her denim dress over her hips. "Don't project."

"Did he?"

"No. Does that make you feel any better?" She walked to the fence, to look out at the road, the dirt and trash blowing in the wind, trash stuck in the weeds on the other side of the road. 'Maybe once or twice, he came by to see if you were all right. But I let him know in no uncertain terms that his presence was no longer appreciated. And that was that."

I thought of him, his sheepish face, the long blond hair. He hadn't meant to hurt me. She could have given him another chance. "You never thought maybe I'd like a father."

"In ancient times there were no fathers. Women copulated with men in the fields, and their babies came nine months later. Fatherhood is a sentimental myth, like Valentine's Day." She

473

turned back to me, her aquamarine eyes pale behind her tanned face, like a crime in a lit room behind curtains. "Have I answered enough, or is there more?"

"He never came back?" I asked quietly, praying it wasn't true, that there was more, just a scrap more. "Never called you, later on, wanting to see me?"

She squatted down again, put her arm around me, propped her head against mine. We sat like that for a while.

"He called once when you were, I don't know. Seven or eight?" She ran her fingers through my hair. "He was visiting from Denmark with his wife and his two small children. He wanted us to meet at a park, that I should sit on the park bench and play with you, so he could see you."

"Did we go?" I just wanted her to hold me.

"It sounded like the plot of a bad movie," she said. "I told him to go to hell."

He had called, he had wanted to see me, and she said no. Without asking me, without mentioning it. It struck me across the throat like a blow with a pipe.

I got up and went to lean on the tree trunk, on the other side of the trunk. She could hardly see me from there. But I could hear her. "You wanted to know. Don't turn over rocks if you don't want to see the pale creatures who live under them."

"Do you know where he is now?"

"Last I heard he bought a farm somewhere on one of the Danish islands. Aero, I think." When I looked around the trunk, she was playing with her shoes, walking them on her hands. "Picturesque, but unless his wife knows something about farming, I'm sure they've lost it by now." She looked up just in time to catch my glance, and smiled her knowing half-smile, not my father's wide-open smile, but the one that said she had read your mind, knew what you were thinking. "Why, are you planning to descend upon your long-lost father and his family? Don't be surprised if they don't kill the fatted calf."

"Better than you and your new children," I said. The heat rippled off the blacktop, I could smell asphalt loosened by heat.

"Ah," she said and lay back on the grass, her arms folded underneath her head, her legs crossed at the ankle. "I told them you wouldn't necessarily greet them with open arms. But they're a tender lot. Idealistic. They thought they'd give you a try. They were so proud of the article. Did you like it, by the way?"

"Threw it out."

"Pity."

The crows suddenly flew out of the tree in a series of shots, we listened to their rough calls doppler away. A truck went by on the frontage road, a club cab with dual back wheels, trailing ranchero music, absurdly cheerful. Like Guanajuato, I thought, and knew my mother was thinking the same.

My shirt didn't absorb sweat; it pooled and was soaked into the waistband of my skirt. I felt I'd been wading. "Tell me about Annie."

"Why do you have to hold on to the past?" She sat up, twisted her hair back, skewered it with the pencil. Her voice was sharp, irritated. "What's the past, just a pile of moldy newspapers in some old man's garage."

"The past is still happening. It never stopped. Who was Annie?"

The wind shook the dense glossy foliage of the ficus, there was no other sound. She ran her fingers over her hair, pulling

475

tight, like she was climbing out of a pool. "She was a neighbor. She took in kids, did people's laundry."

The smell of laundry. The laundry basket, sitting in the laundry basket with other children, playing we were in a boat. The little squares. It was yellow. We scooted it across the kitchen floor. "What did she look like?"

"Small. Talkative." She shaded her eyes with one hand. "She wore those Dr. Scholl's sandals."

Wooden clopping on the linoleum. Yellow linoleum with a multicolored paint-splotch pattern. The floor was cool when you put your cheek against it. And her legs. Tanned. Bare legs in cutoffs. But I couldn't see her face. "Dark or fair?"

"Dark. Straight hair with little bangs."

I couldn't get the hair. Just the legs. And the way she sang all day long to the radio.

"And where were you?"

My mother was silent. She pressed her hand down on her eyes. "How could you possibly have remembered this."

Everything she knew about me, everything she walked around with in that thin skull case like a vault. I wanted to crack her open, eat her brain like a soft-boiled egg.

"Imagine my life, for a moment," she said, quietly, cupping her long fingers like a boat, like she was holding her life in a shell. "Imagine how unprepared I was to be the mother of a small child. The demand for the enactment of the archetype. The selfless eternal feminine. It couldn't have been more foreign. I was a woman accustomed to following a line of inquiry or inclination until it led to its logical conclusion. I was used to having time to think, freedom. I felt like a hostage. Can you understand how desperate I was?"

476

I didn't want to understand, but I remembered Caitlin, tugging, always tugging, *Assi, juice! Juice!* Her imperiousness. On the other side of the fence, past my mother's head, the young women in Reception watched one of them sweeping the concrete courtyard, sweeping, sweeping, like it was a penance. "That's what babies are like. What were you thinking, that I would amuse you? That you and I could exchange thoughts on Joseph Brodsky?"

She sat up, crossed her legs, and rested her hands on her knees. "I thought Klaus and I were going to live happily ever after. Adam and Eve in a vine-covered shack. I was walking the archetypes. I was out of my fucking mind."

"You were in love with him."

"Yes, I was in love with him, all right?" she yelled at me. "I was in love with him and baby makes three and all that jazz, and then we had you and I woke up one morning married to a weak, selfish man, and I couldn't stand him. And you, you just wanted, wanted, wanted. Mommy Mommy Mommy until I thought I would throw you against the wall."

I felt sick. I had no trouble believing it, seeing it. I saw it all too clearly. And I understood why she never told me about this, had simply, kindly, refrained.

"So you left me there."

"I hadn't really intended to. I dropped you at her house just for the afternoon, to go to the beach with some friends, and one thing led to another, they had some friends down in Ensenada, and I went, and it felt wonderful, Astrid. To be free! You can't imagine. To go to the bathroom by myself. To take a nap in the afternoon. To make love all day long if I wanted, and walk on the beach, and not to have to think, where's Astrid?

What's Astrid doing? What's she going to get into? And not having you on me all the time, Mommy Mommy Mommy, clinging to me, like a spider . . ."

She shuddered. She still remembered my touch with revulsion. It made me dizzy with hatred. This was my mother. The woman who raised me. What chance could I ever have had.

"How long were you gone?" My voice sounded flat and dead in my own ears.

"A year," she said quietly. "Give or take a few months."

And I believed it. Everything in my body told me that was right. All those nights, waiting for her to come home, listening for her key in the lock. No wonder. No wonder they had to tear me away from her when I started school. No wonder I always worried she was going to leave me one night. She already had.

"But you're asking the wrong question," she said. "Don't ask me why I left. Ask me why I came back."

A truck with a four-horse trailer rattled up the road toward the highway. We could smell the horses, see their sleek rumps over the rear gate, and I thought about that day at the races, Medea's Pride.

"You should have been sterilized."

Suddenly she was up, pinning me by my shoulders to the tree trunk. Her eyes were a sea in fog. "I could have left you there, but I didn't. Don't you understand? For once, I did the right thing. For you."

I was supposed to forgive her now, but it was too late. I would not say my line. "Bully. For. You," I replied dryly.

She wanted to slap me, but she couldn't. They'd end the visit right now. I lifted my head, knowing the white scars were gleaming.

She dropped her grip on my arms. "You were never like this before," she said. "You're so hard. Susan told me, but I thought it was just a pose. You've lost yourself, your dreaminess, that tender quality."

I stared at her, not letting her look away. We were the same height, eye to eye, but I was bigger-boned, I probably could have beaten her in a fair fight. "I would have thought you'd approve. Wasn't that the thing you hated about Claire? Her tenderness? Be strong, you said. I despise weakness."

"I wanted you to be strong, but intact," she said. "Not this devastation. You're like a bomb site. You frighten me."

I smiled. I liked the idea that I frightened her. The tables were truly turned. "You, the great Ingrid Magnussen, goddess of September fires, Saint Santa Ana, ruler over life and death?"

She reached out her hand, as if to touch my face, like a blind woman, but she couldn't reach me. I would burn her if she touched me. The hand stayed in the air, hovering in front of my face. I saw, she was afraid. "You were the one thing that was entirely good in my life, Astrid. Since I came back for you, we've never been apart, not until this."

"The murder, you mean."

"No, this. You, now." The gesture, the attempt to reach me, faded like sunset. "You know, when I came back, you knew me. You were sitting there by the door when I came in. You looked up, and you smiled and reached for me to pick you up. As if you were waiting for me."

I wanted to cut through this moment with the blue flame of an acetylene torch. I wanted to burn it to ash and scatter it into the wind, so the pieces would never come back together again. "I was always waiting for you, Mother. It's the constant in my life. Waiting for you. Will you come back, will you forget that you've tied me up in front of a store, left me on the bus?"

The hand came out again. Tentatively, but this time it lightly touched my hair. "Are you still?"

"No," I said, brushing her hand away. "I stopped when Claire showed me what it felt like to be loved."

Now she looked tired, every day of forty-nine years. She picked up her shoes. "Is there anything else you want? Have I fulfilled my end of the bargain?"

"Do you ever regret what you've done?"

The expression in her eyes was bitter as nightshade. "You ask me about regret? Let me tell you a few things about regret, my darling. There is no end to it. You cannot find the beginning of the chain that brought us from there to here. Should you regret the whole chain, and the air in between, or each link separately, as if you could uncouple them? Do you regret the beginning which ended so badly, or just the ending itself? I've given more thought to this question than you can begin to imagine."

I never thought I'd hear the day my mother, Ingrid Magnussen, would admit to regret. Now that she stood in front of me, shaking with it, I couldn't think of anything to say. It was like watching a river run backwards.

We stood there staring out at the empty road.

"What are you going to do when you get out?" I asked her. "Where are you going to go?"

She wiped the sweat off her face with the collar of her dress. Secretaries and office workers and COs were coming out of the brick administration building. They leaned into the hot wind, holding their skirts down, heading for lunch, a nice air-conditioned Coco's or Denny's. When they saw me with my mother, they drew closer together, talking among themselves. She was already a celebrity, I could see it. We watched them start up their cars. I knew she imagined herself with those keys in her hand, accelerator, gas tank marked Full.

She sighed. "By the time Susan is done, I'll be a household icon, like Aunt Jemima, the Pillsbury Doughboy. I'll have my choice of teaching positions. Where would you like to go, Astrid?" She glanced at me, smiled, my carrot. Reminding me which end of the plank and so on.

"That's years away," I said.

"You can't make it alone," she said. "You need an environment, a context. People invested in your success. God knows, look at me. I had to go to prison to get noticed."

The cars started up, crunched over the gravel. Camille came out of the shelter, pointed at her watch. It was over. I felt empty and used. Whatever I thought knowing the truth would do for me, it hadn't. It was my last hope. I wanted her to hurt the way I did. I wanted it very much.

"So, how does it feel, knowing I don't give a damn anymore?" I said. "That I'll do anything to get what I want. Even lie for you, I won't blink an eye. I'm like you now, aren't I? I look at the world and ask what's in it for me."

She shook her head, gazed down at her bare tanned feet. "If I could take it all back, I would, Astrid." She lifted her eyes to mine. "You've got to believe me." Her eyes, glinting in the sun, were exactly the color of the pool we swam in together the summer she was arrested. I wanted to swim there again, to submerge myself in them.

"Then tell me you don't want me to testify," I said. "Tell me you don't want me like this. Tell me you would sacrifice the rest of your life to have me back the way I was."

She turned her blue gaze toward the road, that road, the beautiful road, the road women in prison dreamed about. The road she had already left me for once. Her hair like smoke in the wind. Overhead, the foliage blew back and forth like a fighter working a small bag in air that smelled of brushfire and dairy cattle. She pressed her hands over her eyes, then slid them down her face to her mouth. I watched her staring out at the road. She seemed lost there, sealed in longing, searching for an exit, a hidden door.

And suddenly I felt panic. I'd made a mistake, like when I'd played chess with Ray and knew a second too late I'd made the wrong move. I had asked a question I couldn't afford to know the answer to. It was the thing I didn't want to know. The rock that never should be turned over. I knew what was under there. I didn't need to see it, the hideous eyeless albino creature that lived underneath. "Listen, forget it. A deal's a deal. Let's leave it at that."

The wind crackled its dangerous whip in the air, I imagined I could see the shower of sparks, smell the ashes. I was afraid she hadn't heard me. She was still as a daguerreotype, arms crossed across her denim dress. "I'll tell Susan," she said quietly. "To leave you alone."

I knew I had heard her but I didn't believe it. I waited for something, to make me believe it was true.

My mother came back to me then, put her arms around me,

rested her cheek against my hair. Although I knew it was impossible, I could smell her violets. "If you could go back, even partway, I would give anything," she said into my ear.

Her large hands gently stroked my hair. It was all I ever really wanted, that revelation. The possibility of fixed stars.

32

⟿

THE YEAR my mother's new trial was held, February was bitter cold. I was living in Berlin with Paul Trout, in a fourth-story flat in the old Eastern sector, a sublet of a sublet some friends found for us. It was crumbling and coal-heated, but we could afford it most of the time. Ever since Paul's graphic novels had become the codebook of a new secret society among European art students, we'd made friends in every city. They passed us along from squat to sublet to spare couch like torches in a relay race.

I liked Berlin. The city and I understood each other. I liked that they had left the bombed-out hulk of the Kaiser Wilhelm Church as a monument to loss. Nobody had forgotten anything here. In Berlin, you had to wrestle with the past, you had to build on the ruins, inside them. It wasn't like America, where we scraped the earth clean, thinking we could start again every time. We hadn't learned yet, there was no such thing as an empty canvas.

I had begun turning to sculpture, an outgrowth of my time with Rena Grushenka. I'd developed an obsessive fondness for scavenged materials, for flea markets and curbside treasures and haggling in six different languages. Over time, this flotsam worked its way into my art, along with bits of German and worship of the Real and twenty-four kinds of animal scat. At the Hochschule der Künste, our art student friends had a professor, Oskar Schein, who liked my work. He smuggled me into classes there as sort of a shadow student, and was lobbying for my acceptance as a bona fide scholar working toward a degree, but in a perverse way, my current status suited me. I was still a foster child. The Hochschule der Künste was Cal Arts in German, students with funny haircuts making ugly art, but I was developing a context, as my mother would have said. My classmates knew about Paul and me, we were the wild children with all the talent, living on my waitress tips and sidewalk sales of our handmade rearview-mirror ornaments. They wished they could be us. *We are the free birds,* I could still hear Rena say.

That year, I craved suitcases. I haunted the flea market near the Tiergarten, bargaining and trading for old-fashioned suitcases — there were thousands for sale now, since unification. Leather with yellow celluloid handles. Train cases and hatboxes. In the old Eastern sector, no one had ever thrown them out, because there had been nothing to replace them with. Now they sold cheap, the Easterners were buying the latest carryons, uprights with wheels. Along the flea market booths of the Strasse des 17 Juni, the dealers all knew me. *Handkofferfräulein,* they called me. Suitcase girl.

I was making altars inside them. Secret, portable museums. Displacement being the modern condition, as Oskar Schein liked to say. He kept wanting to buy one, but I couldn't sell, though Paul and I were quite obviously broke. I needed them. Instead, I made Oskar one of his own for his birthday, with Louise Brooks as Lulu, and inflation marks in denominations of hundreds of thousands, toy train tracks like veins, and a black plastic clay swamp in the bottom printed with a giant boot-print that I'd filled with clear, green-tinted gel. Through the Lucite you could see the submerged likenesses of Goethe, Schiller, and Rilke.

All winter long I sat on the floor in the corner of the flat with my glue and my clay, resins and solvents and paint and thread and bags of scavenged materials, my coat still on, my fingerless gloves. I could never decide whether to work with the windows open to ventilate fumes, or closed to stay warm. It depended. Sometimes my sense of futurity was stronger, sometimes my sense there was only the past.

I was creating my personal museum. They were all here: Claire and Olivia, my mother and Starr, Yvonne and Niki and Rena, Amelia Ramos, Marvel. The Musée de Astrid Magnussen. I'd had to leave everything behind at Rena's when I went to New York to find Paul, all my boxes and souvenirs, everything but my mother's four books and the jewelry I'd acquired, the aquamarine ring, the amethyst, and the stolen necklace, plus eight hundred dollars in cash. Before I left, Sergei slipped me the name of a Russian fence in Brighton Beach, Ivan Ivanov, who would help me transfer my stash into cash. "He don't speak much of English, but he give you good price." *The phoenix must burn to emerge,* I kept thinking as I took a bus across the country with nothing but the address of a comic book store on St. Marks Place to steer by.

But now I'd assembled it again, my museum. There, against the wall, in this cold northern city, I'd re-created my life.

Here was Rena, a brown leather case lined in green figured velvet holding a spread-eagled wax nude with a white cat head made in white bunny fur. The lid was lined with doll furniture and decorated in fanned phony greenbacks. Niki was an American Tourister glazed in magenta enamel, metal-flaked like a drumkit. Inside, it had knackwursts made from condoms stuffed with foam rubber. For Yvonne, I'd found a child's suit-case and covered it in pastel blanket fuzz. Inside stretched guitar wire, and little baby dolls were tangled there. I was looking for a music box, so that when you opened the lid, it would play "Michelle."

Marvel's was turquoise, it opened to reveal white gravel stuck to the bottom, and a battery-powered flashlight signaling SOS in Morse code. One of our art student friends helped me wire it. Girl toy soldiers — free giveaways from an American movie — crawled among the moon rocks with their AK-47s. I'd painted tiny swastikas on their arms. There was a little TV screen in the lid, where a decoupaged Miss America beamed, her face dotted with clear nail polish tears.

Starr and Ray shared a plastic cloth suitcase with cracked leather bindings, bleached tan with a faded plaid. When you propped it open, it released a heady scent of raw wood and Obsession. Against bright op-art jersey I'd crisscrossed strips of a Pendleton plaid. Inside the lid, a prom-pink satin rose uncoiled, richly vaginal, under a glow-in-the-dark Jesus. The edges were furred with wood shavings from a local cabinet-maker, poodle curly. The base held a tiny reliquary chest, filled with chunks of scrap lead. You couldn't get bullets in Europe,

I'd had to make do. In a glass terrarium on the bottom, a snake crawled over yellow sand, broken glass, and a half-buried pair of wire-rimmed glasses.

Like Berlin, I was layered with guilt and destruction. I had caused grief as well as suffering it. I could never honestly point a finger without it turning around in mid-accusation.

Olivia Johnstone was a hatbox covered in green crocodile plastic that released Ma Griffe when you opened it. Dagmar, the perfume counter girl at the Wertheim Department Store, let me wet cotton balls with the sample perfumes, which I stashed in film canisters in my pockets. Inside, I'd woven a nest of taupe and black stockings, which surrounded a Carnival mask of black feathers, and a beaker that held the white ocean. On its surface floated a gumball ring, also white.

They were all here. A lunchbox decoupaged in flea market postcards of fin de siècle aristocracy was the Amelia Ramos. Inside, antique forks thrust up through a mat of black wig hair striped in white. The forks looked like hands reaching out, begging.

And Claire. I built her memorial from a train case from the thirties, white leather with red patent trim. It cost me 50DM, but it opened to watermarked mauve moiré silk, like the grain in wood, like a funeral in a box. Inside the lid, I'd glued pieces of white-painted record vinyl to resemble the wings of butterflies. Each tiny cache drawer had a secret inside. A reticulated, miniature fish. A drawer full of pills. A strand of pearls. A fern fiddle. A sprig of rosemary. A picture of Audrey Hepburn in *Two for the Road*. And in one drawer, twenty-seven names for tears. *Heartdew. Griefhoney. Sadwater. Die Tränen. Eau de douleur. Los rios del corazón.* It was the one Oskar Schein kept wanting to buy.

All my mothers. Like guests at a fairy-tale christening, they had bestowed their gifts on me. They were mine now. Olivia's generosity, her knowledge of men. Claire's tenderness and faith. If not for Marvel, how would I have penetrated the mysteries of the American family? If not for Niki, when might I have learned to laugh? And Yvonne, *mi hermosa*, you gave me the real mother, the blood mother, that wasn't behind wire, but somewhere inside. Rena stole my pride but gave me back something more, taught me to salvage, glean from the wreckage what could be remade and resold.

I carried all of them, sculpted by every hand I'd passed through, carelessly, or lovingly, it didn't matter. Amelia Ramos, that skunk-streaked bitch, taught me to stand up for myself, beat on the bars until I got what I needed. Starr tried to kill me, but also bought me my first high heels, made me entertain the possibility of God. Who would I give up now?

And in a blue suitcase with a white handle, the first and last room of the Astridkunsthalle. Lined in white raw silk, edges stained red, scented with violet perfume.

I sat on the floor in the gathering dusk of a gray afternoon on the threadbare carpet splotched in paint by generations of art students. This was my mother's time, dusk, though in Berlin winter it was dark by four, no timeless western twilights, surf on yellow sand. I opened the lid.

The scent of her violets always made me feel sad. The vial of tinted water was the exact color of the pool on Hollywood Boulevard. I sat in front of my mother's altar and built a set of drawings on clear plastic, watched the disjointed lines come together, until they formed the image of her in profile. Letters tied in barbed wire nestled in the suitcase bottom along with a

489

spread of tarot cards, the queen of wands prominently featured. A row of glass fragments hung from the lid, I ran my fingers along them so they chimed, and imagined wind through the eucalyptus on a hot summer night.

We wrote a couple of times a month, using the comic book shop near the university as a letter-drop. Sometimes she had her lawyer send me a little money via Hana Gruen in Cologne, from her poems or more likely scammed off a fan. I told her I didn't want to know about her preparations for trial, but her letters boasted of offers lined up — Amherst, Stanford, Smith. Dangling the carrot of green college campuses. I imagined myself a professor's daughter, riding a bike to my classes. I could wear a camel's hair coat at last, have a roommate, play intramural volleyball, all paid for in advance. How safe it would be, contained, everything decided for me. I could be a child again, I could start over. Sure I wouldn't want to come home?

I reached out and touched a tine of the barbed wire, rang the chimes. The beauty and the madness, wasn't it. What was being weighed on the scales of the night.

LATER, I LAY under the feather bed, fully clothed, not for sleep but just to stay warm. The space heater buzzed and threw out the familiar smell of burned hair. The windowpanes were frosted over, and I could see my breath in the room. I was listening to a tape, a band called Magenta, our friends thought it was far out we knew the singer, Niki Colette. They were playing in Frankfurt next month, we already had tickets, a place to crash. I still heard from Yvonne at Christmastime, she was living in Huntington Beach with an ex-Marine named Herbert, with whom she had a son, Herbert, Jr.

I was waiting for Paul to come home, I was hungry. He was supposed to pick up some food after his appointment with a printer for his next graphic book. He was trying to get someone to print it cheap and take a piece of the sales. His last German publisher had OD'd in the fall, leaving us back at square one. But he had presold two hundred copies, not bad at all.

He came home about nine, took off his boots and climbed under the covers. He had a greasy paper bag of kebabs from the local Turkish fast food. My stomach growled. Paul threw a newspaper on top of me. "Guess who?" he said.

It was tomorrow's *International Herald Tribune*, still smelling of wet ink. I looked at the front page. Croatia, OPEC, bomb threat at La Scala. I opened it and there she was on page three: JAILED POET FOUND INNOCENT AFTER NINE YEARS. Smiling her half-smile, waving like royalty returning from exile, happy but still mistrusting the masses. She had made it through trial without me. She was free.

Paul ate his kebab sandwich, dropping pieces of salad back onto the bag as I quickly read the story, more shocked than I'd thought I would be. They'd taken the defense that Barry had committed suicide and made it look like murder. I was appalled that it worked. My mother was quoted saying how grateful she was that justice had been done, she looked forward to taking a bath, she thanked the jurors from the bottom of her heart. She said she'd received offers to teach, to publish her autobiography, to marry an ice-cream millionaire and pose for *Playboy*, and she was going to accept them all.

491

Paul offered me a falafel, I shook my head. Suddenly, I wasn't hungry anymore. "Save it for later," he said, and dropped the bag by the side of the bed. His rich brown eyes asked every question. He didn't have to say a word.

I rested my head in the crook of his shoulder and gazed at the squares of blue TV light shining through the frost blossoms on our window from the windows just across the way. I tried to imagine what she was feeling right now. In Los Angeles it was noon. A bright sunny February, it looked from the picture. I imagined her in a hotel room, courtesy Susan D. Valeris, some luxury suite full of flowers from well-wishers, waking up on fresh sheets. She would have her bath in a double-wide tub, and write a poem overlooking the winter roses.

Then she might take a few interviews, or rent a white convertible for a spin down the beach, where she'd pick up a young man with clear eyes and sand in his hair, and make love to him until he wept with the beauty of it. What else would you do when you were acquitted of murder?

It was too much to imagine her tempering her joy with a moment of grief, a moment for the knowledge of what her triumph had cost. I couldn't expect that from her. But I had seen her remorse, and it had nothing to do with Barry or anyone else, it was a gift offered despite a price she had had no way to estimate then, it could have been heavy as mourning, final as a tomb. No matter how much she had damaged me or how flawed she was, how violently mistaken, my mother loved me, unquestionably.

I thought of her, facing a court of law without the pawn formation of my lies. The queen stripped bare, she had mastered the end game on her own.

Paul rolled a Drum cigarette, the shreds like hair as he lifted them from the bag, tore the shag from the ends, lit it with a match scraped under the box that served as our end table. "You want to go call her?" We couldn't afford a phone. Oskar Schein let us use his.

"Too cold."

He smoked, the ashtray resting on his chest. I reached over and took a puff, handed it back. We had come such a long way together, Paul and I. From the apartment on St. Marks to the squat in South London, an uninsulated barge in Amsterdam, now Senefelderstrasse. I wished we knew someone in Italy, or Greece. I hadn't been warm since I left L.A.

"Do you ever want to go home?" I asked Paul.

He brushed an ash from my face. "It's the century of the displaced person," he said. "You can never go home."

He didn't have to tell me, he was afraid I was going to go back. Become an American college coed on the three-meal plan, field hockey and English comp, and leave him holding the foster kid bag. There it was. On the one hand, there was Frau Acker and the rent, my cough, Paul's print run. On the other, a place with heat, a degree, decent food, and someone taking care of me.

I'd never told him, sometimes I felt old. How we lived was depressing. Before, I couldn't afford to think about it, but now that she was out, how could I not. And now Oskar Schein was asking if he could see me alone, take me to dinner, he wanted to talk to me about a gallery show. I'd put him off, but I didn't know how long I could hold out. I found him attractive, a bearish man with a cropped silver beard. Lying down for the father again. If it weren't for Paul, I'd have

493

done it months ago. But Paul was more than my boyfriend. He was me.

And now my mother was calling me, I didn't have to get on the phone. I could hear her. My blood whispered her name.

I stared at her photograph, waving in the California sunlight. At this very moment, she was out. Driving around, ready to start again fresh, so American after all. I thought of my life bundled in suitcases against the wall, the shapes I had taken, the selves I had been. Next I could be Ingrid Magnussen's daughter at Stanford or Smith, answering the hushed breathless questions of her new children. She's your mother? What's she really like? I could do it. I knew how to trade on my tragic past, skillfully revealing my scars, my foster kid status, I'd perfected the art with Joan Peeler. People took me up, made me their project, their pet. They cast themselves as my champions, and I let them. I hadn't come this far to be left at some river bottom among the wrecked cars.

To be my mother's daughter again. I played with the idea like a child with a blanket, running it between my fingers. To be lost in the tide of her music again. It was an idea more seductive than any man. Was it really too late for childhood, to crawl back into the crucible, to dissolve into the fire, to rise without memory? *The phoenix must burn* . . . How would I dare? It had taken me this long to be free of her shadow, to breathe on my own, even if in this singed-hair space-heater Europe.

I lay in Paul's arms, thinking how we'd gone up to Denmark last summer to find Klaus Anders. We located him in Copenhagen. He was living in a shabby flat with his children, it smelled of turpentine and stale milk. His wife was off working. It was three in the afternoon when we came calling, he had on a blue seersucker bathrobe covered with paint. There were two kids under five, my half sister and brother from his third or fourth marriage, on the couch watching TV. The girl had strawberry jam in her hair, the baby needed changing, and I saw the chain of disaster could move laterally as well as up and down.

He'd been painting, a biomorphic abstraction that looked like an old shoe with hair. He offered us Carlsbergs and asked about my mother. I drank and let Paul do most of the talking. My father. His handsome forehead, his Danish nose, just like mine. His voice lilting with its accent, humorous even when expressing regret. A man who never took anything seriously, least of all himself. He was pleased I was an artist, unsurprised my mother was in prison, sorry we'd never met. He wanted to make up for lost time, offered to let us stay, we could sleep on the couch, I could help out with the kids. He was sixty-one years old, and so ordinary.

I had felt like my mother, sitting in his living room, judging him and his sticky children and the TV that never turned off. The old futon-couch, scarred teak coffee table with rings. Canvases on the walls, encrustations like brain coral and colon cancer. We ate cheese and bread, the large jar of strawberry jam. I gave him the address of the comic book store, said I'd be in touch. It was the first time I'd ever wanted to move on, be the first person out of the room.

Afterward we went to a student bar near the university and I got thoroughly, sloppily drunk, and threw up in the alley. Paul got me on the last train back to Berlin.

Now I took Paul's hand in the bed, his right in my left, laced my fingers through his, my hands large and pale as winter, my identity stitched in the whorls of their fingertips, Paul's hands dark from graphite and fragrant with Drum and kebabs. Our palms were the same size but his fingers were two inches longer. His beautiful hands. I always thought if we ever had children, I hoped they'd have them.

"So what happened with the printer?" I asked.

"He wants cash," Paul said. "Imagine."

I turned our hands, so we could examine them from each side. His fingers practically touched my wrists. I traced along the sinews of his hand, thinking how in less than a day I could be back in the States. I could be like my mother, like Klaus. It was my legacy, wasn't it, to shed lives like snakeskin, a new truth for each new page, a moral amnesiac?

But a disgrace. I'd rather starve. I knew how to do it, it wasn't that hard.

I looked around our flat, the rain-ruined walls, the few bits of furniture, battered pressboard chest we found in an alley, the dusty velvet curtain concealing our tiny kitchen. Paul's drawing table, his papers and pens. And the suitcases, ranged against the wall, filling the rest of the floor. Our life. *The phoenix must burn*, my mother had said. I tried to imagine the flames, but it was too cold.

"Maybe I'll sell the museum," I said.

Paul traced the lacy dogbite scars on my hand. "I thought you told Oskar you wouldn't."

I shrugged. I would never reach the end of what was in those suitcases, those women, those men, what they meant to me. These rooms were only the start. There were suitcases inside of suitcases I had not even begun to unpack. *You want remember, so just remember.*

I slipped my hands up under the wool shirt I'd bought him at the flea market. He flinched with the cold, then allowed me to warm them against his skinny ribs. As we drew close, murmuring softly into each other's necks, the *Herald Tribune* slid off the feather bed and fell to the floor in a soft cascade, burying my mother among her headlines, news of other crises and personages. We shed our jackets and our pants to make love, but kept our shirts and socks on. I knew I was making a choice. This, now, suitcases, Paul. It was my life, a trait and not an error, written by fire on stone.

AFTERWARD, I lay gazing at the patterns cast on the stained walls, the effect of the light from the street shining through our windows, the etched designs like bird feet. Next to me, Paul slept with a pillow crammed tightly over his head, product of his years in foster care, not to hear more than he had to. I slipped out from under the covers, pulled on my icy stiff jeans and a sweater, put on the fire under the kettle for a Nescafé. What I would give for a cup of Olivia's thick black coffee, so dark it didn't even turn pale when you put the cream in. I rolled myself a cigarette from Paul's Drum tobacco, and waited for the water to boil.

It was three in California. I would never tell Paul how much I wanted to be there, how much I wanted to drive in a top-down Mustang with my mother along the coast in sun-warmed, sage-scented February, and pick up some sea-washed stranger with a shell strand laced around his beautiful neck. If I told Paul how much I missed L.A., he would think I was crazy. But I missed it, that poisoned place, gulag of abandoned children, archipelago of regret. I craved it even now, the hot wind smelling of creosote and laurel sumac, the rustle of eucalyptus, the nights of mismatched stars. I thought of that ruined dovecote behind the house on St. Andrew's Place that my mother once wrote a poem about. How it bothered her the doves would not leave, though the chicken wire had long since collapsed, the two-by-fours fallen. But I understood them. It was where they belonged, shade in summer, their sad wooden flute calls. Wherever they were, they would try to get back, it was like the last piece of a puzzle that had been lost.

The kettle whistled and I made my instant coffee, stirred in some evaporated milk from a can, and gazed out at the flats opposite ours across the courtyard — the old man watching TV and drinking peppermint schnapps, a man washing dishes, a woman painting — while on the other side of the globe, California shimmered, hoarding the ragged edge of the century in a bright afternoon scented with love and murder. In the flat downstairs, the neighbors' newborn was crying, rhythmically, a high thin chant.

I pressed my hand to the frosted pane, let the heat from my body melt the ice, leaving a perfect outline against the darkness. But I was thinking about light coming in through white curtains, the smell of ocean and sage and fresh laundry. Voices and music, a scratchy recording of Dietrich singing *"Ich bin von Kopf bis Fuss,"* rose into the sound well of the courtyard, but inside my head, I could hear the repetitive cries of a red-shouldered hawk, the faint rustle of lizards in a dry wash, a click of palms and the almost imperceptible sigh of rose petals falling. In the dark palmprint, I could see my blurred image, but also my mother's face shimmering on a rooftop over an

498

unknowable city, talking to the three-quarter moon. I wanted to hear what she was saying. I wanted to smell that burnt midnight again, I wanted to feel that wind. It was a secret wanting, like a song I couldn't stop humming, or loving someone I could never have. No matter where I went, my compass pointed west. I would always know what time it was in California.

Acknowledgements

I profoundly thank the following people for making this book possible:

My generous friend and colleague Jeffrey Merrick, who read the enormous draft of *White Oleander* and helped me through the labyrinth. My mentor, Kate Braverman, who taught me the art of fiction, and my literary family, particularly Les Plesko, the Hard Words writing collective, and Donald Rawley, a comrade sorely missed. My literary agent, Bill Reiss, who believed in me throughout the long years. My friend Warwick Downing, champion of writerly search and rescue. My sagacious editor, Michael Pietsch, and all the staff at Little, Brown. For research assistance, Ruby Owens, M.S.W., Department of Children and Family Services, MacLaren Children's Center; Dr. John Berecochea, Chief of the Research Branch, State of California Department of Corrections; the California Institution for Women at Corona-Frontera; Dr. Elizabeth Leonard; Dr. Denise Johnston, Director of the Center for Children of Incarcerated Parents; and especially the many respondents who shared their diverse experiences with me as part of the Foster Daughters Project. My wonderful and supportive friends and family; my mother and father, Alma and Vernon Fitch; and most of all, my husband and daughter, Steve and Allison Strauss, who love me whether or not the chapter's any good.

ALIAS GRACE

Margaret Atwood

'Oh brilliant! I cannot rave enough . . . with its explosive mixture of sex, murder and class conflict, Alias Grace is an absolute winner' – Val Hennessy, *Daily Mail*

'A sensuous, perplexing book, at once sinister and dignified, grubby and gorgeous, panoramic yet specific . . . I don't think I have ever been so thrilled . . . This, surely, is as far as a novel can go' – Julie Myerson, *Independent on Sunday*

'The oustanding novelist of our age' – Peter Kemp, *Sunday Times*

'Sometimes I whisper it over to myself: Murderess. Murderess. IT rustles, like a taffeta skirt along the floor' Grace Marks. Female fiend? Femme fatale? Or weak and unwilling victim? Around the true story of one of the most enigmatic and notorious women of the 1840s, Margaret Atwood has created an extraordinarily potent tale of sexuality, cruelty and mystery.

THE CURE FOR DEATH BY LIGHTNING

Gail Anderson-Dargatz

'I loved it from the first page, she's fluent and graceful and there's passion and tension, in fact all I want from a novel. The writing is so powerful and yet shows a restraint that tightens the whole atmosphere. An excellent read – I was gripped' – Margaret Forster

The remote Turtle Valley in British Columbia is home to fifteen-year-old Beth Weeks and a community of eccentric but familiar characters. There, amidst a stunning landscape of purple swallows and green skies, strange and unsettling events occur: children go missing, a girl is mauled by a crazy bear and Beth too is being pursued . . .

The Cure for Death by Lightning is a rich and thrilling novel, as filled with strange deeds and dark fears as with beauty and magic.

Now you can order superb titles directly from Virago

☐ Alias Grace	Margaret Atwood	£
☐ Cure for Death by Lightning	Gail Anderson-Dargatz	£
☐ Fair Exchange	Michèle Roberts	£
☐ Stuck up a Tree	Jenny McLeod	£
☐ Cowboys are My Weakness	Pam Houston	£
☐ Like	Ali Smith	£
☐ Pandora's Box	Alice Thompson	£
☐ Little Sister	Carol Birch	£
☐ The Magic Toyshop	Angela Carter	£
☐ Oyster	Janette Turner Hospital	£

Please allow for postage and packing: **Free UK delivery**.
Europe; add 25% of retail price; Rest of World; 45% of retail price.

To order any of the above or any other Virago titles, please call ou
credit card orderline or fill in this coupon and send/fax it to:

Virago, 250 Western Avenue, London, W3 6XZ, UK.
Fax 0181 324 5678   Telephone 0181 324 5516

☐ I enclose a UK bank cheque made payable to Virago for £ ....

☐ Please charge £.............. to my Access, Visa, Delta, Switch Card

☐☐☐☐☐☐☐☐☐☐☐☐☐☐☐☐☐☐☐

Expiry Date ☐☐☐☐   Switch Issue No. ☐☐

NAME (Block letters please) ....

ADDRESS ....

....

....

Postcode ....Telephone ....

Signature ....

Please allow 28 days for delivery within the UK. Offer subject to price and availability.

Please do not send any further mailings from companies carefully selected by Virago